CU00832633

The
RON RASH
READER

The
RON RASH
READER

Edited by Randall Wilhelm

The University of South Carolina Press

© 2014 University of South Carolina

Published by the University of South Carolina Press
Columbia, South Carolina 29208

www.sc.edu/uscpress

Manufactured in the United States of America

23 22 21 20 19 18 17 16 15 14   10 9 8 7 6 5 4 3 2 1

Library of Congress Cataloging-in-Publication data can be found in the back of this book.

"Badeye," "The Night the New Jesus Fell to Earth," and "My Father's Cadillacs" from *The Night the New Jesus Fell to Earth and Other Stories from Cliffside, North Carolina* by Ron Rash. © 1994 by Ron Rash. Reprinted with permission of the author. All rights reserved.

"The Way Things Are," "Summer Work," and "Casualties and Survivors" from *Casualties* by Ron Rash. © 2000 by Ron Rash. Reprinted with permission of the author. All rights reserved.

Section One from *One Foot in Eden* by Ron Rash. © 2002 by Ron Rash. Reprinted with permission of the author. All rights reserved.

Nonfiction selections: "The Gift of Silence," "Lost Moments in Basketball History: David Thompson, Dynamite, and a Summer Night in Carolina Where Only the Spring Didn't Boil," "Coal Miner's Son," and "In the Beginning" by Ron Rash. © by Ron Rash. Reprinted with permission of the author. All rights reserved.

Uncollected Stories: "Outlaws," "The Far and the Near," "The Gatsons," "White Trash Fishing," and "The Harvest" by Ron Rash. © by Ron Rash. Reprinted with permission of the author. All rights reserved.

"Invocation," "Eureka," "Mill Village," "Bearings," "Brown Lung," and "July, 1949" from *Eureka Mill* by Ron Rash. 1998 by Ron Rash. Reprinted with permission of Hub City Press.

"Resolution," "First Memory," "Watauga County: 1959," "Spillcorn," "White Wings," "Three A.M. and the Stars Were Out," "The Code," and "Good Friday, 2006: Shelton Laurel" from *Waking* by Ron Rash. © 2011 by Ron Rash. Reprinted with permission of Hub City Press.

"Plowing on Moonlight," "The Exchange," "A Preacher Who Takes Up Serpents Laments the Presence of Skeptics in His Church," "Return," "The Fox," "August, 1959: Morning Service," "Among the Believers," and "Good Friday, 1995: Driving Westward" from *Among the Believers* by Ron Rash. © 2000 by Ron Rash. Reprinted with permission of Iris Press.

"Last Service," "Under Jocassee," "Jocassee: 1916," "Watauga County: 1803," "In Dismal Gorge," "Black-Eyed Susans," "At Reid Hartley's Junkyard," "Madison County: June, 1999," and "A Homestead on the Horsepasture" from *Raising the Dead* by Ron Rash. © 2002 by Ron Rash. Reprinted with permission of Iris Press.

Chapter 1 and Prologue from *Saints at the River* by Ron Rash. © 2004 by Ron Rash. Reprinted by permission of Henry Holt and Company, LLC.

Chapter 1 from *The World Made Straight* by Ron Rash. © 2006 by Ron Rash. Reprinted by permission of Henry Holt and Company, LLC.

"Chemistry" and "Their Ancient, Glittering Eyes" from the book *Chemistry and Other Stories* by Ron Rash. © 2007 by Ron Rash. Reprinted by permission of Henry Holt and Company, LLC.

"Hard Times," "The Ascent," "The Woman Who Believed in Jaguars," "Burning Bright," and "Lincoln-ites" from *Burning Bright* by Ron Rash. © 2010 by Ron Rash. Reprinted with permission of HarperCollins Publishers.

"The Trusty," "Where the Map Ends," and "The Woman at the Pond" from *Nothing Gold Can Stay* by Ron Rash. © 2013 by Ron Rash. Reprinted with permission of HarperCollins Publishers.

Chapters 1 to 3 from *Serena* by Ron Rash. © 2009 by Ron Rash. Reprinted with permission of Harper-Collins Publishers.

Chapters 1 to 3 from *The Cove* by Ron Rash. © 2012 by Ron Rash. Reprinted with permission of Harper-Collins Publishers.

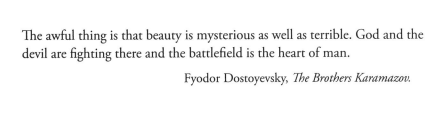

The awful thing is that beauty is mysterious as well as terrible. God and the devil are fighting there and the battlefield is the heart of man.

Fyodor Dostoyevsky, *The Brothers Karamazov.*

CONTENTS

Contents

Contents

ACKNOWLEDGMENTS

For my mother, Sarah Wyly Cashin Wilhelm, and to the memory of my father, Bill Wilhelm, Legend: 1929–2010.

Gracious thanks to all those who worked with me on this project. Without the help of my good friend, Ron Rash, this book would simply not exist so my sincere thanks go out to him—and to Ann Rash, the ever-ready answer woman. Thanks also to my friends, colleagues, and mentors who have taught me so much—Bill Koon, Mark Powell, Jesse Graves, John Lang, Hallman Bryant, Danny Marion, Anna Higgins Dunlap, Casey Clabough, and all the other readers, and speakers at conferences I have had the pleasure to talk with and listen to over the years. Special thanks also to Lisa Graves, and to Renee, as always.

I'd also like to express my sincere gratitude to the kind folks at USC Press who took up this project so earnestly and professionally. It has been truly a pleasure to work with such kind, helpful, and brilliant people. My warmest thanks and appreciation to Linda Fogle, Jim Denton, Jonathan Haupt, and everyone else at USC Press who worked on making this book a reality.

I am also indebted to those kindred souls who worked with me on providing permissions without regard to financial gain. Thank you Betsy Teeter of Hub City Press and Robert Cumming of Iris Press for your kindness and generosity. I'd also like to thank Marly Rusoff and Associates, Peter London, Karen Maine, and James Meader at HarperCollins, and Mimi Ross at Henry Holt.

Introduction

Blood Memory

At first he may not have believed it. The sounds may not have felt quite right. But then he rose slowly from the table and made his way to the podium at the head of the ballroom. Before him, seated at a swirl of tables bedecked with fine china, slender candles, and sleek glasses of wine and champagne, sat the sophisticated elite of the international literary establishment. Looking out from the podium Ron Rash must have thought—if only for an instant—of the long journey it had taken to arrive at such a place. Then he graciously accepted the world's most prestigious literary prize for short fiction, the Frank O'Connor International Short Story Award, for his stunning 2010 collection of stories *Burning Bright*. Bursting through the often reductive categories of "Appalachian," "Southern," and even "American" writer, Rash's work has earned him a place on the global literary mountain and is reaching even new heights, and rightfully so.

Rash's poems, short stories, and novels straddle the best of both worlds—international critical acclaim and a readership the world over.[1] His work is widely recognized for his thrilling poetic images, for his craftsmanship, and for his highly distinctive voice, qualities that mark Rash as a force to be reckoned with on the regional, national, and global stages of contemporary literature. But certainly the journey has been a long one from the harsh and beautiful Appalachian region of western North Carolina, its shining waterfalls, granite outcrops, and rolling waves of blue-misted ridges a far cry from an elegant ballroom filled with tuxedo-wearing dignitaries in the heart of downtown Cork, Ireland.

To begin to understand the many threads running throughout Rash's body of work, it is illuminating to look into the natural world from which he comes, to Rash's fierce and primal connection to place, to the land through

1

which he came to know the world, and to his strong ties to family and the "blood memory" of his ancestors. Rash's love of the Appalachian landscape and his dedication to the memory of family and regional history forms the backbone of his work as a poet, short story writer, and novelist. For Rash, art and life are one continuous weave, as inseparable as air and breathing, and his work is shaped by a fertile interplay between familial and regional history, a vivid and narrative imagination, and a hard won skill for storytelling. When questions turn to place in his work, Rash often quotes Eudora Welty, saying that "one place comprehended can make us understand other places better."[2] In an interview with Thomas Bjerre, Rash responded at length when asked of his connection to the natural world:

> I was very lucky in that I grew up in a rural area [Boiling Springs, N.C.]. But I also spent a lot of time, pretty much spent my summers, with my grandmother on her farm [in Aho in Watauga County, N.C.]. There was no car there, and I was just allowed to roam these mountains. . . . I'd eat a big breakfast, and [my grandmother would] give me a sandwich, and I'd take off. I'd come back at five o'clock. She just let me go. It was a different world, but what it did for me, you know, I was just out in that world, and I observed it. But it wasn't like I was self-consciously identifying trees or anything, but I was just in it, and I felt very comfortable there. I probably felt more comfortable there than I did around other human beings.
>
> The other thing that happened up there was that, particularly with a lot of my older relatives, you got this sense of the world, there's almost a kind of shimmering sentience in the land. I can remember, for instance, as a child, I'd like to catch salamanders in the springhouse, and my grandmother would tell me that I wasn't supposed to do that. What was going on there was this idea that those salamanders were like guardian spirits of the purity of that water. All this folklore I grew up with made for a very mysterious world, and also a world that was very alive . . . to me the natural world is the most universal of languages.[3]

For Rash, the Appalachian landscape performs as a type of conduit, a place of conjuring where the ghosts and mysteries of the past live on both in memory and imagination, which he fuses together in tightly crafted works of art that "raise the dead" and give them human voice. Rash has called his mountain heritage his own "spirit world" where his ancestors still remain, ghostly figures who emerge from the rolling fogbanks of the past and who assume flesh and blood and stubborn bone in Rash's writing.[4] "Invocation," from his first book of poetry *Eureka Mill* (1998), tells of this kind of ritual summoning of James Moody Rash where the poet pools moonshine into a mason jar lid and lights it, a blue flame rising that merges all elements of the mysterious night and which curls

> northward to seep six feet
> into the black bony dirt
> and guide his spirit across
> the declining mountains to this room,
> where I sit and sip, await
> a tobacco-breathed haint, shadowless shadow,
> bloodless blood-kin I have summoned
> to hear my measured human prayer:
> *Grandfather guide my hand*
> *to weave with words a thread*
> *of truth as I write down*
> *your life and other lives*
> *close kin but strangers too,*
> *those lives all lived as gears*
> *in Springs' cotton mill*
> *and let me not forget*
> *your lives were more than that.*[5]

"Invocation" is an important poem, not only because of its position as prologue into the vibrant and haunting world of *Eureka Mill*, or because of its craft, distinctive speech rhythms, and remarkable sound sense. The poem is also a clear and achingly tender *ars poetica* of Rash's project as a writer—that of recovering lost voices who have been "erased" from history and who deserve better than a thoughtless forgetting. It is a project built on Rash's determination and perseverance to his writing and by his fierce attachment to the land and lives of his ancestors, who first began to arrive in the Appalachian mountains in the mid-1700s. They migrated from regions in Wales and Scotland and built their lives on the hardscrabble farms and black loamy soil in the shadows of the blue mountains that reminded them of home. They recorded their births and deaths in family bibles and were witnesses to war, natural disasters, and gruesome deaths. They also fought silent battles against the fear and worries that ride the demons of displacement, superstition, and change in a mysterious and unforgiving land.

Rash dips into this vibrant past as into a vast Jungian sea. The thematic material he pulls from its depths ranges widely but all of Rash's work is distinctly characterized by his ability to penetrate into the lonely spaces of the human heart with a force and clarity few writers can match. With Rash's characters there are no easy answers—only tough choices, desperate schemes, and dances with the devil. Some are downright losers, some try hard and play fair, and some yield to the inevitable pull of corruption and evil. Most fail, some endure, some prevail, all suffer. There are stories of floodings, droughts, murders, and betrayals, of lust, greed, violence, and regret. There are also stories of love, courage, duty, and heart-rending beauty. Rash knows this world well and has spent his youth and most of his adult life writing, researching, and reclaiming it.

Over the years stories about Rash himself have emerged. These stories have shaped a portrait of the writer as a man preternaturally connected to the natural world, a man who moves through the land with ease and reverence and who communes with the dead swirling about him like some type of Appalachian Wordsworth. Anna Higgins Dunlap tells it particularly well: "Rash has tramped this [Appalachian] landscape, poking around the cairns of old homesteads, looking down dilapidated wells, studying old barbed wire fences, trying to sense the lives lived. He has spent a lot of time, too, walking among the dead, tracing his fingers along the names and dates on crumbling stones, imagining the lives and deaths that brought them to that place."[6]

Rash has been called "one of the hardest working writers in America," a claim that stands tall when one realizes that since his debut story collection *The Night the New Jesus Fell to Earth* in 1994 he has published fourteen books in twenty years: *Eureka Mill* (poems, 1996); *Casualties* (stories, 2000); *Among the Believers* (poems, 2000); *Raising the Dead* (poems, 2002); *One Foot in Eden* (novel, 2002); *Saints at the River* (novel, 2004); *The World Made Straight* (novel, 2006); *Chemistry and Other Stories* (stories, 2007); *Serena* (novel, 2009); *Burning Bright* (stories, 2010); *Waking* (poems, 2011); *The Cove* (novel, 2012); and *Nothing Gold Can Stay* (2013).[7] It is a staggering achievement and one that attests to his intense desire to capture what he sees as a vanishing culture and to cast, as Faulkner said, "a last look back" to save the past from disappearing into the maw of oblivion. For Rash, "literature—prose or poetry—is a way to preserve our identity. For all good writers, it is a way of holding on, a way to cope with change."[8]

This collection provides an illuminating map of Rash's work over the years. It allows readers access in one edition to his development as a writer and craftsman and to the themes and concerns that run obsessively throughout his poetry and fiction. Rash has spoken about the "mirroring" effect he has consciously developed from his earliest writings to his most recent celebrated publications, a type of recycling that generates a compelling resonance so that his body of work shapes thematic material that is constantly interwoven. The stories, poems, and novel excerpts included in this edition allow readers to see for themselves this kind of nuanced and subtle weaving. These carefully chosen selections exhibit some of the best of Rash's work and provide readers the opportunity to explore how Rash's writing rewards close examination and offers even greater insights into his concerns as a writer. Readers of this volume can see how the various strands wind, loop, and cross and deepen both our understanding of Rash's literary world and our own enjoyment of his writing.

Although Rash first began to publish stories in small magazines during the late seventies and early eighties, he was working largely under the radar of critical attention until the release of his first collection *The Night the New Jesus Fell to Earth* (1994), which showcases his impressive storytelling gifts and features his remarkable ability to adapt a variety of influences to form his own unique voice. The collection also features some of Rash's most salient early characteristics, perhaps most importantly the formal structure of assimilating different stories, speakers, or themes into distinct sections, often with a prologue and an epilogue, a tendency that speaks to his desire for a mirroring effect and a formal complexity that both invites and rewards rereadings. In this case, the book is structured by three narrative voices—Tracy, Vincent, and Randy—who each tell stories about the eccentric characters and strange events surrounding the community of Cliffside, North Carolina.

The stories show a variety of early and abiding influences. There are touches of Flannery O'Connor, William Faulkner, Jesse Stuart, Eudora Welty, and Anton Chekhov. Contemporary writers such as Robert Morgan, Doris Betts, Wendell Berry, and Barry Hannah are evident as well. Fred Chappell's influence is particularly strong, especially in his sequence of tales spun by the child narrator Jess Sorrells in *I Am One of You, Forever* that depicts a fascinating host of Appalachian character types with the rich and detailed texture of a mountain community. The cycle of interpolated stories blends a coming-of-age narrative with poignant scenes of loss and an evocative sense of humor indicative of the best Appalachian writing in the tall tale tradition. Rash's mature work has been praised for its use of a Southern Gothic sensibility and the compelling nature of Rash's rendering of the darkness and gloom of nature and the human heart.[9] However, what Rash learned, at least in part, from these early influences is the power and necessity of using humor in telling a story. The stories in *The Night the New Jesus Fell to Earth* are by far Rash's most charming and humorous, qualities especially prominent in writers such as Chappell, Stuart, and Welty.

"Badeye" is perhaps Rash's most autobiographical story, one initially conceived as a first novel but which later found its form as a brilliant short story. In this story Rash sets the scene of Cliffside, North Carolina, which is actually Boiling Springs, North Carolina, the small town where Rash grew up. It is a coming-of-age story, a narrative that Rash has used repeatedly in his work, that tells of an eight-year old's fascination with both snowcones and snakes, rebellious acts against his mother's wishes that ultimately lead the young boy to a frightful but illuminating conclusion. In "The Night the New Jesus Fell to Earth," Tracy, the town's only female carpenter, tells how her ex-husband Larry nearly kills himself posing as Christ on a rickety cross set up to advertise his own used car lot. Both stories show Rash's ability to blend humor with serious thematic content. In "Badeye," it is the rebellious nature of humans and a thirst for knowledge and experience colliding with parental authority and the primacy of the family unit as the ultimate source of protective love. In the titular story, it is the commodification of religion, a group-think mentality that isolates characters from the common fold, sexism, betrayal, and a tough-minded resolve that may lead to a kind of personal redemption.

In "My Father's Cadillacs," Rash reworks his father's own unique taste for unusual cars and other oddities into a hilarious coming-of-age story where the fifteen-year old narrator ends up driving a black Cadillac bought from a funeral home in what turns out to be a unique riff on the disastrous prom story experience. By turns satirical and poignant, the stories in *The Night the New Jesus Fell to Earth* are by far Rash's most autobiographical and humorous tales. But they are bound together by some of Rash's most enduring themes—change, love, pain, and a sense of enduring loss. In this case, the focus is on a "razing of the past" following a fire that burns down Greene's café, a site that registers the vanishing of a beloved era and the necessary thrust into the future that Vincent painfully realizes as he cranks up his truck and heads "up Highway Ten, watch[ing] Cliffside disappear in the rearview mirror."[10]

Although Rash develops his material from many familial and biographical sources, he never actually writes about himself. It is part of his genius as a writer that he so deftly veils, shifts, and reforms personal and familial history and events into works that are masked behind what Keats termed "negative capability," or what Coleridge described as "secondary genius," where the author "disappears" from the text and enters the consciousness of the characters. This ability is apparent in the poems of *Eureka Mill* (1998), which document, through a sequence of forty poems grouped into five thematic sections, the story of his grandparents' move off the family farm to join other dispossessed families in the textile mills of the South Carolina Piedmont. Like his fiction, Rash's poetry is highly narrative, driven through the use of precise images and evocative metaphors, structured through multiple speakers capturing the disjunction, isolation, and anger of Appalachian farmers bereft of their land and turned into clone-like cogs in a capitalist machine.

Rash's poetry is characterized by an elegiac and somber sensibility and is informed by many sources, particularly by the dark vision of Irish poets such as Seamus Heaney, Patrick Kavanagh, Dylan Thomas, and William Butler Yeats. The influence of Faulkner is also in these poems, not only through the use of multiple speakers and the fleshing out of a specific place (like Faulkner's Yoknapatawpha County, which he referred to as his "own little postage stamp of native soil") but also for their Depression-era desperation and hardship, and for the ironic use of black humor and violence that speakers use to maintain a sense of psychic balance and pride.[11] There are also echoes of D. H. Lawrence and Thomas Hardy, whose dark landscapes teem with brutality and human cruelty, qualities that spin the stark and unforgiving fates of its inhabitants.

In "Eureka," for instance, Rash's grandfather finds himself standing amidst the roaring hum of the weave room, "thinking *This is my life* / and catching himself before he was caught / lost wages or fingers the risk of reflection."[12] Although Rash is aware of the complex economic nature of the mill system, his sympathies clearly rest with the workers, particularly his grandfather, who realizes "his spatial enclosure, his loss of autonomy, the large-scale shift in his world from agrarian to industrial values, where people who were once self-sustaining individuals are now conceived of as 'irregular solids' who are measured, shaped, and distributed much like the goods they produce in the weaving rooms in which they labor."[13] The accessibility and surprising depths of Robert Frost's poems are also at work here as Rash self-consciously rejects the self-absorbed and often showy over-complexity of much of contemporary American poetry by using a strong narrative and lyric thrust. In "Brown Lung," for example, the speaker relates his failing health from years spent in the unhealthy conditions of the weave room, admitting in common speech the nightmare of his approaching death: "But even though I slept more I'd still wake / gasping for air at least one time a night, / and when I dreamed I dreamed of bumper crops / of Carolina cotton in my chest."[14]

Rash's knowledge of and virtuosity with a range of poetic forms is on display in these poems as he employs free verse, the villanelle, iambic pentameter, the Anglo-Saxon split line, the caesura, kennings, and other devices for specific thematic effects. For instance, in the first section, the poems are written in a looser verse that evokes the farmers' sense of freedom and independence as self-reliant owners of their own land and labor. As they move into the restrictive mill villages, forms such as the villanelle tighten and constrict, registering their loss of freedom and spatial enclosure. In the sections that feature the repetitive tasks and unceasing labor of the mill's mechanical world, Rash uses iambic pentameter to reinforce the rhythms of such work and the persistent drudgery of their daily routines. In other poems, Rash mirrors the former farmers' frustrations and anger by using the Anglo-Saxon split line and the caesura to evoke a type of primitive and tribal sensibility where violence erupts in a variety of startling ways.

But despite the often grim nature of his writing, Rash does not leave the reader trapped in despair. There is nearly always a glimmer of hope or a suggestion of endurance despite the circumstances. The closing poem in *Eureka Mill,* for instance, ends on a note of one of Rash's most trenchant and hopeful themes—a fierce love for the past and a duty to memorialize his parents' lives as crucial foundations for the present. Just as in "Invocation," Rash the poet, the man, the son, appears again in "July, 1949," as if summoned by all the speakers haunting the book's pages. In this poem Rash imagines what he cannot remember, an achingly tender recreation of the young woman who would become his mother, dreaming a life where her future husband waits for her unknowingly in the weave room, both of them unable to hear "the world's soft click, / fate's tumbler's falling into place, / soft as the sound of my mother's / bare feet as she runs, / runs toward him, toward me."[15]

One of Rash's most distinguishing traits is his force as a fierce triple threat in contemporary literature—prize-winning poet, short story writer, and novelist. While *The Night the New Jesus Fell to Earth* won several awards, including the Sherwood Anderson Prize (1996), Rash was originally recognized as a poet due to his voluminous output in regional and national journals, poems that were later shaped into the stunning collections *Among the Believers* (2000) and *Raising the Dead* (2002). Anthony Hecht's introduction to *Among the Believers* heralded Rash's poetry as "a gift matched with skills of the first order."[16] This acclaim was due in large part to what Hecht described as Rash's formal brilliance and his development and mastery of a seven-syllable line adopted from the traditional Welsh alliterative form, *cynghanedd* (literally "harmony"). This technique allows Rash to connect familial and regional Appalachian subject matter with the greatness of the Welsh and English poetic traditions, perhaps best exemplified in the medieval collection *The Mabinogion* and in the sprung rhythms and inscapes of Gerard Manley Hopkins. Rash's syllabic line creates a rhythmic structure where dramatic enjambments, clusters of evocative imagery, and surprising internal rhymes spill over each other in a forest of brilliant sound chimes.

Rash has discussed the importance of sound in his poetry, and has noted that many of his poems begin with "just some sounds strung together." His admiration of Welsh poets such as Thomas and Henry Vaughn rest largely on the musicality in their work.[17] In fact, Rash often explains his idea of writing poems through the metaphor of music: "To me, it's almost like having stereo speakers and unplugging one of them. In the poems I love the most, the sound gives a pleasure just in itself that makes it worthwhile just to hear, to read. And then you've got meaning or language, and the poets I love most are always working stereo."[18] Rash's "stereo sound" and his syllabic line are especially fine in his poem "Scarecrow":

> He said this land would kill him,
> and when it did his widow
> left the hoe where he dropped it
> on his death-row, staked his clothes
>
> to raise his stark shade over
> tall corn stalks like the black pall
> she laid across his casket.
> All that summer into fall
>
> she allowed no harrowing plow
> where his heart failed, not until
> five Aprils passed and the last
> rag on that rotting cross fell.[19]

Both the structure (three four-line stanzas) and the sounds in these lines exemplify the power and skill of Rash's poetic brilliance. Each stanza describes a scene in this three part tale of life, death, grief, and the landscape of this tragedy, which the "he" in line one ominously narrates to us. Each line in the poem employs the seven-syllable rhythm, except for line nine, which stretches to eight syllables because of the word "harrowing," the only three-syllable word in the poem, and one which connects the action of the man's farming (a harrow is a farm tool used for breaking up hard ground) to the grief of the widow (to "harrow" is to inflict great distress and torment). The dramatic enjambments push the narrative forward into clusters of imagery—the widow "stakes" the man's "clothes" to a scarecrow frame that casts a "stark shade" over the "tall corn stalks" and waits for the seasons to change from "summer into fall"—before revealing the inevitable change that awaits us all, indicated by images of time and decay portrayed by "passing," "rag," and "rotting."

But the syllabic line and the haunting images only tell half of the story, only give us one speaker of Rash's poetic "stereo." The sounds themselves push this tale of grief even deeper into the emotional chambers of our minds. There is a delicate interweaving of long vowel sounds ("he," "she"; "staked," "raise," "shade," "laid, "failed"; "widow," "death-row," "clothes," "over," "no,") with short ones ("kill," "him," "it," "did," "into," "until," "Aprils"; "stark," "stalks"; "black," "casket," "passed," "last," "rag"; "dropped," "across," "rotting," "cross"). These sounds ring and chime into a rhythmic scheme with the longer vowels mainly associated with the living characters, types of purposeful action, and places or objects associated with life, and the short vowels indicative of death, time's passage, grief, and decay. The "widow" hangs the man's "clothes" over his "death-row" and waits for the "last" "rag" to "rot" on the "cross." There are too many of these rhymes or near-rhymes to discuss here, but one final construction is particularly evocative and generates much of the emotional intensity of the poem: the "tall . . . stalks" are like the "pall" of grief that lingers into "fall" until the scarecrow "fell." The softness of the last word not only ends the poem and contrasts with the energetic diction driving most of its action, but with its off-rhyme and past tense, it releases the man, the widow's grief, and our witness to the tragic event. This interweaving of sound and sense is the stuff of poetic genius and shows the subtle, startling, and powerful complexity of Rash's work as a poet of the "first order."

In *Among the Believers,* Rash continues to develop his poetic music and his exploration of the familial but he also moves deeper into the regional history and folklore of the western North Carolina mountains, where speakers range from the grief-stricken to the amorous to the fanatical to the elegiac. The poems offer glimpses into the complex history of the region with its paradoxical mix of spirituality and paganism, its stark and primal landscapes, and its enduring families that tell stories rife with somber mystery, sudden violence, and unsettling moments of unexpected beauty. Ceremonial rites such as foot washing, baptisms, and serpent handling blend with Civil War-era violence and a host of bodies strewn throughout, victims of flood, matricide, bad luck, murder, the supernatural, and the wilderness itself.

Rash has discussed his ability to write poetry and fiction at the same time by using the musical metaphor of radio frequencies which he characterizes as AM or FM, the signals transmitting whether the sounds and images he receives are better suited for poetry or fiction, although he isn't always certain. This is a fundamental trait of Rash's work, a type of recycling, where an idea may begin as a poem, but which he later often reworks as a story, a few of which turn into fully realized novels as well. For instance, Rash's second collection of stories, *Casualties* (2000), features an impressive array of finely tuned tales that both look back to his Cliffside stories and forward into new territories explored in his poetry. For instance, the poem "Last Rite" in *Among the Believers* becomes a story by the same name in *Casualties,* where a grieving mother journeys deep into the mountains to mark the exact spot of her son's murder so she can record it in her family bible. The poem "Return" also changes frequencies and becomes a story as well, the tale of Rash's uncle, a World War II veteran who, haunted by the war, makes a slow and steady ascent to his home atop the mountain where he cleanses himself by drinking deeply from the pure water of the family spring.[20]

The stories in *Casualties* selected for this reader relate to themes Rash had previously explored in both *The Night the New Jesus Fell to Earth* and in *Eureka Mill.* "The Way Things Are," for example, is set in a grayish mountain town reminiscent of Cliffside, and features two working class characters, whose glory days as high school football players are long gone. Like many of Rash's characters, these men become invisible working class outcasts, trapped in a present age defined by dead end jobs, aching bodies, alienated selves, and a powerlessness they strive to overcome through defiance, violence, and genuine good-heartedness. "Summer Work" is set in Cliffside and features teenage characters that play a mean-spirited practical joke that goes desperately wrong. The story also displays one of Rash's most prevalent structural devices, a "set-up" first line or paragraph that establishes character and context, and provides a tension or hook (to use a Rash metaphor) that propels the reader into a state of wonder regarding how the story will flesh out: "I saw Cecil Ledbetter last week for the first time since I'd seen him dragged unconscious and bleeding from a truck eleven years ago, and I thought again of my role in what happened to him."[21]

"Casualties and Survivors" shows Rash's movement away from previous stories and into new territory. While this story maintains a strong connection to the earlier ones, Rash's use of third-person narration filtered through the main character, Rachel, allows him to explore issues that would become increasingly important to him—loneliness, trauma, separation, and a seemingly overwhelming despair met with hope, courage, and a trenchant love that refuses to yield. Although these stories build on earlier themes and settings, they also evoke a new resonance and show fresh and evocative developments in his writing. Rash continues to use the first-person narrator who speaks directly and evocatively to the reader, but he also works through a third-person point of view that provides more distance, although the slippage from narrative voice to character's mind maintains the immediacy of a character's actions and emotions as if it were a first-person account. Rash also continues working through familiar themes, narrative strategies, and metaphors: the pressures of enduring loss and economic hard times; the coming-of-age story reflected through an adult narrator's painful admission of complicity; and the emerging metaphor of water that would lead Rash into a new world of lost voices and cultural erasure.[22]

In 2002, Rash published two books of poetry and fiction that led to widespread critical acclaim and propelled him into the national spotlight. In the poetry collection *Raising the Dead* (2002), Rash stakes claim to the Appalachian underwater world of Jocassee Valley (the Cherokee word for "valley of the lost") in northwestern South Carolina, which was flooded for hydroelectric power in the 1960s. In these evocative poems, mountain residents speak with dignity of a lost world, a place of intense belonging filled with mystery, beauty, love, and death. As in *Eureka Mill* and *Among the Believers*, Rash continues to use various poetic forms to generate both mood and meaning, and although his mastery of the seven-syllable line is even more evident in this collection than the previous two, he is not bound to it exclusively.

In "Under Jocassee," for example, the lines shift between five to seven syllables, a technique that both maintains the rhythms and sound effects of the *cynghanedd* and the Welsh and Appalachian past but also allows a freedom suggestive of the shift to the contemporary. The poem is emblematic of the book's nostalgic sense and features a present-day boater skimming the surface of Lake Jocassee, unaware of the past below before the poet guides him to bow his head and look deep into the water "as through a mirror" where "all that's changed is time."[23] He drifts sixty years into the past, seeing the farm life of the submerged mountain valley, his boat casting a shadow upon a woman below who feels it as an omen of approaching disaster: "She believes someone / has crossed her grave, although / she will go to her grave, / a grave you've just passed over, / wondering why she looked up."[24]

Like the poems in *Eureka Mill* and *Among the Believers*, the speakers in *Raising the Dead* continue to enlarge Rash's project of recovering lost voices, but without histrionics or accusation. Rash's fascination with this lost world is painfully and eloquently evident in poems ranging from the loss of rare flora like the "Shee-Show" (or "Oconee Bell"), to the extinction of the native catamounts and Carolina parakeets, to a reverence for the hardships of lives ravaged by the toil and turmoil of settlement, war, and disease, and which are ultimately drowned beneath a controlled but devastating flood reminiscent of Old Testament punishment. Rash's obsessive use of water as both physical setting and metaphor is one of his most notable and noticeable thematic devices. The biblical connotations of redemption and rebirth are potent signifiers that capture the region's devout Christian belief system but Rash's use of water also hearkens back to Welsh folklore, where it functions as a conduit between the two worlds of the living and the dead.

As in *Raising the Dead,* Rash's first novel *One Foot in Eden* (2002) is set in Jocassee Valley where water is a foreboding presence as characters fear the encroaching flood that will drown their land, their ancestors, and their agrarian way of life. The novel expresses Rash's genuine fear of cultural erasure—that an entire way of life and its people can vanish so easily. He has spoken about this with characteristic wonder and empathy: "After an exodus like that of the Cherokee, or the peoples before the Cherokee, something remains. Arrowheads, pottery—artifacts the earth holds. We find these and remember. We have their names, too, things they named, Jocassee, Oconee, Chattooga, Watauga, the Shee-Show. It's the same with the European settlers, roads especially. At Jocassee, there is only the water; not even the place names remain. It's simply terrifying to me, at Jocassee—the erasure—of lives, of graves, of farmland, of flowers, of names. All erased."[25]

One Foot in Eden won many awards, including the Appalachian Book of the Year, and garnered attention from across the country with a review by the *Los Angeles Times* calling this Southern gothic murder mystery, "a veritable garden of earthly disquiet."[26] Just as Rash writes poetry with strong characters and a narrative thrust, he writes novels with a poetic language of intense eloquence and penetrating beauty. The book, perhaps more than any of Rash's previous work, pivots on the twin themes of hard times and tough choices, concerns that would dominate his fiction until the present day. The presence of Faulkner, O'Connor, and Morgan remain but other influences such as Cormac McCarthy and Fyodor Dostoyevsky charge this disappearing world with a complex and intense sense of foreboding and corrupting malevolence.

Through five sections, each narrated by a different speaker, the novel tells the story of Billy Holcombe and his wife Amy, who, unable to produce a child, find themselves increasingly desperate. They are thrust into an implacable situation that spawns bad decisions and nearly unthinkable choices as they commit crimes and sins of the heart that enmesh them in a fateful web of seduction, betrayal, and murder. Elemental and tragic, Rash's sensual language is rich with images of earth and water and plunges the reader into a world rife with superstition and human frailty while also evoking a profound sense of the power of love and a deeply felt belief in forgiveness and redemption. One scene is particularly evocative of these themes and showcases Rash's haunting gothic sensibility: "The rope spread [his] arms out. They was stiff now as fire-pokers and as he raised higher his arms spread out like wings. I remembered Preacher Robertson reading from Revelation how on Judgment Day the dead would raise from earth and sea and fly to Heaven and what a glorious sight that would be. But as I parted Sam's flank and [he] lifted another few yards into the sky, his face gouged by barbed wire, the hole in his chest boiling with bluebottle flies and yellow jackets, I reckoned a man might witness no more terrible sight than the dead resurrected."[27]

In *Saints at the River* (2004), Rash continues developing the themes of love, death, and redemption with the story of Maggie Glenn's return to her home in the South Carolina mountains to cover the story of a young girl's drowning in the primitively harsh but spiritually-resonant Tamassee River. Maggie's reluctant homecoming reconnects her with "the Dark Corner" of her youth and with her dying father, after she had left the area full of resentment because of several traumatic childhood experiences.[28] As she tells us in the beginning, she thought she deserved better and remembers herself as "twenty years old and want[ing] my Friday and Saturday nights for something other than helping my mother die."[29] In this novel Rash breaks away from multiple speakers and uses the female voice as narrator, something Robert Morgan had tremendous success with in his acclaimed novel *Gap Creek* (1998). As a photographer for the state newspaper in Columbia, Maggie is "a woman who spent much of her life focusing on surfaces to reveal deeper meanings."[30] This is an enduring theme in Rash's work but Maggie has trouble with maintaining her objectivity when returning to the rich, fecund earth of her youth where she realizes that she "couldn't let things go. I didn't even want to. Forgetting, like forgiving, only blurred things."[31]

Another distinguishing trait is Rash's refusal to trade in worn-out, mythic stereotypes built atop rocking chairs, banjo strummers, and feuding clans bathed in a warm fog of nostalgia, types that continue to plague too much of Appalachian writing. Rash self-consciously deconstructs this type of characterization through Billy Watson, owner of a general store and host to Saturday night musical hoe-downs, which would seem the epitome of stereotyping if "Uncle Billy" wasn't so shrewdly aware of such a constructed identity. Billy's family is well off, and although he "had a degree in agriculture from Clemson University" he had decided "that his true calling was playing Snuffy Smith to fleece tourists."[32] Rash's refusal to play to type or draw oversimplified solutions to life's difficulties is also evident in this novel as he shows both the flaws and virtues of everyone involved in the tragedy, from Ruth Kowalski's grief-stricken parents to Luke Miller, an impassioned environmentalist and self-appointed savior of the wild river, to the calculating and opportunistic developer Tony Bryan.

Even though *Saints at the River* had its predecessor in the story "Something Rich and Strange," *The World Made Straight* (2006) offers an even better example of Rash's recycling methods.[33] In this case, Rash revises his O. Henry Award winning short story "Speckled Trout," which originally began as the short poem "Speckled Trout," and turns it into a thrilling novel that looks into the past of a Civil War massacre at Shelton Laurel in "Bloody Madison" county in western North Carolina. Rash uses italicized entries from a Confederate doctor who is an unwilling witness to the atrocity to connect past to present, but the novel is firmly set in the contemporary world of Appalachia, where bad luck, poverty, personal failures, illiteracy, and the drug trade command the field.

Like the swirling fog and mists whose tendrils form and reform over the meadow at Shelton Laurel, Rash knits together a tale of fragments, of broken characters bucking forces beyond their control, of spaces marked by ghosts and violence, of a history forged through brutality and ignorance. All this is in Madison County, North Carolina, a backwoods region along the Tennessee border, where in 1863 members of a Confederate force massacred thirteen Union sympathizers—all children and aged men—in the middle of a snow-swept field, their rifle reports echoing into nothingness. "I feel haunted by ghosts" Rash has said.[34] His ancestors were themselves participants in the tragic events of Shelton Laurel, a communal act of internecine violence that weighed on this area for a generation. Rash captures the essence of that weight—the tug and pull at every step—in the bleakness of this mountain land, how its stark spaces are rife with time, pockets of history swimming with the past like a mirror that conjures the dead. As one character states, "you know a place is haunted when it feels more real than you are."[35]

The novel is thick with some of Rash's most poignant and enduring themes, particularly the pull of the past and the imprint of history on the land, and how its grip tangles and complicates the present world likes snags on a trout line. Travis Shelton, a high school dropout who prefers fishing deep in the woods for the elusive speckled trout, one day stumbles upon a cash crop of marijuana plants lining the creek bottom, a bounty he quickly appropriates for himself, much to the displeasure of the tough backwoods moonshiner-turned-drug dealer Carlton Toomey. Shortly after, Travis finds refuge with Leonard Shuler, a disgraced high school teacher who now deals dime bags and six-packs to a host of mountain kids like Travis, bent on copping buzzes as they barrel down the long road to nowhere. But Travis, like Leonard himself, is different, and soon Leonard begins to speak of "Bloody Madison" County, the Civil War, and a history that begins to shape both characters in ways neither is fully aware of.

One particular episode drives this point home with compelling force and profundity. During a visit to Shelton Laurel, Travis, using Leonard's own metal detector to sweep the meadow for remnants, discovers a pair of small eyeglasses with one lens missing. Travis puts on the glasses, squinting. "It's kind of blurry," he tells Leonard, "like looking through water."[36] But then something amazing happens as Travis, previously nothing much more than another angry self-destructive teen, is suffused with an overwhelming sense of empathy for the twelve-year boy whose life was taken at this very spot. "Travis opened his left eye. 'David Shelton could have been looking through these glasses when they shot him. Standing right where I'm standing.'"[37] It is an eerie scene, the glasses performing like a talisman summoning revenants from the grave, long silenced. Past and present, victim and victimizer, family and country, duty and survival—all cohere in a poetic intensity that evokes the novel's larger concerns regarding the preciousness of hope, the fragility of dreams, and the moral responsibilities we all must face.

Rash's third book of short fiction, *Chemistry and Other Stories* (2007), reprints eight of the fourteen stories from *Casualties* but adds several new tales that forge ahead in new directions. The title story is one of Rash's best, where a young narrator tries to come to grips with his father's mental illness and his father's subsequent embracing of Pentecostal fervor that leads him in search of a type of salvation scuba-diving in the deep waters of Lake Jocassee. "Their Ancient, Glittering Eyes" shows Rash's ability to use humor in a wry and comical way and as a tool for evoking a sense of reverence for the past. In this case, the cast of characters is a bunch of old timers who sit around a store, reminiscent of some of Barry Hannah's striking tales such as "Water Liars" and "High-Water Railers."[38] In this story, Rash transforms the old southern stereotype of porch-sitting, tale-spinning cut-ups past their prime into a big fish tale where the men are mocked and dismissed because no one believes their sighting of a monster fish in the river that runs alongside the Riverside

Gas and Grocery store. This may be one of Rash's funniest stories, with lines and scenes of knee-slapping hilarity, but like all of his work, under the surface swims a host of darker themes, including the present's dismissal of the past, the need for human community and solace, the determination of desire, and the perseverance that can lead to a type of salvation and dignity.

Rash's masterpiece to date is unquestionably the epic and ambitious *Serena,* a sweeping novel of Olympian proportions that pits the Nietzchean "will to power" of 1930s timber barons against the nascent environmental movement and the building of the Great Smokies National Park. Reviews of the book catapulted Rash into the top rank of southern and American novelists and introduced in dramatic and hypnotizing ways perhaps the most powerful and dominating female character in southern literature, Serena Pemberton. Wife of the Boston-bred and privileged George Pemberton, Serena's ruthless quest for all-consuming power reminds one of Marlowe's Doctor Faustus or Tamburlaine, of the corrosive relationships that darken the stages of Shakespeare's *MacBeth,* and of *King Lear*'s malevolent co-conspirators Edmund, Regan, and Goneril.

Serena's single-minded obsession with the denuding of virgin forest lands in the Appalachians (and later in Brazil) evokes the type of destructive compulsion of Ahab's quest in *Moby Dick.* The novel's body count, which begins in the first few pages where Pemberton ruthlessly guts an older local, "his intestines spilled onto his lap in loose gray ropes," builds throughout the novel in an unrelenting fury of recklessness and human evil that recalls the stunning violence of McCarthy's *Blood Meridian.*[39] The dead man turns out to be the father of a young woman, Rachel Hampton, who Pemberton has carelessly impregnated before Serena's arrival and the act begins the turning of fate's wheel as the familiar themes of violence, infertility, obsession, and environmental destruction tumble and click into place, gaining thrilling momentum as the novel churns its way to its inevitable bloody conclusion.

If Rash's concern with evil and its sometimes unwitting agents is balanced or tempered in *One Foot in Eden* and *Saints at the River,* and becomes more obvious in drug lords such as Carlton Toomey in *The World Made Straight,* *Serena*'s villains are cast in a fever pitch, whether backed by a trained European education like Serena or by a visceral will to maim, murder, and destroy like her henchman, a one-handed killer appropriately named Galloway. The connections to Elizabethan drama and the revenge tragedy are not accidental. Rash has commented on his intention to write "an Elizabethan play" in novel form, with the book's thematic sections performing as "acts" in this drama of overweening violence and moral corruption in the obsessive pursuit of material gain and worldly power.[40] In the Pembertons' hands, the natural world is literally scalped, recalling the crater-like landscapes of World War One. Early in the book, Pemberton takes the newly arrived Serena to an overlook to survey their holdings. It is a nightmare vision that evokes Armageddon and the end of the world: "At the valley's center was the camp, surrounded by a wasteland of stumps and branches. To the left, Half Acre Ridge had been cut bare as well. On the right, the razed lower quarter of Noland Mountain. As it crossed the valley, the railroad track appeared sewn into the lowland like stitches."[41]

Rash's concerns with environmental destruction and the subsequent loss of humanity that arises from such disconnection to the natural world of which we are part are themes "writ large" in this epic novel. One scene is especially revealing of the human attitude that views nature as purely raw material for exploitation, a conception that we employ at our own peril. As Serena is recovering from an illness, Pemberton looks through her trunk and finds a map (reminiscent of a similar one in *Tamburlaine*) that illustrates the dangerous human lust for power and domination. It was "a wax-engraved map of South America, which, once unfolded, consumed half the front room. The map covered the room for days, a caneback chair set upon it so Serena could peruse its expanse more diligently, the chair occasionally lifted like a chess piece and set back down on a different square of the map."[42]

If one of Rash's distinguishing characteristics is that he does not provide readers with easy answers and clearly drawn heroes and villains, he makes the exception in *Serena*, even though this killing goddess has her own moments of humanity. However, if one looks through the body of Rash's writing, characters who knowingly and willfully abuse their power come through, as Cormac McCarthy says in *The Road*, as "the bad guys."[43] Serena, Galloway, and Cheney are the villains in this Elizabethan power play, but as in Shakespeare or Marlowe, there is always a price to pay. Mark Powell has commented on Rash's ability to create these types of characters, ones who often rise to the mythic but who cannot escape their humanity: "Rash's characters are often dynamic individuals, bending the world to their will while simultaneously crashing against the constraints of their own bodies. No matter how close a character approaches myth, the indelible marks of human suffering are always visible."[44]

In addition to enlarging his usual themes—hard times, tough choices, human goodness and malignity, reverence and concern for the natural world, power and infertility, violence and forgiveness—to epic proportions, Rash also displays his ability to write about past events with such an immediacy of detail and language that his works never come close to falling into the trap of genre. His writing does the work implicit in all great historical novels in that he captures a precise moment in time, but that moment also provides a lens for readers to view similar issues of significance in contemporary society. If Rash is a kind of history writer, then he is one unconstrained by genre, and his writing of the past mirrors the present for a deeper look into both. The robber barons and their unbridled desire for power fueled by greed are mirrors of the first decade of the twenty-first century where the "winner-take-all" ideology resulted in economic, societal, and cultural damage that is still under repair. However, despite these potential forces of destruction, in *Serena*—as in all of his novels—he offers the reader hope and a way out.[45] Rachel's flight with her baby from Serena's henchmen has been said to be "the single sign of hope that the powerless might at times, with the help from others who make strong moral choices, be able to win against the power mongers."[46] Rash's use of universal themes and archetypal conflicts such as those between father and son, individual and community, male and female, power and the powerless, imbue his work with a tough and clear-sighted resonance that is one of the many reasons why his stories project a life and immediacy far beyond the bounds of regional or historical fiction.

Burning Bright's international acclaim cemented Rash's reputation as a master of the short story form. It is a brilliant book containing a host of mesmerizing stories that won him global reviews and awards. The stories in *Burning Bright,* like the themes of Blake's poem "The Tyger," flash with a brutal intensity and create a "fearful symmetry" that plunges the reader into the churning depths of the trials and vicissitudes of the human experience. Many of the stories show new influences, particularly from the work of William Gay, Donald Harington, and Edna O'Brien. The first story, "Hard Times," is emblematic of the entire collection and of Rash's work as a whole. In this Depression-era story the "tough choice" theme threading throughout Rash's work is given a new intensity when a beleaguered farmer must contend with loss, poverty, and the choice between human sympathy and survival. The stories in this collection form a type of patchwork quilt of Appalachian history. Rash's constant probing of the past and the present in this mountainous region, from the Civil War era to the 1930s and 1950s to a contemporary Appalachia beset with economic collapse, loneliness, addiction, and desperate schemes for survival, gives the collection a distinct and finely-tuned locality but also a universality that reminds one of Joyce's Dublin or Philip Roth's Newark.

Rash's concern with the proliferation of the contemporary drug trade, first addressed in stories such as "Speckled Trout" and "Deep Gap" and in *The World Made Straight,* are developed with an even deeper gothic sensibility in

Burning Bright. In stories such as "Back of Beyond" and particularly in "The Ascent," Rash writes hauntingly of the new plague ravaging the region. "The Ascent" tells the story of a young boy's imaginative escape from his meth-addled parents and into the surrounding mountainside where he finds a downed plane with frozen corpses inside. He prefers the company of the dead to his near-dead parents who repeatedly break promises and sell the family's belongings under the influence of addiction and the desperate need for higher and more intense binges. Rash has commented on how the meth plague is ravaging Appalachia in ways just as deep and profound as the coal, natural gas, and other corporate powers that have exploited the region for generations. In this story Rash combines a coming-of-age narrative with the contemporary drug scourge to create a haunting portrait of a diseased Appalachia where the once dominant center of the culture—the family—is wasting away amid self-destruction and traumatic loneliness.

The loneliness in "The Ascent," as in many of Rash's previous stories, finds its most eloquent and perfect form in "The Woman Who Loved Jaguars," a story laden with loss, alienation, and despair. Ruth Lealand returns from her mother's funeral, vacant-eyed and hollow, tormented by the memory of her stillborn child and the resulting collapse of her marriage. She lives an invisible life and wears a stoic façade to the outside world. She searches desperately for some connection to life even if it is by hunting for an extinct species that has simply vanished from history. "Burning Bright" recasts the theme in a more sinister tone, as Marcie, a recent widow and outsider to the region, finds herself desperately seeking human connection to stave off an all-consuming loneliness. Her desire is so extreme that she willingly endangers her life by pursuing a relationship with a mysterious young man half her age who is a clear suspect for a series of fires that flare in deadly repetition in the mountains surrounding her home, each one creeping nearer and nearer. But this uncertain fate is better than the one awaiting her as a widowed outsider shaped by the fundamentalist values of a small mountain community. After her first husband dies, "Marcie [had] learned then what true loneliness was. Five miles from town on a dead-end dirt street. . . . She bought extra locks for the doors because at night she sometimes grew afraid, though what she feared was as much inside the house as outside it. Because she knew what was expected of her—to stay in this place, alone, waiting for the years, perhaps decades, to pass until she herself died."[47] As Ruth fights loneliness and despair in a "lost cause" scheme to prove jaguars once existed in South Carolina, so Marcie responds to emptiness by making a seemingly hopeless and far more dangerous attempt to take control over her life and fate's cruel hand.

In "Linconites," though, Rash rewrites this "lost cause' response to life's vicissitudes by ironically using a "Lost Cause" character to stage a scene of violence and victory. Lily, several months pregnant, wife of a Southerner-turned Union solider, waits alone in their mountain cabin for his rare visits, worrying for his safety and her own from Confederate outliers in the area, who are hardly distinguishable from common brigands and criminals. Rash's interest in writing about the Civil War ties him emphatically to the great tradition of southern literature, particularly the work of Faulkner, whose obsessions with the sins of the South soar to heights of dizzying complexity, especially in the masterful novels *Light in August* and *Absalom, Absalom!* But Rash's interest in the "War Between the States" takes a different slant by focusing on Union sympathizers in the mountains, or "Lincolnites," whose allegiance to the Federal Army led to disasters like Shelton Laurel and to other atrocities described by contemporary writers such as Charles Frazier in *Cold Mountain* and Daniel Woodrell in *Woe to Live On*. In Rash's story, Lily must face Vaughan, who has been watching her hoeing in the fields alone and has decided to requisition her horse and other things for the Confederate cause. But Lily's "tough decision due to troubled circumstances" is not self-destructive and illusory, and by the end she thinks: "Bad as it was that had happened, there'd been some luck in it too. . . . She could it get it done by noon . . . maybe even have time to plant some tomato and squash before supper."[48] These three stories clearly show Rash's ability to write convincingly from the female perspective in different settings and eras, each facing problems with a profound dignity, even if their hardships seem to overcome them. Lily, though, is an exception and in her will to survive and to nourish the fetus fluttering inside her she proves more than capable and shows Rash's rewriting of helpless women characters as capable, creative, determined, and dangerous depending on the circumstances.

Rash's recent work both continues his life-long concerns and recycling of thematic material while breaking into new territory and climbing ever higher on the global literary mountain. *Waking* (2011) is Rash's first book of poems since 2002 and shows the poet at the height of his powers. Many of the poems in this collection display a tight and condensed intensity that offers readers a penetrating glimpse into the beauty and brutality of the region but the focus remains on the respect and holiness of the natural world and the complex interrelationship between humans and the land upon which their lives depend. The book includes fifty-eight poems structured in thematic sections, and is bookended by poems emphasizing Rash's continuous fascination and reverence for water, the wellspring that sustains human life. In "Resolution," the poet writes of the humility necessary to recognize nature's power and mystery as the reader is told to peer into a stream that expresses the firmness of purpose and clarification of vision implicit in all of Rash's work: "Watch the crayfish prance across the sand, / the mica flash, the sculpen blend with stone. / It's all beyond your reach though it appears / as near and known as your outstretched hand."[49] The poem is an *ars poetica*—its metaphor of seeing more clearly, in both meaning and form, are qualities that embody Rash's aspirations as a poet from his beginnings as a writer.

In other poems Rash writes with a lyrical texture, determined spirit, and narrative thrust indicative of his best poetry. "Watauga County: 1959" and "The Code" are infused with several of Rash's major thematic concerns—death, grief, violence, and suffering. Death is imagined both as an absence, "an open parenthesis / no father, uncle could close" and as a result of history and its unswerving allegiance to traditions of family honor as men in "MacGregor tartan" appear on an old man's doorstep at night, "kin seeking one who killed one of their own."[50] The long poem "Three A.M. and the Stars Were Out" is another fine example of "green" Rash, where the poem's narrative of an old veterinarian answering the call of a desperate farmer is later recycled into the final short story in *Nothing Gold Can Stay*. Both "Spillcorn" and "White Wings" show Rash's ingenious ability to transform the narrative action of the poems into literary metaphors, with the leaves of the trees morphing into pages in a book, and the "white wings" of hymnal pages contrasting with the marble wings of angels over tombstones where death is not forgiven.

In *The Cove*, Rash propels the reader headlong into mystery, danger, violence, and desperation as this thriller deftly tells the story of love, sacrifice, hardship, and determination in the haunting backwoods of western North Carolina during the years of World War One. Rash employs the third-person limited perspective that he had been using since *The World Made Straight* and tells the story of Laurel Shelton, her brother Hank (a wounded veteran), an escapee from a German prisoner of war camp, and a zealous army recruiter bent on rooting out any trace of "the Hun" in the region. For *The World Made Straight* Rash coined the phrase "landscape as destiny"—which means, in that novel and in other stories, that the power of the Appalachian landscape is as much a determinant of a person's fate as his or her character, perhaps even more so.[51] In *The Cove*, landscape is a character itself, its gloom and mystery evocative of the power and darkness in Thomas Hardy's Egdon Heath, where fate moves its characters across the dark and unforgiving land like chess pieces in the hands of a sadist.

The land in *The Cove* carves itself into the people who inhabit it in many ways, some visible, some not. For Laurel, everyone believes the cove has marked her face and neck, a sign that she is bad luck at best, a witch at worst, troubles reminiscent of Eustacia Vye in Hardy's *The Return of the Native*.[52] The steep and winding trails, rushing creek beds, granite outcrops, and mysterious events in the cove and their effects on the characters show a conscious development toward moving the setting from background to foreground as a force itself. In an early scene, the interrelations and symbolic resonance between nature and human are intertwined as Laurel moves from the darkness of her past self into the light of new experience: "Emerging from the mountain's vast shadow was, as always, like stepping from behind a curtain. She winced from the sunlight, and her bare feet felt the strangeness of treading a surface not aslant."[53]

But Rash is doing other things in this novel too. He is working in both historical and contemporary modes but he is also developing his earlier themes, or "threads," in the larger weave of his work. In this case, the outcast/underdog Laurel Shelton's loneliness and the characters' desperate gambles for love reveal a landscape of despair that has appeared in previous work and taps into a universal fear that we all understand. The workings of a type of Greek-like fate are at work in Rash's mountain world where even though most are motivated by a need for acceptance and belonging, few escape failure and doom. In *The Cove,* Rash trims the epic sweep of *Serena* into a stripped down thriller crossed with a romance that becomes a dark and disturbing fairy tale. But this is a Ron Rash love story and troubles abound along with a strong sense of *carpe diem*. As one character thinks as he stares at the mountains, "how small and fleeting human life was. Forty or fifty years, a blink of time for these mountains, and there'd be no memory of what had happened here."[54] The pacing and ferocity of the novel shows, as in *Waking*, a slight twinge of direction, or at least a tweak in volume. There is a patient, lyrical plotting, a precision and control that belies the work of a master who has indeed come a long way since his days as a "mountain boy."

The stories in *Nothing Gold Can Stay* (2013) show Rash at the top of his game. As in *Burning Bright*, these tightly controlled, haunting and brutal tales stun the reader with an honesty and directness that spares no one and which often end on the teetering cusp of resolution. The pared down language and poetic allure of these stories show a writer with full confidence in his vision and abilities. One reviewer has marveled at the way "Rash can create a character in a single sentence," and in these new stories Rash exhibits a power of expression and precision of metaphor startling in its brilliance.[55] "The Trusty," for example, provides readers with a creative take on Grant Wood's famous painting "American Gothic," where the farmer and his wife gaze weirdly at the viewer behind the upraised prongs of a pitchfork. In this case, it is a "trusted" convict, working on a chain gang, who appeals to the young and seemingly unhappy farmer's wife, first for water from her well, then for her help in a planned double escape. Rash works the classic "grifter grifted" theme in this story and the convict's growing concerns about the young girl's dedication to the plan is expressed in a tight but telling metaphor, when he thinks, "a girl her age could turn quick as a weathervane."[56]

In "Where the Map Ends", Rash again taps into the South's most traumatic event but he approaches the effects of the Civil War in different ways than his predecessors such as Faulkner, Allen Tate, and Robert Penn Warren. Rash's world is not the Deep South but the Appalachian mountains, a land that was largely Union, a territory he had explored before in stories such as "Lincolnites" and in poems such as "The Dowry."[57] But here it is not Lily and her baby who are in danger from a haggard Confederate but two slaves in the traditional "runaway slave caught on the road" drama that turns out to be anything but traditional. As part of a growing number of Civil War era stories, "Where the Map Ends" shares many similar themes and strategies as the others but is unique in its focus from the African-American point of view. The story is not told in first person, though. It is another example of Rash's strategy of using a seemingly objective narrator, whose voice appears to be merely telling the story, but one which usually has an apparent sympathy for a character, although this sympathy is often complex and paradoxical as well.[58] In this story, it is Vitticus, the older fugitive, in which the narrative voice merges and readers are plunged into a tale of desire, remorse, grief, hatred, violence, and redemption paid for in blood.

In "The Woman at the Pond," Rash returns to his trademark metaphor of water and recasts the familiar themes of surface and depth, loss and pain, and past and present in the symbolic draining of a local pond. The story begins with one of Rash's most evocative statements about his favorite metaphor. The narrator, another adult looking back on a teenage encounter gone wrong, tells us: "Water has its own archaeology, not a layering but a leveling, and thus truer to our sense of the past, because what is memory but near and far events spread and smoothed beneath the present's surface."[59] The Rudisells are back too, a family that crops up in Rash's fiction like the Snopes clan in Faulkner's Yoknapatawpha but without the malice and materialism, except for perhaps Larry the car salesman in "The Night the New Jesus Fell to Earth." Wallace Rudisell is draining a pond at the behest of an old woman, both signs of better days gone by. But Rudisell drains the pond in a kind of ritual way and the narrator, a local boy now grown up, performs as the witness like so many characters in Rash's work.[60] For the narrator, the draining of the pond is like a slow seepage of time pooling in the opposite direction. The more the water recedes, the more memories are dredged up of a night long forgotten and the narrator's complicity in a possible act of violence, even murder, which he could have prevented and now must reflect on helplessly: "Shadows deepen where the water was, making it appear that the pond has refilled. By the time I'm over the barbed wire fence, I look back and can no longer tell what was and what is."[61]

Rash's nonfiction writing offers readers an unusually personal glimpse into his fascination with and practice of writing as well as a peek into other aspects of his life. Ironically while Rash strives to remove himself from his creative work he usually inserts himself into his nonfiction writing, whether the subject matter is about himself or someone else. Two of the selections, "The Gift of Silence" and "In the Beginning," frame Rash's experience with reading and writing. The first tells of the young Rash's speech impediment that forced him into the role of an active listener who became fully immersed in the magic of a story's world, and the second offers readers a rare commentary on Rash's writing methods. In the other selections Rash writes about his personal interest and involvement with matters other than literature—sports (in this case, basketball) and country music.[62] It should be noted, though, that these nonfiction pieces bear striking resemblance to Rash's creative work. The stories of both David Thompson and Gary Stewart are rife with themes Rash has explored in nearly all of his work. In fact, they could each be characters in a Rash story, ones who must suffer through failure, cope with the ravages of inner turmoil and the illusory escape of alcohol and drugs, and who persevere or succumb to mental anguish and despair.

This collection also offers readers five of Rash's stories that remain unpublished in book form. While three of these selections were published in journals, magazines, or newspapers, two others have never seen print and remain unknown by most readers of Rash's work. The stories also provide a range in both scope, from 1998 to 2013, and tenor, from tragedy to humor to redemption. "Outlaws" is one of Rash's most recent stories and showcases all of these qualities as an adult narrator tells of his youthful initiation into the world of pain and suffering, a transition only hinted at in the story's opening line: "When I was sixteen, my summer job was robbing trains."[63] In "The Far and the Near," Rash combines characters and themes previously explored in "Chemistry"—a young narrator, an older man (this time the narrator's

grandfather), mental illness, religion, an unusual attempt to regain a sense of
sanity, and the ultimate failure to defeat the swirling demons of a tortured
mind. It is a compelling story and "a sad one" too as Rash has said, but the
story's concerns with love, faith, determination, and family duty are ones that
pulse throughout Rash's work and give this story a strength and power that
strikes deep into the human heart.[64]

"The Gatsons" and "White Trash Fishing" both showcase Rash's distinct
brand of humor, a quality that reviewers regularly overlook. In fact, "The
Gatsons," with its focus on the nightmarish pet, "Princess Kittymus Angel,"
is surely one of Rash's most comical tales and is reminiscent of the type of
small town humor in *The Night the New Jesus Fell to Earth*. Written in 1998,
the story shares many of the fundamental elements in those previous stories—the strong connection between father and son, the family and neighborhood as center of the universe, and eccentric but well-meaning characters
that stick out from the common fold due to some unusual quality. One can
also notice the growth of Rash's pacing, characterization, dialogue, and other
strategies that amplify the humor and his storytelling skills. In places there is
sheer slapstick, as when cat meets sandbox meets firecrackers; in others, the
stories are comically cinematic as when the narrator catches the finger from a
young girl with an intense hostility reminiscent of Flannery O'Connor's
Mary Grace in her celebrated story "Redemption."

In "White Trash Fishing," Rash is again working with one of his favorite
metaphors but in this story the narrator is not searching for something or
someone who has drowned or been forgotten. Rather, his fishing expedition
is an escape from a bloodless technocratic society to the rank natural world
complete with chiggers, mosquitoes, and the dirt, sweat, and muck of fishing
for catfish in a primal way that others who use expensive gear in sport boats
can never know. The story is unique in the Rash canon as the unnamed narrator spins a determined and detailed rant (emphasized by the pervasive
refrain "what I'm talking about is") on how to *really* fish, using for bait
"doughballs textured with anything from motor oil to ketchup" and "killing
what you catch and eating it right there on the riverbank."[65] The humor in
this story is not as overt and conventional as that in "The Gatsons." Rash's
narrator, with his training guide-like commentary and his desperation to
immerse himself in a world of slime and stink, revels in the comic tradition
of one frantically trying to escape a false self, of talking to oneself in an excited
state about unusual experiences that seem like jibberish, and of commenting
in precise detail about the experience itself. In this story, Rash rewrites a type
of long vanished frontier humor by staging the scene in a stink creek on the

margins of a technology-saturated and over-civilized society that has lost touch with the natural world, especially in its most rank state.

Written over twenty years later, "The Harvest" shows Rash in more familiar territory, featuring the emotionally and physically bleak landscape of loss, despair, and hardship in the western North Carolina mountains. It is one of Rash's most compressed stories and is indicative of a type of minimalist aesthetic that resonates far beyond the borders of the story. Some critics have begun to make connections between Rash and the stories of Raymond Carver, while others continue to praise Rash's ability to create memorable and powerful characters and stories that seem much larger than the pages that contain them. Rash's work as a poet and his reading of contemporary writers such as O'Brien and Alice Munro also contribute to this aesthetic, a stripping down to essentials, a workman honing his craft to razor clarity. When asked recently about creating stories, Rash spoke about the precision of words crucial to making a story "work," and that in addition to syntax and diction, "every word [should be in the] service of the story."[66]

"The Harvest" would make a good object lesson for this dictum because it is a tale of kindness amidst despair, of purposeful and necessary action as a familial and communal duty to the suffering of a child's unspoken initiation into a world where adults are as fragile as children, powerless to the vagaries, vicissitudes, and uncertainties of life. Early in the story, Rash captures it all—plot, character, place, culture, and theme—in one stark image of a tractor: "It laid on its side, one big black wheel raised up, the harrow's tines like long fingers."[67] We are never told explicit details surrounding the old man's death and for good reason—the image does it for us.

The story also shows one of Rash's greatest strengths as a writer, a tough-minded love and respect for the damaged and downtrodden, a resiliency to fight the blows of life with an unspoken empathy and pragmatic action that runs deep in the Appalachian blood line. The story confirms Rash's commitment to the power of family and love, where human kindness can help to salve the wounds of the suffering, as the father tells his son in the last line: "You done good."[68]

Rash's work is rich with influences without being captive to any one of them. What readers of this edition can see as they move through these selected texts is the brilliance that occurs when a poetic sensibility of the highest order turns itself to the creation of narratives concerning the deepest and most fundamental aspects of the human condition. Unlike much contemporary fiction, which too often depends on surface flash, shock value, gimmickry, and an obsession with the inanities of popular culture, Rash's work runs counter to those impulses in deeply human, deeply crafted ways. Like the ancients and the great books he devoured in his youth, Rash's writing throbs with an intensity and immediacy that promises a longevity beyond the temporary whims and fads that flash and fade in trendy fashion. It is Rash's fierce confrontation with the old pull of human blood and its endless struggle with pain, loss, and tragedy, punctuated by moments of grace and beauty, that infuses his work with a richness that is the mark of a distinctly powerful writer.

Notes

1. Many of Rash's works have been published internationally to rave reviews. Rash is a favorite of the French, who may see in his fiction the same type of force and clarity of vision they so admired in writers such as Poe and Faulkner. In Great Britain, Denmark, and other European countries, Rash also enjoys a strong readership and ongoing critical praise. Even farther away, Rash's work still connects—he has a strong following in Australia and New Zealand as well as in China. It is a curious sight to see *Serena* published in Chinese characters, but such is the global presence of Rash's writing.

2. Welty, "Place in Fiction," 128.

3. Bjerre, "The Natural World," 224.

4. Wilhelm and Graves, "Words with Ron Rash," 217. In my interview and in other conversations with Mr. Rash, we discussed his mountain heritage at length, but he also spoke of the importance of his early years as a child of mill workers. Having a foot in "both worlds" he said, allowed him to see more clearly the differences between the lifestyles of the piedmont and mountain cultures, and sharpened his senses to the struggles and uniqueness of both ways of life. See also, Marion, "Interview with Ron Rash," 18–40.

5. Rash, *Eureka Mill,* xv–xvi.

6. Dunlap, "Anything But Surrender," 50.

7. Wilhelm and Graves, "Words with Ron Rash," 225.

8. Dunlap, "Anything But Surrender," 54.

9. Although the work of Edgar Allan Poe is seen by contemporary scholars as the beginning of the Southern Gothic tradition, the term was first coined by Ellen Glasgow to describe her macabre story "Jordan's End" (1928), which featured such disturbing elements as a mysterious illness, a brooding and bleak landscape with dead trees, forbidding and impenetrable woods, eccentric and bizarre characters, family secrets, the supernatural, and winding, lonely roads that lead to a decaying mansion. William Faulkner took these elements to new heights in *The Sound and the Fury, As I Lay Dying,* and *Absalom, Absalom!* and became known as the master of Southern Gothic style, with the curse of slavery and racism as the underlying malaise responsible for the region's decay and madness. Contemporary writers who employ the Southern Gothic sensibility such as Ron Rash, Cormac McCarthy, William Gay, Dorothy Allison, Barry Hannah, and Tom Franklin, among others, relate the disease of the South to other sources such

as the scourge of drugs, poverty, incest, ignorance, violence, mental illness, and class inequality, among other themes.

10. Rash, *The Night the New Jesus Fell to Earth,* 143.

11. Faulkner, *Lion in the Garden,* 255.

12. Rash, *Eureka Mill,* 3.

13. Wilhelm, "Ghostly Voices," 25.

14. Rash, *Eureka Mill,* 49.

15. Ibid., 62.

16. Hecht, "Introduction," xi–xv.

17. Wilhelm and Graves, "Words with Ron Rash," 227.

18. Ibid., 231.

19. Rash, *Among the Believers,* 5.

20. Rash's recycling of this poem exemplifies his intense work ethic and sense of getting the narrative not only into its proper form, but also into its most perfect rendering. Even after publishing the poem in *Among the Believers* and the story in *Casualties,* he revised it a third time for the prize-winning collection *Burning Bright.*

21. Rash, *Casualties,* 36.

22. Rash has recently revised one of the stories from *Casualties,* "My Father Like a River," that pivots on the metaphor of water as memory, loss, and sacrifice, themes he would continue to develop in his later work. The story is available from Harper Collins as an e-book and also includes "The Trusty" from *Nothing Gold Can Stay,* which is reprinted in this reader.

23. Rash, *Raising the Dead,* 4.

24. Ibid.

25. Dunlap, "Anything But Surrender," 56.

26. Rozzo, "First Fiction," R.10.

27. Rash, *One Foot in Eden,* 136.

28. The term "The Dark Corner" refers to the upstate mountain region of South Carolina, which had been relatively unmapped and had a much sparser population than other areas of the state such as Columbia and the lowcountry regions around Charleston. With little political representation, the people of these areas were stigmatized as violent, uneducated, moonshiners, and outlaws, stereotypes that kept them "in the dark" regarding civilization, and which kept "outsiders" from venturing into the area as well.

29. Rash, *Saints at the River,* 38.

30. Ibid., 13.

31. Ibid., 31.

32. Ibid., 21.

33. The story was first published in *Shade 2004 An Anthology.* (New York: Four Way Books, 2003): 69–75. Rash revised and developed the story of the drowned girl to shape *Saints at the River* (2004). He later revised the initial short story for inclusion in *Nothing Gold Can Stay* (2012).

34. Randall Wilhelm, personal interview with Ron Rash, June 12, 2006. Clemson, South Carolina.

35. Rash, *The World Made Straight,* 202.

36. Ibid., 205.

37. Ibid., 205.

38. Hannah, "Water Liars," 3–7; and "High-Water Railers," 3–11.

39. Rash, *Serena,* 10.

40. Wilhelm and Graves, "Words with Ron Rash," 240.

41. Rash, *Serena,* 13–14.

42. Ibid., 215.

43. Among these "villain types," one could easily place the developer Tony Bryan in *Saints at the River;* the drug lord Carlton Toomey in *The World Made Straight;* Chauncey Feith in *The Cove;* Colonel Springs in *Eureka Mill;* the brigand Confederate Vaughn in "Lincolnites"; and perhaps, most obviously, the corporate giant Carolina Power in *One Foot in Eden,* whose utility man gleefully exults in his power over others: "You don't belong here anymore. Every last one of you hillbillies is going to be flushed out of this valley like shit down a commode" (184).

44. Powell, "Serena," 203.

45. In *One Foot in Eden,* for instance, Isaac is left to carry on in the larger world outside the mountains; in *Saints,* Maggie leaves the "dark corner" after having finally made peace with her father and her past there; in *The World Made Straight,* Travis gets his GED and is able to escape the trap of poverty that his friends and their dead end lifestyles embody; in *Serena,* Jacob eludes certain doom and even turns the table against it; and in *The Cove,* Walter, an escaped prisoner of war who is hunted throughout the novel, ultimately finds release from his seemingly certain capture.

46. Dunlap and Powell, "Ron Rash's *Serena,*" 86.

47. Rash, *Burning Bright,* 120.

48. Ibid., 205.

49. Rash, *Waking,* xv.

50. Rash, *Waking,* 13, 52.

51. Randall Wilhelm, personal interview with Ron Rash, June 12, 2006. Clemson, South Carolina.

52. Rash has commented on the magnificence of Hardy's work, particularly of Hardy's use of the tensions between setting and character, how the power of landscape affects the fateful actions of its people. A favorite instance is the opening of Hardy's *The Return of the Native,* which shows Eustacia Vye standing atop Rainbarrow, the largest of the many Celtic burial mounds in the area, silhouetted against the sky "like an organic part of the entire motionless structure" (12).

53. Rash, *The Cove,* 8.

54. Ibid., 255.

55. Saunders, "*Burning Bright* by Ron Rash."

56. Rash, *Nothing Gold Can Stay,* 17.

57. Rash has built a small corpus of Civil War stories and poems that reveal both a knowledge and reverence for the past and a rewriting of it as well, a dilemma faced by

many postmodern southern writers. Rash's interest in the Civil War dates back to his youth and stories he heard from family and community, particularly the "secret" tale of the Shelton Massacre. In that regard, *The World Made Straight* is Rash's "Civil War Book" but it also reveals how he and other contemporary writers are working within the gap of mythic and stereotypical history and the current age of technology saturation, diversity, and antihistory. Rash's other Civil War stories struggle with similar issues: "Cold Harbor"; Dead Confederates"; "Lincolnites"; "Where the Map Ends"; and "The Dowry." Significant poems written on the Civil War include "Madison County: 1864"; "Allen's Command"; "Antietam"; "Shelton Laurel"; "The Dowry"; "Shiloh: 1801"; "Cold Harbor"; "The Crossing"; and "Good Friday, 2006: Shelton Laurel," among others.

58. The literary term for this strategy is "free indirect discourse," which, in simpler terms, means the weaving in and out of a character's mind by the narrator. Rash's narrators do this often, a classic technique of persuading readers to like a character even if he or she is grave- robbing, stealing drugs, running a con job, or committing murder. By repeatedly telling the seemingly objective story through a character's thoughts and perceptions, readers become sympathetic to a character's thoughts and actions although the character's perceptions may be inaccurate, misguided, biased, or (self) deceptive.

59. Rash, *Nothing Gold Can Stay,* 193.

60. The witness in Rash's work is a significant theme and is used in many stories and poems in different ways for various effects. Rash's tendency to include a witness character is most likely a result of growing up in an oral culture and by writing from the first-person point of view in his earlier days. For more on the witness in Rash's work, see Vernon, "The Role of Witness," 19–24.

61. Rash, *Nothing Gold Can Stay,* 208.

62. Sports appear in Rash's work on more than a few occasions. Rash's own experience as a high school and college track athlete instilled him with an ability to train and work hard, qualities he uses as a writer as well (See Wilhelm and Graves, "Words with Ron Rash"). Early stories show this link more overtly as in "The Way Things Are" and in "My Father's Cadillacs" when Vincent comes home from "track practice." Rash's story "Overtime," in *Chemistry and Other Stories,* is a fictional account of similar thematic concerns addressed in Rash's nonfiction piece on David Thompson. Music runs throughout Rash's work even more than sports. From characters that play musical instruments, to people and small communities coming together through song, to "name dropping" specific song titles or lyrics, to mentioning musicians' names, music in Rash's work ranges from folk, gospel, blues, country, ballad, classical, and even metal. If country music dominates it is a hard driving non-Nashville kind that has much in common with the electric guitar-sliding blues of 1970s icons such as the Allman Brothers, the Rolling Stones, Traffic, and Lynyrd Skynyrd. The honky tonk in Rash's memoir of Stewart is rewritten into a comic story called "The Graveyard Shift" where the singer is forced to play renditions of "Free Bird." This story was revised again and included in *Burning Bright* as the humorous homage "Waiting for the End of the World."

63. Rash "Outlaws," 84.

64. Randall Wilhelm, personal interview with Ron Rash, March 15, 2013. Clemson, South Carolina.

65. Rash, "White Trash Fishing," 2D.

66. Rash, "In the Beginning."

67. Rash, "The Harvest."

68. Ibid.

BIBLIOGRAPHY

Works by Ron Rash

"Outlaws." *The Oxford American*. No. 81 (2013): 84–90. Summer Edition.

"The Harvest." 2013. Unpublished manuscript. Author's collection.

"In the Beginning." *Wall Street Journal*. 8 March 2013.

Nothing Gold Can Stay. New York: Ecco Press, 2013.

"My Father Like a River." Accessed May 12, 2013, http://www.amazon.com/s/ref=nb_
   sb_noss_2?url=search-lias%3Dstripbooks&fieldkeywords=rash+%22my+father
   +like+a+river%.

"The Gift of Silence." Accessed May 26, 2013, http://www.harpercollins.com/author/
   mirrosite/readingguide.aspx? authorID=33503&displayType=essay&articleId
   =6058.

The Cove. New York: Ecco Press, 2012.

Waking. Spartanburg, S.C.: Hub City Press, 2011.

"Lost Moments in Basketball History: David Thompson, Dynamite, and a Summer
   Night in Carolina Where Only the Spring Didn't Boil." *Grantland*. 16 November
   2011. Accessed May 30, 2013, http://search. espn.go.com/ron-rash/grantland/136.

Burning Bright. New York: Ecco Press, 2010.

Serena. New York: Ecco Press, 2009.

Chemistry and Other Stories. New York: Picador, 2007.

"Coal Miner's Son." *The Oxford American* 54 (Fall 2006): 109–111.

The World Made Straight. New York: Picador, 2006.

"The Far and the Near." In *CrossRoads: A Southern Culture Annual*. Ted Olson. Macon,
   Ga.: Mercer University Press, 2006. 21–38.

Saints at the River. New York: Picador, 2004.

"Something Rich and Strange." In *Shade 2004 An Anthology*. David Dodd Lee. New
   York: Four Way Books, 2003. 69–75. Rev. in *Nothing Gold Can Stay*. New York:
   Ecco Press, 2013. 27–42.

Raising the Dead. Oak Ridge, Tenn.: Iris Press, 2002.

One Foot in Eden. New York: Picador, 2002.

Among the Believers. Oak Ridge, Tenn.: Iris Press, 2000.

Casualties. Beaufort, S.C.: The Bench Press, 2000.

"White Trash Fishing." *The (Raleigh) News & Observer* 9 May 1999: 2D.

"The Gatsons." Unpublished Manuscript, Author's Collection, 1998.

Eureka Mill. Corvallis, Ore.: The Bench Press, 1998.

The Night the New Jesus Fell to Earth and Other Stories from Cliffside, North Carolina. Beaufort, S.C.: The Bench Press, 1994.

Other Works Cited

Bjerre, Thomas. "'The Natural World is the Most Universal of Languages': An Interview with Ron Rash." *Appalachian Journal* 34, no. 2 (2007): 216–227.

Brown, Joyce Compton, and Mark Powell. "Ron Rash's *Serena* and the 'Blank and Pitiless Gaze' of Exploitation in Appalachia." *North Carolina Literary Review.* No. 19 (2010): 70–89.

Dunlap, Anna Higgins. "'Anything But Surrender': Preserving Southern Appalachia in the Works of Ron Rash." *North Carolina Literary Review.* No. 13 (2004): 49–58.

Faulkner, William. *Lion in the Garden: Interviews with William Faulkner, 1926–1962.* Edited by James B. Meriwether and Michael Millgate. New York: Random House, 1968.

Hannah, Barry. "Water Liars." In *Airships.* 1978. New York: Grove Press, 1994.

———. "High-Water Railers." In *Bats Out of Hell.* New York: Grove Press, 1994.

Hardy, Thomas. *The Return of the Native.* 1878. Reprint, Oxford: Oxford University Press, 1990.

Hecht, Anthony. "Introduction: A Gift Matched with the Skills of the First Order." In *Among the Believers*, xi–xv. Oak Ridge, Tenn.: Iris Press, 2000.

Marion, Jeff Daniel. "Interview with Ron Rash." *Mossy Creek Reader* 9 (Spring 2000): 18–40.

Powell, Mark. "Serena." *The Southern Quarterly* 47, no. 3 (2010): 202–204.

Rozzo, Mark. "First Fiction." *Los Angeles Times* 29 Dec. 2002: Book Review, R 10.

Saunders, Kate. "Burning Bright by Ron Rash." *The Times* (London). 20 August 2011. www.thetimes.co.uk/tto/arts/books/fiction/acticle3134983.ece. Accessed December 18, 2013

Vernon, Zackary. "The Role of Witness: Ron Rash's Peculiarly Historical Consciousness." *The South Carolina Review* 42, no. 2 (2010): 19–24.

Welty, Eudora. "Place in Fiction." In *The Eye of the Story.* New York: Vintage International. 1990.

Wilhelm, Randall. "Ghostly Voices and Worker Bodies: Power and Resistance in Ron Rash's *Eureka Mill.*" *The South Carolina Review* 42, no. 2 (2010): 25–36.

Wilhelm, Randall and Jesse Graves. "Words with Ron Rash." In *Grist: The Journal for Writers* 1, no. 1 (2008): 214–40.

SHORT STORIES

From *The Night the New Jesus Fell to Earth and Other Stories from Cliffside, North Carolina* (1994)

BADEYE

I remember Badeye Carter. I remember his clear eye, the patch, the serpent tattooed on his shoulder, the long, black fingernails. I remember his black '49 Ford pickup, the rusty cowbell dangling from the sideview mirror, the metal soft drink chest in the back filled with shaved ice, the three gallon jars of flavoring—cherry, lemon, and licorice, the Hav-a-Tampa cigar box he kept his money in. I remember how he always came that summer at bullbat time, those last moments of daylight when the streetlight in our neighborhood came on and the bats began to swoop, preying on moths attracted to the glow.

That summer was the longest of my life. Time seemed to sleep that summer. Sometimes a single afternoon seemed a week. June was an eternity. It must have seemed just as endless for my mother, for this was the summer when my obsession with snakes reached its zenith, and our house seemed more a serpentarian than a home. And then there was Badeye, to my mother just as slippery, and as dangerous.

I was eight years old. Every evening when I heard the clanging of the cowbell, I ran to the edge of the street, clutching the nickel I had begged from my father earlier that day. I never asked my mother. To her Badeye was an intruder, a bringer of tooth decay, bad eating habits, and other things.

Every other mother in Cliffside felt the same way, would refuse to acknowledge Badeye's hat-tipping "how you doing, ma'ams" as he stopped his truck in front of their houses.

They would either stare right at him with a look colder than anything he ever put in his paper cones, as my mother did, or, like our next door neighbor Betty Splawn, turn her back to him and walk into the house.

Their reasons for disliking Badeye went beyond his selling snowcones to their children. They knew, as everyone in Cliffside knew, that while Badeye was new to the snowcone business, he had been the town's bootlegger for over a decade. Being hard-shell Southern Baptists, these women held him responsible for endangering their husbands' eternal souls with his moonshine brought up from Scotland County.

There was also the matter of his right eye, which had been blinded ten years earlier when Badeye's wife stabbed him with an ice pick as he slept. Badeye had not pursued charges, and the ex-Mrs. Carter had not explained her motivation before heading to Alabama to live with a sister, leaving the women of Cliffside to wonder what he must have done to deserve such an awakening.

Cliffside's fathers viewed Badeye more sympathetically. They tended to believe his snow cones would cause no lasting harm to their children, sometimes even eating one themselves. As for the bootlegging, some of these men were Badeye's customers, but even those who did not drink, such as my father, felt Badeye was a necessary evil in a town where the nearest legal alcohol was fifteen miles away. These men also realized that each of them had probably done something during their years that warranted an icepick in the eye. Badeye's right eye had died for all their sins.

So it was our father we went to, waiting until our mothers were washing the supper dishes or were otherwise occupied. Our fathers would fish out nickels from the pants pockets, trying not to jingle the change too loudly, listening, like us, for the sound of our mothers' approaching footsteps.

Badeye always stopped between our house and the Splawns'. Donnie Splawn, who was my age, his younger brother, Robbie, and I would gather around the tailgate of Badeye's truck, our bare feet burning on the still-hot pavement. Sometimes we would be joined by another child, one who had gotten his nickel only after Badeye had passed by his house, forced to chase the truck through the darkening streets, finally catching up with him in front of our houses. It was worth it—that long, breathless run we had all made at some time when our mothers had not washed the dishes right away or when we had been playing and did not hear the cowbell until too late, worth it because Badeye's snowcones were the most wonderful thing we had ever sunk our teeth into.

Donnie and I were partial to cherry, while Robbie liked lemon best. Donnie and Robbie tended to suck the syrup out of their snowcones, while I let the syrup in mine pool in the bottom of the paper cone, a last, condensed gulp so flavorful that it brought tears to my eyes.

Our mothers tried to fight back. They first used time-honored scare tactics, handed down from mother to daughter for generations. My mother's version of the "trip to the dentist with snowcone-rotted teeth" horror story was vividly rendered, but while it did cause me to brush my teeth more frequently for a while, it did not slow my snowcone consumption. The story's only lasting impact on me was a lifelong fear of dentists.

When my mother realized this conventional story had failed, she assumed the cause was overexposure, that stories, like antibiotics, tended to become less effective on children they more they were used, so she came up with a new story, one unlike any heard in the collective memory of Cliffside's children. The story concerned an eight-year old boy in the adjoining county who had contracted a rare disease carried specifically by flies that lit on snowcones. The affliction reduced the boy's backbone to jelly in a matter of days. He now spent all of his time in a wheelchair, looking mournfully out of his bedroom window at all the non-snowcone-eating children who played happily in the park across the street from his house. The setting of the story in Rutherford County was a stroke of genius on my mother's part, for it helped create a feeling of "if it could happen there, it could happen here" while at the same time being far enough away from Cliffside so as not to be easily discredited. The park across the street was also a nice touch.

But even at eight I realized the story was too vivid, the details too fully realized (my mother even knew the victim's middle name) to be anything other than fiction. I continued to eat Badeye's snow cones.

My mother, along with other mothers, realized another strategy was needed, so in an informal meeting after Sunday School in late June, Hazel Wasson, Dr. Wasson's wife, was appointed to find out if the law could accomplish what the horror stories had failed to do. Mrs. Wasson spent the following Monday morning in the county courthouse in Shelby. To her amazement as well as everyone else's, Badeye had all the necessary licenses to sell his snowcones. Mrs. Wasson's next stop, this time accompanied by Clytemnestra Ely, was to call on the country sheriff, who appeased the women by promising to conduct an illegal-liquor search on Badeye's premises the following afternoon, and, according to my mother, about thirty minutes after calling to let Badeye know they were coming. The sheriff and two of his deputies conducted their raid and claimed to have found nothing.

"I don't know why we even bothered to try," I heard my mother tell Betty Splawn the following morning, "what with Cleveland County politicians being his most loyal customers."

In the first week of July my mother spearheaded a last, concerted effort against Badeye. She found a recipe for freezing Kool-Aid in ice-cube trays. The cubes were then broken up in a blender or placed inside a plastic bag and crushed with a hammer. According to the final sentence of the recipe, which my mother chanted again and again, trying to convince not only me but herself as well, the result was "an inexpensive taste treat every bit as good as the commercial snowcone all children love." As the Kool-Aid hardened in the freezer, my mother called other mothers. By late afternoon every child in Cliffside had been served a dixie cup filled with my mother's recipe, but while we condescendingly ate these feeble imitations, they only served to whet our appetite for the real thing. My mother threw away the recipe and dumped the remaining trays of Kool-Aid cubes into the kitchen sink.

After this fiasco, Badeye seemed invincible. There were occasional minor victories: a husband might be coaxed or bullied into not giving his children nickels for a few days, or a son or daughter might wake up in the middle of the night with a toothache, which the mother could blame on Badeye's snowcones. The child would promise to repent, to never eat another one. But he or she always did, just as the fathers, after a day or two of ignoring their children's pleas, began to slip nickels to their offspring.

At my house, my mother had simply given up her battle against Badeye. Being a deeply religious person, she accepted the biblical edict that the husband was the decision maker in a household. She could explain to my father the reasons she did want me to eat Badeye's snowcones, but whether he gave me the nickels was a decision he as head of the household would have to make, and she would have to abide by that decision, no matter how wrongheaded it was.

There was also the matter of the weather. Our house, like almost all in Cliffside, was unairconditioned. The energy that had fueled my mother's horror stories and her recipe search was being steadily sapped away by the fierce heat of the North Carolina summer.

But, most of all, my mother had another problem that made Badeye seem little more than a nuisance—my growing snake collection. The previous summer I had caught a green snake in our backyard and brought it into our kitchen. My mother had screamed, dropped the plate she had been drying, and run out the front door. She did not stop running until she reached the Splawns' house, where she called my father at the junior college where he taught. My father rushed home and ran inside, my mother watching from the Splawns' front yard. When my father and I had come out a few minutes later, the snake was, to my mother's horror, still very much alive, although safely contained in a mason jar.

That snake was the first of a dozen garter and green snakes I would catch in our back and side yards that summer. Despite my mother's pleas, my father refused to kill them. Instead, he punched holes in the jar lids and encouraged me to keep them a couple of days before turning them loose again. My father tired to assure my mother, lectured her on the value of snakes, how most were non-poisonous, were friends of mankind who helped control mice and rats. He had even brought a book on reptiles home from the college library to support his views. But my mother had her own book to refer to—the Bible, and in its first chapters found enough evidence to convince her that snakes had been, since the Garden of Eden, mankind's worst enemy. Now, with the aid of her husband, her son was making "pets" out of them, further proof to her of man's fallen nature.

My mother had hoped that my fascination with reptiles was, like the hula hoop, a passing fad that would be forgotten once the snakes went underground for the winter. This might have happened except for my father.

Up to this point in my life, my father and I had been rather distant. Part of the problem was that, possessing an artistic temperament, he was distant towards everyone, his mind fixed on some personal vision of truth and beauty. But even the times he had tried to establish some kind of rapport with me had been unsuccessful, since these attempts consisted of Saturday morning trips to the basement of the college's fine arts building. Once there my father sat me on a stool and placed a football-sized lump of clay in front of me, assuming that a five- or six-year old boy would find a morning spent making pottery as enjoyable as he did.

He was wrong, of course. I quickly became bored and wished I were home watching cartoons. I watched the clock hands crawl towards lunchtime, daydreaming of fathers such as Mr. Splawn, who had taught Donnie how to throw a curve ball and took him bass fishing at Washburn's pond.

It was the snakes that brought us together. To my amazement my father shared my interest in reptiles and even spoke of having caught snakes when he was a child. And it was he who, during that long, snakeless winter of my seventh year, kindled my interest with books checked out of the college's library.

By March I rivaled Dr. Brown, the college's biology teacher, as Cliffside's leading herpetologist. With my father's assistance, I had read every book on reptiles in Cliffside Junior College Library. I also owned a book on snakes better than any found there, a massive tome big as our family Bible, a Christmas present from my father titled *Snakes of the World*.

It was this book, more than anything else, that turned my hobby into an obsession.

Unlike most of the books from the college's library which had been small, black-and-white photographs, *Snakes of the World* had 14 × 18 inch color plates. Opening the dull reddish-brown cover of that book was the visual equivalent of biting into one of Badeye's snowcones, for though my mother could never have comprehended it, I found these creatures indescribably beautiful. Not all of them, of course. Some, like the water moccasins or timber rattlesnakes, had thick, bloated bodies and flattened heads and were black or dull brown. There were others, however, that were stunning in their beauty: the bright-green tree boa, for instance, found in the Amazon; or the gaboon viper, an Asian snake, its dark-blue color prettier than the stained glass windows of our church.

The most beautiful one of all, however, the coral snake, was found not in Australia, or Asia, or Africa, but in the American South. A picture of a coral snake appeared on page 137 of my book, and in the right-hand corner of that page was a paragraph that I quickly memorized:

> Because of its alternating bands of black, red, and yellow, the North American Coral Snake (*micrirus fulvius*) is one of the most brilliantly colored snakes in the World. A secretive, nocturnal creature found in the Southern United States, it is rarely encountered by humans. The North American Coral Snake is a member of the cobra family, and thus, despite its small size (rarely exceeding three feet in length), is the most venomous reptile in the Northern Hemisphere.

I celebrated my eighth birthday in late March. As the fried chicken cooled and the candles started to droop on top of the cake, my mother and I assumed my father was in the basement of the fine arts building throwing pots, having forgotten it was his only child's birthday. But we were wrong. Just as we started to go ahead and eat, my father came in the back door, grinning, a wire mesh cage in his right hand. He placed it on the dining room table between the green beans and my cake.

"Happy Birthday, son," he said.

It took me a few seconds to identify the creature coiled in the bottom of the cage as a hog-nosed snake, but it only took my mother about half a second to drop her fork, shove back her chair, and make a frantic exit into the kitchen. After taking a moment to compose herself, she appeared at the doorway separating the kitchen from the dining room.

"I will not have a live snake inside my house, James," she said. "Either me or that snake is leaving right now."

It was clear my mother was not bluffing, so my father carried the cage out to the carport, moving some stacks of old art magazines to clear a space in the corner farther from the door. When I asked my father where the snake had come from, he told me he had driven to Charlotte that afternoon and had visited three pet shops before finally finding what he wanted.

As March turned into April, the temperatures began to rise. The dogwood tree in our sideyard blossomed, and snakes began to crawl out of their burrows. Because my father had absolutely no interest in keeping up his property, our back and side yards were a kudzu-filled jungle, a reptile heaven. It was here that I spent most of my spring afternoons. My reading had made me a much more successful snake hunter than I had been the previous summer. Instead of wandering around hoping to get lucky and spot a sunning snake, my method became much more sophisticated. I covered the back and side yards with large pieces of tin and wood as well as anything else that might provide a snake shelter. Each piece was placed carefully so that a snake could crawl under it with little difficulty. My efforts paid almost immediate dividends, for I now not only caught green snakes and garter snakes but also other species, including several small king snakes, and in late May, a five-foot-long black snake.

My father had borrowed a dozen wire cages from Dr. Brown, so I was able to keep the snakes I caught for several weeks at a time, longer if they ate well in captivity. I cleared out more space on the carport as I filled cage after cage. When school let out the first week of June, my snake-hunting range extended beyond my own yard. I caught thick-bodied water snakes in Sandy Run Creek, red-tongued green snakes in the vacant lot next to my grandmother's mill house in Shelby, orange and white corn snakes in my Uncle Earl's barn, tiny ring-necked snakes in the dense woods behind Laura Bryant's house. My father borrowed more cages from the junior college.

By this time the hot weather had brought out Badeye as well, and for a while my mother fought a spirited battle against both, using similar tactics. Having grown up in the rural South, she had a rich repository of snake stories to draw on, so every night before I went to sleep, my mother would pull a chair beside my bed and try to frighten me out of my hobby. She told of timber rattlesnakes dropping out of trees, strangling children by wrapping around their necks, of copperheads lying camouflaged in leafpiles, waiting for someone to step close enough so they could inject their always-fatal poison, of blue racers, almost as poisonous as copperheads, so swift they could chase down the fastest man, and hoop snakes, capable of rolling up in a hoop, their tails poison-filled stingers.

My mother's bedtime stories were graphic, and there is little doubt they would have cured most children of not only snake collecting but sleep as well. But I found them only humorous, even less convincing than her snowcone horror stories because I knew her tales had absolutely no basis in fact. Timber rattlesnakes did not climb trees, and they were vipers, not constrictors. Blue racers were non-poisonous, incapable of speeds greater than five miles an hour, even in short bursts. Hoop snakes were non-poisonous also, and unable to roll into a hoop, though as page 72 of *Snakes of the World* made clear, "Reports to the contrary continue to persist in primitive, superstitious regions of the United States."

My mother bought baseball cards and a half-dozen Indianhead pennies, trying to get me interested in collecting something besides snakes. She purchased a chemistry set, believing the possibility of my blowing myself up a lesser danger than my snake collecting. Her efforts were futile. I traded the baseball cards to Jimbo Miller for a half-dozen rat snake eggs he found in a sawdust pile and bought bubblegum with the pennies. The chemistry set gathered dust in the basement.

By this time my mother was having nightmares about snakes several times a week. Dark circles began to appear under her eyes. For the first time in my life, I watched her refuse to defer to my father, the view of serpents in Genesis evidently balancing out the command that wives should obey their husbands, the danger to her son tipping the scales. Every evening at supper she would lecture my father on the catastrophe that was about to occur.

Sometimes she even succeeded in breaking through the trance-like state he spent most of his waking hours in. At these times my father related the information he had gleaned from the books he had read to me the past winter. He tried to convince my mother that her fears were groundless, that the only poisonous snake in the county was the copperhead whose bite was rarely serious enough to require medical treatment, that the truly dangerous snakes—water moccasins, rattlesnakes, and coral snakes were at least two counties away. He assured my mother that she didn't have to worry about the copperheads because I had promised him that if I did come across one I would not try and catch it, would keep my distance.

My mother's sense of impending doom was not assuaged. Her fear of snakes was more than cultural and religious; it was instinctual as well, too deeply embedded in her psyche to be dealt with on a rational level. Facts and statistics were useless. She threatened to get rid of the snakes, gather up the cages and take them away herself, but I knew she wouldn't do it, couldn't do it. Her fear of snakes was so great she had not even set foot in the carport since the arrival of the hog-nosed snake in March.

By the dog days of August I had thirty-three cages in the carport, and every one had a snake in it. The feeding of the snakes and the cleaning of the cages left me little time for snake-collecting field trips, but by this time the snakes were coming to me.

Not by themselves, of course, slithering by the hundreds toward our house. That occurred only in my mother's dreams. In late July Frank Moore, who owned, published, and wrote in the *Cleveland County Messenger,* had done an article about me and my hobby, making me a county-wide celebrity and bringing a steady stream of visitors to our carport. Most came empty-handed, just wanting to see my collection, but others brought milk pails and wash buckets, mason jars and once even a cookie tin. Inside were snakes, some alive, some dead. The live ones I put into cages; the dead ones that were not too badly mangled by hoe, buckshot, or tire I placed, depending on their size, in quart or gallon jars filled with alcohol. Though months earlier my mother had told my father and me that she would not allow a "live" snake in her house, she had said nothing about dead ones, so I kept these snakes in my room where, almost every night, they crawled out of their jars and into my mother's dreams.

Badeye came too. One night after completing his rounds, he drove back by the house and, seeing me alone in the carport, parked his truck across the street. The carport lightbulb was burned out, the only light coming from the streetlamp across the road, so I took each snake out of its cage so Badeye could see them better. Unlike the other people who visited the carport that summer, Badeye did not keep his distance from the snakes once I took them into my hands. He moved closer, his blue eye only inches away as he studied each one intently.

When I had put the last snake back in its cage, Badeye rolled up one of the sleeves of his soiled, white t-shirt.

"Look here," he said, pointing to a king cobra, hood flared, tattooed on his upper arm. I moved closer and saw, incredibly, the cobra uncoil slightly, its great head sway back and forth. Badeye grinned as I stepped back, stumbled over a stack of newspapers.

"I've got to go," he said. "I've got a long drive downstate to make tonight." I watched him slowly walk back to the truck, slide behind the steering wheel, then disappear into the darkness. As I walked back to the carport, I saw my mother watching from the living room window. Tears flowed down her cheeks.

I did not sleep much that night. Part of the reason was the heat. The temperature had been over ninety-five every day for three weeks. Rain was only a memory. The night brought no cool breezes, only more hot, stagnant air. But it was more than the heat. It was the cobra on Badeye's arm and my mother's tears. I sweated through the night as if I had a fever, listening to the window fan beat futilely against the darkness.

The following evening Badeye gave Donnie and Robbie their snowcones first, even though I had beaten them to his truck. After they left, Badeye jumped out of the truckbed and opened the door on the passenger side.

"I've got something for you," he said. "Saw it on the road last night when I was driving back from Laurinburg."

Badeye held an uncapped quart whiskey bottle up to my face.

"It's the prettiest snake I ever saw," he said.

And so it was, for a coral snake that looked to be a foot long lay in the bottom of the bottle.

"Is it alive?" I asked, hoping for a second miracle.

Badeye shook the bottle. The snake pushed its black head against the glass, tried to climb upward before collapsing on itself.

"Here," he said, placing the bottle in my hand, though still gripping it with his own. "It's yours if you will do one thing for me."

"Anything," I said, meaning it.

"You know Bub Ely, don't you, and where he lives, that white house next to Marshall Hamrick's?"

I nodded. It was only a half mile away.

"Well, I need to get something to him, but I can't take it by right now." Badeye grinned. "His wife don't approve of me. Tonight, say about eleven, after everyone goes to sleep, could you take it over to his house? Just put it in the garage. Bub will find it in the morning."

I said I would. Badeye ungripped the whiskey bottle, opened the glove compartment.

"Here," he said, handing me a mason jar filled with clear liquid that looked like water but I already knew it had to be moonshine.

"You know what it is?" Badeye asked.

I nodded.

"Good," he said, sliding behind the steering wheel. "You'll know to be careful with it." Badeye's voice suddenly sounded menacing. "Don't get careless and drop it."

After checking to make sure my parents were not watching out the window, I carried the moonshine and placed it in the high grass beside the dogwood tree in the sideyard. Then I carried the whiskey bottle into the carport. I opened a cage with a king snake in it and didn't even watch it disappear into the nearby stacks of books and newspapers. I tipped the bottle, watched the coral snake out of the bottle's neck into the cage. I carried the cage to the edge of the carport so that more of the glow from the streetlight would fall on the snake.

The coral snake was everything I had dreamed it would be, and much, much more. As beautiful as it had appeared in the photographs. I saw now how the camera had failed. The black, red, and yellow bands were a denser hue than any camera could capture. The small, delicate body gave the snake a grace of movement lacking in larger, bulkier snakes.

I lost all track of time and did not hear my father open and close the carport door. I was unaware of his presence until he crouched beside me and peered into the cage.

"That looks like a coral snake," he said in an alarmed voice as he picked up the cage for a better look.

"It's a scarlet king snake," I quickly lied.

"Are you sure?" my father said, still looking intently at the snake.

"I'm sure, Dad. Positive."

"But the bands are black, red, and yellow. I thought only coral snakes had those."

"Look," I said, trying to sound as convincing as possible, "scarlet king snakes have the same colors. Besides, coral snakes don't live this far west. You know that."

"That's true," my father said, putting the cage down. "Come on in," he said, standing up. "It's already past your bedtime."

I followed my father inside and waited in my darkened room three hours until my parents finally went to sleep. Then I sneaked into the kitchen, took the flashlight from the cupboard, and eased out the back door. I found the moonshine and walked up the street towards Bub Ely's. It was 11:30 according to my Mickey Mouse watch.

The lights were off at the Ely house, but there was enough of a moon that I did not need the flashlight to make my way to the garage. Once there, however,

I did not lay the jar down in the corner. Instead, I unscrewed it. Everything that Badeye had put in my hands before had been magical. I wanted to know what magic the jar held. I pressed it to my lips, poured a mouthful. I held it there for a moment, and despite the kerosene taste, made a split-second decision to swallow instead of spit it out. When I did, I gagged, almost dropped the jar. My eyes teared. My throat and stomach burned. When the burning finally stopped, I placed the jar in a corner, walked slowly home.

I will never know for sure if what I did next would have happened had I not sampled Badeye's moonshine, but I did not go inside when I got home. Instead, I went to the carport to look at the coral snake, placing the flashlight against the cage for a better view. Finally, just looking wasn't good enough. I opened the cage and gently placed my right thumb and index finger behind the snake's head, but my hold was too far behind the head. The coral snake's mouth gripped my index finger.

I snatched my hand out of the cage, slung the snake from my finger, and screamed loud enough to be heard over the window fan in my parent's room. My scream was not one of pain but of knowledge. I knew the small, barely bleeding mark would not cause the agonizing swelling of a copperhead or rattlesnake bite. The coral snake's poison affected the nervous system, the heart. I also knew that four out of twenty people recently bitten by coral snakes in the Southeast had died. It was this knowledge that paralyzed me, made me unable to move, for my books had assured me the chances of a child's dying from a coral snake's bite were even greater.

And I very well might have died, if my father had not been able to act in a focused manner. He ran out into the carport in his underwear, took my trembling hands and asked what had happened. I pointed to the snake coiled on the concrete floor.

"It's a coral," I whimpered, and showed him the bite mark.

My mother was at the doorway in her nightgown, asking my father in a frantic voice what was the matter, though a part of her already knew.

"He's been bitten," my father said, walking rapidly towards my mother. "I've got to call the hospital, tell them they need to get antivenom rushed here from Charlotte."

My father was now on the carport steps. He turned to my mother. "Get him to the hospital. Quick. I'll get over there fast as I can."

My father brushed by my mother, who had not moved, only stood there looking at me. He brought her the car keys. "Go," he shouted, almost shoving her out into the carport.

My mother saw the coral snake coiled on the concrete between us, but she did not hesitate. She stepped right over it and caught me as I collapsed in her arms.

The sound of rain pelting the windows woke me. I opened my eyes to whiteness, the unadorned walls of Cleveland County Hospital. My father and mother were sitting in metal chairs placed beside my bed. Their heads were bowed, and at first I thought they were asleep, but when I stirred they looked up, offered weary smiles.

Three days later I was released, and in a week I was feeling healthy enough to help my father fill my Uncle Earl's pickup truck with my snake collection. We first drove down to Broad River, taking the bumpy dirt road that followed the river until we were several miles from the nearest house. We opened the cages, watched the contents slither away.

Then we drove back towards home, stopping a mile from Cliffside at the town dump. My father backed the truck up to the edge of the landfill and we lowered the tailgate. We threw the snake-and-alcohol-filled jars out of the truck, watched them shatter against the ground, and knew they would soon be buried forever under tons of other things people no longer wanted.

As for Badeye, I ignored his offers of free snowcones. My parents ignored his apologies.

After several attempts at reconciliation failed, Badeye stopped slowing down as he approached our house, even sped up a little as his truck glided past into the twilight.

That October Badeye left Cliffside. When he pulled into Heddon's Gulf station, his possessions piled into the back of his truck, Charlie Heddon asked him where he was moving to.

Badeye only shrugged his shoulders and muttered, "Somewhere where it's warmer." No one ever saw him again.

I remember my mother staring out the kitchen window that autumn as the dogwood tree began to shed its leaves. It would not be until years later that I would understand how wonderful those falling leaves made her feel, for they signaled summer's end and the coming of cold weather, the first frost that would banish snakes (including the coral snake which we never found), as well as Badeye and his snowcones. But I also remember the first bite of my first snowcone that June evening when Badeye suddenly appeared on our street. Nothing else has ever tasted so good.

THE NIGHT THE NEW JESUS FELL TO EARTH

The day after it happened, and Cliffside's new Jesus and my old husband was in the county hospital in fair but stable condition, Preacher Thompson, claiming it was all his fault, offered his resignation to the board of deacons. But he wasn't to blame. He'd only been here a couple of months, fresh out of preacher's college, and had probably never had to deal with a snake like Larry Rudisell before. A man or a woman, as I've found out the hard way, usually has to get bit by a snake before they start watching out for them.

What I mean is, Preacher Thompson's intentions were good. At his very first interview the pulpit committee had told him what a sorry turn our church had taken in the last few years, and they hadn't left out much either. They told him about Len Deaton, our former choir director, who left his choir, wife, and eight children to run off to Florida with a singer at Harley's Lounge who wasn't even a Baptist. And they told about Preacher Crowe, who had gotten so senile he had preached the same sermon four weeks in a row, though they didn't mention that a lot of the congregation hadn't even noticed. The committee told him about how membership had been slipping for several years, how the church was in a rut, and how when Preacher Crowe had finally retired in November, it had been clear that some major changes had to be made if the church was going to survive. And this was exactly why they wanted him to be the new minister, they told him. He was young and energetic and could bring some fresh blood into the church and help get it going in the right direction. Which was exactly what he tried to do, and exactly why Larry was able to talk his way onto that cross.

It did take a few weeks, though. At first Preacher Thompson was so nervous when he preached that I expected him to bolt for the sanctuary door at any moment. He wouldn't even look up from his notes, and when he performed his first baptism he almost drowned poor little Eddie Gregory by holding him under the water too long. Still, each week you could see him get a little more comfortable and confident, and by the last Sunday in February, about two months ago, he gave the sermon everybody had been waiting for. It was all about commitment and the need for new ideas, about how a church was like a car, and our church was in reverse and we had to get it back in forward. You could tell he was really working himself up because he wasn't looking at his notes or his watch. It was 12:15, the first time he'd ever kept us up after twelve, when he closed, telling us that Easter, a month away, was a time of rebirth, and he wanted us all to go home and think of some way our church could be reborn too, something that would get Cliffside Baptist Church back in the right gear.

Later I wondered if maybe all the car talk had something to do with what happened, because the next Sunday Preacher Thompson announced he'd gotten many good suggestions, but there was one in particular that was truly inspired, one that could truly put the church back on the right road, and he wanted the man who had come up with the idea, Larry Rudisell, to stand up and tell the rest of the congregation about it.

Like I said earlier, once you've been bitten by a snake you start looking out for them, but there's something else too. You start to know their ways. So I knew right off that whatever Larry was about to unfold, he was expecting to get something out of it, because having been married to this snake for almost three years, I knew him better than he knew himself. Larry's a hustler. Always has been. He came out of his momma talking out of both sides of his mouth, trying to hustle her, the nurse, the doctor, whichever one he saw first. He hasn't stopped talking or hustling since.

Larry stood up, wearing a sport coat he couldn't button because of his beer gut, no tie, and enough gold around his neck to fill every tooth in Cleveland County. He was also wearing his sincere "I'd swear on my dead momma's grave I didn't know that odometer had been turned back" look, which was as phony as the curls in his brillo-pad hairdo, which he'd done that way to cover up his bald spot.

Then Larry started telling about what he was calling his "vision," claiming that late Friday night he'd woke up, half blinded by bright flashing lights and hearing a voice coming out of the ceiling, telling him to recreate the crucifixion on the front lawn of Cliffside Baptist Church, at night, with lights shining on the three men on the crosses. The whole thing sounded more like one of those U.F.O. stories in *The National Examiner* than a religious experience, and about as believable. Larry looked around and started telling how he just knew people would come from miles away to see it, just like they went to McAdenville every December to see the Christmas lights, and then he said he believed in his vision enough to pay for it himself.

Then Larry stopped to see if his sales pitch was working. He was selling his crucifixion idea the same way he would sell a '84 Buick in his car lot. And it was working. Larry has always been a smooth talker. He talked me into the back seat of his daddy's car when I was seventeen, talked me into marrying him when I was eighteen, and talked me out of divorcing him on the grounds of adultery a half dozen times. I finally got smart and plugged up my ears with cotton so I couldn't hear him while I packed my belongings.

Larry started talking again, telling the congregation he didn't want to take any credit for the idea, that he was just a messenger and that the last thing God had told him was that he wanted Larry to play Jesus, and his mechanic, Terry Wooten, to play one of the thieves, a role, as far as I was concerned, Terry had been playing as long as he'd worked for Larry. When I looked over at Terry, the expression on his face made it quite clear that God hadn't bothered to contact him about all of this. Then I looked up at the ceiling to see if it was about to collapse and bury us all. Everybody was quiet for about five seconds. Then the whole congregation started talking at once, and it sounded more like a tobacco auction than a church service.

After a couple of minutes people remembered where they were, and it got a little more civilized. At least they were raising their hands and getting acknowledged before they started shouting. The first to speak was Jimmy Wells, who had once bought an Olds 88 from Larry and had the transmission fall out not a half-mile from where he had driven it off Larry's lot. Jimmy was still bitter about that, so I wasn't too surprised when he nominated his brother-in-law Harry Bayne to play Jesus.

As soon as Jimmy sat down, Larry popped up like a jack-in-the-box, claiming Harry couldn't play Jesus because Harry had a glass eye. When Jimmy asked why that mattered, Larry said they didn't have glass eyes back in olden times and Jimmy said nobody would notice and Larry said yes they would because the color in Harry's real eye was different than in the glass eye. Jimmy and Larry kept arguing. Harry finally got up and said if it meant that much to Larry to let him do it, that he was too hungry to care anymore.

Preacher Thompson had pretty much stayed out of all this till Harry said that, but then he suggested that Harry play the thief who gets saved, leaving Terry as the other one. The Splawn brothers, Donnie and Robbie, were nominated to be the Roman soldiers. To the credit of the church, when Preacher Thompson asked for a show of hands as to whether we should let this be our Easter project, it was close. My hand wasn't the only one that went up against it, and I still believe it was empty stomachs as much as a belief in Larry and his scheme that got it passed.

But it did pass, and a few days later Preacher Thompson called me up and asked, since I was on the church's building and grounds committee, if I would help build the crosses. You see, I'm a carpenter, the only full-time one, male or female, in the church, so whenever the church's softball field needs a new backstop or the parsonage needs some repair work, I'm the one who usually does it. And I do it right. Carpentry is in my blood. People around here say my father was the best carpenter to ever drive a nail in western North

Carolina, and after my mother died when I was nine, he would take me with him every day I wasn't in school. By the time I was fourteen, I was working fulltime with him in the summers. I quit school when I was sixteen. I knew how I wanted to make my living. I've been a carpenter for the last fifteen years.

It was hard at first. Since I was a woman, a lot of men didn't think I could do as good a job as they could. But one good thing about being a carpenter is someone can look at your work and know right away if you know what you're doing. Nowadays, my reputation as a carpenter is as good as any man's in the county.

Still, I was a little surprised that Preacher Thompson asked me to work on a project my ex-husband was so involved in. But, being new, he might not have known we had once been married. I do go by my family's name now. Or maybe he did know, figuring since the divorce was over five years ago we had forgiven each other like Christians should. Despite its being Larry's idea, I did feel obligated since I was on the building and grounds committee, so I said I would help. Preacher Thompson thanked me and said we would meet in front of the church at ten on Saturday morning.

On Saturday, me, Preacher Thompson, Larry, and Ed Watt, who's an electrician, met on the front lawn. From the very start, it was obvious Larry was going to run the show, telling us the way everything should be, pointing and waving his arms like he was a Hollywood director. He had on a white, ruffled shirt that was open to his gut, his half-ton of gold necklaces, and a pair of sunglasses. Larry was not just trying to act like but look like he was from California, which meant, as far as I was concerned, that, unlike Jesus, he actually deserved to be nailed to a cross.

Larry showed me where he wanted the three crosses, and he gave me the length he wanted them. His was supposed to be three feet taller than the other two. Preacher Thompson was close by, so we acted civil to one another till I walked over to my truck to go get the wood I'd need. Larry followed me, and as soon as I got in the truck and cranked it, he asked me how it felt to have only a pillow to hold every night. "Lot of advantages to it," I said as I drove off. "A pillow don't snore and it don't have inch-long toenails and it don't smell like a brewery." I was already out of shouting distance before he could think of anything to say to that.

I was back an hour later with three eight-inch-thick poles, just like the ones I used to build the backstop for the softball field, and a railroad crosstie I'd sawed into three lengthwise pieces for the part the arms would be stretched out on. I'd also gotten three blocks of wood I was going to put where their feet would be to take the strain off their arms.

As I turned into the church parking lot, I saw that Wanda Wilson's LTD was parked in the back of the church. She was out by the car with Larry, wearing a pink sweatshirt and a pair of blue running shorts, even though it was barely 60 degrees, just to show off her legs. When they saw me they started kissing and putting their hands all over each other. They kept that up for a good five minutes, in clear view of not just me but Ed Watt and Preacher Thompson too, and I thought we were going to have to get a water hose and spray them, the same way you would two dogs, to get them apart.

Finally, Wanda got into her LTD and left, maybe to get a cold shower, and Larry came over to the truck. As soon as he saw the poles in the back of the truck he got all worked up, saying they were too big around, that they looked like telephone poles, that he was supposed to be Jesus, not the Wichita Lineman. That was enough for me. I put my toolbox back in the cab and told Preacher Thompson Benny Brown was coming over with his post-hole digger around noon. I pointed at Larry. "I forgot all about Jesus being a carpenter," I said. "I'm taking all of this back over to Hamrick's Lumberyard." Then I drove off and didn't look back.

Why is it that some men always have to act like they know more than another human being just because that other human being happens to be a woman? Larry's never driven a nail in his life, but he couldn't admit that I would know what would make the best and safest cross. I guess some people never change. Ever since the divorce was made final, Larry has gone out of his way to be as ugly as possible to me. The worst thing about being divorced in a small town is that you're always running into your ex. Sometimes it seems I see him more now than I did when I was married to him. I can live with that.

But it's been a lot harder to live with the lies he's been spreading around town, claiming things about me that involved whips and dog collars and Black Sabbath albums. You'd think nobody would believe such things, but like the Bible says, it's a fallen world. A lot of people want to believe the worst, so a lot of them believed Larry when he started spreading his lies. I couldn't get a date for almost two years, and I lost several girlfriends too. Like the song says, "Her hands are callused but her heart is tender." That rumor caused me more heartache than you could believe.

I have no idea what they did after I drove off that Saturday, but the Sunday before Easter the crosses were up, so after church let out just about everybody in the congregation went out on the front lawn to get a better look. I've always said you can tell a lot about a person by how carefully they build something or put something together, but looking at Larry's crosses didn't tell me a thing I didn't already know. Instead of using a pole for the main section, he had gotten four-by-eight boards made out of cedar, which anybody who knows anything about wood can tell you is the weakest wood you can buy. The crossties and footrests were the same. I'm not even going to mention how sorry the nailing was.

I walked over to the middle cross, gave it a push, and felt it give like a popsicle stick in sand. I kneeled beside it and dug up enough dirt to see they hadn't put any cement in the hole Benny Brown had dug for them but had just packed dirt in it. I got up and walked over to the nearest spigot and washed the red dirt off my hands while everybody watched me, waiting for me to pass judgment on Larry's crosses. "All I'm going to say is this," I said as I finished drying my hands. "Anybody who gets up on one of those things had better have a whole lot of faith."

Of course Larry wasn't going to let me have the last word. He started saying I was just jealous that he'd done such a good job, that I didn't know the difference between a telephone pole and a cross. I didn't say another word, but as I was walking to my truck I heard Harry Bayne tell Larry he was going to have to find somebody else to play his role, that he'd rather find a safer way to prove his faith, like maybe handling a rattlesnake or drinking strychnine. I went back that night to look at the crosses some more. I left convinced more than ever that the crosses, especially the taller middle one, wouldn't support the weight of a full-grown man.

On Good Friday I went on over to the church about an hour before they were scheduled to start, mainly because I didn't believe they would be able to get up there without at least one of the crosses snapping like a piece of dry kindling. There were already a good number of people there, including Larry's cousin Kevin, who wasn't a member of our church or anybody else's, but who worked part-time for Larry and was enough like Larry to be a good salesman and a pitiful excuse for a human being. Kevin was spitting tobacco juice into a paper cup while Mrs. Murrel, who used to teach drama over at the high school, dabbed red paint on his face and hands and feet, trying to make him look like the crucified thief Larry had talked, paid, or threatened him into playing. Besides the paint, the only thing he was wearing was a sweatshirt with a picture of Elvis on it and what looked like a giant diaper, though I'd already heard the preacher explain to several people it was supposed to be what the Bible called a loincloth. Terry Wooten was standing over by the crosses, dressed up the same way, looking like he was about to vomit as he stared up at where he would be hanging in only a few more minutes.

Then I saw the sign and suddenly everything that had been going on for the last month made sense. It was one of those portable electric ones with about a hundred colored light bulbs bordering it. "The Crucifixion of JESUS CHRIST Is Paid for and Presented by LARRY RUDISELL's Used Cars of Cliffside, North Carolina" was spelled out in red plastic letters at the top of the message board. Near the bottom in green letters it said, "If JESUS Had Driven A Car, He Would Have Bought It At LARRY's." It was the tackiest, most sacrilegious thing I'd ever seen in my life.

Finally, the new Jesus himself appeared, coming out of the church with what looked like a brown, rotting halo on his head—it was his crown of thorns—fifty yards of extension cord covering his shoulder, and a cigarette hanging out of his mouth. He unrolled the cord as he came across the lawn, dressed like Kevin and Terry except he didn't have any red paint on his face. Larry didn't have a fake beard either. He wanted everyone to know it was Larry Rudisell up on that cross. He walked over to the sign and plugged the extension cord into it.

You know what it's like when the flashbulb goes off when you're getting a picture taken and you stagger around half blind for a while? Well, that's about the effect Larry's sign had when it came on. The colored lights were flashing on and off, and you could have seen it from a mile away. Larry watched for a minute to make sure it was working right and then announced it was twenty minutes to show time so they needed to go ahead and get up on the crosses. Preacher Thompson and the Splawn brothers went and got the stepladders and brought them over to where the crosses were. Terry and Kevin slinked over behind the sign, trying to hide. It was obvious Larry was going to have to get up there first.

Larry took off his sweatshirt, and I realized for the first time they were going to go up there with nothing except the bedsheets wrapped around them. It wasn't that cold right then, but like it always is in March, it was windy. I knew that in a few minutes, when the sun went down, the temperature would really fall fast.

While Donnie and Robbie Splawn steadied the cross, Larry crawled up the ladder. With only the loincloth wrapped around him, he looked more like a Japanese Sumo wrestler on *Wide World of Sports* than Jesus. When he got far enough up, Larry reached over, grabbed the crosstie, and put his feet on the board he was going to stand on. He turned himself around until he faced us. I'll never know how the cross held, but it did.

It was completely dark, except of course for Larry's sign, by the time Terry and Kevin had been placed on their crosses. As I watched I couldn't help thinking that if they ever did want to bring back crucifixion, the three hanging up there in the dark would be as good a bunch to start with as any. I looked over my shoulder and saw the traffic was already piled up, and the whole front lawn was filled with people. There was even a TV crew from WSOC in Charlotte.

At 6:30 the music began, and the spotlights Ed Watt had rigged up came on. I had to admit it was impressive, especially if you were far enough away so you didn't see Larry's stomach or Terry's chattering teeth. The WSOC cameras were rolling, and more and more people were crowding onto the lawn and even spilling out into the road, making the first traffic jam in Cliffside's history even worse.

The crucifixion was supposed to last an hour, but after twenty minutes the wind started to pick up, and the crosses began making creaking noises, moving back and forth a little more with each gust of wind. It wasn't long before Terry began to make some noises too, screaming over the music for someone to get a ladder and get him down. I didn't blame him. The crosses were really starting to sway, and Terry, Kevin, and Larry looked like acrobats in some circus high-wire act. But there wasn't a net for them to land in if they fell.

Preacher Thompson and Ed Watt were running to get the ladders, but at least for Larry, it was too late. His cross swung forward one last time, and then I heard the sound of wood cracking. Donnie Splawn heard it too, and he tripped on his Roman Soldier's robe as he ran to get out of the way. Larry screamed out "God help me," probably the sincerest prayer of his life. But it went unanswered. The crosses began to fall forward, and Larry, with his arms outstretched, looked like a man doing a swan dive. I closed my eyes at the last second but heard him hit.

Then everything was chaos. People were screaming and shouting and running around in all directions. Janice Hamrick, who's a registered nurse, came out of the crowd to tend to Larry till the rescue squad could get there and take him to the county hospital. Several other people ran over to stabilize the other two crosses. When Terry saw what happened to his boss, he stained his loincloth. His eyes were closed, and he was praying so fast only God could understand what he was saying. Kevin wasn't saying or doing anything because he had fainted dead away the second his cousin hit the ground.

It's been three weeks now since all this happened. Larry got to leave the county hospital, miraculously, alive, on Easter morning, but his jaw is still wired shut, and it's going to stay that way for at least another month. But despite the broken jaw and broken nose, he still goes out to his car lot every day. Since people over half the state saw him hit the ground, in slow motion, on WSOC's six o'clock news, Larry's become western North Carolina's leading tourist attraction. They come from more miles away than you would believe just to see him, and then he gets his pad and pencil out and tries to sell them a car. Quite a few times he does. As a matter of fact, I hear he's sold more cars in the last two weeks than any two-week period in his life, which is further proof that, as the Bible tells us, we live in a fallen world.

Still, some good things have happened. When Preacher Thompson offered to resign, the congregation made it clear they wanted him to stay, and he has. But he's toned down his sermons a good bit, and last Sunday, when Larry handed him a proposal for an outdoor manger scene with you know who playing Joseph, Preacher Thompson just crumpled it up and threw it in the trashcan.

As for me, a lot of people remember that I was the one who said the crosses were unsafe in the first place, especially one person, Harry Bayne. Two weeks ago Harry took me out to eat as a way of saying thank you. We hit it off and have spent a lot of time together lately. We're going dancing over at Harley's Lounge tonight. I'm still a little scared, almost afraid to hope for too much, but I'm beginning to believe than even in a fallen world things can sometimes look up.

MY FATHER'S CADILLACS

I was 15 when I came home from track practice one late April afternoon to find a big, light-gray car under the blooming dogwood tree where our blue Plymouth was usually parked. That the car might be ours didn't occur to me, because everybody I'd ever seen who owned this kind of car had money and a big white house to go along with it. No one in my family ever had either.

Our cars had been battered Plymouths and Mercurys which came with six-digit mileage figures and engines that broke down on long trips. The seat covers were ripped, the tires were bald, and the heaters seldom worked. But I had never been ashamed of our cars because most of the people around Cliff-side owned similar ones. Doctor Wasson was the exception, and he was the man I thought of when I hurried into the house, expecting to find my mother or father sick or injured. I didn't even remember that his car was light green. Inside, however, I found only my mother and father.

The car belonged to my family.

"It's a Cadillac, isn't it," I asked, "like Doctor Wasson's?" My father proudly answered that indeed it was. My mother said nothing. It was clear that she was not nearly as happy about our new car as my father was. I ran back outside.

It was a Cadillac, but hardly the equal of Doctor Wasson's. This one was almost 10 years old, and though it had electric windows like Doctor Wasson's, only two of ours worked. Ours had a cigarette lighter, clock, and an AM/FM radio; none of these accessories worked either. Nevertheless, being used to Plymouths and Mercurys, I was impressed with the fact that these gadgets had ever worked.

My enthusiasm for our new car was short-lived, however. Within three days, Jimbo Miller, who sat behind me in homeroom, poked the back of my head with a pencil.

"Why did your old man buy that bone car?" Jimbo asked.

"What are you talking about, Jimbo?" I said, knowing I really didn't want to know.

"That Cadillac," he hissed, because Miss Blanton was looking our way. "Everybody in town is talking about it. That car could only come from one place. I know. When my uncle died last year, I rode in a car just like it."

"Doctor Wasson has a Cadillac," I said.

"Yeah, but his is green, and he bought his brand-new, not from a funeral home. Besides, he's a doctor. I think there's some law that they have to drive Cadillacs."

I was too stunned to speak. At the handful of funerals I had attended, undertakers had always terrified me. Dressed in their black suits, they always seemed to be tall, thin, pale men whose smiles were as phony and awful as the smiles on my dead relatives' faces. Once a funeral director had shaken my hand, and his soft, clammy hand had made me shudder.

"Face it, boy" Jimbo said. "Your old man has done lost his mind and bought an undertaker's car, and you're going to have to ride in it. Hey, there might even be a body or two in the trunk."

Jimbo snickered, stopping only to repeatedly whisper "bone car" into my ear until I finally turned around and punched him in the nose. Bleeding from both nostrils, Jimbo finally shut up, at least for a little while, but I had to stay after school a week for hitting him, and Jimbo made it absolutely clear to all my classmates exactly what kind of car my family now owned.

In the next few days I wondered why my father hadn't just made me wear a sign around my neck with "not normal" written on it, instead of buying a 1960 Cadillac. I suffered the cruelest blow when Laura Bryan, a girl I had been secretly in love with since the sixth grade, asked if my family's new car really had once been owned by a funeral home. I survived fifth and sixth periods only because it was Friday, and I knew that as soon as I stayed my extra 30 minutes after school for hitting Jimbo, I could skip track practice, walk home, lock myself in my bedroom, and never come out for the rest of my life.

I did, of course. The smell of pork chops brought me out. But while eating supper I told my parents that our new car had wrecked my life. My mother said nothing, though she was obviously less than thrilled about the Cadillac herself. My father was staring out the window at the dogwood tree, deep in thought about something else. This made it worse. He wasn't even listening to what I was saying. As soon as I finished my banana pudding, I went to my room, locked the door, and brooded the rest of the evening over the tragic turn my life had taken. I came out the next morning, but only after I heard the roar of the Cadillac's 450 engine, signaling that my father was on his way to the art department where he spent most Saturday mornings and afternoons painting and throwing pots.

I found my mother in the kitchen drinking coffee and reading the newspaper, used to these husbandless Saturdays. Why, I asked her, had my father picked, of all the thousands of used cars in western North Carolina, the one that would make my life miserable? But she had no idea why. He had just driven the Plymouth up to Asheville one morning, and in the afternoon had come back with the Cadillac.

"Your father doesn't always have a reason for the things he does. You surely know that by now," she said.

I did know. I understood exactly what my mother meant. This was the man who had taught classes in his bedroom slippers, forgetting to put his shoes on before he left home, who on trips kept my mother and I constantly on the alert, knowing from experience that my father might drive right by our destination.

And there were other things, caused not so much by forgetfulness as by just not knowing how normal human beings were supposed to act. Several times late at night I had gotten up to get a drink of water, turned on the kitchen light, and found my father in his underwear leaning against the kitchen sink and staring out the window at the moon as he ate a banana. Or we would go to visit my mother's family and my father, after barely saying hello, would sit down in the nearest chair and read a book about Italian painting until it was time to leave.

Nevertheless, I was convinced there was something different about my father's recent behavior. For one thing, buying a car was something you had to know you were doing. No one, not even my father, could go out and buy a car without realizing it. I knew my parents had recently paid off the final installment of my father's student loans, but we were still far from being well off. His income was no better than most of the mill workers or farmers around Cliffside. Our new car clearly made this point. It was a Cadillac in name only, and my father could have gotten a nicer, newer Plymouth or Mercury for less money and less trouble. Cadillacs, even used one, were rare in rural North Carolina.

So why a beat-up old Cadillac? I'd always believed that in his own quiet way he loved me. When I was younger he had always been the one who woke me from my nightmares and stayed with me, sitting on the corner of the bed until I fell asleep. He had even shared my intense though short-lived interest in snakes. Had this man secretly hated me all the while, and was he only now allowing himself to show it by buying a car that would make me an outcast among my peers?

"You know," my mother said, trying to cheer me up, "it could be worse."

"I doubt it," I said.

"He wanted to name you when you were born, and the name he picked out for you was Hieronymus Michelangelo Hampton. I told him no child of mine was going to go through life with a name like that."

My mother was right. With a name like Hieronymus I wouldn't have survived past the first grade, much less adolescence, at least not in Cliffside, North Carolina.

"You see, it could have been worse," she said.

Despite my vow never to leave my room again, I was in school on Monday morning. I sulked down the hallways between classes, expecting the worst. But except for a few remarks, I found my family's Cadillac no longer a hot topic of conversation. Evidently our car had been talked about around town for a few days and then dismissed by the adults as just another example—like Professor Hamrick's unzipped pants and Professor Abrams' refusal to get a driver's license—of the bizarre behavior of the college's teachers, behavior they forgave because they had come to view it as an inevitable affliction of the overeducated. Their children followed suit.

Still, I was already beginning to dread the day, now ten months off, when I would turn 16 and be eligible for my driver's license. Knowing my classmates, I was convinced that as soon as I slipped behind the Cadillac's steering wheel, I would immediately be greeted by ridicule and laughter, just as I knew that my not getting a license would cause a similar reaction. Either way, I did not believe I could bear it.

The following Saturday I went with my father to the art department, vowing not to leave there until I knew why I was being tormented. When I was younger, I had sometimes spent rainy Saturdays with him in the basement of the college's fine arts building where he had taught me to throw and glaze a pot, mix oil paints, and work a kiln.

It was also a place where we had been able to talk to each other in a way we never could anywhere else. As we worked, he would tell me stories, sometimes about Leonardo, who died lamenting the failure of his life, wishing that he had more time, or Michelangelo, who, after finishing one of the last statues he would ever create, had to be stopped by his apprentices from destroying it, because the statue "wouldn't breathe." The story he told most often, however, was about a potter in ancient China who invented a beautiful, dark-red glaze, only to find that the pottery coated with the glaze would crack each time it was fired. The potter lowered and raised the temperature of the kiln, changed the composition of the pots, and even burned different kinds of wood. After years of failure, the potter threw himself into the kiln, where his final load of glazed pots was baking. Later, all of the pots his friends took out of the kiln possessed the dark-red color, and all were unbroken. The charred bones his friends found in the kiln had been the missing ingredient.

We had been throwing pots for about an hour when I felt the time was right.

"Why did you buy a Cadillac, Dad?" I asked. "Why not a Mercury or Plymouth, or even a Ford?"

My father walked over to the sink to wash his hands. I followed, not about to leave without an answer.

"You've got to tell me," I said.

He picked up a paper towel and dried his hands.

"Because owning a Cadillac shows exactly how far I've come from that mill village where I grew up."

"But, Dad," I said, not sure how what I was about to say would be taken. "It's got over a hundred thousand miles on it, hardly anything works the way it should, and it's the wrong color."

My father smiled.

"That's true. Maybe it also shows how far I have to go."

One month before I turned 16 my father, who had been carefully checking the used-car advertisements in the Asheville and Charlotte papers for months, traded cars again. This Cadillac was only seven years old, not ten like the other, and its interior and exterior were in much better shape than its predecessor. It did have its drawbacks, however. It was also gray, but a darker, gloomier gray, and only one of its electric windows would close all the way.

This car was the first I ever drove, and much of the humiliation I had expected became a reality. I found myself able to make my classmates laugh hysterically almost anytime they saw me behind the wheel of the big, dark-gray Cadillac, with three windows partially down even in the middle of winter. I drove only when I absolutely had to, and then I slumped behind the wheel in the feeble hope that I could hide myself. I watched with envy as my classmates drove their families' normal cars.

In the next two years my father traded cars three more times, all were Cadillacs. Each was newer, and despite some drawbacks, better. In the spring of my last year of high school, only two weeks before my senior prom, my father traded for the last of these.

I had just gotten home from track practice when he drove up, slowly turning into our driveway. As my father got out of the car, I noticed for the first time that his hair was almost completely gray. I had been so caught up in my own life that I hadn't even noticed. The car was a Cadillac Fleetwood, the "Cadillac of Cadillacs," according to the owner's manual I found in the glove compartment. It was a 1973, meaning the car was less than three years old, and the odometer had fewer than 30,000 miles on it, beating the previous family record by 20,000 miles. All the electric windows worked, and the interior looked almost new.

But like all our Cadillacs, this one had its drawbacks too. The main one was its color—black. Why it was black became all too clear when I was putting the owner's guide back in the glove compartment and found a stack of business cards with "Harris Funeral Home, Charlotte, North Carolina" printed on them.

Well, time had proven Jimbo right. Nevertheless, I wasn't nearly as upset as I would have been two years earlier, for in my last half-year of high school I gained a great deal of confidence in myself. The Cadillacs had been a godsend as far as my track career went. Instead of spending my afternoons and evenings cruising around Cliffside in a car, like so many of my classmates, I ran, sometimes more than 100 miles a week in the winter of my senior year. Now, in the spring, after running several fast times in the mile, I was receiving letters from a dozen schools about possible track scholarships. Nothing was definite yet, but in my last race I had set a conference record while an assistant coach from Chapel Hill was in the stands.

I was just as hopeful about impressing another person in the stands that day—Laura Bryan—and after the meet I asked her to go with me to our senior prom. She accepted. But the confidence I had the day of the race quickly disappeared. I soon began to have second thoughts about my date. Did she realize that going to the prom with me meant going in my father's car? I agonized over this question and several times almost asked her.

I had never taken a girl out in one of our Cadillacs. The few dates I'd been on, I arranged it so I wouldn't have to drive. My date and I just met somewhere.

But you couldn't just meet at your senior prom. Perhaps, finally, I had overcome the stigma of my father's Cadillacs and was about to become a normal teenager. So even though I had just found out that our newest Cadillac didn't just look like a car used in a funeral but actually had been, I was not too worried. I was the best high school miler in western North Carolina, and one of the prettiest and smartest girls at Cliffside High was going to the prom with me. Not even a black, ex-funeral car could stop me now.

The weekend before my senior prom, my father decided to drive over to Shelby to see my grandmother. My mother, anticipating that he would spend most of the weekend at the art department, had already made other plans. Then he came into my room and asked if I wanted to go. I was surprised; he usually assumed that if I wanted to go I would be in the car when he backed out of the driveway. I told him yes, I always enjoyed going to see my grandmother, but that I would need to get back before too late to make some plans with Laura for the prom.

We visited until late afternoon. As we were driving away from my grandmother's house, we turned right, onto a street I had never been on before. It was an old section of town; dogwood and oak trees lined the sidewalks, and behind them were huge, two-story, wooden houses, five times the size of my grandmother's home a half-mile away. For a few seconds I thought my father had once again forgotten where he was going. But he slowed the Fleetwood down until it was barely moving and pointed out the window at the largest of the houses.

"That is where Old Man Calhoun lived, the owner of the mill, when I was growing up."

My father didn't say anything else. Instead, he stopped the car and stared up at the big, white house. We stayed there for about a minute, saying nothing. I looked at my watch. I was supposed to call Laura at 6:30. I broke the silence, telling my father that we needed to go.

The prom was the following weekend. We picked up our tuxedos at school on Friday, a tradition at our school, and on Saturday morning my mother drove to a greenhouse outside Cliffside and bought Laura's corsage. The sky had been overcast all day, and as I drove to Laura's house, it began to drizzle. Fortunately, my mother made me take an umbrella as I went out the door. I took having the umbrella with me as a good omen, ignoring the sky as a possible omen too.

When I got to Laura's, her parents took our picture. I gave her the corsage, and she gave me a white carnation. The umbrella kept Laura dry, and she said nothing about my family's newest car as we began the ten-mile drive to the country club. It was only seven o'clock, but because of the cloudy skies it was already getting hard to see. I looked over at Laura, and she smiled at me in a way that made my legs feel weaker than they had ever felt after a race. I turned on the Fleetwood's headlights. Everything was going too well to risk even the slightest chance of another driver not seeing me and wrecking what promised to be one of the most enjoyable nights of my life.

Though heavily traveled, the road to the country club was only two lanes. I hadn't felt the need to drive the Fleetwood before this evening, but I was soon wishing I had, for the steering wheel was much looser than the ones on our previous cars. This, along with the wet, narrow road, made me more and more nervous. The road was, except for a few curvy stretches, a 55-mile an hour zone, but I was only going 35. Soon a small line of cars was behind me, unable or unwilling to pass me on the rain-slick roads.

We were five miles from our destination when the first car coming from the other direction pulled off the road. I didn't think anything of it, figuring the driver was having car trouble. A quarter of a mile further, however, two more cars did the same thing.

Around Cliffside, it had long been a custom when you met a funeral procession coming in the other direction to pull off the road as a sign of respect for the departed and the departed's family. Whether you knew the person or not did not matter. It was a matter of manners, which the people I grew up around took very seriously. Three more cars pulled off the road before I realized what was happening. At that moment I prayed to God that Laura Bryan wasn't as smart as I thought she was and would not realize why those cars were pulling off the road.

For a few more minutes she watched, puzzled, while several more cars did the same thing. Then she turned to me.

"They think this is a funeral, and that we're leading it! And you," she shrieked, pointing to my carnation, "they think you're the funeral director."

She started shaking with laughter. I was too upset to try to speak. I was suddenly back in the ninth grade. It didn't matter that I had set a conference record in the mile run and might get a scholarship to Chapel Hill. It wouldn't have mattered if I had set a world's record. And it certainly didn't matter that my prom date was Laura Bryan, for Laura, who was bent over with laughter at that very moment, would never take me seriously again.

Five minutes passed before I was able to ask her if she wanted to go back home. I was hoping she would say yes, but between spasms of laughter Laura told me she had to go now to tell everyone what had happened. I tore the carnation off my lapel and switched off the headlights, hoping to stop the pulloffs, each of which now caused Laura to howl even louder. I no longer cared if I had an accident or not. I was almost hoping for one. Death or serious injury seemed preferable to what awaited me at the prom.

Once we got there, Laura wasted no time telling the story to everyone she could. After an hour of being the butt of the same joke, I hated her enough not to feel obligated to stay any longer. I told her I was leaving, and if she wanted to stay she would have to find her own way home. I had to stand near the punch bowl until she was sure she had a ride arranged. She came back a few minutes later with Jimbo Miller, now wearing the white carnation I had torn off. He had come alone and was only too happy to take Laura home.

I was back home before 9:30. I took the keys to what was now known as the "funeral director's car" and handed them to my father. When my mother asked why I was home so early, I didn't even answer her. I went to my room and locked the door.

The following Monday afternoon I went to the bank and withdrew all the money from my savings account. I had been saving for college, but college was no longer the number-one priority in my life; never having to drive one of my father's Cadillacs again was. As soon as I left the bank, I went over to the Gulf station where a 1967 Volkswagen Beetle was for sale. I had the right amount of money, but Johnny Heddon, the owner of the station who also owned the Beetle, refused to sell it to me without my parents' permission. At first, my parents were reluctant, but I was so adamant—and, after all, it was my money—that they soon gave in. Two weeks later Chapel Hill wrote and offered me a full scholarship. I accepted and left Cliffside in mid-August, in my Volkswagen.

The Fleetwood was the last car my father ever bought. He died during my senior year at Chapel Hill. In the fall of 1981, the Fleetwood was broadsided when a college student ran Cliffside's one stop light. My mother, who was driving the car, was uninjured, but the Fleetwood was too damaged to justify repairing it. My mother bought a 1976 Ford Pinto with the insurance money.

I drove the Volkswagen for a decade, until it blew a rod and ended up in a junkyard outside Greenville, South Carolina. For weeks, I prowled used car lots looking for a replacement, always gravitating to the battered gas-guzzlers on the back rows.

I settled on a 1978 Cadillac Coup De Ville. Two of the electric windows worked when I bought it four years ago. Now only one does, the left rear window.

This is the car I drove last spring when I came up from South Carolina to visit my relations. I spent the night at my mother's house in Cliffside, and the

66

next day she and I drove over to Shelby, picked up my grandmother, and spent the day visiting kin. We ended up at the cemetery outside Cliffside. My grandmother placed some jonquils on my father's grave, flowers she picked that morning.

It was starting to get dark as we drove back into Shelby from the cemetery. My grandmother asked to ride down Lee Street to look at the dogwoods, which were now in full bloom. I didn't know where Lee Street was, but she gave me directions and five minutes later I was on the same street I had been on years earlier with my father.

"That's where the owner of the mill lived, wasn't it?" I asked my grandmother as I pointed to the biggest house. My grandmother nodded that it was. I suddenly realized I had stopped the car in the middle of the street. A car was coming up behind me, so I pressed the accelerator and drove down to the end of the block.

My grandmother looked out the window at the dogwoods. "You know," she said, "there is something about a dogwood in the spring that fills a body with hope. It makes you feel like all your dreams can still come true."

When she said that I thought of my grandfather, working most of his life in the card room of the cotton mill, breathing the cotton dust that eventually killed him, dreaming of a son who would never have to see the inside of a cotton mill, but never living long enough to see his dream come true, to see his son, my father teaching at a college.

I thought of my father sitting in the art class with the mill owner's daughter and the other children whose fathers were doctors or lawyers or store owners and whose mothers stayed home, who did not have to work in a cotton mill to make ends meet. My father, too, dreaming of a life beyond the mill village.

As I waited to turn left, the dogwoods held my gaze, their blossoms blazing, bright as dreams against the darkness.

From *Casualties* (2000)

THE WAY THINGS ARE

The second we walk in I know it's all wrong. The two girls riding the bikes, the others trapped in the machines, they're trying too hard not to look at us.

"Shit," Clifford says out of the corner of his mouth. "I didn't know we were supposed to wear a costume."

Clifford's trying to make a joke, but like me he's looking in the mirror that covers the back wall. He sees what I see—two guys getting a little big in the belly wearing t-shirts and cut-off jeans. One of them has hands and arms black from working on lawn mowers all day, the other, me, mortar on his arms, some in my beard. They don't put mirrors in port-a-johns.

"Damn if I don't believe these people shower before they work out," Clifford says.

Two guys wearing tight shirts with Nautilus written on the front are standing in the middle of the room. The older looking one, about our age, helps a woman do some negatives.

The younger guy sits on the free-weight bench, doing nothing. We wait.

"Let's get out of here," I say. Clifford shakes his head like a bull starting to madden up.

"I paid five dollars for that coupon book," he says. "All I got so far is a half-price burger at Hardee's."

I know Clifford. We played six years of junior high and high school football together, most of the time side by side on the offensive line. I know there's no use in saying anything else. He ain't leaving.

And they realize it too, the coaches, the trainers, the whatever you call them. The younger one gets off his ass, like maybe we're just lost and come in to get directions.

Clifford takes out the book and tears out the coupon. He's got muscles, this guy, the kind that you can see right through his clothes, but when he opens his hand to take Clifford's coupon you can tell he's never done the kind of work we do. He reads the coupon.

"OK," he says. "But you understand this coupon is good for only one workout. A year's membership is three hundred dollars."

I almost say that we're not that stupid. And then I almost say we can read, too. But I end up not saying a damn thing. He starts Clifford on the first machine, but not before he goes and gets a towel so he can wipe each machine when Clifford finishes. They start down the line, him talking to Clifford, explaining the machines, but he ain't looking at Clifford, like if he keeps looking away maybe Clifford will disappear.

I walk over to where Clifford's pushing a ton on the leg machine, sweating and stinking and grunting till he finally can lock his legs. I tell him I'm going out to the car. Clifford lets the weights clang back down, rubs his knee.

"But the coupon's for two people," he says, trying to catch his breath.

"I done sweated enough today just to make a living," I say, then walk out into the heat.

The air conditioner's been broke for a year, so I roll down the window. It's still hot, but not hotter than it's been the last eight hours. I lower my hat brim over my eyes and rest. Clifford comes hobbling out thirty minutes later.

"Sorry you had to wait," he says. He's gritting his teeth when he says it, flexing his leg. He don't have to tell me he's rehurt the knee the doctor's cut on after our senior year.

"No problem," I say. "I ain't got nothing better to do."

"I showed that candy-ass a thing or two," he says. "Asked him what he did on that leg machine, then did ten more pounds."

Clifford reaches into a paper bag he's got his work clothes in, pulls out two cans of Gatorade.

"Little treat," he says.

Even warm Gatorade tastes good when you been working out in the sun all day. It takes about two swallows to empty the can, and I'm wishing I had another.

"Don't think I'm going to join," Clifford says, crushing his can and putting it in the bag. "It ain't like when we lifted for football. Hell, it don't even smell right in there. No Atomic Balm. No Ben-Gay. Nobody yelling. Nobody sweating. It just ain't for me."

"Me either," I say, getting my keys out.

"Those girls on the bikes were sure pretty, though," Clifford says. "College girls, I'd guess."

"I reckon," I say, cranking up the car, not wanting to talk about it any more. "Where are we going?"

"You got something else to wear in the trunk?" Clifford asks.

I nod.

"Let's go over to my apartment then," Clifford says. "Get something to eat, then go to the Firefly. Hell, I'll even let you take a shower provided you ain't got any cooties."

Bocephus is singing "The Pressure is On," so I turn it up and burn some rubber leaving the parking lot.

I almost feel decent by the time we turn into Clifford's apartment. A couple of black guys are out front drinking Schlitz Malt Liquors. They got their backs to us but they can see me and Clifford because one of those mirrors that lets you see around corners is right above them. They're in Clifford's yard, if you can call dirt and weeds a yard, but they move on out into the parking lot, their backs still to us, keeping their distance. Luther, the black guy who works with me, he swears the only white guys black dudes are scared of is guys like us with long hair and beards. Too many guys that look like that are crazy, Luther says, like Charlie Manson. I don't know if that has anything to do with it or not, but the black guys keep their distance, don't even look our way.

We get a shower, eat a couple of TV dinners apiece. Clifford turns on his television and we watch the end of *Gunsmoke.* Then we head over to the Firefly.

It's Tuesday so Freeda's working the bar by herself. We come in and it takes her a little too long to get up from her stool. You can tell she's bone-tired, but ain't we all. She knows what we drink so she opens two long-neck Buds, puts them on the counter. Clifford gets his and limps over to the poker machine. His leg's starting to stiffen, and I hope like hell he hasn't messed it up bad, because he don't have a dime's worth of insurance.

Freeda sits back down on the stool. She's filling out some kind of government form, like what they give you for taxes, but it's probably something to do with her kids. She's got three of them and no husband, at least not anymore, and lives with her mother and works here two-to-two, six days a week.

I used to think Freeda was a lot older than me and Clifford, but she says she saw us play ball in high school, screaming her school, Burns, to kick our asses. Clifford likes to remind her they never did.

I'm thinking all this when two necktie types come in, sit in one of the booths in the far corner. Instead of going up to the bar, they make Freeda come to them, then start giving her lip about not having any imported beers, like she owns the place and decides what beers to carry. But that's the way things are. If you work there's always somebody giving you shit about something. And if you're like Freeda and you got three kids and an ex-husband who won't pay his alimony, you smile when they rub your face in it. And that's what Freeda is doing, smiling, hoping for a good tip.

They finally order and Freeda brings their beers. The one closest to the door says something to Freeda, but I can't hear what it is because Clifford's cussing the poker machine.

Then he rubs his hand across one of her breasts. I can't believe it. It's dark so maybe I'm just thinking I saw him do it. But Freeda's coming back toward me and her head is down. She's trying not to let them see she's crying.

I'm off the stool and in his face. "What can I do for you?" the necktie closest to the door says. He talks smooth, like a lawyer.

"Give me a chance to kick your ass," I say, loud, right in his face. He's as big as me but soft, and not just in the belly. I can take him. Clifford's coming up behind me. Even with a bum knee he can take care of the other one.

"I don't want any trouble," the necktie says.

No, I'm thinking, you just want to give it.

Freeda's beside me now with their drinks. She heard enough to know what's going on.

"It's OK," she says. "He didn't mean nothing by it."

The necktie finally catches on, understands why I'm pissed off.

"The lady's right," he says. "I didn't mean anything."

Freeda wedges between me and him, puts the drinks on the table.

"Please," she says. "You're making trouble for me."

She turns to Clifford.

"Help me, Clifford," she says.

Clifford don't know half of what's going on, but he's ready to fight, at least until Freeda says that. He untightens his fist, backs off a little.

"Come on back to the bar," she tells me and Clifford. "I'll get you boys a beer, on the house."

Freeda takes my hand like I'm a little kid, leads me back over to the bar. She gets our beers then goes back to the booth. She's talking soft but I hear enough to know she's apologizing. Clifford loses some more money playing the poker machine while I sip my beer and try not to look in the mirror.

SUMMER WORK

I saw Cecil Ledbetter last week for the first time since I'd seen him dragged unconscious and bleeding from a truck eleven years ago, and I thought again of my role in what happened to him. I was back home in western North Carolina, visiting my parents and sister. I've lived in southwest Virginia for the last decade, a region completely ignorant of red cole-slaw and ketchup-based pork, so on my infrequent trips back to Cliffside I indulge myself by eating lunch at Henson's Barbeque Lodge.

I drove uptown with my sister, past the closed-down theater and new supermarket, on past Hamrick Mill where my father worked. At Cliffside's one stoplight we turned right, parking in front of Cliffside Junior College's administration building. We crossed the street and stepped into Henson's.

Cecil was sharing the table closest to the door with a couple of college-aged boys. They had spent the morning cutting grass. Their tee-shirts were sweat-stained, and I could smell the gasoline lingering on their hands and clothing. As I passed the table Cecil looked up at me, but there was no blink of recognition in his eyes. Whatever link he had to me had been severed when his skull cracked the windshield. He looked back down at his plate, my face one more lost connection. In a few minutes I watched him take short steps toward the door, his gait slow and deliberate, like a man who'd suffered a stroke.

In my mind I followed him across the street, across eleven summers to my junior year at Chapel Hill, the summer my college roommate Ben Grier and I worked on the maintenance crew at Cliffside Junior College.

Our plan was to work at Hamrick Mill as we'd done the last two summers. Ben's father and mine were shift supervisors, and they'd been able to get us work in the past. But during the spring there had been layoffs at the mill. The only summer jobs we could find was working at the junior college for minimum wage.

Our mill jobs had paid a dollar an hour better, so I had to recalculate my student loan. Ben didn't have that worry. He'd scored 1560 on his SAT and received a full scholarship to Chapel Hill. He was, however, saving money for medical school. Like me, Ben was already ticked off about making less money.

But I don't think that had anything to do with what happened that summer. I'd known Ben since second grade. In high school we'd been lab partners and in the Beta Club together, but I'd never thought of him as a friend. I didn't know anyone who had.

We, students and teachers, had known even in grammar school that he was different, smart in a way the rest of us would never be no matter how many books we read, how hard we studied. Ben didn't draw attention to his brilliance. He never raised his hand in class, though he always knew the answer if he were called on. But sometimes when a teacher or student said something he found stupid he'd make a sardonic comment, as much to himself as to anyone else, and you wondered if in that moment he'd shown what he thought of all of us.

In the spring of our senior year in high school Ben asked me to room with him at Chapel Hill. I was surprised and flattered but shouldn't have been. He was already planning for medical school and didn't want to risk a roommate who'd be cranking up the stereo at 2 A.M. or bringing a bunch of drunk friends back to the room. I suspect he saw me as dull enough to have to have to spend a lot of time studying, introverted enough to keep to myself.

So one Monday in late May Ben and I punched in at the junior college's physical plant office. Mr. Priester, who'd hired us, nodded toward the other man in the office.

"Cecil will show you boys what to do," Mr. Priester said, then disappeared into the air-conditioned office he strayed from as little as possible.

We walked out to the blue truck with *Maintenance* painted on the side.

"Get in," Cecil said but didn't unlock the passenger door, so Ben and I climbed in the back. We rode past the gym and curved around the math and science building and on past the springhouse the college had restored years earlier. Cecil stopped the truck abruptly in front of a quonset hut, causing Ben and me to slide against the cab window. We jumped out of the truck as Cecil unlocked the quonset hut's sliding metal door.

"Listen, college boys," he said as we stepped inside. "This machinery don't care how smart you are. You get careless and you can get hurt bad."

We stood among the big Yazoo riding mowers, the push mowers and weed eaters. It was already hot inside the hut, and the reek of oil and gasoline made me nauseous.

"I reckon you boys know all about equipment like this but I'm going to tell you anyway, once. That way my ass is covered if you cut your fingers off doing something stupid."

Cecil bent down on one knee beside the weed eater.

"Come over here," he said to me. "You too, four eyes," Cecil added, not even looking at Ben. If he'd looked up he might have been surprised at the anger that flashed across Ben's face, but it didn't surprise me. Ben was tall and skinny and had worn glasses since the second grade, but his looks were deceiving. He was quiet but not timid. Yes, he looked the way you'd expect someone who'd nearly aced the SAT to look, but he was also an athlete, hard-nosed and competitive, something you wouldn't expect. Our senior year he'd been the best pitcher on the baseball team. He was smart and knew how to keep hitters guessing, but he also knew how to intimidate his opponent. Rutherford County had a first baseman that year who was all-state. The first time up, he hit a home run off Ben. The second time he came to the plate Ben threw two head-high fastballs right at the guy. Ben rattled him so bad he fanned on called strikes the rest of the game.

Cecil tugged six inches of monofilament from each of the three holes on the weed eater's plastic head.

"That's the length you need." Cecil looked up at us. "Wait till you got it running full speed before you try to trim. You understand?"

Ben smiled at him.

"Do you mean do we understand the concept of centrifugal force?" Ben said, still smiling. "Yeah, I think we understand that, Cecil."

As soon as the words were out I knew Cecil Ledbetter would be a long time in forgiving Ben for what he'd said, would make him, and maybe me, pay for those words the rest of the summer. Ben's words didn't surprise me. He'd said similar things in a similar tone to other men when we'd worked at the mill. A couple of times I'd thought his words were leading to a fight, and maybe they would have if his daddy hadn't had some rank in the mill.

Cecil looked up from where he kneeled. He was in his late twenties but he looked older, his forehead already creased, his long hair and beard flecked with gray. He was almost as tall as Ben and outweighed him by fifty pounds.

"Well," Cecil said to Ben. "Since you know so much about weed eaters we'll let you run one this summer. Me and your buddy will ride the Yazoos."

Ben shrugged his shoulders. "Fine," he said.

So that Monday morning our routine was set for the summer. I'd do trim with a push mower, but most of the time I was atop one of the Yazoos making a week-long journey that started at the springhouse, then around the dorms and classroom buildings, across the acre of open ground at the campus center, and ending at the administration building facing Cliffside's main street. It would be Friday afternoon when I finished and the following Monday I'd start over. Always somewhere behind me was Ben, moving around the trees and buildings with the weed eater. Meanwhile, Cecil kept the machinery running, changing oil, tightening belts, and sharpening mower blades, usually down at the springhouse where we worked in the shade of century-old oaks. The rest of the time he drove around campus in the blue maintenance truck, ogling sunbathing co-eds or trying to catch us slacking off.

By lunchtime that first day I was feeling guilty about riding while Ben lugged the weed eater in my wake, so I decided to say something. We got our bag lunches out of the office refrigerator and walked down to the spring-house. You weren't supposed to drink the water because there might be bacteria in it, but most people did anyway. When the college had repaired the springhouse years back they'd built a roofed lattice with a door. A concrete bench curved around the spring like a horseshoe. Ben and I bent down and filled our hands with water so cold it hurt our teeth when we drank. We sat on the concrete and opened our bags.

"I'm going to talk to Cecil about us switching off this afternoon," I said. "It's not fair for me to ride the Yazoo all day."

"No," Ben said sharply. "He'll think I asked you to say something. I don't want you to give him the satisfaction of thinking that. You just keep your mouth shut."

Ben looked up.

"Here comes the bastard now."

I turned and saw the blue maintenance truck curving around the math and science building and heading towards us. Cecil drove onto the grass and parked in the shade of an oak ten yards from where we sat. He opened the truck door but did not get out. His metal lunch box lay open on his lap.

Ben stashed his sandwich back in his lunch bag, the paperback he'd brought to read in his back pocket.

"I'll be damned if I'm going to spend any time around him I don't have to," he said, getting up from the bench. "I'm going to sit outside the library and eat." Ben walked out the door.

"I'll go too," I said, packing up my lunch.

"Suit yourself," Ben said, not looking back.

After that first day Ben and Cecil pretty much stayed clear of one another, but in early June Cecil caught us talking to a couple of co-eds in front of the cafeteria. He bumped the truck over the curve and drove straight up to us.

"Get back to work," he said. "You can chase poontang on your own time."

The girls and I were embarrassed. Ben was too, but was also angry.

"You ignorant redneck," Ben said.

"What?" Cecil cut off the ignition.

"Don't say it again," one of the girls said.

"You heard me," Ben said.

"Yeah, well, just remember this ignorant redneck gets to tell you what to do."

"Only one summer, Cecil," Ben said.

"A summer can be a damn long time, college boy." Cecil cranked the truck and drove off.

For the next ten weeks Cecil made sure we worked every minute we were on the clock. He watched us take our breaks at ten and three and saw to it they were exactly fifteen minutes. He wouldn't let us take our equipment back to the quonset hut until five minutes before lunch or quitting time.

By mid-July the temperature was over ninety every afternoon. I was riding at least part of the day, but I was still exhausted by five. The mill work had been hard, but we'd been out of the sun and our bosses, probably out of deference to our fathers, had cut us some slack when we got tired. At lunchtime Ben no longer read. He ate quickly and then napped under an elm tree in front of the library. At five minutes to one I'd shake him awake and we'd walk down to the quonset hut.

He never complained, not to Mr. Priester, Cecil, or me, and he never eased up. Sometimes on afternoons it was so hot I could see heat rolling across the campus in waves, I'd risk Cecil's wrath by parking the Yazoo under a tree for a few minutes, but Ben never stopped. He was always moving, always wearing his eight-pound albatross.

It was in late July that I caught the snake. Ben and I were walking to the office to check out. I thought it was dead, but when I stepped closer I saw the red tongue flicker. I picked it up to take home and let go in the woods behind my house.

Mr. Priester and Cecil were in the office when we walked in, the snake coiled around my hand.

Cecil stumbled back against the refrigerator.

"Keep that damn thing away from me," he said.

At first I thought he was joking.

"Keep it away from me," he said again, and I saw he was truly frightened. He punched out and left the office.

"It's just a green snake," I told Mr. Priester, holding the snake up for him to see.

"Cecil's scared shitless of snakes," Mr. Priester said. "He got bit by a copperhead when he was a kid. It almost killed him."

"A green snake isn't a copperhead,' Ben said. "Even Cecil should be able to figure that out."

Mr. Priester shook his head.

"What kind it is don't make a difference to Cecil," Mr. Priester said.

Cecil had been right. A summer can be a long time, but August finally came. Whatever battle of wills between Cecil and Ben was over. Ben had won and even Cecil realized it, and though he'd have died before admitting it, you could tell Cecil respected Ben for sticking it out, for never once complaining. Those last days he no longer checked our breaks. If we saw him at all he was bringing us a cooler filled with water from the springhouse, some paper cups to drink from.

It was eleven-thirty of our last day when Ben waived me toward the quonset hut. He carried our lunch bags in his right hand.

"It's a little early, isn't it?" I asked as I climbed off the Yazoo.

"It's our last day, " Ben said. "What can they do to us. Besides, I've got some lunchtime entertainment planned you might enjoy. It's going to be at the spring so we better get going."

"Is Cecil in on this?" I asked.

"Oh yeah," Ben said. "He just doesn't know it."

I followed Ben up the road past the springhouse. We went up the hill to the side of the math and science building.

"This will give us a good view," Ben said and sat down on the grass.

"What are we waiting to see?" I asked.

"I added something to Cecil's lunch box a few minutes ago when I went to get ours. A snake."

Ben grinned.

"Don't worry. It's just a hog-nose snake, but it looks enough like a copperhead to give Cecil a good scare."

"He'll know who did it," I said.

Ben looked at me. He was no longer grinning.

"I don't care. I'll risk a concussion just to see that asshole when he opens that lunch bag."

"This is a bad idea," I said. "This is wrong."

"Well," Ben said, looking up the road. "Here he comes. If you want to tell him, flag him down."

And I almost did, because I realized at that moment that I liked Cecil more than I liked Ben, that a part of me would enjoy watching Cecil kick Ben's ass. But I didn't. I just sat there and let it happen.

The blue maintenance truck curved around the math and science building and passed thirty yards below us. I saw Cecil in the cab, the window open, only his left hand on the steering wheel. I watched him glance down at the passenger seat.

People who have been in wrecks talk about how everything slows down, but to watch a wreck happen is a different matter. It happens so fast you can't believe what you've seen. Cecil's truck swerved then accelerated across the grass and crashed through the springhouse lattice and into the concrete bench. The impact was so loud faces appeared at the doors and windows of the math and science building. In the few seconds I sat there trying to get my brain to believe what my eyes had just seen, students and teachers ran out the doors toward the crumpled truck, its doors flung open.

Ben and I followed. Inside the cab I saw Cecil slumped over the steering wheel, the windshield cracked where his head had hit.

One of the students was a nursing major. She checked Cecil's pulse and kept anyone from trying to move him.

"He's alive," I heard her say.

Mr. Priester showed up a few minutes later and pushed his way through the students and teachers. He was talking to Cecil but getting no response. An ambulance finally arrived, and we all backed up to let the EMS crew work.

They gently removed Cecil from the truck, placed him in the ambulance and drove off. At the stoplight the ambulance wailed eastward toward Charlotte, not west toward the county hospital.

The students and teachers went back to their classes.

Ben leaned toward me.

"You're not going to tell," he said, and whether his words were a question was unclear.

"No," I said, as Mr. Priester walked toward us.

"You boys know what happened?"

"No, sir," Ben said. "We heard the crash and came to see what was going on."

"Well, he wasn't wearing his seat built. That's a school regulation," Mr. Priester said, looking at the truck.

"Do you know what to do this afternoon?"

We nodded.

"Well, go do it. I'll probably be in Charlotte."

At five o'clock I walked into the physical plant office and punched a time clock for the last time in my life. Ben and I stepped into the parking lot where Mr. Priester and the college's vice president were talking. Mr. Preister waved us over.

"The doctors say he'll live, but they're pretty sure there's brain damage. They don't know how bad yet."

The vice-president looked at his watch.

"It's time to leave," he said, and it was.

Three months passed before Cecil left the hospital, and it was almost a year before the college, whether out of compassion or fear of a lawsuit, rehired him. He no longer worked on the equipment, however, or drove a truck or a Yazoo. They let him use the push mowers and weed eaters. In the fall and winter he raked leaves.

The night we were to go back to Chapel Hill, Ben called.

"Listen," he said. "Don't take this personal but I put in a request to live in Johnson Dorm. It's closer to my labs. They told me it would take a couple of weeks to make the switch, so we'll be rooming together a few days. Is that O.K.?"

"Sure," I said. "I never asked you to room with me. That was your idea."

"I guess you're right," Ben said, as if he had forgotten.

"I think we need to talk about what happened," I said.

"What do you want me to say?" Ben asked, then answered his own question. "You want me to say that I'm eaten up with guilt. Well, I don't feel bad at all, and I'm not hypocritical enough to pretend I do. It was an accident, and it happened to a dumb, mean redneck. It's not like the world's lost some great contributor to mankind. But do I wish it had never happened? Sure, and that's more than Cecil would have felt if it had happened to me."

"You don't know that," I said. "I feel bad about this even if you don't."

"You shouldn't," Ben said. "It's on my conscious, not yours, and if you're stupid enough to feel bad about not telling about what happened, let me ease your mind. All that would have done was risk ruining two lives instead of one."

I didn't say anything else to Ben about the wreck, not that night or any other night. There didn't seem to be any point.

Ben went on to medical school at Emory. He did his internship at Boston General, marrying a fellow intern. He's now a G. P. in a Boston suburb.

I do not know if Ben is haunted by what happened that summer. I do not know if when he worked the emergency room at Boston General he was reminded of Cecil each time he looked into the face of a wreck victim. Perhaps he saw so many damaged humans that Cecil became one more blurred face on the emergency room's assembly line of catastrophe, an unlikable man who from his point of view—unlike the eight year-old child or pregnant woman he might minister to—had some responsibility for what had happened to him.

As my sister and I walked out to my car last week, I saw Cecil running a weed eater in front of the junior college's administration building. He held it in front of him as if it were a metal detector. He looked like a man searching for something lost long ago.

CASUALTIES AND SURVIVORS

Rachel is learning sign language. She stands in the basement of the Cleveland County Library between two long, metal book shelves marked H, the bright-yellow paperback *Signing for Kids* held like a hymnal in her left hand, her right hand raised as if conducting some imaginary choir as she mimics the drawings. Footsteps approach the stack where she'd cloistered, so she closes the paperback, picks up the brown hardback lain sideways on the shelf.

Rachel waits in line to check out the sign language book and the book Dr. Watson suggested she and Allen read. She likes Dr. Watson. He's different from the other specialists who bustle into the room and never sit down, older men who check their watches and ease out the door even as they ask, "Any Questions?" Dr. Watson always sits down, crossing his left leg over his right, his fingers meshed over his kneecap as if to say, "What's on your mind, folks. I've got all the time in the world." His youth and obvious good health are especially heartening to Rachel because the hospital's coronary care wing is crowded with people who drag their damaged bodies, the very equipment that keeps them alive, through the hall as if participating in some kind of painful waltz.

"I don't want you trying to climb Chimney Rock," Dr. Watson had said to Allen on their last visit two weeks ago, but just about anything else will be fine." Yardwork, driving, sex, all that's O.K. Keep increasing the length of your walk, eat right, and in a month you'll be back at your desk full-time."

Dr. Watson had torn a page from his prescription pad.

"Read this book," he'd said, writing the title and author on the paper. "I believe it will help both of you."

Rachel hands the librarian her two books, and he waves a machine the size of a telephone over the inside jackets until there's a beep. She finds the noise irritating. It bothers her that she cannot get a book checked out without a machine being involved. That is why when she'd entered the library twenty minutes ago she'd walked right past the blue computer screens that hummed and beeped with the same efficiency and coldness of the technology that had monitored and managed the damage to Allen's heart. The chairs in front of the computers had been filled, the occupants calling up words that appeared and vanished in an eyeblink. Rachel had wanted something more tangible, the enduring solidity of wood and thick manila file cards, so she'd made her way to the library's far corner.

There she had removed the *S* tray from the card catalogue and lain it on a nearby study table. She'd glanced at the cards whose raised left corners marked particular subjects: Sex, Sign Language, Surgery. There had not been one for surviving, so she'd thumbed through the back of the tray until she found *Surviving a Heart Attack: The Road to Recovery.* She'd written down the call number and was about to put the tray up when she'd paused and placed it back on the study table. She'd parted the cards behind sign language, reading five before she picked up her pen.

Rachel is back home by 12:30, her hands cradling the books, the two Styrofoam containers filled with vegetables from Hinton's Café. She knocks on the door with her elbow and hears Allen's bedroom slippers, a sound like a whisper as he shuffles across the carpet.

"Come on in," he says, opening the door wide, stepping back, it seems to her, warily, as if she were some stranger who'd asked to borrow the phone. He still wears what he slept in, and this bothers her. He's never been the kind of man to laze around in his pajamas all morning, not even on weekends.

Rachel lays the books and food on the kitchen table where she and Allen eat both of their meals now that the children have left home. She opens the styrofoam containers and feels the steam of the vegetables moisten her face.

"It's still hot," she calls down the hallway. "Let's go ahead and eat."

She hears Allen coming up the hall, moving with short, measured steps, as though he believed the floor, the very earth itself, might suddenly buckle, give way. Maybe that's what it felt like, she thinks, and remembers again how she'd found him, slumped on the bathroom floor, dressed only in his pajama bottoms, his lips blue, his lips gray as November, the electric razor still clutched in his hand, its cord yanked from the socket above the mirror.

"I miss fried chicken," Allen says as he sits down.

"You wouldn't be a self-respecting Southerner if you didn't," Rachel says, but he does not return her smile.

She lifts *Surviving a Heart Attack: The Road to Recovery* and shows him the cover.

"They had it."

"I'll look at it later," Allen says, barely glancing at the cover.

Rachel raises the bright yellow paperback between them.

"I got this too."

He smiles, almost his old smile.

"You haven't had enough to do lately?"

"I just thought it would be interesting to try and learn something new."

Allen lays down his plastic fork.

Rachel almost tells him he needs to eat more to keep his strength up, but she doesn't want to seem a nag. She looks at the eight pill bottles lined up across the windowsill like tombstones in a cemetery.

"Alecia called," Allen said. "She made a C on her speech."

"Well, she comes by it honest. We're not the most vocal bunch around here. Was she upset?"

"More relieved than anything else. She's just glad to have it over with."

Allen nods toward the yellow paperback.

"Maybe she can use sign language in her next speech. It would take care of her stammering problem."

"She have any other news?"

"No. Mainly just checking on me, same as Steven last night."

"They're good kids," Rachel says, remembering how supportive Steven and Alecia have been. They were at the hospital before sundown that first day, Steven having driven from southwest Virginia, Alecia the four hours from Chapel Hill. For the next two months the kids had alternated weekends. Steven and Alecia bought groceries, washed dishes, got prescriptions filled. They had come through when she and Allen needed them the most, their essential decency confirmed in small, quiet acts of consideration and generosity.

Neither Steven nor Alecia has come home the last few weeks, and Rachel knows that is how it should be, for now is the time for her children to reclaim their own lives, for Allen and her to try and reclaim theirs.

"Did Matt call?" Rachel asks. This conversation is as long as any they've had in weeks, and she does not want it to end.

Matt is Allen's younger brother. He once worked for Allen but left eight years ago to sell insurance full time. Matt was the one who had convinced Rachel and Allen to increase their health coverage. Whatever else Allen's heart attack has done to them, at least it has not devastated them financially.

"No," Allen says, looking down at his half-eaten lunch, the glimpse of his old self gone now. "Matt's too busy running his own business to play nursemaid," he says. Allen gets up from the table, places the stryofoam container in the trash can. "I'm going to take a nap," he says.

Rachel thinks how insured and assured sound so alike yet are so completely different in meaning as Allen's footsteps pass Alecia's, then Steven's room before entering their bedroom. The bedsprings creak as he lies down.

Rachel remembers three months ago when the doctor in the emergency room had avoided her eyes, her questions as he checked her husband's vital signs. If someone could have assured her he would be alive in three months she could not have imagined asking for anything more. But now she does want more. Her marriage has been a good one, as good as any she knows. She and Allen had always been able to sustain each other when bad times had come, be it the deaths of parents, Alecia's car wreck, or the December they'd feared he'd lose his business.

Sometimes it was words, sometimes a gesture, but they had found a way to heal.

Now, for the first time in their marriage, she has been unable to comfort him. When she tries to talk to him he is terse and distant. Her hardly acknowledges her presence in afternoons she comes home from work or evenings when they sit across the room from each other in the living room. The night of their last visit to Dr. Watson she had kept her lips open to his after she'd kissed him goodnight, but he had turned his back to her. It is as if he were a ghost still burdened by a body.

Rachel picks up the paperback and carries it into the bathroom. She lays it open on the vanity and places a hairbrush between the pages to hold her place. She looks into the mirror, the same mirror Allen looked into three months ago. What had he seen that moment his heart stalled? Had he watched the color drain from his face? Had he looked at his chest and actually seen his heart fluttering against his chest like a trapped bird? When Dr. Watson had asked Allen what he'd felt those last moments before losing consciousness he'd said "afraid" and volunteered nothing more.

Rachel looks down at the book and then at the mirror. She moves her hands in gestures as slow and careful as Allen's footsteps. After thirty minutes she believes she is getting the hang of it. She strings together three different signs without looking at the book. She is communicating but only with herself. She turns her palms toward her and looks at the back of her hands, the loose skin and prominent veins, the hands of a woman no longer young.

Rachel lets her hands fall to her sides. She looks at her face in the mirror, the crow's feet, the lines across her brow. She looks at her hair streaked with gray and wonders if Allen thinks she is still pretty.

As she stares into the mirror Rachel remembers a hotel room cold and sterile as a doctor's office. She remembers a chest of drawers and a mirror large as a window, a table with a vase of flowers already wilting, flowers she knew the maid would throw out come morning. She and Allen sat in the room's two chairs, their conversation as awkward as on their first date, as they tried not to look at the bed that seemed to loom big as an island in the center of the room. They had changed after the reception. Allen wore a blue dress shirt and brown slacks, she a blouse and the plaid skirt he had given her the previous Christmas.

This had been the moment she'd truly realized the safe, known world was behind her now. She was in a strange room in a strange city with a man she suddenly felt she hardly knew.

She had not felt this way that morning as her sisters and mother fussed about her, smoothing her wedding dress, adjusting her veil, or during the ceremony itself—the preacher she'd known all her life reading the words, the church filled with familiar faces. She wondered if she could have said "yes" had she felt this way six months earlier when he'd proposed, eight hours earlier when her father had let go of her hand and stepped back.

Rachel remembered how she'd looked across the hotel room into the mirror, and seen a young, frightened face, a bride beginning her marriage in a room shared with decades of people she'd never know, a room where nothing but the furniture stayed long. She'd been looking in the mirror when Allen had walked across the room and stood behind her chair. He leaned down, his face close to hers, both looking at the mirror as if posing for a photograph.

"You're so beautiful," he'd said, and she'd seen his face in the mirror, his gray eyes bright with tears.

Rachel turns from the bathroom mirror. She walks softly into the bedroom where Allen sleeps on the bed. She opens the closet door and raises her hand. Quietly as possible, three or four at a time, she rakes the clothes-heavy hangers to the right side until she comes to the farthest hanger. She lifts the plaid skirt from the metal rod, removes the plastic cover, the hanger.

Allen does not stir as she sheds her shirt and pants, her underclothes and puts on a blouse and the skirt. She stands before the bureau's small mirror. The skirt is tight, especially around hips widened by two children and twenty-five years. She looks in the mirror, smooths the plaid cloth as best she can. She cannot say if Allen will remember that he gave the skirt to her so many Christmases ago, or remember that she wore it when their life together was little more than a promise of untarnished rings.

"Allen," she says.

He opens his eyes.

Rachel raises her right hand, the palm facing forward, her thumb, index finger, and little finger extended. She crosses both hands over her heart, palms facing in, then covers the fingers on her right hand with her left fingers and thumb.

The curtains are partially open. She wonders for a moment how a neighbor or stranger would interpret a forty-eight-year-old woman in a dress two decades too small gesturing to a man lying on a bed. What would Steven and Alecia make of this scene? Would it seem bizarre, comic, or sad? Or would they sense if not understand the message in the weave of her fingers and hands, as she believes Allen will as he watches her intently.

She removes the blouse and skirt and lies down beside him. He starts to speak but she gently presses her forefinger against his lips. She unbuttons his pajama top and traces the incision with her fingertip. She moves her body closer, her chest against his, feeling the scarred ridge of flesh pressed into her flesh, her heart inches from his scarred heart. Allen's eyes are closed but his lips find hers. They lay their hands upon each other's bodies and speak love's old, final language.

From *Chemistry and Other Stories* (2007)

CHEMISTRY

The spring my father spent three weeks at Broughton Hospital, he came back to my mother and me pale and disoriented, two pill bottles clutched in his right hand as we made our awkward reunion in the hospital lobby. A portly, gray-haired man wearing a tie and a tweed jacket soon joined us. Dr. Morris pronounced my father "greatly improved, well on his way to recovery," but even in those few first minutes my mother and I were less sure. My father seemed to be in a holding pattern, not the humorous, confident man he had been before his life swerved to some bleak reckoning, but also not the man who'd lain in bed those April mornings when my mother called the high school to arrange for a substitute. He now seemed like a shipwreck survivor, treading water but unable to swim.

"All he needs is a hobby," Dr. Morris said, patting my father's back as if they were old friends, "to keep his mind off his mind." The doctor laughed and straightened his tie, added as if an afterthought, "and the medicine, of course." Dr. Morris patted my father's back again. "A chemistry teacher knows how important that is."

My father took half of Dr. Morris's advice. As soon as we got home, he brought the steel oxygen tank clanging down from the attic and gathered the wet sit, mask, and flippers he hadn't worn since his navy days. He put it all on to check for leaks and rips, his webbed feet flapping as he moved around the living room like some half-evolved creature.

"I'm not sure this was the kind of hobby Dr. Morris had in mind," my mother said, trying to catch the eyes behind the mask. "It seems dangerous."

My father did not reply. He was testing the mouthpiece while adjusting the straps that held the air tanks. That done, he made swimming motions with his arms as he raised his knees toward his chest like a drum major.

"I've got some repairs to make," he said, and flapped on out to the garage. While my mother cooked a homecoming supper of pork chops and rice, he prepared himself to enter the deep gloaming of channels and drop-offs with thirty minutes of breath strapped to his back.

My father still wore his wet suit and fins when he sat down at the supper table that evening. He ate everything on his plate, which heartened my mother and me, and drank glass after glass of iced tea as if possessed of an unquenchable thirst. But when he lay his napkin on the table, he did not refill his glass with more tea and reach for the pill bottles my mother had placed beside his plate.

"You've got to take the medicine," my mother urged. "It's going to heal you."

"Heal me," my father mused. "You sound like Dr. Morris. He said the same thing right before they did the shock treatments."

My mother looked at her plate.

"Can't you see that's exactly why you need to take the pills? So you won't ever have to do that again." She raised her napkin to blot a tear from her cheek, her voice a mere whisper now. "This is not something to be ashamed of, Paul. It's no different from taking penicillin for an infection."

But my father was adamant. He pushed the tinted bottles to the center of the table one at a time as if they were chess pieces.

"How can I teach chemistry if I'm so muddled I can't find the classroom?" he said.

That spring my allegiances were with my mother, who anchored our family in ways I had not appreciated until my father lost his moorings. The following Monday my father resumed teaching, and I was her confederate at school. Between bells I peeked into a classroom filled with Styrofoam carbons and atoms wired together like fragile solar systems. In March Mr. Keller, the vice principal, had found my father crouched and sobbing in the chemical storage room, a molecular model of oxygen clutched in his hands, so it was with relief in those last weeks of my junior year that I found my father manning his desk between breaks, braced and ready for the next wave of students.

One morning he was looking up when my halved face appeared at his door. He saluted me sharply.

"Petty Office Hampton reports no men overboard, sir," he said to me.

"Well, at least he's got his sense of humor back," my mother said when I reported the incident.

In mid-June my father announced at Sunday breakfast he was no longer a Presbyterian. Instead of sitting with us on the polished oak pews of Cliffside

Presbyterian, he would be driving up to Cleveland County's mountainous northern corner to attend a Pentecostal church.

"It's something I've got to do,' he said.

My mother laid her napkin on the table, looked at my father as if he'd just informed us he was defecting to Cuba.

"We need to talk, Paul," she said. "Alone."

My parents disappeared behind a closed bedroom door. I could hear my father's voice, moderate and reassuring, or at least attempting to be. My mother's voice, in contrast, was tense and troubled. They talked an hour, then dressed for church. I was unsure who'd prevailed until my father came out of the bedroom wearing not a suit but a shirt and tie. He cranked our decade-old Ford Fairlane and headed north into the mountains, as he would Sunday mornings and Wednesday nights for the rest of his life. Meanwhile, my mother and I drove our newer Buick Le Sabre in the opposite direction, down toward Broad River to Cliffside Presbyterian.

I was not made privy to what kind of understanding, if any, my parents had reached about my father's change in church affiliation, but it was obvious as well as inevitable that my mother found this religious transmutation troubling. A lifelong Presbyterian, she distrusted religious fervor, especially for a man in such a tenuous mental state, but I suspect she also felt something akin to betrayal—a rejection of much of the life his marriage to her had made possible.

My mother had been baptized in Cliffside Presbyterian church, but my father, who'd grown up in the high mountains of Watauga County, had been Pentecostal before their marriage. His conversion signaled a social as well as religious transformation, a sign of upward mobility form hardscrabble Appalachian beginnings, for in this Scots-Irish community where Episcopalians were rare as Eskimos, he worshiped with the Brahmins on the county's Protestant hierarchy.

My father had appeared a dutiful convert, teaching Sunday school, helping prepare the men's breakfasts, even serving a term as an elder, but he'd been a subversive convert as well. On Sunday mornings he would entertain me with caustic remarks about the propriety of the services and Presbyterian's inability to sing anything remotely resembling a "joyful noise." When the choir rose to sing, my father winked at me, pretended to stuff plugs in his ears. My mother looked straight ahead at such times, trying to ignore my father's shenanigans, but her lips always tightened.

"That wafer might as well be a burnt marshmallow for all the passion it evokes in that crowd," my father said one Sunday as we drove home. "If Jesus

Christ and his disciples marched in during a service, the ushers would tell them to have a seat, that the congregation would be glad to hear what they had to say as soon as the monthly business meeting was over."

My mother glared at my father but addressed her words to the backseat, where I sat.

"Just because a service is orderly or dignified doesn't mean it isn't heart-felt," she said. "Don't trust people who make a spectacle of what they believe, Joel. Too often it's just a show, a way of drawing attention to themselves."

As we entered summer, our lives took on a guarded normality. My father taught a six-week summer school session. My mother resumed, after a two-month absence, her part-time job as a book-keeper for my uncle Brad's construction firm. I worked for my uncle as well, driving nails and pouring concrete. My uncle also gave us free reign of the lake house he'd bought years earlier, when he'd had the time to use it, so on Saturday mornings we drove up Highway Ten to spend the day at South Mountain Reservoir, where cool mountain breezes and teeth-chattering water might revive us after a week of wilting piedmont humidity. No doubt my mother packed up food and swim-suits each Saturday in hopes the lake might be beneficial to my father after a week of remedial teaching in an unairconditioned classroom.

My father was eager that I share his new hobby. He gave me demonstra-tions on how to use the scuba apparatus. At supper he spoke excitedly of water's other side. He often wore his diving equipment around the house, once opening the door to a startled paperboy while wearing a mask and fins. My mother was reluctant to let me participate, but she acquiesced when I promised not to go into the reservoir's deep heart, where a diver had drowned the previous summer. So on Saturday afternoons she read paperbacks on the screened porch and cast nervous glances toward the lake as my father and I shared the diving equipment. When my turn came, I fell backward off the dock and into the lake, watching a rushing away sky as I hit the water and sank, air bubbles rising above my head like thoughts in a comic strip.

I could never see more than a few yards, but that was enough. Arm-long catfish swam into view sudden as a nightmare, their blunt, whiskered faces rooting the bottom. Loggerheads big as hubcaps walked the lake floor, their hand-grenade heads ready to bite off a careless finger. I found what no longer lived down there as well: fish suspended like kites, monofilament trailing from their mouths to line-wrapped snags below; drowned litters of kittens and puppies; once an out-of-season deer, a gash on its head where the antlers had been. On the reservoir's floor even the familiar startled. Gaudy bass plugs hung on limbs and stumps like Christmas ornaments; branches snapped off like black icicles; a refrigerator yawned open like an unsprung trap.

Each time I entered the water my foreboding increased, not chest-tightening panic, but a growing certainly that many things in the world were better left hidden. By August I'd joined my mother on the porch, playing board games and drinking iced tea as my father disappeared off the dock toward mysteries I no longer wished to fathom.

On one of these August afternoons after he'd finished diving, my father decided to drive out to the highway and buy ice so we could churn ice cream. "Come with me, Joel," he said. "I might need some help."

Once we turned onto the blacktop, my father passed two convenience stores before pulling in to what once had been a gas station. Now only a weedy cement island remained, the pumps long uprooted. HOLCOMBE'S STORE, nothing more, appeared on a rusting black-and-white sign above the door. REDWORMS AND MINNERS FOR SALE was scrawled eye level on a second sign made of cardboard.

We stepped inside, adjusting our eyes to what little light filtered through the dusty windows. A radio played gospel music. Canned goods and paper plates, toilet paper and boxes of cereal lined the shelves. A man about my father's age sat behind the counter, black hair combed slick across his scalp, a mole above his right eyebrow the size and color of a tarnished penny. The man stood up from his chair and smiled, his two front teeth chipped and discolored.

"Why, hi, Brother Hampton," he said warmly in a thick mountain accent. "What brings you up this way?"

"Spending Saturday on the lake," my father said, then nodded toward me. "This is my son, Joel."

"Carl Holcombe," the man said, extending his hand. I felt the calluses in his palm, the wedding ring worn on his right hand.

"We're going to make ice cream," my father said. "I was hoping you had some ice."

"Wish I could help you but I weren't selling enough to keep the truck coming by," Mr. Holcombe said.

"How about some worms then?"

"That I can help you with." Mr. Holcombe came around the corner, walking with a slight limp as he made his way to the back of the store.

"How many boxes?" he asked, opening a refrigerator.

"Four," my father said.

My father laid a five-dollar bill on the counter. Mr. Holcombe rang up the sale.

"See you at church tomorrow?" Mr. Holcombe asked, dropping coins into my father's hand. My father nodded.

I tried not to stare at the mole as Mr. Holcombe filled my hands with the cardboard containers.

"Your daddy," he said to me, "is a Godly man, but I suspect you already know that."

He closed the cash register and walked with us to the entrance.

"I hope you all catch something" he said, holding the tattered screen door open.

"Why did you buy the worms?" I asked my father as we drove off.

"Because he needs the money," my father said. "We'll let them go in the garden."

"Mr. Holcombe's a friend of yours?" I asked, wondering if my father would note the surprise in my voice.

"Yes," my father said. "He's also my pastor."

The following Wednesday my father left to attend his midweek church service. I'd already asked my mother if I could borrow the Buick that evening, so when he departed so did I, following the Fairlane through town. At the stoplight I too turned right onto Highway Ten. Since the previous Saturday I'd been perplexed about what could compel my father, a man with a university education, to drive a good half hour to hear a preacher who, if his spelling and grammar were any indication, probably hadn't finished high school.

Outside of town it began to rain. I turned on the Buick's windshield wipers and headlights. Soon hills became mountains, red clay darkened to black dirt. I swallowed to relieve the ear pressure from the change in altitude as the last ranch-style brick house, the last broad, manicured lawn, vanished from my rearview mirror. Stands of oaks and dogwoods crowded the roadsides. Gaps in the woods revealed the green rise of corn and tobacco, pastures framed by rusty barbed-wire fences. Occasionally I passed a prosperous looking two-story farmhouse, but most homes were trailers or four room A-frames, often with pickups, cars, and appliances rusting in the side yards, scrawny beagles and blueticks chained under trees.

The rain quit so I cut off the windshield wipers, let the Fairlane get further ahead of me. I came over a rise and the Fairlane had already disappeared around a curve. I sped up, afraid I'd lost my father, but coming out the curve I saw his car stopped in the road a hundred yards ahead, the turn signal on though our Buick was the closest car behind him. My father turned into a dirt road and I followed, still keeping my distance though I wondered if it were really necessary. He slowed in front of a cinder-block building no bigger than a woodshed, pulling into a makeshift parking lot where our ancient Fairlane looked no older than the dozen other cars and trucks. I eased off the road on a rise above the church and watched my father walk hurriedly toward the building. A white cross was nailed above the door he entered.

I could hear an out-of-tune piano, a chorus of voices rising from the open door and the windows into the August evening, merging with the songs of crickets and cicadas. I waited half and hour before I got out of the Buick and walked down the road to the church. At the front door I paused, then stepped into a foyer small and dark as a closet. A half-open room led to the main room. The singing stopped, replaced by a single voice.

I peered into a thick-shadowed room whose only light came from a single bare bulb dangling from the ceiling. Mr. Holcombe stood in front of three rows of metal chairs where the congregation sat. At his feet lay a wooden box that looked like an infant's coffin. Holes had been bored in its lid. Mr. Holcombe wore no coat or tie, just a white, short-sleeved shirt, brown slacks, and scuffed black loafers. His arm outstretched, he waved a Bible as if fanning an invisible flame.

"The word of the Lord," he said, then opened the Bible to a page marked by a paper scrap. "And they cast out many devils, and anointed with oil many that were sick, and healed them," Mr. Holcombe read. He closed the Bible and went down on one knee in front of the wooden box, but his head bowed, like an athlete resting on the sidelines.

"Whoever is afflicted, come forward," he said. "Lord, if it is your will, let us be the instrument of your healing grace."

"Amen," the congregation said as my father left the last row and kneeled beside Mr. Holcombe. Without a word, the congregation rose and gathered around my father. An old woman, gray hair reaching her hips, opened a bottle and dabbed a thick, clear liquid on my father's brow. The other members laid their hands on his head and shoulders.

"Oh Lord," shouted Mr. Holcombe, raising the Bible in his hand. "Grant this child of God continued victories over his affliction. Let not his heart be troubled. Let him know your abiding presence."

The old woman with the long hair began speaking feverishly in a language I couldn't understand, her hands straining upward as if she were attempting to haul heaven down into their midst.

"Praise God, praise God," a man in a plaid shouted as he did a spastic dance around the others.

My father began speaking the strange, fervent language of the old woman. The congregation removed their hands as my father rocked his torso back and forth, sounds I could not translate pouring from his mouth.

Mr. Holcombe, still kneeling beside my father, unclasped the wooden box. The room suddenly became silent, then a whirring sound like a dry gourd being shaken. At first I did not realize where the noise came from, but when Mr. Holcombe dipped his hand and forearm into the box the sound increased. Something was in there, something alive and, I knew even before seeing it, dangerous.

Mr. Holcombe's forearm rose from out of the box, a timber rattlesnake coiled around his wrist like a thick, black vine. The reptile's head rose inches above Mr. Holcombe's open palm, its split tongue probing the air like a sensor.

I turned away, stepped out of the foyer and into the parking lot. My eyes slowly adjusted to being outside the church's dense shadows. I stood there until the scraping of chairs signaled the congregation's return to their seats. They sang a hymn, and then Mr. Holcombe slowly read a long passage from the book of Mark.

I walked back to the Buick, halfway there when I saw the headlights were on. I tried the battery five times and gave up, dragging the jumper cables from the trunk and opening the hood in the hope someone might stop and help me. No cars or truck passed, however, and in a few minutes people came out of the church, some pausing to speak but most going straight to their vehicles. I sat in the car and waited until I saw our Fairlane leave the parking lot.

My father pulled off the road in front of the Buick, hood to hood, as though he already knew the problem. I stepped out of the car.

"What happened?" he asked.

I wasn't sure how to answer his question, but I gave the simplest answer.

"The battery's dead," I said, holding up the jumper cables as if to validate my words.

He opened the Fairlane's hood. We clamped the cables to the batteries, then got back in the cars and cranked the engines. My father unhooked the cables and came around to the Buick's side. He dropped the jumper cables on the floorboard and sat down beside me. Both engines were running, the cars aimed at each other like a wreck about to happen.

"Why did you follow me?" my father asked, looking out the window. There was no anger in his voice, just curiosity.

"To find out why you come here."

"Do you know now?"

"No."

The last two cars left the church. The drivers slowed as they passed, but my father waved them on.

"Dr. Morris says I have too much salt in my brain, a chemical imbalance," my father said. "It's an easy problem for him with an easy solution, so many milligrams of Elavil, so many volts of electricity. But I can't believe it's that simple."

Perhaps it was the hum of the engines, my father looking out as he spoke, but I felt as though we were traveling although the landscape did not change. It was like I could feel the Earth's slow revolution as August's strange, pink glow tinted the evening's last light.

My father shut his eyes for a moment. He'd aged in the last year, his hair gray at the edges, his brow lined.

"Your mother believes the holy rollers got me too young, that they raised me to see the world only the way they could see it. But she's wrong about that. There was a time I could understand everything from a single atom to the whole universe with a blackboard and a piece of chalk, and it was beautiful as any hymn the way it all came together.

My father nodded toward the church, barely visible now in the gloaming.

"You met Carl Holcombe. His wife and five-year-old daughter got killed eleven years ago in a car wreck, a wreck that was Carl's fault because he was diving too fast. Carl says there are whole weeks he can't remember he was so drunk, nights he put a gun barrel under his chin and held it there an hour. There was nothing in this world to sustain him, so he had to look somewhere else. I've had to do the same."

Though the cars still idled, we sat there in silence a few more minutes, long enough to see the night's first fireflies sparking like matches in the woods. My father's face was submerged in shadows when he spoke again.

"What I'm trying to say is that some solutions aren't crystal clear. Sometimes you have to search for them in places where only the heart can go."

"I still don't think I understand," I said.

"I hope you never do," my father said softly, "but from what the doctors at Broughton told me there's a chance you will."

My father leaned over, switched on the Buick's headlights.

"We need to get home," he said. "Your mother will be worried about us."

The pill bottles remained unopened the rest of the summer, and there were no more attempts to cauterize my father's despair with electricity. Which is not to say my father was a happy man. His was not a religion of bliss but one that allowed him to rise from his bed on each of those summer mornings and face two classes of hormone-ravaged adolescents, to lead those students toward solutions he himself no longer felt adequate. I did not tell my mother what I had seen that Wednesday evening, or what I refused to see. I have never told her.

My father died that September, on an afternoon when the first reds and yellows flared in the maples and poplars. We'd driven up to the lake house that morning. My father graded tests until early afternoon. When he'd finished he went inside and put on his diving gear, then crossed the brief swath of grass to the water—moving slow and deliberate on the land like an aquatic creature returning to its natural element. Once on the dock he turned toward the lake house, raised a palm, and fell forever from us.

My mother and I sat on the porch playing Risk and drinking tea. When my father hadn't resurfaced after a reasonable time, my mother cast frequent glances toward the water.

"It hasn't been thirty minutes yet," I said more than once. But in a few more minutes a half an hour had passed, and my father still had not risen.

I ran down to the lake while my mother dialed the county's EMS unit. I dove into the murky water around the dock, finding nothing on the bottom but silt. I dove until the rescue squad arrived, though I dove without hope. I was seventeen years old. I didn't know what else to do.

The rest of the afternoon was a loud confusion of divers and boats, rescue squad members and gawkers. The sheriff showed up and, almost at dusk, the coroner, a young man dressed in khakis and a blue cotton shirt.

"Nitrogen narcosis, sometimes called rapture of the deep," the coroner said, conversant in the language of death despite his youth. "A lot of people wouldn't think a reservoir would be deep enough to cause that, but this one is." He and the sheriff stood with my mother and me on the screened porch, cups of coffee in their hands. "If you go down too far you can take in too much nitrogen. It causes a chemical imbalance, an intoxicating effect." The coroner looked out toward the reservoir. "It can happen to the most experienced diver."

The coroner talked to us a few more minutes before he and the sheriff stepped off the screened porch, leaving behind empty coffee cups, no doubt hoping what inevitable calamity would reunite them might wait until after a night's sleep.

Once he had no further say in the matter, my father was again a Presbyterian. His funeral service was held at Cliffside Presbyterian, his burial in the church's cemetery. Mr. Holcombe and several of his congregation attended. They sat in the back, the men wearing short-sleeved shirts and ties, the women cotton dresses that reached their ankles. After the burial they awkwardly shook my hand and my mother's before departing. I've never seen any of them since.

In my less generous moments I perceive my mother's insistence on Presbyterian last rites as mean-spirited, a last rebuke to my father's Pentecostal reconversion. But who can really know another's heart? Perhaps it was merely her Scots-Irish practicality, less trouble for everyone to hold the rites in Cliffside instead of twenty miles away in the mountains.

After my father's death my mother refused to go back to the lake house, but I did and occasionally still do. I sit out on the screened porch as the night starts its slow glide across the lake. It's a quiet time, the skiers and most of the fishermen gone home, the echoing trombone of frogs not yet in full volume. I listen to sounds unheard any other time—the soft slap of water against the dock, a muskrat in the cattails.

I sometimes think of my father down in that murky water as his lungs surrendered. I think of what the coroner told me that night on the porch, that the divers found the mask in the silt beside him. "Probably didn't even know he was doing it," the coroner said matter-of-factly. "People do strange things like that all the time when they're dying."

The coroner is probably right. But sometimes as I sit on the porch with darkness settling around me, it is easy to imagine that my father pulling off the mask was something more—a gesture of astonishment at what he drifted toward.

THEIR ANCIENT, GLITTERING EYES

Because they were boys, no one believed them, including the old men who gathered each morning at the Riverside Gas and Grocery. These retirees huddled by the potbellied stove in rain and cold, on clear days sunning out front like reptiles. The store's middle-aged owner, Cedric Henson, endured the trio's presence with a resigned equanimity. When he'd bought the store five years earlier, Cedric assumed they were part of the purchase price, in that way no different from the leaky roof and the submerged basement whenever the Tuckaseegee overspilled its banks. The two boys, who were brothers, had come clattering across the bridge, red-faced and already holding their arms apart as if carrying huge, invisible packages. They stood gasping a few moments, waiting for enough breath to tell what they'd seen.

"This big," the twelve-year-old said, his arms spread wide apart as he could stretch them.

"No, even bigger," the younger boy said.

Cedric had been peering through the door screen but now stepped outside.

"What you boys talking about?" he asked.

"A fish," the older boy said, "in the pool below the bridge."

Rudisell, the oldest of the three at eighty-nine, expertly delivered a squirt of tobacco between himself and the boys. Creech and Campbell simply nodded at each other knowingly. Time had banished them to the role of spectators in the world's affairs, and from their perspective the world both near and far was now controlled by fools. The causes of this devolution dominated their daily conversations. The octogenarians Rudisell and Campbell blamed Franklin Roosevelt and fluoridated water. Creech, a mere seventy-six, leaned toward Elvis Presley and television.

"The biggest fish ever come out of the Tuckaseegee was a thirty-one-inch brown trout caught in nineteen and forty-eight," Rudisell announced to all present. "I seen it weighed in this very store. Fifteen pounds and two ounces."

The other nodded in confirmation.

"This fish was twice bigger than that," the younger boy challenged.

The boy's impudence elicted another spray of tobacco from Rudisell.

"Must be a whale swum up from the ocean," Creech said. "Though that's a long haul. It'd have to come up the Gulf Coast and the Mississippi, for the water this side of the mountain flows west."

"Could be one of them log fish," Campbell offered. "They get that big. Them rascals will grab your bait and then turn into a big chunk of wood afore you can set the hook."

"They's snakes all over that pool, even some copperheads," Rudisell warned. "You younguns best go somewhere else to make up your tall tales."

The smaller boy pooched out his lower lip as if about to cry.

"Come on," his brother said. "They ain't going to believe us."

The boys walked back across the road to the bridge. The old men watched as the youths leaned over the railing, took a last look before climbing atop their bicycles and riding away.

"Flouridated water," Rudisell wheezed. "Makes them see things."

On the following Saturday morning, Harley Wease scrambled up the same bank the boys had, carrying the remnants of his Zebco 202. Harley's hands trembled as he laid the shattered rod and reel on the ground before the old men. He pulled a soiled handkerchief from his jeans and wiped his bleeding index finger to reveal a deep slice between the first and second joints. The old men studied the finger and the rod and reel and awaited explanation. They were attentive, for Harley's deceased father had been a close friend of Rudisell's.

"Broke my rod like it was made of balsa wood," Harley said. "Then the gears on the reel got stripped. It got down to just me and the line pretty quick." Harley raised his index finger so the men could see it better. "I figured to use my finger for the drag. If the line hadn't broke, you'd be looking at a nub."

"You sure it was a fish?" Campbell asked. "Maybe you caught hold of a muskrat or snapping turkle."

"Not unless them critters has got to where they grow fins," Harley said.

"You saying it was a trout?" Creech asked.

"I only got a glimpse, but it didn't look like no trout. Looked like a alligator but for the fins."

"I never heard of no such fish in Jackson County," Campbell said, "but Rudy Nicholson's boys seen the same. It's pretty clear there's *something* in that pool."

The men turned to Rudisell for his opinion.

"I don't know what it is either," Rudisell said. "But I aim to find out."

He lifted the weathered ladder-back chair, held it aloft shakily as he made his slow way across the road to the bridge. Harley went into the store to talk with Cedric, but the other two men followed Rudisell as if all were deposed kings taking their thrones into some new kingdom. They lined their chairs up at the railing. They waited.

Only Creech had undiminished vision, but in the coming days that was rectified. Campbell had not thought anything beyond five feet of himself worth viewing for years, but now a pair of thick, round-lensed spectacles adorned his head, giving him a look of owlish intelligence. Rudisell had a spyglass he claimed once belonged to a German U-boat captain. The bridge was now effectively one lane, but traffic tended to be light. While trucks and cars drove around them, the old men kept vigil morning to evening, retreating into the store only when rain came.

Vehicles sometimes paused on the bridge to ask for updates, because the lower half of Harley Wease's broken rod had become an object of great wonder since being mounted on Cedric's back wall. Men and boys frequently took it down to grip the hard plastic handle. They invariably pointed the jagged fiberglass in the direction of the bridge, held it out as if a divining rod that might yet give some measure or resonance of what creature now made the pool its lair.

Rudisell spotted the fish first. A week had passed with daily rains clouding the river, but two days of sun settled the silt, the shallow tailrace clear all the way to the bottom. This was where Rudisell aimed his spyglass, setting it on the rail to steady his aim. He made a slow sweep of the sandy floor every fifteen minutes. Many things came into focus as he adjusted the scope: a flurry of nymphs rising to become mayflies, glints of fool's gold, schools of minnows shifting like migrating birds, crayfish with pincers raised as if surrendering to the behemoth sharing the pool with them.

It wasn't there, not for hours, but then suddenly it was. At first Rudisell saw just a shadow over the white sand, slowly gaining depth and definition, and then the slow wave of the gills and pectoral fins, the shudder of the tail as the fish held its place in the current.

"I see it," Rudisell whispered, "in the tailrace." Campbell took off his glasses and grabbed the spyglass, placed it against his best eye as Creech got up slowly, leaned over the rail.

"It's long as my leg," Creech said.

"I never thought to see such a thing," Campbell uttered.

The fish held its position a few more moments before slowly moving into deeper water.

"I never seen the like of a fish like that," Creech announced."

It ain't a trout," Campbell said.

"Nor carp or bass," Rudisell added.

"Maybe it is a gator," Campbell said. "One of them snowbirds from Florida could of put it in there."

"No," Rudisell said. "I seen gators during my army training in Louisiana. A gator's like us, it's got to breathe air. This thing don't need air. Beside, it had a tail fin."

"Maybe it's a mermaid," Creech mused.

By late afternoon the bridge looked like an overloaded barge. Pickups, cars, and two tractors clotted both sides of the road and the store's parking lot. Men and boys squirmed and shifted to get a place against the railing. Harley Wease recounted his epic battle, but it was the ancients who were most deferred to as they made pronouncements about size and weight. Of species they could speak only by negation.

"My brother works down at that nuclear power plant near Walhalla," Marcus Price said. "Billy swears there's catfish below the dam near five foot long. Claims that radiation makes them bigger."

"This ain't no catfish," Rudisell said. "It didn't have no big jug head. More lean than that."

Bascombe Greene ventured the shape called to mind the pikefish caught in weedy lakes up north. Stokes Hamilton thought it could be a hellbender salamander, for though he'd never seen one more than twelve inches long he'd heard tell they got to six feet in Japan. Leonard Coffey told a long, convoluted story about a goldfish set free in a pond. After two decades of being fed corn bread and fried okra, the fish had been caught and it weighed fifty-seven pounds.

"It ain't no pike nor spring lizard nor goldfish," Rudisell said emphatically.

"Well, there's but one way to know," Bascombe Greene said, "and that's to try and catch the damn thing." Bascombe nodded at Harley. "What bait was you fishing with?"

Harley looked sheepish.

"I'd lost my last spinner when I snagged a limb. All I had left in my tackle box was a rubber worm I use for bass, so I put it on."

"What size and color?" Bascombe asked. "We got to be scientific about this."

"Seven inch," Harley said. "It was purple with white dots."

"You got any more of them?" Leonard Coffey asked.

"No, but you can buy them at Sylva Hardware."

"Won't do you no good," Rudisell said.

"Why not?" Leonard asked.

"For a fish to live long enough to get that big, it's got to be smart. It'll not forget that a rubber worm tricked it."

"It might not be near smart as you reckon," Bascombe said. "I don't mean no disrespect, but old folks tend to be forgetful. Maybe that old fish is the same way."

"I reckon we'll know the truth of that soon enough," Rudisell concluded, because fishermen already cast from the bridge and banks. Soon several lines had gotten tangled, and a fistfight broke out over who had claim to a choice spot near the pool's tailrace. More people arrived as the afternoon wore on, became early evening. Cedric, never one to miss a potential business opportunity, put a plastic fireman's hat on his head and a whistle in his mouth. He parked cars while his son Bobby crossed and recrossed the bridge selling Cokes from a battered shopping cart.

Among the later arrivals was Charles Meekins, the county's game warden. He was thirty-eight years old and had grown up in Madison, Wisconsin. The general consensus, especially among the old men, was the warden was arrogant and a smart-ass. Meekins stopped often at the store, and he invariably addressed them as Wynken, Blynken, and Nod. He listened with undisguised condescension as the old men, Harley, and finally the two boys told of what they'd seen.

"It's a trout or carp," Meekins said, "carp" sounding like "cop." Despite four years in Jackson County, Meekins still spoke as if his vocal cords had been pulled from his throat and reinstalled in his sinus cavity. "There's no fish larger in these waters."

Harley handed his reel to the game warden.

"That fish stripped the gears on it."

Meekins inspected the reel as he might an obviously fraudulent fishing license.

"You probably didn't have the drag set right."

"It was bigger than any trout or carp," Campbell insisted.

"When you're looking into water you can't really judge the size of something,"

Meekins said. He looked at some of the younger men and winked. "Especially if your vision isn't all that good to begin with."

A palmful of Red Mule chewing tobacco bulged the right side of Rudisell's jaw like a tumor, but his apoplexy was such that he swallowed a portion of his cud and began hacking violently. Campbell slapped him on the back and Rudisell spewed dark bits of tobacco onto the bridge's wooden flooring.

Meekins had gotten back in his green fish and wildlife truck before Rudisell recovered enough to speak.

"If I hadn't near choked to death I'd have told that shitbritches youngun to bend over and we'd see if my sight was good enough to ram this spyglass up his ass."

In the next few days so many fishermen came to try their luck that Rudisell finally bought a wire-bound notebook from Cedric and had anglers sign up for fifteen-minute slots. They cast almost every offering imaginable into the pool. A good half of the anglers succumbed to the theory that what had worked before could work again, so rubber worms were the single most popular choice. The rubber-worm devotees used an array of different sizes, hues, and even smells. Some went with seven-inch rubber worms while others favored five- or ten-inch. Some tried purple worms with white dots while others tried white with purple dots and still others tried pure white and pure black and every variation between including chartreuse, pink, turquoise, and fuchsia. Some used rubber worms with auger tails and others used flat tails. Some worms smelled like motor oil and some worms smelled like strawberries and some worms had no smell at all.

The others were divided by their devotion to live bait or artificial lures. Almost all the bait fishermen used night crawlers and red worms in the belief that if the fish had been fooled by an imitation, the actual live worm would work even better, but they also cast spring lizards, minnows, crickets, grubs, wasp larvae, crawfish, frogs, newts, toads, and even a live field mouse. The lure contingent favored spinners of the Panther Martin and Rooster-tail variety though they were not averse to Rapalas, Jitterbugs, Hula Poppers, Johnson Silver Minnows, Devilhorses, and a dozen other hook-laden pieces of wood or plastic. Some lures sank and bounced along the bottom and some lures floated and still others gurgled and rattled and some made no sound at all and one lure even changed colors depending on depth and water temperature. Jarvis Hampton cast a Rapala F 14 he'd once caught a tarpon with in Florida. A subgroup of fly fishermen cast Muddler Minnows, Woolly Boogers, Woolly Worms, Royal Coachmen, streamers and wet flies, nymphs and dry flies, and some hurled nymphs and dry flies together that swung overhead like miniature bolas.

During the first two days five brown trout, one speckled trout, one ball cap, two smallmouth bass, ten knotty heads, a bluegill, and one old boot were caught. A gray squirrel was snagged by an errant cast into a tree. Neither the squirrel nor the various fish outweighed the boot, which weighed one pound and eight ounces after the water was poured out. On the third day Wesley McIntire's rod doubled and the drag whirred. A rainbow trout leaped in the pool's center, Wesley's quarter-ounce Panther Martin spinner embedded in its upper jaw. He fought the trout for five minutes before his brother Robbie could net it. The rainbow was twenty-two inches long and weighed five and a half pounds, big enough that Wesley took it straight to the taxidermist to be mounted.

Charles Meekins came by an hour later. He didn't get out of the truck, just rolled down his window and nodded. His radio played loudly and the atonal guitars and screeching voices made Rudisell glad he was mostly deaf, because hearing only part of the racket made him feel like stinging wasps swarmed inside his head. Meekins didn't bother to turn the radio down, just shouted over the music.

"I told you it was a trout."

"That wasn't it," Rudisell shouted. "The fish I seen could of eaten that rainbow for breakfast."

Meekins smiled, showing a set of bright white teeth that, unlike Rudisell's, did not have to be deposited in a glass jar every night.

"Then why didn't it? That rainbow has probably been in that pool for years." Meekins shook his head. "I wish you old boys would learn to admit when you're wrong about something."

Meekins rolled up his window as Rudisell pursed his lips and fired a stream of tobacco juice directly at the warden's left eye. The tobacco hit the glass and dribbled a dark, phlegmy rivulet down the window.

"A fellow such as that ought not be allowed a guvment uniform," Creech said.

"Not unless it's got black and white stripes all up and down it," Crenshaw added.

After ten days no other fish of consequence had been caught and anglers began giving up. The notebook was discarded because appointments were no longer necessary. Meekins's belief gained credence, especially since in ten days none of the hundred or so men and boys who'd gathered there had seen the giant fish.

"I'd be hunkered down on the stream bottom too if such commotion was going on around me," Creech argued, but few remained to nod in agreement. Even Harley Wease began to have doubts.

"Maybe that rainbow *was* what I had on," he said heretically.

By the first week in May only the old men remained on the bridge. They kept their vigil but the occupants of cars and trucks and tractors no longer paused to ask about sightings. When the fish reappeared in the tailrace, the passing drivers ignored the old men's frantic waves to come see. They drove across the bridge with eyes fixed straight ahead, embarrassed by their elders' dementia.

"That's the best look we've gotten yet," Campbell said when the fish moved out of the shallows and into deeper water. "It's six feet long if it's a inch."

Rudisell set his spyglass on the bridge railing and turned to Creech, the one among them who still had a car and driver's license.

"You got to drive me over to Jarvis Hampton's house," Rudisell said.

"What for?" Creech asked.

"Because we're going to rent out that rod and reel he uses for them tarpon. Then we got to go by the library, because I want to know what this thing is when we catch it."

Creech kept the speedometer at a steady thirty-five as they followed the river south to Jarvis Hampton's farm. They found Jarvis in his tobacco field and quickly negotiated a ten-dollar-a-week rental for the rod and reel, four 2/0 vanadium-steel fishhooks, and four sinkers. Jarvis offered a net as well but Rudisell claimed it wasn't big enough for what they were after. "But I'll take a hay hook and a whetstone if you got it," Rudisell added, "and some bailing twine and a feed sack.

"They packed the fishing equipment in the trunk and drove to the county library, where they used Campbell's library card to check out an immense tome called *Freshwater Fish of North America*. The book was so heavy that only Creech had the strength to carry it, holding it before him with both hands as if it were made of stone. He dropped it in the backseat and, still breathing heavily, got behind the wheel and cranked the engine.

"We got one more stop," Rudisell said, "that old millpond on Spillcorn Creek."

"You wanting to practice with that rod and reel?" Campbell asked.

"No, to get our bait," Rudisell replied. "I been thinking about something. After that fish hit Harley's rubber worm they was throwing night crawlers right and left into the pool figuring that fish thought Harley's lure was a worm. But what if it thought that rubber worm was something else, something we ain't seen one time since we been watching the pool though it used to be thick with them?"

Campbell understood first. "I get what you're saying, but this is one bait I'd rather not be gathering myself, or putting on a hook for that matter."

"Well, if you'll just hold the sack I'll do the rest."

"What about baiting the hook?"

"I'll do that too."

Since the day was warm and sunny, a number of reptiles had gathered on the stone slabs that had once been a dam. Most were blue-tailed skinks and fence lizards, but several mud-colored serpents coiled sullenly on the largest stones. Creech, who was deathly afraid of snakes, remained in the car. Campbell carried the burlap feed sack, reluctantly trailing Rudisell through broom sedge to the old dam.

"Them snakes ain't of the poisonous persuasion?" Campbell asked.

Rudisell turned and shook his head.

"Naw. Them's just your common water snake. Mean as the devil but they got no fangs."

As they got close the skinks and lizards darted for crevices in the rocks, but the snakes did not move until Rudisell's shadow fell over them. Three slithered away before Rudisell's creaky back could bend enough for him to grab hold, but the fourth did not move until Rudisell's liver-spotted hand closed around its neck. The snake thrashed violently, its mouth biting at the air. Campbell reluctantly moved closer, his fingers and thumbs holding the sack open, arms extended out from his body as if attempting to catch some object falling from the sky. As soon as Rudisell dropped the serpent in, Campbell gave the snake and sack to Rudisell, who knotted the burlap and put it in the trunk.

"You figure one to be enough?" Campbell asked.

"Yes," Rudisell replied. "We'll get but one chance."

The sun was beginning to settle over Balsam Mountain when the old men got back to the bridge. Rudisell led them down the path to the riverbank, the feed sack in his right hand, the hay hook and twine in his left. Campbell came next with the rod and reel and sinkers and hooks. Creech came last, the great book clutched to his chest. The trail became steep and narrow, the weave of leaf and limb overhead so thick it seemed they were entering a cave.

Once they got to the bank and caught their breath, they went to work. Creech used two of the last teeth left in his head to clamp three sinkers onto the line, then tied the hook to the monofilament with an expertly rendered hangman's knot. Campbell studied the book and found the section on fish living in southeastern rivers. He folded the page where the photographs of relevant species began and then marked the back section where corresponding printed information was located. Rudisell took out the whetstone and sharpened the metal with the same attentiveness as the long-ago warriors who once roamed these hills had honed their weapons, those bronze men who'd flaked dull stone to make their flesh-piercing arrowheads. Soon the steel tip shone like silver.

"All right, I done my part," Creech said when he'd tested the drag. He eyed the writhing feed sack apprehensively. "I ain't about to be close by when you try to get that snake on a hook."

Creech moved over near the tailwaters as Campbell picked up the rod and reel. He settled the rod tip above Rudisell's head, the fishhook dangling inches from the older man's beaky nose. Rudisell unknotted the sack, then pinched the fishhook's eye between his left hand's index finger and thumb, used the right to slowly peel back the burlap. When the snake was exposed, Rudisell grabbed it by the neck, stuck the fishhook through the midsection, and quickly let go. The rod tip sagged with the snake's weight as Creech moved farther down the bank.

"What do I do now?" Campbell shouted, for the snake was swinging in an arc that brought the serpent ever closer to his body.

"Cast it," Rudisell replied.

Campbell made a frantic sideways, two-handed heave that looked more like someone throwing a tub of dishwater off a back porch than a cast. The snake landed three feet from the bank, but luck was with them for it began swimming underwater toward the pool's center. Creech came back to stand by Campbell, but his eyes nervously watched the line. He flexed his arthritic right knee like a runner at the starting line, ready to flee up the bank if the snake took a mind to change direction. Rudisell gripped the hay hook's handle in his right hand. With his left he began wrapping bailing twine around metal and flesh. The wooden bridge floor rumbled like low thunder as a pickup crossed. A few seconds later another vehicle passed over the bridge. Rudisell continued wrapping the twine. He had no watch but suspected it was after five and men working in Sylva were starting to come home. When Rudisell had used up all the twine, Creech knotted it.

"With that hay hook tied to you it looks like you're the bait," Creech joked. "If I gaff that thing it's not going to get free of me," Rudisell vowed.

The snake was past the deepest part of the pool now, making steady progress toward the far bank. It struggled to the surface briefly, the weight of the sinkers pulling it back down. The line remained motionless for a few moments, then began a slow movement back toward the heart of the pool.

"Why you figure it to turn around?" Campbell asked as Creech took a first step farther up the bank.

"I don't know," Rudisell said. "Why don't you tighten your line a bit."

Campbell turned the handle twice and the monofilament grew taut and the rod tip bent. "Damn snake's got hung up."

"Give it a good jerk and it'll come free," Creech said. "Probably just tangled in some brush."

Campbell yanked upward, and the rod bowed. The line began moving upstream, not fast but steady, the reel chattering as the monofilament stripped off.

"It's on," Campbell said softly, as if afraid to startle the fish.

The line did not pause until it was thirty yards upstream and in the shadow of the bridge.

"You got to turn it," Rudisell shouted, "or it'll wrap that line around one of them pillars."

"Turn it," Campbell replied. "I can't even slow it down."

But the fish turned of its own volition, headed back into the deeper water. For fifteen minutes the creature sulked on the pool's bottom. Campbell kept the rod bowed, breathing hard as he strained against the immense weight on the other end. Finally, the fish began moving again, over to the far bank and then upstream. Campbell's arms trembled violently.

"My arms is give out," he said and handed the rod to Creech. Campbell sprawled out on the bank, his chest heaving rapidly, limbs shaking as if palsied. The fish swam back into the pool's heart and another ten minutes passed. Rudisell looked up at the bridge. Cars and trucks continued to rumble across. Several vehicles paused a few moments but no faces appeared at the railing.

Creech tightened the drag and the rod bent double.

"Easy," Rudisell said. "You don't want him breaking off."

"The way it's going, it'll kill us all before it gets tired," Creech gasped.

The additional pressure worked. The fish moved again, this time allowing the line in its mouth to lead it into the tailrace. For the first time they saw the behemoth.

"Lord amercy," Campbell exclaimed, for what they saw was over six feet long and enclosed in a brown suit of prehistoric armor, the immense tail curved like a scythe. When the fish saw the old men it surged away, the drag chattering again as the creature moved back into the deeper water.

Rudisell sat down beside the book and rapidly turned pages of color photos until he saw it.

"It's a sturgeon," he shouted, then turned to where the printed information was and began to call out bursts of information. "Can grow over seven feet long and three hundred pounds. That stuff that looks like armor is called scutes. They's even got a Latin name here. Says it was once in near every river, but now endangered. Can live a hundred and fifty years."

"I ain't going to live another hundred and fifty seconds if I don't get some relief," Creech said and handed the rod back to Campbell.

Campbell took over as Creech collapsed on the bank. The sturgeon began to give ground, the reel handle making slow, clockwise revolutions.

Rudisell closed the book and stepped into the shallows of the pool's tailrace. A sandbar formed a few yards out and that was what he moved toward, the hay hook raised like a metal question mark. Once he'd secured himself on the sandbar, Rudisell turned to Campbell.

"Lead him over here. There's no way we can lift him up the bank."

"You gonna try to gill that thing?" Creech asked incredulously.

Rudisell shook his head."I ain't gonna gill it, I'm going to stab this hay hook in so deep it'll have to drag me back into that pool as well to get away."

The reel handle turned quicker now, and soon the sturgeon came out of the depths, emerging like a submarine. Campbell moved farther down the bank, only three or four yards from the sandbar. Creech got up and stood beside Campbell. The fish swam straight toward them, face-first, as if led on a leash. They could see the head clearly now, the cone-shaped snout, barbels hanging beneath the snout like whiskers. As it came closer Rudisell creakily kneeled down on the sandbar's edge. As he swung the hay hook the sturgeon made a last surge toward deeper water. The bright metal raked across the scaly back but did not penetrate.

"Damn," Rudisell swore.

"You got to beach it," Creech shouted at Campbell, who began reeling again, not pausing until the immense head was half out of the water, snout touching the sandbar. The sturgeon's wide mouth opened, revealing an array of rusting hooks and lures that hung from the lips like medals.

"Gaff it now," Creech shouted.

"Hurry," Campbell huffed, the rod in his hands doubled like a bow. "I'm herniating myself."

But Rudisell appeared not to hear them. He stared intently at the fish, the hay hook held overhead as if it were a torch allowing him to see the sturgeon more clearly.

Rudisell's blue eyes brightened for a moment, and an enigmatic smile creased his face. The hay hook's sharpened point flashed, aimed not at the fish but at the monofilament. A loud twang like a broken guitar string sounded across the water. The rod whipped back and Campbell stumbled backward, but Creech caught him before he fell. The sturgeon was motionless for a few moments, then slowly curved back toward the pool's heart. As it disappeared, Rudisell remained kneeling on the sandbar, his eyes gazing into the pool. Campbell and Creech staggered over to the bank and sat down.

"They'll never believe us," Creech said, "not in a million years, especially that smart-ass game warden."

"We had it good as caught," Campbell muttered. "We had it caught."

"None of them spoke further for a long while, all exhausted by the battle. But their silence had more to do with each man's reflection on what he had just witnessed than with weariness. A yellow mayfly rose like a watery spark in the tailrace, hung in the air a few moments before it fell and was swept away by the current. As time passed crickets announced their presence on the bank, and downriver a whippoorwill called. More mayflies rose in the tailrace. The air became chilly as the sheltering trees closed more tightly around them, absorbed the waning sun's light, a preamble to another overdue darkness.

"It's okay," Campbell finally said.

Creech looked at Rudisell, who was still on the sandbar.

"You done the right thing. I didn't see that at first, but I see it now."

Rudisell finally stood up, wiped the wet sand from the knees of his pants. As he stepped into the shallows he saw something in the water. He picked it up and put it in his pocket.

"Find you a fleck of gold?" Campbell asked.

"Better than gold," Rudisell replied and joined his comrades on the bank.

They could hardly see their own feet as they walked up the path to the bridge. When they emerged, they found the green fish and wildlife truck parked at the trail end. The passenger window was down and Meekins's smug face looked out at them.

"So you old boys haven't drowned after all. Folks saw the empty chairs and figured you'd fallen in."

Meekins nodded at the fishing equipment in Campbell's hands and smiled.

"Have any luck catching your monster?"

"Caught it and let it go," Campbell said.

"That's mighty convenient," Meekins said. "I don't suppose anyone else actually saw this giant fish, or that you have a photograph."

"No," Creech said serenely. "But it's way bigger than you are."

Meekins shook his head. He no longer smiled. "Must be nice to have nothing better to do than make up stories, but this is getting old real quick."

Rudisell stepped up to the truck's window, only inches away from Meekins's face when he raised his hand. A single diamond-shaped object was wedged between Rudisell's gnarled index finger and thumb. Though tinted brown, it appeared to be translucent. He held it eye level in front of Meekins's face as if it were a silty monocle they both might peer through.

"Acipenser fulvescens," Rudisell said, the Latin uttered slowly as if an incantation. He put the scute back in his pocket and, without further acknowledgment of Meekins's existence, stepped around the truck and onto the hardtop. Campbell followed with the fishing equipment and Creech came last with the book. It was a slow, dignified procession. They walked westward toward the store, the late-afternoon sun burnishing their cracked and wasted faces. Coming out of the shadows, they blinked their eyes as if dazzled, much in the manner of old-world saints who have witnessed the blinding brilliance of the one true vision.

From *Burning Bright* (2010)

HARD TIMES

Jacob stood in the barn mouth and watched Edna leave the hen house. Her lips were pressed tight, which meant more eggs had been taken. He looked up at the ridgetop and guessed eight o'clock. In Boone it'd be full morning now, but here light was still splotchy and dew damped his brogans. This cove's so damn dark a man about has to break light with a crowbar, his daddy used to say.

Edna nodded at the egg pail in her hand.

"Nothing under the bantam," Edna said. "That's four days in a row."

"Maybe that old rooster ain't sweet on her no more," Jacob said. He waited for her to smile. When they'd first started sparking years ago, Edna's smile had been what most entranced him. Her whole face would glow, as if the upward turn of her lips spread a wave of light from mouth to forehead.

"Go ahead and make a joke," she said, "but little cash money as we got it makes a difference. Maybe the difference of whether you have a nickel to waste on a newspaper."

"There's many folks worse off," Jacob said. "Just look up the cove and you'll see the truth of that."

"We can end up like Hartley yet," Edna replied. She looked past Jacob to where the road ended and the skid trail left by the logging company began. "It's probably his mangy hound that's stealing our eggs. That dog's got the look of a egg-sucker. It's always skulking around here."

"You don't know that. I still think a dog would leave some egg on the straw. I've never seen one that didn't."

"What else would take just a few eggs at a time? You said your ownself a fox or weasel would have killed the chickens."

"I'll go look," Jacob said, knowing Edna would fret over the lost eggs all day. He knew if every hen laid three eggs a night for the next month, it wouldn't matter. She'd still perceive a debit that would never be made up. Jacob tried to be generous, remembered that Edna hadn't always been this way. Not until the bank had taken the truck and most of the livestock. They hadn't lost everything the way others had, but they'd lost enough. Edna always seemed fearful when she heard a vehicle coming up the dirt road, as if expecting the banker and sheriff were coming to take the rest.

Edna carried the eggs to the springhouse as Jacob crossed the yard and entered the concrete henhouse. The smell of manure thickened the air. Though the rooster was already outside, the hens clucked dimly in their nesting boxes. Jacob lifted the bantam and set it on the floor. The nesting box's straw had no shell crumbs, no albumen or yellow yoke slobber.

He knew it could be a two-legged varmint, but hard as times were Jacob had never known anyone in Barker's Cove to steal, especially Hartley, the poorest of them all. Besides, who would take only two or three eggs when there were two dozen more to be had. The bantam's eggs at that, which were smaller than the ones under the Rhode Island Reds and leghorns. From the barn, Jacob heard the Guernsey lowing insistently. He knew she already waited beside the milk stool.

As Jacob came out of the henhouse he saw the Hartleys coming down the skid trail. They made the two-mile trek to Boone twice a week, each, even the child, burdened down with galax leaves. Jacob watched as they stepped onto the road, puffs of gray dust rising around their bare feet. Hartley carried four burlap pokes stuffed with galax. His wife carried two and the child one. With their ragged clothes hanging loose on bony frames, they looked like scarecrows en route to another cornfield, their possessions in tow. The hound trailed them, gaunt as the people it followed. The galax leaves were the closest thing to a crop Hartley could muster, for his land was all rock and slant. You couldn't grow a toenail on Hartley's land, Bascombe Lindsey had once said. That hadn't been a problem as long as the sawmill was running, but when it shut down the Hartleys had only one old swaybacked milk cow to sustain them, that and the galax, which earned a few nickels of barter at Mast's General Store. Jacob knew from the Sunday newspapers he bought that times were rough everywhere. Rich folks in New York had lost all their money and jumped out of buildings. Men rode boxcars town to town begging for work. But it was hard to believe any of them had less than Hartley and his family.

When Hartley saw Jacob he nodded but did not slow his pace. They were neither friends nor enemies, neighbors only in the sense that Jacob and Edna were the closest folks down the cove, though closest meant a half mile. Hartley had come up from Swain County eight years ago to work at the sawmill. The child had been a baby then, the wife seemingly decades younger than the cronish woman who walked beside the daughter. They would have passed without further acknowledgement except Edna came out on the porch.

"That hound of yours," she said to Hartley, "is it a eggsucker?" Maybe she wasn't trying to be accusatory, but the words sounded so.

Hartley stopped in the road and turned toward the porch. Another man would have set the pokes down, but Hartley did not. He held them as if calculating their heft.

"What's the why of you asking that," he said. The words were spoken in a tone that was neither angry nor defensive. It struck Jacob that even the man's voice had been worn down to a bare-boned flatness.

"Something's got in our henhouse and stole some," Edna said. "Just the eggs so it ain't a fox nor weasel."

"So you reckon my dog."

Edna did not speak, and Hartley set the pokes down. He pulled a barlow knife from his tattered overalls. He softly called the hound and it sidled up to him. Hartley got down on one knee, closed his left hand on the scruff of the dog's neck as he settled the blade against its throat. The daughter and wife stood perfectly still, their faces blank as bread dough.

"I don't think it's your dog that's stealing the eggs," Jacob said.

"But you don't know for sure. It could be," Hartley said, the hound raising its head as Hartley's index finger rubbed the base of its skull.

Before Jacob could reply the blade whisked across the hound's windpipe. The dog didn't cry out or snarl. It merely sagged in Hartley's grip. Blood darkened the road.

"You'll know for sure now," Hartley said as he stood up. He lifted the dog by the scruff of the neck, walked over to the other side of the road and laid it in the weeds. "I'll get it on the way back this evening," he said, and picked up the pokes. Hartley began walking and his wife and daughter followed.

"Why'd you have to say something to him," Jacob said when the family had disappeared down the road. He stared at the place in the weeds where flies and yellow jackets began to gather.

"How'd I know he'd do such a thing," Edna said.

"You know how proud a man he is."

Jacob let those words linger. In January when two feet of snow had shut nearly everyone in, Jacob had gone up the skid trail on horseback, a salted pork shoulder strapped to the saddle. "We could be needing that meat soon enough ourselves," Edna had said, but he'd gone anyway. When Jacob got to the cabin he'd found the family at the plank table eating. The wooden bowls before them held a thick liquid lumped with a few crumbs of fatback. The milk pail hanging over the fire was filled with the same gray-colored gruel. Jacob had set the pork shoulder on the table. The meat had a deep wood-smoke odor, and the woman and child swallowed every few seconds to conceal their salivating. "I ain't got no money to buy it," Hartley said. "So I'd appreciate you taking your meat and leaving." Jacob had left, but after closing the cabin door he'd laid the pork on the front stoop. The next morning Jacob had found the meat on his own doorstep.

Jacob gazed past Hartley's dog, across the road to the acre of corn where he'd work till suppertime. He hadn't hoed a single row yet but already felt tired all the way to his bones.

"I didn't want that dog killed," Edna said. "That wasn't my intending."

"Like it wasn't your intending for Joel and Mary to leave and never darken our door again," Jacob replied. "But it happened, didn't it."

He turned and walked to the woodshed to get his hoe.

The next morning the dog was gone from the roadside and more eggs were missing. It was Saturday, so Jacob rode the horse down to Boone, not just to get his newspaper but to talk to the older farmers who gathered at Mast's General Store. As he rode he remembered the morning six years ago when Joel dropped his bowl of oatmeal on the floor. Careless, but twelve-year-olds did careless things. It was part of being a child. Edna made the boy eat the oatmeal off the floor with his spoon. "Don't do it," Mary had told her younger brother, but he had, whimpering the whole time. Mary, who was sixteen, eloped two weeks later. "I'll never come back, not even to visit," a note left on the kitchen table said. Mary had been true to her word.

As Jacob rode into Boone, he saw the truck the savings and loan had repossessed from him parked by the courthouse. It was a vehicle made for hauling crops to town, bringing back salt blocks and fertilizer and barbed wire, but he'd figured no farmer could have afforded to buy it at auction. Maybe a store owner or county employee, he supposed, someone who still used a billfold instead of a change purse like the one he now took a nickel from after tying his horse to the hitching post. Jacob entered the store. He nodded at the older men, then laid his coin on the counter. Erwin Mast handed him last Sunday's *Raleigh News.*

"Don't reckon there's any letters?" Jacob asked.

"No, nothing this week," Erwin said, though he could have added, "or the last month or last year." Joel was in the navy, stationed somewhere in the Pacific. Mary lived with her husband and her own child on a farm in Haywood County, sixty miles away but it could have been California for all the contact Jacob and Edna had with her.

Jacob lingered by the counter. When the old men paused in their conversation, he told them about the eggs.

"And you're sure it ain't a dog?" Sterling Watts asked.

"Yes. There wasn't a bit of splatter or shell on the straw."

"Rats will eat a egg," Erwin offered from behind the counter.

"There'd still be something left, though," Bascombe Lindsey said.

"They's but one thing it can be," Sterling Watts said with finality.

"What's that," Jacob asked.

"A big yaller rat snake. They'll swallow two or three eggs whole and leave not a dribble of egg."

"I've heard such myself," Bascombe agreed. "Never seen it but heard of it."

"Well, one got in my henhouse," Sterling said. "And it took me near a month to figure out how to catch the damn thing."

"How did you?" Jacob asked.

"Went fishing," Sterling said.

That night Jacob plowed in his cornfield till dark. He ate his supper, then went to the woodshed and found a fishhook. He tied three yards of line to it and went to the henhouse. The bantam had one egg under her. Jacob took the egg and made as small a hole as possible with the barb. He slowly worked the whole hook into the egg, then tied the line to a nail head behind the nesting box. Three yards, Watson had said. That way the snake would swallow the whole egg before a tight line set the hook.

"I ain't about to go out there come morning and deal with no snake," Edna said when he told her what he'd done. She sat in the ladderback rocking chair, her legs draped by a quilt. He'd made the chair for her to sit in when she'd been pregnant with Joel. The wood was cherry, not the most practical for furniture, but he'd wanted it to be pretty.

"I'll deal with it," Jacob said.

For a few moments he watched her sew, the fine blue thread repairing the binding of the Bear's Claw quilt. Edna had worked since dawn, but she couldn't stop even now. Jacob sat down at the kitchen table and spread out the newspaper. On the front page Roosevelt said things were getting better, but the rest of the news argued otherwise. Strikers had been shot at a cotton mill. Men whose crime was hiding in boxcars to search for work had been beaten with clubs by lawmen and hired railroad goons.

"What you claimed this morning about me running off Joel and Laurel," Edna said, her needle not pausing as she spoke, "that was a spiteful thing to say. Those kids never went hungry a day in their lives. Their clothes was patched and they had shoes and coats."

He knew he should let it go, but the image of Hartley's knife opening the hound's throat had snared in his mind.

"You could have been easier on them," Jacob said.

"The world's a hard place," Edna replied. "There was need for them to know that."

"They'd have learned soon enough on their own," Jacob said.

"They needed to be prepared, and I prepared them. They ain't in a hobo camp or barefoot like Hartley and his clan. If they can't be grateful for that, there's nothing I can do about it now."

"There's going to be better times," Jacob said. "This depression can't last forever, but the way you treated them will."

"It's lasted nine years," Edna said. "And I see no sign of it letting up. The price we're getting for corn and cabbage is the same. We're still living on half of what we did before."

She turned back to the quilt's worn binding and no other words were spoken between them. After a while Edna put down her sewing and went to bed. Jacob soon followed. Edna tensed as he settled his body beside hers.

"I don't want us to argue," Jacob said, and laid his hand on her shoulder. She flinched from his touch, moved farther away.

"You think I've got no feelings," Edna said, her face turned so she spoke at the wall. "Stingy and mean-hearted. But maybe if I hadn't been we'd not have anything left."

Despite his weariness, Jacob had trouble going to sleep. When he finally did, he dreamed of men hanging onto boxcars while other men beat them with sticks. Those beaten wore muddy brogans and overalls, and he knew they weren't laid-off mill workers or coal miners but farmers like himself.

Jacob woke in the dark. The window was open and before he could fall back asleep he heard something from inside the henhouse. He pulled on his overalls and boots, then went out on the porch and lit a lantern. The sky was thick with stars and a wet moon lightened the ground, but the windowless henhouse was pitch dark. It had crossed his mind that if a yellow rat snake could eat an egg a copperhead or satinback could as well, and he wanted to see where he stepped. He went to the woodshed and got a hoe for the killing.

Jacob crossed the foot log and stepped up to the entrance. He held the lantern out and checked the nesting box. The bantam was in it, but no eggs lay under her. It took him a few moments to find the fishing line, leading toward the back corner like a single strand of a spider's web. He readied the hoe in his hand and took a step inside. He held the lamp before him and saw Hartley's daughter huddled in the corner, the line disappearing into her closed mouth.

She did not try to speak as he kneeled before her. Jacob set the hoe and lantern down and took out his pocketknife, then cut the line inches above where it disappeared between her lips. For a few moments he did nothing else.

"Let me see," he said, and though she did not open her mouth she did not resist as his fingers did so. He found the hook's barb sunk deep in her cheek and was relieved. He'd feared it would be in her tongue or, much worse, deep in her throat.

"We got to get that hook out," Jacob told her, but still she said nothing. Her eyes did not widen in fear and he wondered if maybe she was in shock. The barb was too deep to wiggle free. He'd have to push it the rest of the way through.

"This is going to hurt, but just for a second," he said, and let his index finger and thumb grip the hook where it began to curve. He worked deeper into the skin, his thumb and finger slickened by blood and saliva. The child whimpered. Finally the barb broke through. He wiggled the shank out, the line coming last like thread completing a stitch.

"It's out now," he told her.

For a few moments Jacob did not get up. He thought about what to do next. He could carry her back to Hartley's shack and explain what happened, but he remembered the dog. He looked at her cheek and there was no tear, only a tiny hole that bled little more than a briar scratch would. He studied the hook for signs of rust. There didn't seem to be, so at least he didn't have to worry about the girl getting lockjaw. But there could still be infection.

"Stay here," Jacob said and went to the woodshed. He found the bottle of turpentine and returned. He took his handkerchief and soaked it, then opened the child's mouth and dabbed the wound, did the same outside to the cheek.

"Okay," Jacob said. He reached out his hands and placed them under her armpits. She was so light it was like lifting a rag doll. The child stood before him now, and for the first time he saw that her right hand held something. He picked up the lantern and saw it was an egg and that it was unbroken. Jacob nodded at the egg.

"You don't ever take them home, do you," he said. "You eat them here, right?"

The child nodded.

"Go ahead and eat it then," Jacob said, "but you can't come back anymore. If you do, your daddy will know about it. You understand?"

"Yes," she whispered, the first word she'd spoken.

"Eat it then."

The girl raised the egg to her lips. A thin line of blood trickled down her chin as she opened her mouth. The shell crackled as her teeth bit down.

"Go home now," he said when she'd swallowed the last bit of shell. "And don't come back. I'm going to put another hook in them eggs and this time there won't be no line on it. You'll swallow that hook and it'll tear your guts up."

Jacob watched her walk up the skid trail until the dark enveloped her, then sat on the stump that served as a chopping block. He blew out the lantern and waited, though for what he could not say. After a while the moon and stars faded. In the east, darkness lightened to the color of indigo glass. The first outlines of the corn stalks and their leaves were visible now, reaching up from the ground like shabbily-dressed arms.

Jacob picked up the lantern and turpentine and went back to the house. Edna was getting dressed as he came back into the bedroom. Her back was to him.

"It was a snake," he said.

Edna paused in her dressing and turned. Her hair was down and her face not yet hardened to face the day's demands and he glimpsed the younger, softer woman she'd been twenty years ago when they'd married.

"You kill it?" she asked.

"Yes."

Her lips tightened.

"I hope you didn't just throw it out by the henhouse. I don't want to smell that thing rotting when I'm gathering eggs."

"I threw it across the road."

He got in the bed. Edna's form and warmth lingered on the feather mattress.

"I'll get up in a few minutes," he told her.

Jacob closed his eyes but did not sleep. Instead, he imagined towns where hungry men hung on boxcars looking for work that couldn't be found, shacks where families lived who didn't even have one swaybacked milk cow. He imagined cities where blood stained sidewalks beneath buildings tall as ridges. He tried to imagine a place worse than where he was.

THE ASCENT

Jared had never been this far before, over Sawmill Ridge and across a creek glazed with ice, then past the triangular metal sign that said *Smoky Mountains National Park*. If it had still been snowing and his tracks were being covered up, he'd have turned back. People had gotten lost in this park. Children wandered off from family picnics, hikers strayed off trails. Sometimes it took days to find them. But today the sun was out, the sky deep and blue. No more snow would fall, so it would be easy to retrace his tracks. Jared heard a helicopter hovering somewhere to the west, which meant they still hadn't found the airplane. They'd been searching all the way from Bryson City to the Tennessee line, or so he'd heard at school.

The land slanted downward and the sound of the helicopter disappeared. In the steepest places, Jared leaned sideways and held on to trees to keep from slipping. As he made his way into the denser woods, he was not thinking of the lost airplane or if he'd get the mountain bike he'd asked for as his Christmas present. Not thinking about his parents either, though they were the main reason he was spending his first day of Christmas vacation out here— better to be outside on a cold day than in the house where everything, the rickety chairs and sagging couch, the gaps where the TV and microwave had been, felt sad.

He thought instead of Lyndee Starnes, the girl who sat in front of him in fifth grade homeroom. Jared made believe that she was walking beside him and he was showing her the tracks in the snow, telling her which markings were squirrel and which rabbit and which deer. Imagining a bear track too, and telling Lyndee that he wasn't afraid of bears and Lyndee telling him she was so he'd have to protect her.

Jared stopped walking. He hadn't seen any human tracks, but he looked behind him to be sure no one was around. He took out the pocketknife and raised it, making believe that the pocketknife was a hunting knife and that Lyndee was beside him. If a bear comes, I'll take care of you, he said out loud. Jared imagined Lyndee reaching out and taking his free arm. He kept the knife out as he walked up another ridge, one whose name he did not know.

He imagined Lyndee still grasping his arm, and as they walked up the ridge Lyndee saying how sorry she was that at school she'd told him his clothes smelled bad. At the ridge top, Jared pretended a bear suddenly raised up, baring its teeth and growling. He slashed at the bear with the knife and the bear ran away. Jared held the knife before him as he descended the ridge. Sometimes they'll come back, he said aloud.

He was halfway down the ridge when the knife blade caught the midday sun and the steel flashed. Another flash came from below, as if it was answering. At first Jared saw only a glimmer of metal in the dull green of rhododendron, but as he came nearer he saw more, a crumpled silver propeller and white tailfin and part of a shattered wing.

For a few moments Jared thought about turning around, but then told himself that an eleven-year-old who'd just fought a bear shouldn't be afraid to get close to a crashed airplane. He made his way down the ridge, snapping rhododendron branches to clear a path. When he finally made it to the plane, he couldn't see much because snow and ice covered the windows. He turned the passenger side's outside handle, but the door didn't budge until Jared wedged in the pocketknife's blade. The door made a sucking sound as it opened.

A woman was in the passenger seat, her body bent forward like a horseshoe. Long brown hair fell over her face. The hair had frozen and looked as if it would snap off like icicles. She wore blue jeans and a yellow sweater. Her left arm was flung out before her and on one finger was a ring. The man across from her leaned toward the pilot window, his head cocked against the glass. Blood stains reddened the window and his face was not covered like the woman's. There was a seat in the back, empty. Jared placed the knife in his pocket and climbed into the back seat and closed the passenger door. It's so cold. That's why they don't smell much, he thought.

For a while he sat and listened to how quiet and still the world was. He couldn't hear the helicopter, or even the chatter of a gray squirrel or caw of a crow. Here between the ridges not even the sound of the wind. Jared tried not to move or breathe hard to make it even quieter, quiet as the man and woman up front. The plane was snug and cozy, warmer than outside. After a while he heard something, just the slightest sound, coming from the man's side. Jared listened harder, then knew what it was. He leaned forward between the front seats. The man's right forearm rested against a knee. Jared pulled back the man's shirt sleeve and saw the watch. He checked the time, almost four o'clock. He'd been sitting in the back seat two hours, though it seemed only a few minutes. The light that would let him follow the tracks back home would be gone soon.

As he got out of the back seat, Jared saw the woman's ring. Even in the cabin's muted light it shone. He took the ring off the woman's finger and placed it in his jean pocket. He closed the passenger door and followed his boot prints back the way he came. Jared tried to step exactly in his earlier tracks, pretending that he needed to confuse a wolf following him.

It took longer than he'd thought, the sun almost down when he crossed the park boundary. As he came down the last ridge, Jared saw that the pickup was parked in the yard, the lights on in the front room. He remembered it was Saturday and his father had gotten his pay check. When Jared opened the door, the small red glass pipe was on the coffee table, an empty baggy beside it. His father kneeled before the fireplace, meticulously arranging and rearranging kindling around an oak log. A dozen crushed beer cans lay amid the kindling, balanced on the log itself three red-and-white fishing bobbers. His mother sat on the couch, her eyes glazed as she told Jared's father how to arrange the cans. In her lap lay a roll of tinfoil she was cutting into foot-long strips.

"Look what we're making," she said, smiling at Jared. "It's going to be our Christmas tree."

When he didn't speak, his mother's smile quivered.

"Don't you like it, honey?"

His mother got up, strips of tin foil in her left hand. She kneeled beside the hearth and carefully draped them on the oak log and kindling.

Jared walked into the kitchen and took the milk from the refrigerator. He washed a bowl and spoon left in the sink and poured some cereal. After he ate Jared went into his bedroom and closed the door. He sat on his bed and took the ring from his pocket and set it in his palm. He placed the ring under the lamp's bulb and swayed his hand slowly back and forth so the stone's different colors flashed and merged. He'd give it to Lyndee when they were on the playground, on the first sunny day after Christmas vacation so she could see how pretty the ring's colors were. Once he gave it to her, Lyndee would finally like him, and it would be for real.

Jared didn't hear his father until the door swung open.

"Your mother wants you to help light the tree."

The ring fell onto the wooden floor. Jared picked it up and closed his hand.

"What's that?" his father asked.

"Nothing," Jared said. "Just something I found in the woods."

"Let me see."

Jared opened his hand. His father stepped closer and took the ring. He pressed the ring with his thumb and finger.

"That surely a fake diamond, but the ring looks to be real gold."

His father tapped it against the bedpost as if the sound could confirm its authenticity. His father called his mother and she came into the room.

"Look what Jared found," he said, and handed her the ring. "It's gold."

His mother set the ring in her palm, held it out before her so they all three could see it.

"Where'd you find it, honey?"

"In the woods," Jared said.

"I didn't know you could find rings in the woods," his mother said dreamily. "But isn't it wonderful that you can."

"That diamond can't be real, can it?" his father asked.

His mother stepped close to the lamp. She cupped her hand and slowly rocked it back and forth, watching the different colors flash inside the stone.

"It might be," his mother said.

"Can I have it back?" Jared asked.

"Not until we find out if it's real, son," his father said.

His father took the ring from his mother's palm and placed it in his pants pocket. Then he went into the other bedroom and got his coat.

"I'm going down to Bryson City and find out if it's real or not."

"But you're not going to sell it," Jared said.

"I'm just going to have a jeweler look at it," his father said, already putting on his coat. "We need to know what it's worth, don't we? We might have to insure it. You and your momma go ahead and light our Christmas tree. I'll be back in just a few minutes."

"It's not a Christmas tree," Jared said.

"Sure it is, son," his father replied. "It's just one that's chopped up, is all."

He wanted to stay awake until his father returned, so he helped his mother spread the last strips of tinfoil on the wood. His mother struck a match and told him it was time to light the tree. The kindling caught and the foil and cans withered and blackened, the fishing bobbers melting. His mother kept adding kindling to the fire, telling Jared if he watched closely he'd see angel wings folding and unfolding inside the flames. Angels come down the chimney sometimes, just like Santa Claus, she told him. Midnight came and his father still wasn't back. Jared went to his room. I'll lay down just for a few minutes, he told himself, but when he opened his eyes it was light outside.

He smelled the methamphetamine as soon as he opened his bedroom door, thicker than he could ever remember. His parents had not gone to bed.

He could tell that as soon as he came into the front room. The fire was still going, kindling piled around the hearth. His mother sat where she'd been last night, wearing the same clothes. She was tearing pages out of a magazine one at a time, using scissors to make ragged stars she stuck on the walls with Scotch tape. His father sat beside her, watching intently.

The glass pipe lay on the coffee table, beside it four baggies, two with powder still in them. There'd never been more than one before.

His father grinned at him.

"I got you some of that cereal you like," he said, and pointed to a box with a green leprechaun on its front.

"Where's the ring?" Jared asked.

"The sheriff took it," his father said. "When I showed it to the jeweler, he said the sheriff had been in there just yesterday. A woman had reported it missing. I knew you'd be disappointed, that's why I bought you that cereal. Got something else for you too."

His father nodded toward the front door where a mountain bike was propped against the wall. Jared walked over to it. He could tell it wasn't new, some of the blue paint chipped away, one of the rubber handle grips missing, but the tires didn't sag and the handlebars were straight.

"It didn't seem right for you to have to wait till Christmas to have it," his father said. "Too bad there's snow on the ground, but it'll soon enough melt and you'll be able to ride it."

Jared's mother looked up.

"Wasn't that nice of your daddy," she said, her eyes bright and gleaming. "Go ahead and eat your cereal, son. A growing boy needs his breakfast."

"What about you and daddy?" Jared asked.

"We'll eat later."

Jared ate as his parents sat in the front room passing the pipe back and forth. He looked out the window and saw the sky held nothing but blue, not even a few white clouds. He thought about going back to the plane, but as soon as he laid his bowl in the sink his father announced that the three of them were going to go find a real Christmas tree.

"The best Christmas tree ever," his mother told Jared.

They put on their coats and walked up the ridge, his father carrying a rusty saw. Near the ridge top, they found Frazier firs and white pines.

"Which one do you like best, son?" his father asked.

Jared looked over the trees, then picked a Frazier fir no taller than himself.

"You don't want a bigger one?" his father asked.

When Jared shook his head no, his father kneeled before the tree. The saw's teeth were dull but his father finally broke the bark and worked the saw through. They dragged the tree down the ridge and propped it in the corner by the fireplace. His parents smoked the pipe again and then his father went out to the shed and got a hammer and nails and two boards. While his father built the makeshift tree stand, Jared's mother cut more stars from the newspaper.

"I think I'll go outside a while," Jared said.

"But you can't," his mother replied. "You've got to help me tape the stars to the tree."

By the time they'd finished, the sun was falling behind Sawmill Ridge. I'll go tomorrow, he told himself.

On Sunday morning the baggies were empty and his parents were sick. His mother sat on the couch wrapped in a quilt, shivering. She hadn't bathed since Friday and her hair was stringy and greasy. His father looked little better, his blue eyes receding deep into his skull, his lips chapped and bleeding.

"Your momma, she's sick," his father said, "and your old daddy ain't doing too well himself."

"The doctor can't help her, can he?" Jared asked.

"No," his father said. "I don't think he can."

Jared watched his mother all morning. She'd never been this bad before. After awhile she lit the pipe and sucked deeply for what residue might remain. His father crossed his arms, rubbing his biceps as he looked around the room, as if expecting to see something he'd not seen moments earlier. The fire had gone out, the cold causing his mother to shake more violently.

"You got to go see Brady," she told Jared's father.

"We got no money left," he answered.

Jared watched them, waiting for the sweep of his father's eyes to stop beside the front door where the mountain bike was. But his father's eyes went past it without the slightest pause. The kerosene heater in the kitchen was on, but its heat hardly radiated into the front room.

His mother looked up at Jared.

"Can you fix us a fire, honey?"

He went out to the back porch and gathered an armload of kindling, then placed a thick log on the andirons as well. Beneath it he wedged newspaper left over from the star cutting. He lit the newspaper and watched the fire slowly take hold, then watched the flames a while longer before turning to his parents.

123

"You can take the bike down to Bryson City and sell it," he said.

"No, son," his mother said. "That's your Christmas present."

"We'll be alright," his father said. "Your momma and me just did too much partying yesterday is all."

But as the morning passed, they got no better. At noon Jared went to his room and put on his coat.

"Where you going, honey?" his mother asked as he walked toward the door.

"To get more firewood."

Jared walked into the shed but did not gather wood. Instead, he took a length of dusty rope off the shed's back wall and wrapped it around his waist and then knotted it. He left the shed and followed his own tracks west into the park. The snow had become harder, and it crunched beneath his boots. The sky was gray, darker clouds farther west. More snow would soon come, maybe by afternoon. Jared made believe he was on a rescue mission. He was in Alaska, the rope tied around him dragging a sled filled with food and medicine. The footprints weren't his but of the people he'd been sent to find.

When he got to the airplane, Jared pretended to unpack the supplies and give the man and woman something to eat and drink. He told them they were too hurt to walk back with him and he'd have to go and get more help. Jared took the watch off the man's wrist. He set it in his palm, face upward. I've got to take your compass, he told the man. A blizzard's coming, and I may need it.

Jared slipped the watch into his pocket. He got out of the plane and walked back up the ridge. The clouds were hard and granite-looking now, and the first flurries were falling. Jared pulled out the watch every few minutes, pointed the hour hand east as he followed his tracks back to the house.

The truck was still out front, and through the window Jared could see the mountain bike. He could see his parents as well, huddled together on the couch. For a few moments Jared simply stared through the window at them.

When he went inside, the fire was out and the room was cold enough to see his breath. His mother looked up anxiously from the couch.

"You shouldn't go off that long without telling us where you're going, honey."

Jared lifted the watch from his pocket.

"Here," he said, and gave it to his father.

His father studied it a few moments, then broke into a wide grin.

"This watch is a Rolex," his father said.

"Thank you, Jared," his mother said, looking as if she might cry. "You're the best son anybody could have, ain't he Daddy?"

"The very best," his father said.

"How much can we get for it?" his mother asked.

"I bet a couple of hundred at least," his father answered.

His father clamped the watch onto his wrist and got up. Jared's mother rose as well.

"I'm going with you. I need something quick as I can get it." She turned to Jared. "You stay here, honey. We'll be back in just a little while. We'll bring you back a hamburger and a Co-cola, some more of that cereal too."

Jared watched as they drove down the road. When the truck had vanished, he sat down on the couch and rested a few minutes. He hadn't taken his coat off. He checked to make sure the fire was out and then went to his room and emptied his backpack of school books. He went out to the shed and picked up a wrench and a hammer and placed them in the backpack. The flurries were thicker now, already beginning to fill in his tracks. He crossed over Sawmill Ridge, the tools clanking in his backpack. More weight to carry, he thought, but at least he wouldn't have to carry them back.

When he got to the plane, he didn't open the door, not at first. Instead, he took the tools from the backpack and laid them before him. He studied the plane's crushed nose and propeller, the broken right wing. The wrench was best to tighten the propeller, he decided. He'd straighten out the wing with the hammer.

As he switched tools and moved around the plane, the snow fell harder. Jared looked behind him and on up the ridge and saw his footprints were growing fainter. He chipped the snow and ice off the windshields with the hammer's claw. Finished, he said, and dropped the hammer on the ground. He opened the passenger door and got in.

"I fixed it so it'll fly now," he told the man.

He sat in the back seat and waited. The work and walk had warmed him but he quickly grew cold. He watched the snow cover the plane's front window with a darkening whiteness. After a while he began to shiver but after a longer while he was no longer cold. Jared looked out the side window and saw the whiteness was not only in front of him but below. He knew then that they had taken off and risen so high that they were enveloped inside a cloud, but still he looked down, waiting for the clouds to clear so he might look for the pickup as it followed the winding road toward Bryson City.

THE WOMAN WHO BELIEVED IN JAGUARS

On the drive home from her mother's funeral, Ruth Lealand thinks of jaguars. She saw one once in the Atlanta Zoo and admired the creature's movements—like muscled water—as it paced back and forth, turning inches from the iron bars but never acknowledging the cage's existence. She had not remembered then what she remembers now, a memory like something buried in river silt that finally works free and rises to the surface, a memory from the third grade. Mrs. Carter tells them to get out their *History of South Carolina* textbooks. Paper and books shuffle and shift. Some of the boys snicker, for on the book's first page is a drawing of an Indian woman suckling her child. Ruth opens the book and sees a black and white sketch of a jaguar, but for only a moment, because this is not a page they will study today or any other day this school year. She turns to the correct page and forgets what she's seen for fifty years.

But now as she drives west toward Columbia, Ruth again sees the jaguar and the palmetto trees it walks through. She wonders why in the intervening decades she has never read or heard anyone else mention that jaguars once roamed South Carolina. Windows up, radio off, Ruth travels in silence. The last few days were made more wearying because she's had to converse with so many people. She is an only child, her early life long silences filled with books and games that needed no other players. That had been the hardest adjustment in her marriage—the constant presence of Richard, though she'd come to love the cluttered intimacy of their shared life, the reassurance and promise of "I'm here" and "I'll be back." Now a whole day can pass without speaking a word to another person.

In her apartment for the first time in three days, Ruth drops her mail on the bed, then hangs up the black dress, nudges the shoes back into the closet's far corner. She glances through the bills and advertisements, but stops, as she always does, when she sees the flyer of a missing child. She studies the boy's face, ignoring the gapped smile. If she were to see him, he would not be smiling. Her lips move slightly as she reads of a lost child four feet tall and eighty pounds, a boy with blonde hair and blue eyes last seen in Charlotte. Not so far away, she thinks, and places it in her pocketbook that already holds a dozen similar flyers.

No pastel sympathy cards brighten her mail. A personal matter, Ruth had told her supervisor, and out of deference or indifference the supervisor hadn't asked her to explain further. Though Ruth's worked in the office sixteen years, her co-workers know nothing about her. They do not know she was once married, once had a child. At Christmas the people she works with draw names, and every year she receives a sampler of cheeses and meats. She imagines the giver buying one for her and one for some maiden aunt. There are days at the office when Ruth feels invisible. Co-workers look right through her as they pass her desk. She believes that if she actually did disappear and the police needed an artist's sketch, none of them could provide a distinguishing detail.

Ruth walks into the living room, kneels in front of the set of encyclopedias on the bottom bookshelf. When she was pregnant, her mother insisted on making a trip to Columbia to bring a shiny new stroller, huge discount bags of diapers, and the encyclopedias bought years ago for Ruth.

They're for your child now, her mother had said. That's why I saved them.

But Ruth's child lived only four hours. She was still hazy from the anesthesia when Richard had sat on the hospital bed, his face pale and haggard, and told her they had lost the baby. In her drugged mind she envisioned a child in the new stroller, wheeled into some rarely-used hospital hallway and then forgotten.

Tell them they have to find him, she'd said, and tried to get up, propping herself on her elbows for a moment before they gave way and darkness closed around her.

Richard had wanted to try again. We've got to move on with our lives, he'd said. But she'd taken the stroller and bags of diapers to Goodwill. In the end only Richard moved on, taking a job in Atlanta. Soon they were seeing each other on fewer and fewer weekends, solitude returning to her life like a geographical place, a landscape neither hostile or welcoming, just familiar.

That their marriage had come apart was not unusual. All the books and advice columnists said so. Their marriage had become a tangled exchange of sorrow. Ruth knew now that it had been she, not Richard, who too easily had acquiesced to the idea that it always would be so, that solitude was better because it allowed no mirror for one's grief. They could have had another child, could have tried to heal themselves. She'd been the unwilling one.

Ruth rubs her index finger over the encyclopedia spines, reading the time-darkened letters like braille. She pulls the J volume out, a cracking sound as she opens it. She finds the entry, a black and white photograph of a big cat resting in a tree: *Range: South and Central America. Once found in Texas, New Mexico, Arizona, but now only rare sightings near the U.S.-Mexico border.*

There is no mention of South Carolina, not even Florida. Ruth wonders for the first time if perhaps she only imagined seeing the jaguar in the schoolbook. Perhaps it was a mountain lion or bobcat. She shelves the encyclopedia and turns on her computer, types *jaguar South Carolina extinct* into the search engine. After an hour, Ruth has found three references to *Southeast United States* and several more to *Florida* and *Louisiana,* but no reference to South Carolina. She walks into the kitchen and opens the phone book. She calls the state zoo's main number and asks to speak to the director.

"He's not here today," the switchboard operator answers, "but I can connect you to his assistant, Dr. Timrod."

The phone rings twice and a man's voice answers.

Ruth is unsure how to say what she wants, other than some kind of confirmation. She tells her name and that she's interested in jaguars.

"We have no jaguar," Dr. Timrod says brusquely. "The closest would be in Atlanta."

Ruth asks if they were ever in South Carolina.

"In a zoo?"

"No, in the wild."

"I've never heard that," Dr. Timrod says. "I associate jaguars with a more tropical environment, but I'm no expert on big cats." His voice is reflective now, more curious than impatient. "My field is ornithology. Most people think parakeets are tropical too, but once they were in South Carolina."

"So it's possible," Ruth says.

"Yes, I guess it's possible. I do know buffalo were here. Elk, pumas, wolves. Why not a jaguar."

"Could you help me find out?"

As Dr. Timrod pauses, she imagines his office—posters of animals on the walls, the floor concrete just like the big cats' cages. Maybe a file cabinet and bookshelves but little else. She suspects the room reeks of pipe smoke.

"Maybe," Dr. Timrod says. "I can ask Leslie Winters. She's our large animal expert, though elephants are her main interest. If she doesn't know, I'll try to do a little research on it myself."

"Can I come by the zoo tomorrow to see what you've found?"

Dr. Timrod laughs. "You're rather persistent."

"Not usually," Ruth says.

"I'll be in my office from ten to eleven. Come then."

Ruth calls her office and tells the secretary she will be out one more day.

The needs of the dead have exhausted her. Too tired to cook or go out, Ruth instead finishes unpacking and takes a long bath. As she lies in the warm, neck-deep water, she closes her eyes and summons the drawing of the jaguar. She tries to remember more. Was the jaguar drawn as if moving or standing still? Were its eyes looking toward her or toward the end of the page? Were there parakeets perched in the palmetto trees above? She cannot recall.

Ruth does not rest well that night. She has trouble falling asleep and when she finally does she dreams of rows of bleached tombstones with no names, no dates etched upon them. In the dream one of these tombstones marks the grave of her son, but she does not know which one.

Driving through rush-hour traffic the next morning, Ruth remembers how she made the nurse bring her son to her when the drugs had worn off enough that she understood what lost really meant. She'd looked into her child's face so she might never forget it, stroking the wisps of hair blonde and fine as corn silk. Her son's eyes were closed. After a few seconds the nurse had gently but firmly taken the child from her arms. The nurse had been kind, as had the doctor, but she knows they have forgotten her child by now, that his brief life has merged with hundreds of other children who lived and died under their watch. She knows that only two people remember that child and that now even she has trouble recalling what he looked like and the same must be true for Richard. She knows there is not a single soul on earth who could tell her the color of her son's eyes.

At the zoo the woman in the admission booth gives Ruth a map, marking Dr. Timrod's office with an X.

"You'll have to go through part of the zoo, so here's a pass," the woman says, "just in case someone asks."

Ruth accepts the pass but opens her pocketbook. "I may stay a while."

"Don't worry about it," the woman says and waves her in.

Ruth follows the map past the black rhino and the elephants, past the lost-and-found booth where the Broad River flows only a few yards from the concrete path. She walks over a wooden bridge and finds the office, a brick building next to the aviary.

Ruth is twenty minutes early so sits down on a nearby bench, light-headed with fatigue though she hasn't walked more than a quarter-mile, all of it downhill. On the other side of the walkway a wire-mesh cage looms large as her living room. *The Andean Condor is the largest flying bird in the world. Like its American relatives, Vultur gryphus is voiceless,* the sign on the cage says.

The condor perches on a blunt-limbed tree, its head and neck thick with wrinkles. When the bird spreads its wings Ruth wonders how the cage can contain it. She lowers her gaze, watches instead the people who pass in front of her. Her stomach clenches, and she realizes she hasn't eaten since lunchtime yesterday.

She is about to go find a refreshment stand when she sees the child. A woman dressed in jeans and a blue T-shirt drags him along as if a prisoner, their wrists connected by a cord of white plastic. As they pass between her and the condor, Ruth stares intently at the blue eyes and blonde hair, the pale unsmiling face. She estimates his height and weight as she fumbles with her pocketbook snap, sifts through the flyers till she finds the one she's searching for. She looks and knows it is him. She snaps the pocketbook shut as the woman and child cross the wooden bridge.

Ruth rises to follow and the world suddenly blurs. The wire-mesh of the condor's cage wavers as if about to give way. She grips the bench with her free hand. In a few moments she regains her balance, but the woman and child are out of sight.

Ruth walks rapidly, then is running, the pocketbook slapping against her side, the flyer gripped in her hand like a sprinter's baton. She crosses the wooden bridge and finally spots the woman and child in front of the black rhino's enclosure.

"Call the police," Ruth says to the teenager in the lost-and-found booth. "That child," she says, gasping for breath as she points to the boy, "that child has been kidnapped. Hurry, they're about to leave."

The teenager looks at her incredulously, but he picks up the phone and asks for security. Ruth walks past the woman and child, putting herself between them and the park's exit. She does not know what she will say or do, only that she will not let them pass by her.

But the woman and child do not try to leave, and soon Ruth sees the teenager with two gray-clad security guards, guns holstered on their hips, jogging toward her.

"There," Ruth shouts, pointing as she walks toward the child. As Ruth and the security guards converge, the woman in the blue T-shirt and the child turn to face them.

"What is this?" the woman asks as the child clutches her leg.

"Look," Ruth says, thrusting the flyer into the hands of the older of the two men. The security guard looks at it, then at the child.

"What is this? What are you doing?" the woman asks, her voice frantic now.

The child is whimpering, still holding the woman's leg. The security guard looks up from the flyer.

"I don't see the resemblance," he says, looking at Ruth.

He hands the flyer to his partner.

"This child would be ten years old," the younger man says.

"It's him," Ruth says. "I know it is."

The older security guard looks at Ruth and then at the woman and child. He seems unsure what to do next.

"Ma'am," he finally says to the woman, "if you could show me some I.D. for you and your child we can clear this up real quick."

"You think this isn't my child?" the woman asks, looking not at the security guards but at Ruth. "Are you insane?"

The woman shakes as she opens her purse, hands the security guard her driver's license, photographs of her family and two Social Security cards.

"Momma, don't let them take me away," the child says, clutching his mother's knee more tightly.

The mother places her hand on her son's head until the older security guard hands her back the cards and pictures.

"Thank you, ma'am," he says. "I apologize for this."

"You should apologize, all of you," the woman says, lifting the child into her arms.

"I'm so sorry," Ruth says, but the woman has already turned and is walking toward the exit.

The older security guard speaks into a walkie-talkie.

"I was so sure," she says to the younger man.

"Yes, ma'am," the security guard replies, not meeting her eyes.

Ruth debates whether to meet her appointment or go home. She finally starts walking toward Dr. Timrod's office, for no better reason than it is downhill, easier.

When she knocks on the door, the voice she heard on the phone tells her to come in. Dr. Timrod sits at a big wooden desk. Besides a computer and telephone, there's nothing on the desk except some papers and a coffee cup filled with pens and pencils. A bookshelf is behind him, the volumes on it thick, some leather bound. The walls are bare except for a framed painting of long-tailed birds perched on a tree limb, their yellow heads and green bodies brightening the tree like Christmas ornaments, *Carolina Paroquet* emblazoned at the bottom.

Dr. Timrod's youth surprises her. Ruth had expected gray hair, bifocals, and a rumpled suit, not jeans and a flannel shirt, a face unlined as a teenager's. A styrofoam cup fills his right hand.

"Ms. Lealand, I presume."

"Yes," she says, surprised he remembers her name.

He motions for her to sit down.

"Our jaguar hunt cost me a good bit of sleep last night," he says.

"I didn't sleep much myself," Ruth says. "I'm sorry you didn't either."

"Don't be. Among other things I found out jaguars tend to be nocturnal. To study a creature it's best to adapt to its habits."

Dr. Timrod sips from the cup. Ruth smells the coffee and again feels the emptiness in her stomach.

"I talked to Leslie Winters yesterday before I left. She'd never heard of jaguars being in South Carolina, but she reminded me that her main focus is elephants, not cats. I called a friend who's doing field work on jaguars in Arizona. He told me there's as much chance of a jaguar having been in South Carolina as a polar bear."

"So they were never here," Ruth says, and she wonders if there is anything left inside her mind she can believe.

"I'd say that's still debatable. When I got home last night, I did some searching on the computer. A number of sources said their range once included the Southeast. A number of those mentioned Florida and Louisiana, a few Mississippi and Alabama."

Dr. Timrod pauses and lifts a piece of paper off his desk.

"Then I found this."

He stands up and hands the paper to Ruth. The words *Florida, Georgia, and South Carolina* are underlined.

"What's strange is the source is a book published in the early sixties," Dr. Timrod says. "Not a more contemporary source."

"So people just forgot they were here," Ruth says.

"Well, it's not like I did an exhaustive search," Dr. Timrod says. "And the book that page came from could be wrong. Like I said, it's not an updated source."

"I believe they were here," Ruth says.

Dr. Timrod smiles and sips from the styrofoam cup.

"Now you have some support for your belief."

Ruth folds the paper and places it in her purse.

"I wonder when they disappeared from South Carolina?"

"I have no idea," Dr. Timrod says.

"What about them?" Ruth asks, pointing at the parakeets.

"Later than you'd think. There were still huge flocks in the mid 1800's. Audubon said that when they foraged the fields looked like brilliantly colored carpets."

"What happened?"

"Farmers didn't want to share the crops and fruit trees. A farmer with a gun could kill a whole flock in one afternoon."

"How was that possible?" Ruth asks.

"That's the amazing thing. They wouldn't abandon one another."

Dr. Timrod turns to his bookshelf, takes off a volume and sits back down. He thumbs through the pages until he finds what he's looking for.

"This was written in the 1800's by a man named Alexander Wilson," Dr. Timrod says, and begins to read. "'Having shot down a number, some of which were only wounded, the whole flock swept repeatedly around their prostrate companions, and again settled on a low tree, within twenty yards of the spot where I stood. At each successive discharge, though showers of them fell, yet the affection of the survivors seemed rather to increase; for after a few circuits around the place, they again alighted near me.'"

Dr. Timrod looks up from the book.

"'The affection of the survivors seemed rather to increase,'" he says softly. "That's a pretty heartbreaking passage."

"Yes," Ruth says. "It is."

Dr. Timrod lays the book on the desk. He looks at his watch.

"I've got a meeting," he says, standing up. He comes around the desk and offers his hand. "Congratulations. You may be on the cutting edge of South Carolina jaguar studies."

Ruth takes his hand, a stronger, more callused hand than she'd have expected. Dr. Timrod opens the door.

"After you," he says.

Ruth stands up slowly, both hands gripping the chair's arms. She walks out into the bright May morning.

"Thank you," she says. "Thank you for your help."

"Good luck with your search," Dr. Timrod says.

He turns from her and walks down the pathway. Ruth watches him until he rounds a curve and disappears. She walks the other way. When she comes to where the river is closest to the walkway, Ruth stops and sits on the bench. She looks out at the river, the far bank where the Columbia skyline rises over the trees.

The buildings crumble like sand and blow away. Green-and-yellow birds spangle the sky. Below them wolves and buffalo lean their heads into the river's flow. From the far shore a tree limb rises toward her like an outstretched hand. On it rests a jaguar, blending so well with its habitat that Ruth cannot blink without the jaguar vanishing. Each time it is harder to bring it back, and the moment comes when Ruth knows if she closes her eyes again the jaguar will disappear forever. Her eyes blur but still she holds her gaze. Something comes unanchored inside her. She lies down on the bench, settles her head on her forearm. She closes her eyes and she sleeps.

BURNING BRIGHT

After the third fire in two weeks, the talk on TV and radio was no longer about careless campers. Not *three* fires. Nothing short of a miracle that only a few acres had been burned, the park superintendent said, a miracle less likely to occur again with each additional rainless day.

Marcie listened to the noon weather forecast, then turned off the TV and went out on the porch. She looked at the sky and nothing belied the prediction of more hot dry weather. The worst drought in a decade, the weatherman had said, showing a ten-year chart of August rainfalls. As if Marcie needed a chart when all she had to do was look at her tomatoes shriveled on the vines, the corn shucks gray and papery as hornets' nests. She stepped off the porch and dragged a length of hose into the garden, its rubber the sole bright green among the rows. Marcie turned on the water and watched it splatter against the dust. Hopeless, but she slowly walked the rows, grasping the hose just below the metal mouth, as if it were a snake that could bite her. When she finished she looked at the sky a last time and went inside. She thought of Carl, wondering if he'd be late again. She thought about the cigarette lighter he carried in his front pocket, a wedding gift she'd bought him in Gatlinburg.

When her first husband, Arthur, had died two falls earlier of a heart attack, the men in the church had come the following week and felled a white oak on the ridge. They'd cut it into firewood and stacked it on her porch. Their doing so had been more an act of homage to Arthur than concern for her, or so Marcie realized the following September when the men did not come, making clear that the church and the community it represented believed others needed their help more than a woman whose husband had left behind fifty acres of land, a paid-off house, and money in the bank.

Carl showed up instead. Heard you might need some firewood cut, he told her, but she did not unlatch the screen door when he stepped onto the porch, even after he explained that Preacher Carter had suggested he come. He stepped back to the porch edge, his deep-blue eyes lowered so as not to meet hers. Trying to set her at ease, she was sure, appear less threatening to a woman living alone. It was something a lot of other men wouldn't have done, wouldn't even have thought to do. Marcie asked for a phone number and he gave her one. I'll call you tomorrow if I need you, she said, and watched him drive off in his battered black pickup, a chain saw and red five-gallon gas can rattling in the truck bed. She phoned Preacher Carter after Carl left.

"He's new in the area, from down near the coast," the minister told Marcie. "He came by the church one afternoon, claimed he'd do good work for fair wages."

"So you sent him up here not knowing hardly anything about him?" Marcie asked. "With me living alone."

"Ozell Harper wanted some trees cut and I sent him out there," Preacher Carter replied. "He also cut some trees for Andy West. They both said he did a crackerjack job." The minister paused. "I think the fact he came by the church to ask about work speaks in his favor. He's got a good demeanor about him too. Serious and soft-spoken, lets his work do his talking for him."

She called Carl that night and told him he was hired.

Marcie cut off the spigot and looked at the sky one last time. She went inside and made her shopping list. As she drove down the half-mile dirt road, red dust rose in the car's wake. She passed the two other houses on the road, both owned by Floridians who came every year in June and left in September. When they'd moved in, she'd walked down the road with a homemade pie. The newcomers had stood in their doorways. They accepted the welcoming gift but did not invite her in.

Marcie turned left onto the blacktop, the radio on the local station. She went by several fields of corn and tobacco every bit as singed as her own garden. Before long she passed Johnny Ramsey's farm and saw several of the cows that had been in her pasture until Arthur died. The road forked and as Marcie passed Holcombe Pruitt's place she saw a black snake draped over a barbed-wire fence, put there because the older farmers believed it would bring rain. Her father had called it a silly superstition when she was a child, but during a drought nearly as bad as this one, her father had killed a blacksnake himself and placed it on a fence, then fallen to his knees in his scorched cornfield, imploring whatever entity would listen to bring rain.

Marcie hadn't been listening to the radio, but now a psychology teacher from the community college was being interviewed on a call-in show. The man said the person setting the fires was, according to the statistics, a male and a loner. Sometimes there's a sexual gratification in the act, he explained, or an inability to communicate with others except in actions, in this case destructive actions, or just a love of watching fire itself, an almost aesthetic response. But arsonists are always obsessive, the teacher concluded, so he won't stop until he's caught or the rain comes.

The thought came to her then, like something held underwater that had finally slipped free and surfaced. The only reason you're thinking it could be him, she told herself, is because people have made you believe you don't deserve him, don't deserve a little happiness. There's no reason to think such a thing. But just as quickly her mind grasped for one.

Marcie thought of the one-night honeymoon in Gatlinburg back in April. She and Carl stayed in a hotel room so close to a stream that you could hear the water rushing past. The next morning they'd eaten at a pancake house and then walked around the town, looking in the shops, Marcie holding Carl's hand. Foolish, maybe, for a woman of almost sixty, but Carl hadn't seemed to mind. Marcie told him she wanted to buy him something, and when they came to a shop called Country Gents, she led him into its log-cabin interior. You pick, she told Carl, and he gazed into glass cases holding all manner of belt buckles and pocketknives and cuff links, but it was a tray of cigarette lighters where he lingered. He asked the clerk to see several, opening and closing their hinged lids, flicking the thumbwheel to summon the flame, finally settling on one whose metal bore the image of a cloisonné tiger.

At the grocery store, Marcie took out her list and an ink pen, moving down the rows. Monday afternoon was a good time to shop, most of the women she knew coming later in the week. Her shopping cart filled, Marcie came to the front. Only one line was open and it was Barbara Hardison's, a woman Marcie's age and the biggest gossip in Sylva.

"How are your girls?" Barbara asked as she scanned a can of beans and placed it on the conveyor belt. Done slowly, Marcie knew, giving Barbara more time.

"Fine," Marcie said, though she'd spoken to neither in over a month.

"Must be hard to have them living so far away, not hardly see them or your grandkids. I'd not know what to do if I didn't see mine at least once a week."

"We talk every Saturday, so I keep up with them," Marcie lied.

Barbara scanned more cans and bottles, all the while talking about how she believed the person responsible for the fires was one of the Mexicans working at the poultry plant.

"No one who grew up around here would do such a thing," Barbara said.

Marcie nodded, barely listening as Barbara prattled on. Instead, her mind replayed what the psychology teacher had said. She thought about how there were days when Carl spoke no more than a handful of words to her, to anyone, as far as she knew, and how he'd sit alone on the porch until bedtime while she watched TV, and how, though he'd smoked his after-supper cigarette, she'd look out the front window and see a flicker of light rise out of his cupped hand, held before his face like a guiding candle.

The cart was almost empty when Barbara pressed a bottle of hair dye against the scanner.

"Must be worrisome sometimes to have a husband strong and strapping as Carl," Barbara said, loud enough so the bag boy heard. "My boy Ethan sees him over at Burrell's after work sometimes. Ethan says that girl who works the bar tries to flirt with Carl something awful. Of course Ethan says Carl never flirts back, just sits there by himself and drinks his one beer and leaves soon as his bottle's empty." Barbara finally set the hair dye on the conveyor. "Never pays that girl the least bit of mind," she added, and paused. "At least when Ethan's been in there."

Barbara rang up the total and placed Marcie's check in the register.

"You have a good afternoon," Barbara said.

On the way back home, Marcie remembered how after the wood had been cut and stacked she'd hired Carl to do other jobs—repairing the sagging porch, then building a small garage—things Arthur would have done if still alive. She'd peek out the window and watch him, admiring the way he worked with such a fixed attentiveness. He never seemed bored or distracted. He didn't bring a radio to help pass the time and he smoked only after a meal, hand-rolling his cigarette with the same meticulous patience as when he measured a cut or stacked a cord of firewood. She'd envied how comfortable he was in his solitude.

Their courtship had begun with cups of coffee, then offers and acceptances of home-cooked meals. Carl didn't reveal much about himself, but as the days and then weeks passed Marcie learned he'd grown up in Whiteville, in the far east of the state. A carpenter who'd gotten laid off when the housing market went bad, he'd heard there was more work in the mountains so had come west, all he cared to bring with him in the back of his pickup. When Marcie asked if he had children, Carl said he'd never been married.

"Never found a woman who would have me," he said. "Too shy, I reckon."

"Not for me," she told him, and smiled. "Too bad I'm nearly old enough to be your mother."

"You're not too old," he replied, in a matter-of-fact-way, his blue eyes looking at her as he spoke, not smiling.

She expected him to be a shy awkward lover, but he wasn't. The same attentiveness he showed in his work was in his kisses and touches, in the way he matched the rhythms of his movements to hers. It was as though his long silences made him better able to communicate in other ways. Nothing like Arthur, who'd been brief and concerned mainly with satisfying himself. Carl had lived in a run-down motel outside Sylva that rented by the hour or the week, but they never went there. They always made love in Marcie's bed. Sometimes he'd stay the whole night. At the grocery store and church there were asides and stares. Preacher Carter, who'd sent Carl to her in the first place, spoke to Marcie of "proper appearances." By then her daughters had found out as well. From three states away they spoke to Marcie of being humiliated, insisting they'd be too embarrassed to visit, as if their coming home was a common occurrence. Marcie quit going to church and went into town as little as possible. Carl finished his work on the garage but his reputation as a handyman was such that he had all the work he wanted, including an offer to join a construction crew working out of Sylva. Carl told the crew boss he preferred to work alone.

What people said to Carl about their relationship, she didn't know, but the night she brought it up he told her they should get married. No formal proposal or candlelight dinner at a restaurant, just a flat statement. But good enough for her. When Marcie told her daughters, they were, predictably, outraged. The younger one cried. Why couldn't she act her age, her older daughter asked, her voice scalding as a hot iron.

A justice of the peace married them and then they drove over the mountains to Gatlinburg for the weekend. Carl moved in what little he had and they began a life together. She thought that the more comfortable they became around each other the more they would talk, but that didn't happen. Evenings Carl sat by himself on the porch, or found some small chore to do, something best done alone. He didn't like to watch TV or rent movies. At supper he'd always say it was a good meal, and thank her for making it. She might tell him something about her day, and he'd listen politely, make a brief remark to show that though he said little at least he was listening. But at night as she readied herself for bed, he'd always come in. They'd lie down together and he'd turn to kiss her good night, always on the mouth. Three, four nights a week that kiss would linger and then quilts and sheets would be pulled back. Afterward, Marcie would not put her nightgown back on. Instead, she'd press her back into his chest and stomach, bend her knees, and fold herself inside him, his arms holding her close, his body's heat enclosing her.

Once back home, Marcie put up the groceries and placed a chuck roast on the stove to simmer. She did a load of laundry and swept off the front porch, her eyes glancing down the road for Carl's pickup. At six o'clock she turned on the news. There had been another fire set, no more than thirty minutes earlier. Fortunately, a hiker was close by and saw the smoke, even glimpsed a pickup through the trees. No tag number or make. All the hiker knew for sure was that the pickup was black.

Carl did not get home until almost seven. Marcie heard the truck coming up the road and began setting the table. Carl took off his boots on the porch and came inside, his face grimy with sweat, bits of sawdust in his hair and on his clothes. He nodded at her and went on into the bathroom. As he showered, Marcie went out to the pickup. In the truck bed was the chain saw, beside it plastic bottles of twenty-weight engine oil and the red five-gallon gasoline can. When she lifted the can, it was empty.

They ate in silence except for Carl's usual compliment on the meal. She watched him, waiting for a sign of something different in his demeanor, some glimpse of anxiety or satisfaction.

"There was another fire today," she finally said.

"I know," Carl answered, not looking up from his plate.

She didn't ask how he knew, when the truck in his radio didn't work. But he could have heard it at Burrell's as well.

"They say whoever set it drove a black pickup."

Carl looked at her then, his blue eyes clear and depthless.

"I know that too," he said.

After supper Carl sat on the porch while Marcie switched on the TV. She kept turning away from the movie she watched to look through the window. Carl sat in the wooden deck chair, only the back of his head and shoulders visible, less so as the minutes passed and his body merged with the gathering dusk. He stared toward the high mountains of the Smokies, and Marcie had no idea what, if anything, he was thinking about. He'd already smoked his cigarette, but she waited to see if he would take the lighter from his pocket, flick it, and stare at the flame a few moments. But he didn't. Not this night. When she cut off the TV and went to the back room, the deck chair scraped as Carl pushed himself out of it. Then the click of metal as he locked the door.

When he settled into bed beside her, Marcie continued to lie with her back to him. He moved closer, placed his hand between her head and pillow, and slowly, gently, turned her head so he could kiss her. As soon as his lips brushed hers, she turned away, moved so his body didn't touch hers. She fell asleep but woke a few hours later. Sometime in the night she had resettled in the bed's center, and Carl's arm now lay around her, his knees tucked behind her knees, his chest pressed against her back.

As she lay awake, Marcie remembered the day her younger daughter left for Cincinnati, joining her sister there. I guess it's just us now, Arthur had said glumly. She'd resented those words, as if Marcie were some grudgingly accepted consolation prize. She'd also resented how the words acknowledged that their daughters had always been closer to Arthur, even as children. In their teens, the girls had unleashed their rancor, the shouting and tears and grievances, on Marcie. The inevitable conflicts between mothers and daughters and Arthur's being the only male in the house—that was surely part of it, but Marcie also believed there'd been some difference in temperament as innate as different blood types.

Arthur had hoped that one day the novelty of city life would pale and they'd come back to North Carolina. But the girls stayed up north and married and began their own families. Their visits and phone calls became less and less frequent. Arthur was hurt by that, hurt deep, though never saying so. It seemed he aged more quickly, especially after he had a stent placed in an artery. After that Arthur did less around the farm, until finally he no longer grew tobacco or cabbage, just raised a few cattle. Then one day he didn't come back for lunch. She found him in the barn, slumped beside a stall, a hay hook in his hand.

The girls came home for the funeral and stayed three days. After they left, there was a month-long flurry of phone calls and visits and casseroles from people in the community and then days when the only vehicle that came was the mail truck. Marcie learned then what true loneliness was. Five miles from town on a dead-end dirt road, with not even the Floridians' houses in sight. She bought extra locks for the doors because at night she sometimes grew afraid, though what she feared was as much inside the house as outside it. Because she knew what was expected of her—to stay in this place, alone, waiting for the years, perhaps decades, to pass until she died.

It was mid-morning the following day when Sheriff Beasley came. Marcie met him on the porch. The sheriff had been a close friend of Arthur's, and as he got out of the patrol car he looked not at her but at the sagging barn and empty pasture, seeming to ignore the house's new garage and freshly shingled roof. He didn't take off his hat as he crossed the yard, or when he stepped onto the porch.

"I knew you'd sold some of Arthur's cows, but I didn't know it was all of them." The sheriff spoke as if it were intended only as an observation.

"Maybe I wouldn't have if there'd been some men to help me with them after Arthur died," Marcie said. "I couldn't do it by myself."

"I guess not," Sheriff Beasley replied, letting a few moments pass before he spoke again, his eyes on her now. "I need to speak to Carl. You know where he's working today?"

"Talk to him about what?" Marcie asked.

"Whoever's setting these fires drives a black pickup."

"There's lots of black pickups in this county."

"Yes there are," Sheriff Beasley said, "and I'm checking out everybody who drives one, checking out where they were yesterday around six o'clock as well. I figure that to narrow it some."

"You don't need to ask Carl," Marcie said. "He was here eating supper."

"At six o'clock?"

"Around six, but he was here by five thirty."

"How are you so sure of that?"

"The five-thirty news had just come on when he pulled up."

The sheriff said nothing.

"You need me to sign something I will," Marcie said.

"No, Marcie. That's not needed. I'm just checking off folks with black pickups. It's a long list."

"I bet you came here first, though, didn't you," Marcie said. "Because Carl's not from around here."

"I came here first, but I had cause," Sheriff Beasley said. "When you and Carl started getting involved, Preacher Carter asked me to check up on him, just to make sure he was on the up and up. Turns out that when Carl was fifteen he and another boy got arrested for burning some woods behind a ball field. They claimed it an accident, but the judge didn't buy that. They almost got sent to juvenile detention."

"There've been boys do that kind of thing around here."

"Yes, there have," the sheriff said. "And that was the only thing in Carl's file, not even a speeding ticket. Still, his being here last evening when it happened, that's a good thing for him."

Marcie waited for the sheriff to leave, but he lingered. He took out a soiled handkerchief and wiped his brow. Probably wanting a glass of iced tea, she suspected, but she wasn't going to offer him one. The sheriff put up his handkerchief and glanced at the sky.

"You'd think we'd at least get an afternoon thunderstorm."

"I've got things to do," she said, and reached for the screen door handle.

"Marcie," the sheriff said, his voice so soft that she turned. He raised his right hand, palm open as if to offer her something, then let it fall. "You're right. We should have done more for you after Arthur died. I regret that."

Marcie opened the screen door and went inside.

When Carl got home she said nothing about the sheriff's visit, and that night in bed when Carl turned and kissed her, Marcie met his lips and raised her hand to his cheek. She pressed her free hand against the small of his back, guiding his body as it shifted, settled over her. Afterward, she lay awake, feeling Carl's breath on the back of her neck, his arm cinched around her ribs and stomach. She listened for a first far-off rumble, but there was only the dry raspy sound of insects striking the window screen. Marcie had not been to church in months, had not prayed for even longer than that. But she did now. She shut her closed eyes tighter, trying to open a space inside herself that might offer up all of what she feared and hoped for, brought forth with such fervor it could not but help but be heard. She prayed for rain.

LINCOLNITES

Lily sat on the porch, the day's plowing done and her year-old child asleep in his crib. In her hands, the long steel needles clicked together and spread apart in a rhythmic sparring as yarn slowly unspooled from the deep pocket of her gingham dress, became part of the coverlet draped over her knees. Except for the occasional glance down the valley, Lily kept her eyes closed. She inhaled the aroma of fresh-turned earth and dogwood blossoms. She listened to the bees humming around the their box. Like the fluttering she'd begun to feel in her stomach, all bespoke the return of life after a hard winter. Lily thought again of the Washington newspaper Ethan had brought with him when he'd come back from Tennessee on his Christmas furlough, how it said the war would be over by summer. Ethan had thought even sooner, claiming soon as the roads were passable Grant would take Richmond and it would be done. Good as over now, he'd told her, but Ethan had still slept in the root cellar every night of the furlough and stayed inside during the day, his haversack and rifle by the back door, because Confederates came up the valley from Boone looking for Lincolnites like Ethan.

She felt the afternoon light on her face, soothing as the hum of the bees. It was good to finally be sitting, only her hands working, the child she'd set in the shade as she'd plowed now nursed and asleep. After a few more minutes, Lily allowed her hands to rest as well, laying the foot-long needles lengthways on her lap. Reason enough to be tired, she figured, a day breaking ground with a bull-tongue plow and draft horse. Soon enough the young one would wake and she'd have to suckle him again, then fix herself something to eat as well. After that she'd need to feed the chickens and hide the horse in the woods above the spring. Lily felt the flutter again deep in her belly and knew it was another reason for her tiredness. She laid a hand on her stomach and felt the slight curve. She counted the months since Ethan's furlough and figured she'd be rounding the homespun of her dress in another month.

Lily looked down the valley to where the old Boone toll road followed Middlefork Creek. Her eyes closed once more as she mulled over names for the coming child, thinking about how her own birthday was also in September and that by then Ethan would be home for good and they'd be a family again, the both of them young enough not to be broken by the hardships of the last two years. Lily made a picture in her mind of her and Ethan and the young ones all together, the crops she'd planted ripe and proud in the field, the apple tree's branches sagging with fruit.

When she opened her eyes, the Confederate was in the yard. He must have figured she'd be watching the road because he'd come down Goshen Mountain instead, emerging from a thick stand of birch trees he'd followed down the creek. It was too late to hide the horse and gather the chickens into the root cellar, too late to go get the butcher knife and conceal it in her dress pocket, so Lily just watched him approach, a musket in his right hand and a tote sack in the left. He wore a threadbare butternut jacket and a cap. A strip of cow hide held up a pair of ragged wool trousers. Only the boots looked new. Lily knew the man those boots had belonged to, and she knew the hickory tree where they'd left the rest of him dangling, not only a rope around his neck but also a cedar shingle with the word *Lincolnite* burned into the wood.

The Confederate grinned as he stepped into the yard. He raised a finger and thumb to the cap, but his eyes were on the chickens scratching for worms behind the barn, the draft horse in the pasture. He looked to be about forty, though in these times people often looked older than they were, even children. The Confederate wore his cap brim tilted high, his face tanned to the hue of cured tobacco. Not the way a farmer would wear a hat or cap. The gaunt face and loose- fitting trousers made clear what the tote sack was for. Lily hoped a couple of chickens were enough for him, but the boots did not reassure her of that.

"Afternoon," he said, finally letting his gaze settle on Lily briefly before looking westward toward Grandfather Mountain. "Looks to be some rain coming, maybe by full dark."

"Take what chickens you want," Lily said. "I'll help you catch them."

"I plan on that," he said.

The man raised his left forearm and wiped sweat off his brow, the tote sack briefly covering his face. As he lowered his arm, his grin had been replaced with a seeming sobriety.

"But it's also my sworn duty to requisition that draft horse for the cause."

"For the cause," Lily said, meeting his eyes, "like them boots you're wearing."

The Confederate set a boot onto the porch step as though to better examine it.

"These boots wasn't requisitioned. Traded my best piece of rope for them, but I'm of a mind you already know that." He raised his eyes and looked at Lily. "That neighbor of yours wasn't as careful on his furlough as your husband."

Lily studied the man's face, a familiarity behind the scraggly beard and the hard unflinching gaze. She thought back to the time a man or woman from up here could go into Boone. A time when disagreement over what politicians did down in Raleigh would be settled in this county with, at worst, clenched fists.

"You used to work at Old Man Mast's store, didn't you?" Lily said.

"I did," the Confederate said.

"My daddy used to trade with you. One time when I was with him you give me and my sister a peppermint."

The man's eyes didn't soften, but something in his face seemed to let go a little, just for a moment.

"Old Mast didn't like me doing that, but it was a small enough thing to do for the chaps."

For a few moments he didn't say anything else, maybe thinking back to that time, maybe not.

"Your name was Mr. Vaughn," Lily said. "I remember that now."

The Confederate nodded.

"It still is," he said, "my name being Vaughn, I mean." He paused. "But that don't change nothing in the here and now, though, does it?"

"No," Lily replied. "I guess it don't."

"So I'll be taking the horse," Vaughn said, "lest you got something to barter for it, maybe some of that Yankee money they pay your man with over in Tennessee? We might could make us a trade for some of that."

"There ain't no money here," Lily said, telling the truth because what money they had she'd sewn in Ethan's coat lining. Safer there than anywhere on the farm, she'd told Ethan before he left, but he'd agreed only after she'd also sewn his name and where to send his body on the coat's side pocket. Ethan's older brother had done the same, the two of them vowing to get the other's coat home if not the body.

"I guess I better get to it then," Vaughn said, "try to beat this rain back to Boone."

144

He turned from her, whistling "Dixie" as he walked toward the pasture, almost to the split-rail fence when Lily told him she had something to trade for the horse.

"What would that be?" Vaughn asked.

Lily lifted the ball of thread off her lap and placed it on the porch's puncheon floor, then set the half-finished coverlet on the floor as well. As she got up from the chair, her hands smoothed the gingham around her hips. Lily stepped to the porch edge and freed the braid so her blonde hair fell loose on her neck and shoulders.

"You know my meaning," she said.

Vaughn stepped onto the porch, not speaking as he did so. To look her over, Lily knew. She sucked in her stomach slightly to conceal her condition, though his knowing she was with child might make it better for him. A man could think that way in these times, she thought. Lily watched as Vaughn silently mulled over his choices, including the choice he'd surely come to by now that he could just as easily have her and the horse both.

"How old are you?" he asked.

"Nineteen."

"Nineteen," Vaughn said, though whether this was or wasn't in her favor she did not know. He looked west again toward Grandfather Mountain and studied the sky before glancing down the valley at the toll road.

Okay," he finally said, and nodded toward the front door. "Let's you and me go inside."

"Not in the cabin," Lily answered. "My young one's in there."

For a moment she thought Vaughn would insist, but he didn't.

"Where then?"

"The root cellar. It's got a pallet we can lay on."

Vaughn's chin lifted, his eyes seeming to focus on something behind Lily and the chair.

"I reckon we'll know where to look for your man next time, won't we?" When Lily didn't respond, Vaughn offered a smile that looked almost friendly. "Lead on," he said.

Vaughn followed her around the cabin, past the bee box and chopping block and the old root cellar, the one they'd used before the war. They followed the faintest path through a thicket of rhododendron until it ended abruptly on a hillside. Lily cleared away the green-leaved rhododendron branches she replaced each week and unlatched a square wooden door. The hinges creaked as the entrance yawned open, the root cellar's damp earthy odor mingling with the smell of the dogwood blossoms. The afternoon sun revealed an earthen floor lined with jars of vegetables and honey, at the center a pallet and quilt. There were no steps, just a three-foot drop.

"And you think me stupid enough to go in there first?" Vaughn said.

"I'll go in first," Lily answered, and sat down in the entrance, dangling one foot until it touched the packed earth. She held to the door frame and eased herself inside, crouching low, trying not to think how she might be stepping into her own grave. The corn shucks rasped beneath her as she settled on the pallet.

"We could do it as easy up here," Vaughn said, peering at her from the entrance. "It's good as some old spider hole."

"I ain't going to dirty myself rooting around on the ground," Lily said.

She thought he'd leave the musket outside, but instead Vaughn buckled his knees and leaned, set his left hand on a beam. As he shifted his body to enter, Lily took the metal needles from her dress pocket and laid them behind her.

Vaughn set his rifle against the earthen wall and hunched to take off his coat and unknot the strip of cowhide around his pants. The sunlight made his face appear dark and featureless as if in silhouette. As he moved closer, Lily shifted to the left side of the mattress to make room for him. Lily smelled tobacco on his breath as he pulled his shirt up to his chest and lay down on his back, fingers already fumbling to free his trouser buttons. His sunken belly was so white compared to his face and drab clothing it seemed to glow in the strained light. Lily took one of the needles into her hand. She thought of the hog she'd slaughtered last January, remembering how the liver wrapped itself around the stomach, like a saddle. Not so much difference in a hog's guts and a man's, she'd heard one time.

"Shuck off that dress or raise it," Vaughn said, his fingers on the last button. "I ain't got time to dawdle."

"All right," Lily said, hiking up her hem before kneeling beside him.

She reached behind and grasped the needle. When Vaughn placed his thumbs between cloth and hips to pull down his trousers, Lily raised her right arm and fell forward, her left palm set against the needle's rounded stem so the steel wouldn't slip through her fingers. She plunged the steel as deep as she could. When the needle stalled a moment on the backbone, Lily pushed harder and the needle point scraped past bone and went the rest of the way through. She felt the smooth skin of Vaughn's belly and flattened both palms over the needle's stem. Pin him to the floor if you can, she told herself, pushing out the air in Vaughn's stomach as the needle point pierced the root cellar's packed-dirt.

Vaughn's hands stayed on his trousers a moment longer, as though not yet registering what had happened. Lily scrambled to the entrance while Vaughn shifted his forearms and slowly raised his head. He stared at the needle's rounded stem that pressed into his flesh like a misplaced button. His legs pulled inward toward his hips, but he seemed unable to move his midsection, as if the needle had indeed pinned him to the floor. Lily took the rifle and set it outside, then pulled herself out of the hole as Vaughn loosed a long lowing moan.

She watched from above, waiting to see if she'd need to figure out how to use the musket. After almost a minute, Vaughn's mouth grimaced, the teeth locked together like a dog tearing meat. He pushed himself backward with his forearms until he was able to slump his head and shoulders against the dirt wall. Lily could hear his breaths and see the rise of his chest. His eyes moved, looking her way now. Lily did not know if Vaughn could actually see her. He raised his right hand a few inches off the root cellar's floor, palm upward as he stretched his arm toward the entrance, as if to catch what light leaked in from the world. Lily closed and latched the cellar door, covered the entrance with the rhododendron branches before walking back to the cabin.

The child was awake and fretting. Lily went to the crib but before taking up the boy she pulled back the bedding and removed the butcher knife, placed it in her dress pocket. She nursed the child and then fixed herself a supper of cornbread and beans. As Lily ate, she wondered if the Confederate had told anyone in Boone where he was headed. Maybe, but probably he wouldn't have said which particular farm, wouldn't have known himself which one until he found something to take. Ponder something else, she told herself, and thought again of names for the coming child. Girl names, because Granny Triplett had already rubbed Lily's belly and told her this one would be a girl. Lily said those she'd considered out loud and again settled on Mary, because it would the one to match her boy's name.

After she'd cleared the table and changed the child's swaddlings, Lily set him in the crib and went outside, scattering shell corn for the chickens before walking back through the rhododendron to the root cellar. There was less light now, and when she peered though the slats in the wood door she could see just enough to make out Vaughn's body slumped against the earthen wall. Lily watched several minutes for any sign of movement, listened for a moan, a sigh, the exhalation of a breath. Only then did she slowly unlatch the door. Lily opened it a few inches at a time until she could see clearly. Vaughn's chin rested on his chest, his legs splayed out before him. The needle was still in his stomach, every bit as deep as before. His face was white as his belly now, bleached looking. She quietly closed the door and latched it softly, as if a noise might startle Vaughn back to life. Lily gathered the rhododendron branches and concealed the entrance.

She sat on the porch with the child and watched the dark settle in the valley. A last barn swallow swept low across the pasture and into the barn as the first drops of rain began to fall, soft and hesitant at first, then less so. Lily went inside, taking the coverlet and yarn with her. She lit the lamp and nursed the child a last time and put him back in the crib. The supper fire still smoldered in the hearth, giving some warmth against the evening's chill. It was the time of evening when she'd usually knit some more, but since she couldn't do that tonight Lily took the newspaper from under the mattress and sat down at the table. She read the article again about the war being over by summer, stumbling over a few words that she didn't know. When she came to the word *Abraham,* she glanced over at the crib. Not too long before I can call him by his name to anyone, Lily told herself.

After a while longer, she hid the newspaper again and lay down in the bed. The rain was steady now on the cabin's cedar shingles. The young one breathed steadily in the crib beside the bed. Rain hard, she thought, thinking of what she'd be planting first when daylight came. Bad as it was that it had happened in the first place, there'd been some luck in it too. At least it wasn't winter when the ground was hard as granite. She could get it done by noon, especially after a soaking rain, then rest a while doing her inside chores, maybe even have time to plant some tomato and squash before supper.

From *Nothing Gold Can Stay* (2013)

THE TRUSTY

They had been moving up the road a week without seeing another farmhouse, and the nearest well, at least the nearest the owner would let Sinkler use, was half a mile back. What had been a trusty sluff job was now as onerous as swinging a Kaiser blade or shoveling out ditches. As soon as he'd hauled the buckets back to the cage truck it was time to go again. He asked Vickery if someone could spell him and the bull guard smiled and said that Sinkler could always strap on a pair of leg irons and grab a handle. "Bolick just killed a rattlesnake in them weeds yonder," the bull guard said. "I bet he'd square a trade with you." When Sinkler asked if come morning he could walk ahead to search for another well, Vickery's lips tightened, but he nodded.

The next day, Sinkler took the metal buckets and walked until he found a farmhouse. It was no closer than the other, even a bit farther, but worth padding the hoof a few extra steps. The well he'd been using belonged to a hunchbacked widow. The woman who appeared in this doorway wore her hair in a similar tight bun and draped herself in the same sort of flour-cloth dress, but she looked to be in her mid-twenties, like Sinkler. Two weeks would pass before they got beyond this farmhouse, perhaps another two weeks before the next well. Plenty of time to quench a different kind of thirst. As he entered the yard, the woman looked past the barn to a field where a man and his draft horse were plowing. The woman gave a brisk whistle and the farmer paused and looked their way. Sinkler stopped beside the well but did not set the buckets down.

"What you want," the woman said, not so much a question as a demand.

"Water," Sinkler answered. "We've got a chain gang working on the road."

"I'd have reckoned you to bring water with you."

"Not enough for ten men all day."

The woman looked out at the field again. Her husband watched but did not unloop the rein from around his neck. The woman stepped onto the six nailed-together planks that looked more like a raft than a porch. Firewood was stacked on one side, and closer to the door an axe leaned between a shovel and a hoe. She let her eyes settle on the axe long enough to make sure he noticed it. Sinkler saw now that she was younger than he'd thought, maybe eighteen, at most twenty, more girl than woman.

"How come you not to have chains on you?"

"I'm a trusty," Sinkler said smiling. "A prisoner, but one that can be trusted."

"And all you want is water?"

Sinkler thought of several possible answers.

"That's what they sent me for."

"I don't reckon there to be any money in it for us?" the girl asked.

"No, just gratitude from a bunch of thirsty men, and especially me for not having to haul it so far."

"I'll have to ask my man," she said. "Stay here in the yard."

For a moment he thought she might take the axe with her. As she walked into the field, Sinkler studied the house, which was no bigger than a fishing shack. The dwelling appeared to have been built in the previous century. The door opened with a latch, not a knob, and no glass filled the window frames. Sinkler stepped closer to the entrance and saw two ladder-back chairs and a small table set on a puncheon floor. Sinkler wondered if these apple-knockers had heard they were supposed to be getting a new deal.

"You can use the well," the girl said when she returned, "but he said you need to forget one of them pails here next time you come asking for water."

Worth it, he figured, even if Vickery took the money out of Sinkler's own pocket, especially with no sign up ahead of another farmhouse. It would be a half-dollar at most, easily made up with one slick deal in a poker game. He nodded and went to the well, sent the rusty bucket down into the dark. The girl went up on the porch but didn't go inside.

"What you in prison for?"

"Thinking a bank manager wouldn't notice his teller slipping a few bills in his pocket."

"Whereabouts?"

"Raleigh."

"I ain't never been past Asheville," the girl said. "How long you in for?"

"Five years. I've done sixteen months."

Sinkler raised the bucket, water leaking from the bottom as he transferred its contents. The girl stayed on the porch, making sure that all he took was water.

"You lived here long?"

"Me and Chet been here a year," the girl said. "I grew up across the ridge yonder."

"You two live alone, do you?"

"We do," the girl said, "but there's a rifle just inside the door and I know how to bead it."

"I'm sure you do," Sinkler said. "You mind telling me your name, just so I'll know what to call you?"

"Lucy Sorrels."

He waited to see if she'd ask his.

"Mine's Sinkler," he said when she didn't.

He filled the second bucket but made no move to leave, instead looking around at the trees and mountains as if just noticing them. Then he smiled and gave a slight nod.

"Must get lonely being out so far from everything," Sinkler said. "At least, I would think so."

"And I'd think them men to be getting thirsty," Lucy Sorrels said.

"Probably," he agreed, surprised at her smarts in turning his words back on him. "But I'll return soon to brighten your day."

"When you planning to leave one of them pails?" she asked.

"Last trip before quitting time"

She nodded and went into the shack.

"The rope broke," he told Vickery as the prisoners piled into the truck at quitting time.

The guard looked not so much skeptical as aggrieved that Sinkler thought him fool enough to believe it. Vickery answered that if Sinkler thought he'd lightened his load he was mistaken. It'd be easy enough to find another bucket, maybe one that could hold an extra gallon. Sinkler shrugged and lifted himself into the cage truck, found a place on the metal bench among the sweating convicts. He'd won over the other guards with cigarettes and small loans, that and his mush talk, but not Vickery, who'd argued that making Sinkler a trusty would only give him a head start when he tried to escape.

The bull guard was right about that. Sinkler had more than fifty dollars in poker winnings now, plenty enough cash to get him across the Mississippi and finally shed himself of the whole damn region. He'd grown up in Montgomery, but when the law got too interested in his comings and goings he'd gone north to Knoxville and then west to Memphis before recrossing Tennessee on his way to Raleigh. Sinkler's talents had led him to establishments where his sleight of hand needed no deck of cards. With a decent suit, clean fingernails, and buffed shoes, he'd walk into a business and be greeted as a solid citizen. Tell a story about being in town because of an ailing mother and you were the cat's pajamas. They'd take the Help Wanted sign out of the window and pretty much replace it with Help Yourself. Sinkler remembered the afternoon in Memphis when he had stood by the river after grifting a clothing store of forty dollars in two months. Keep heading west or turn back east—that was the choice. He'd flipped a silver dollar to decide, a rare moment when he'd trusted his life purely to luck.

This time he'd cross the river, start in Kansas City or St. Louis. He'd work the stores and cafés and newsstands and anywhere else with a till or a cash register. Except for a bank. Crooked as bankers were, Sinkler should have realized how quickly they'd recognize him as one of their own. No, he'd not make that mistake again.

That night, when the stockade lights were snuffed, he lay in his bunk and thought about Lucy Sorrels. A year and a half had passed since he'd been with a woman. After that long, almost any female would make the sap rise. There was nothing about her face to hold a man's attention, but curves tightened the right parts of her dress. Nice legs, too. Each trip to the well that day, he had tried to make small talk. She had given him the icy mitts, but he had weeks yet to warm her up. It was only on the last haul that the husband had come in from his field. He'd barely responded to Sinkler's "how do you do's" and "much obliged's." He looked to be around forty and Sinkler suspected that part of his terseness was due to a younger man being around his wife. After a few moments, the farmer had nodded at the pail in Sinkler's left hand. "You'll be leaving that, right?" When Sinkler said yes, the husband told Lucy to switch it with the leaky well bucket, then walked into the barn.

Two days passed before Lucy asked if he'd ever thought of trying to escape.

"Of course," Sinkler answered. "Have you?"

She looked at him in a way that he could not read.

"How come you ain't done it, then? They let you roam near anywhere you want, and you ain't got shackles."

"Maybe I enjoy the free room and board," Sinkler answered. He turned a thumb toward his stripes. "Nice duds too. They even let you change them out every Sunday."

"I don't think I could stand it," Lucy said. "Being locked up so long and knowing I still had nigh on four years."

He checked her lips for the slightest upward curve of a smile, but it wasn't there.

"Yeah," Sinkler said, taking a step closer. "You don't seem the sort to stand being locked up. I'd think a young gal pretty as you would want to see more of the world."

"How come you ain't done it?" she asked again, and brushed some loose wisps of hair behind her ear.

"Maybe the same reason as you," Sinkler said. "It's not like you can get whisked away from here. I haven't seen more than a couple of cars and trucks on this road, and those driving them know there's prisoners about. They wouldn't be fool enough to pick up a stranger. Haven't seen a lot of train tracks either."

"Anybody ever try?" Lucy asked.

"Yeah, two weeks ago. Fellow ran that morning and the bloodhounds had him grabbing sky by dark. All he got for his trouble was a bunch of tick bites and briar scratches. That and another year added to his sentence."

For the first time since she'd gone to fetch her husband, Lucy stepped off the porch and put some distance between her and the door. The rifle and axe too, which meant that she was starting to trust him at least a little. She stood in the yard and looked up at an eave, where black insects hovered around clots of dried mud.

"Them dirt daubers is a nuisance," Lucy said. "I knock their nests down and they build them back the next day."

"I'd guess them to be about the only thing that wants to stay around here, don't you think?"

"You've got a saucy way of talking," she said.

"You don't seem to mind it too much," Sinkler answered, and nodded toward the field. "An older fellow like that usually keeps a close eye on a pretty young wife, but he must be the trusting sort, or is it he just figures he's got you corralled in?"

He lifted the full buckets and stepped close enough to the barn not to be seen from the field. "You don't have to stand so far from me, Lucy Sorrels. I don't bite."

She didn't move toward him but she didn't go back to the porch, either.

"If you was to escape, where would you go?"

"Might depend on who was going with me," Sinkler answered. "What kind of place would you like to visit?"

"Like you'd just up and take me along. I'd likely believe that about as much as them daubers flying me out of here."

"No, I'd need to get to know my travelling partner better," Sinkler said. "Make sure she really cared about me. That way she wouldn't take a notion to turn me in."

"You mean for the reward money?"

Sinkler laughed.

"You've got to be a high cloud to have a reward put on you, darling. They'd not even bother to put my mug in a post office, which is fine by me. Buy my train ticket and I'd be across the Mississippi in two days. Matter of fact, I've got money enough saved to buy two tickets."

"Enough for two tickets?" she asked.

"I do indeed."

Lucy looked at her bare feet, placed one atop the other as a shy child might. She set both feet back on the ground and looked up.

"Why come you to think a person would turn you in if there ain't no reward?"

"Bad conscience—which is why I've got to be sure my companion doesn't have one." Sinkler smiled. "Like I said, you don't have to stand so far away. We could even step into the barn for a few minutes."

Lucy looked toward the field and let her gaze linger long enough that he thought she just might do it.

"I have chores to get done," she said and went into the shack.

Sinkler headed back down the road, thinking things out. By the time he set the sloshing buckets beside the prison truck, he'd figured a way to get Lucy Sorrels' dress raised with more than just sweet talk. He'd tell her there was an extra set of truck keys in a guard's front desk he could steal. Once the guards were distracted, he'd jump in the truck, pick her up, head straight to Asheville, and catch the first train out. It was a damn good story, one Sinkler himself might have believed if he didn't know that all the extra truck keys were locked inside a thousand-pound Mosler safe.

When he entered the yard the next morning, Lucy came to the well but stayed on the opposite side. Like a skittish dog, Sinkler thought, and imagined holding out a pack of gum or a candy bar to bring her the rest of the way. She wore the same dress as always, but her hair was unpinned and fell across her shoulders. It was blonder and curlier than he'd supposed. Set free for him, Sinkler knew. A cool, steady breeze gave the air an early-autumn feel and helped round the curves beneath the muslin.

"Your hair being down like that—it looks good," he said. "I bet that's the way you wear it in bed."

She didn't blush. Sinkler worked the crank and the well bucket descended into the earth. Once both his buckets were filled, he laid out his plan.

"You don't much cotton to my idea?" he asked when she didn't respond. "I bet you're thinking we'd have to get past them guards with shotguns but we won't. I'll wait until the chain gang's working up above here. Do it like that and we'll have clear sailing all the way down to Asheville."

"There's an easier way," Lucy said quietly, "one where you don't need the truck, nor even a road."

"I never figured you to be the know-all on prison escapes."

"There's a trail on the yon side of that ridge," Lucy said, nodding past the field. "You can follow it all the way to Asheville."

"Asheville's at least thirty miles from here."

"That's by the road. It's no more than eight if you cut through the gap. You just got to know the right trails."

"Which I don't."

"I do," she said. "I've done it in three hours easy."

For a few moments, Sinkler didn't say anything. It was as though the key he'd been imagining had suddenly appeared in his hand. He left the buckets where they were and stepped closer to the barn. When he gestured Lucy closer, she came. He settled an arm around her waist and felt her yield to him. Her lips opened to his and she did not resist when his free hand cupped a breast. To touch a woman after so long made him feather-legged. A bead of sweat trickled down his brow as she pressed her body closer and settled a hand on his thigh. Only when Sinkler tried to lead her into the barn did Lucy resist.

"He can't see us from down there."

"It ain't just that," Lucy said. "My bleed time's started."

Sinkler felt so rabbity that he told her he didn't care.

"There'd be a mess and he'd know the why of it."

He felt frustration simmer into anger. Sinkler tried to step away but Lucy pulled him back, pressed her face into his chest.

"If we was far away it wouldn't matter. I hate it here. He cusses me near every day and won't let me go nowhere. When he's drunk, he fetches his rifle and swears he's going to shoot me."

"It's all right," Sinkler said, and patted her shoulder.

She let go of him slowly. The only sound was a clucking chicken and the breeze tinking the well bucket against the narrow stone wellhead.

"All you and me have to do is get on that train in Asheville," Lucy said, "and not him nor the law can catch us. I know where he keeps his money. I'll get it if you ain't got enough."

He met her eyes, then looked past her. The sun was higher now, angled in over the mountaintops, and the new well bucket winked silver as it swayed. Sinkler lifted his gaze to the cloudless sky. It would be another hot, dry, miserable day and he'd be out in it. At quitting time, he'd go back and wash up with water dingy enough to clog a strainer, eat what would gag a hog, then at nine o'clock set his head on a grimy pillow. Three and a half more years. Sinkler studied the ridgeline, found the gap that would lead to Asheville.

"I've got money," he told Lucy. "It's the getting to where I can spend it that's been the problem."

That night as he lay in his bunk, Sinkler pondered the plan. An hour would pass before anyone started looking for him, and even then they'd search first along the road. As far out as the prisoners were working, it'd take at least four hours to get the bloodhounds on his trail, and by the time the dogs tracked him to Asheville he'd be on a train. It could be months, or never, until such a chance came again. But the suddenness of the opportunity unsettled him. He should take a couple of days, think it out. The grit in the gears would be Lucy. Giving her the slip in Asheville would be nigh impossible, so he'd be with her until the next stop, probably Knoxville or Raleigh. Which could be all for the better. A hotel room and a bottle of bootleg whiskey and they'd have them a high old time. He could sneak out early morning while she slept. If she took what her husband had hidden, she'd have enough for a new start, and another reason not to drop a dime and phone the police.

Of course, many a convict would simply wait until trail's end, then let a good-sized rock take care of it, lift what money she had, and be on his way. Travelling with a girl that young was a risk. She might say or do something to make a bluecoat suspicious. Or, waking up to find him gone, put the law on him just for spite.

The next morning, the men loaded up and drove to where they'd quit the day before. They weren't far from the farmhouse now, only a few hundred yards. As he carried the buckets up the road, Sinkler realized that if Lucy knew the trail, then the husband did too. The guards would see the farmer in the field and tell him who they were looking for. How long after that would he find out that she was gone? It might be just minutes before the husband went to check. But only if the guards were looking in that direction. When the time came, he'd tell Vickery this well was low and the farmer wouldn't let him use it anymore, so he had to go back down the road to the widow's. He could walk in that direction and then cut into the woods and circle back.

Sinkler was already drawing water when Lucy came out. Primping for him, he knew, her hair unpinned and freshly combed, curtaining a necklace with a heart-shaped locket. She smelled good too, bright and clean smell like honeysuckle. In the distance, the husband was strapped to his horse, the tandem trudging endlessly across the field. From what Sinkler had seen, the man worked as hard as the road crews and had about as much to show for it. Twenty years older and too much of a gink to realize what Lucy understood at eighteen. Sinkler stepped closer to the barn and she raised her mouth to his, found his tongue with her tongue.

"I been thirsting for that all last night and this morning," Lucy said when she broke off the kiss. "That's what it's like—a thirsting. Chet ain't never been able to staunch it, but you can."

She laid her head against his chest and held him tight. Feeling the desperation of her embrace, Sinkler knew that she'd risk her life to help him get away, help them get away. But a girl her age could turn quick as a weathervane. He set his hands on her shoulders and gently but firmly pushed her back enough to meet her eyes.

"You ain't just playing some make-believe with me, because if you are it's time to quit."

"I'll leave this second if you got need to," Lucy said. "I'll go get his money right now. I counted it this morning when he left. It's near seven dollars. That's enough, ain't it, at least to get us tickets?"

"You've never rode a train, have you?" Sinkler asked.

"No."

"It costs more than that."

"How much more?"

"Closer to five each," Sinkler said, "just to get to Knoxville or Raleigh."

She touched the locket.

"This is a pass-me-down from my momma. It's pure silver and we could sell it."

Sinkler slipped a hand under the locket, inspected it with the feigned attentiveness of a jeweler.

"And all this time I thought you had a heart of gold, Lucy Sorrels," Sinkler said and smiled as he let the locket slide off his palm. "No, darling. You keep it around your pretty neck. I got plenty for tickets, and maybe something extra for a shiny bracelet to go with that necklace."

"Then I want to go tomorrow," Lucy said, and moved closer to him. "My bleed time is near over."

Sinkler smelled the honeysuckle and desire swamped him. He tried to clear his mind and come up with reasons to delay but none came.

"We'll leave in the morning," Sinkler said.

"All right," she said, touching him a moment longer before removing her hand.

"We'll have to travel light."

"I don't mind that," Lucy said. "It ain't like I got piddling anyway."

"Can you get me one of his shirts and some pants?"

Lucy nodded.

"Don't pack any of it until tomorrow morning when he's in the field," Sinkler said.

"Where are we going?" she asked. "I mean, for good?"

"Where do you want to go?"

"I was notioning California. They say it's like paradise out there."

"That'll do me just fine," Sinkler said, then grinned. "That's just where an angel like you belongs."

The next morning, he told Vickery that the Sorrelses' well was going dry and he'd have to backtrack to the other one. "That'll be almost a mile jaunt for you," Vickery said, and shook his head in mock sympathy. Sinkler walked until he was out of sight. He found himself a marker, a big oak with a trunk cracked by lightning, then stepped over the ditch and entered the woods. He set the buckets by a rotting stump, close enough to the oak tree to be easily found if something went wrong. Because Sinkler knew that, when it came time to lay down or fold, Lucy might still think twice about trusting someone she'd hardly known two weeks, and a convict at that. Or the husband might notice a little thing like Lucy not gathering eggs or not putting a kettle on for supper, things Sinkler should have warned her to do.

Sinkler stayed close to the road, and soon heard the clink of leg chains and the rasp of shovels gathering dirt. Glimpses of black-and-white caught his eye as he made his way past. The sounds of the chain gang faded, and not long after that the trees thinned, the barn's gray planking filling the gaps. Sinkler did not enter the yard. Lucy stood just inside the farmhouse door. He studied the shack for any hint that the farmer had found out. But all was as it had been, clothing pinned on the wire between two trees, cracked corn spilled on the ground for the chickens, the axe still on the porch beside the hoe. He angled around the barn until he could see the field. The farmer was there, hitched to the horse and plow. Sinkler called her name and Lucy stepped out on the porch. She wore the same muslin dress and carried a knotted bedsheet in her hand. When she got to the woods, Lucy opened the bedsheet and removed a shirt and what was little more than two flaps of tied leather.

"Go over by the well and put these brogans on," Lucy said. "It's a way to fool them hounds."

"We need to get going," Sinkler said.

"It'll just take a minute."

He did what she asked, checking the field to make sure that the farmer wasn't looking in their direction.

"Keep your shoes in your hand," Lucy said, and walked toward Sinkler with the shirt.

When she was close, Lucy got on her knees and rubbed the shirt cloth over the ground, all the way to his feet. Smart of her, Sinkler had to admit, though it was an apple-knocker kind of smart.

"Walk over to the other side of the barn," she told him, scrubbing the ground as she followed.

She motioned him to stay put and retrieved the bedsheet.

"This way," she said, and led him down the slanted ground and into the woods.

"You expect me to wear these all the way to Asheville?" Sinkler said after the flapping leather almost tripped him.

"No, just up to the ridge."

They stayed in the woods and along the field's far edge and then climbed the ridge. At the top Sinkler took off the brogans and looked back through the trees and saw the square of plowed soil, now no bigger than a barn door. The farmer was still there.

Lucy untied the bedsheet and handed him the pants and shirt. He took off his stripes and hid them behind a tree. Briefly, Sinkler thought about taking a little longer before he dressed, suggesting to Lucy that the bedsheet might have another use. Just a few more hours, he reminded himself, you'll be safe for sure and rolling with her in a big soft bed. The chambray shirt wasn't a bad fit, but the denim pants hung loose on his hips. Every few steps, Sinkler had to hitch them back up. The bedsheet held nothing more and Lucy stuffed it in a rock crevice.

"You bring that money?" he asked.

"You claimed us not to need it," Lucy said, a harshness in her voice he'd not heard before. "You weren't trifling with me about having money for the train tickets, were you?"

"No, darling, and plenty enough to buy you that bracelet and a real dress instead of that flour sack you got on. Stick with me and you'll ride the cushions."

They moved down the ridge through a thicket of rhododendron, the ground so aslant that in a couple of places he'd have tumbled if he hadn't watched how Lucy did it, front foot sideways and leaning backward. At the bottom, the trail forked. Lucy nodded to the left. The land continued downhill, then curved and leveled out. After a while, the path snaked into the undergrowth and Sinkler knew that without Lucy he'd be completely lost. You're doing as much for her as she for you, he reminded himself, and thought again about what another convict might do, what he'd known all along he couldn't do. When others had brought a derringer or Arkansas toothpick to card games, Sinkler arrived empty-handed, because either one could take its owner straight to the morgue or to prison. He'd always made a show of slapping his pockets and opening his coat at such gatherings. "I'll not hurt anything but a fellow's wallet," he'd say. Men had been killed twice in his presence, but he'd never had a weapon aimed in his direction.

Near another ridge, they crossed a creek that was little more than a spring seep. They followed the ridge awhile and then the trail widened and they moved back downhill and up again. Each rise and fall of the land looked like what had come before. The mountain air was thin and if Sinkler hadn't been hauling water such distances he wouldn't have had the spunk to keep going. They went on, the trees shading them from the sun, but even so he grew thirsty and kept hoping they'd come to a stream he could drink from. Finally, they came to another spring seep.

"I've got to have some water," he said.

Sinkler kneeled beside the creek. The water was so shallow that he had to lean over and steady himself with one hand, cupping the other to get a dozen leaky palmfuls in his mouth. He stood and brushed the damp sand off his hand and his knees. The woods were completely silent, no murmur of wind, not a bird singing.

"You want any?" he asked, but Lucy shook her head.

The trees shut out much of the sky, but he could tell that the sun was starting to slip behind the mountains. Fewer dapples of light were on the forest floor, more shadows. Soon the prisoners would be heading back, one man fewer. Come suppertime, the ginks would be spooning beans off a tin plate while Sinkler sat in a dining car eating steak with silverware. By then, the warden would have chewed out Vickery's skinny ass but good, maybe even fired him. The other guards, the ones he'd duped even more, would be explaining why they'd recommended making Sinkler a trusty in the first place.

When the trail narrowed again, a branch snagged Lucy's sleeve and ripped the frayed muslin. She surprised him with her profanity as she examined the torn cloth.

"I'd not think a sweet little gal like you to know words like that."

She glared at him and Sinkler raised his hands, palms out.

"Just teasing you a bit, darling. You should have brought another dress. I know I told you to pack light, but light didn't mean bring nothing."

"Maybe I ain't got another dress," Lucy said.

"But you will, and soon, and like I said it'll be a spiffy one."

"If I do," Lucy said, "I'll use this piece of shit for nothing but scrub rags."

She let go of the cloth. The branch had scratched her neck and she touched it with her finger, confirmed that it wasn't bleeding. Had the locket been around her neck, the chain might have snapped, but it was in her pocket. Or so he assumed. If she'd forgotten it in the haste of packing, now didn't seem the time to bring it up.

As they continued their descent, Sinkler thought again about what would happen once they were safely free. He was starting to see a roughness about Lucy that her youth and country ways had masked. Perhaps he could take her with him beyond their first stop. He'd worked with a whore in Knoxville once, let her go in and distract a clerk while he took whatever they could fence. The whore hadn't been as young and innocent-seeming as Lucy. Even Lucy's plainness would be an advantage—harder to describe her to the law. Maybe tonight in the hotel room she'd show him more reason to let her tag along awhile.

The trail curved and then went uphill. Surely for the last time, he figured, and told himself he'd be damn glad to be back in a place where a man didn't have to be half goat to get somewhere. Sinkler searched through the branches and leaves for a brick smokestack, the glint of a train rail. They were both breathing harder now, and even Lucy looked tuckered.

Up ahead, another seep crossed the path and Sinkler paused.

"I'm going to sip me some more water."

"Ain't no need," Lucy said. "We're almost there."

He heard it then, the rasping plunge of metal into dirt. The rhododendron was too thick to see through. Whatever it was, it meant they were indeed near civilization.

"I guess we are," he said, but Lucy had already gone ahead.

As Sinkler hitched the sagging pants up yet again, he decided that the first thing he'd do after buying the tickets was find a clothing store or gooseberry a clothesline. He didn't want to look like a damn hobo. Even in town, they might have to walk a ways for water, so Sinkler kneeled. Someone whistled near the ridge and the rasping stopped. As he pressed his palm into the sand, he saw that a handprint was already there beside it, his handprint. Sinkler studied it awhile, then slowly rocked back until his buttocks touched his shoe heels. He stared at the two star-shaped indentations, water slowly filling the new one.

No one would hear the shot, he knew. And, in a few weeks, when autumn came and the trees started to shed, the upturned earth would be completely obscured. Leaves rustled as someone approached. The footsteps paused, and Sinkler heard the soft click of a rifle's safety being released. The leaves rustled again but he was too worn out to run. They would want the clothes as well as the money, he told himself, and there was no reason to prolong any of it. His trembling fingers clasped the shirt's top button, pushed it through the slit in the chambray.

WHERE THE MAP ENDS

They had been on the run for six days, traveling mainly at night, all the while listening for the baying of hounds. The man, if asked his age, would have said forty-eight, forty-nine or fifty, he wasn't sure. His hair was close-cropped, like gray wool stitched above a face dark as mahogany. A lantern swayed by his side, the twine securing it chafing the bullwhip scar ridging his left shoulder. With his right hand he clutched a tote sack. His companion was seventeen and of a lighter complexion, the color of an oft-used gold coin. The youth's hair was close cropped as well, the curls tinged red. He carried the map.

As foothills became mountains, the journey became more arduous. What food they'd brought had been eaten days earlier. They filled the tote with corn and okra from fields, eggs from a henhouse, apples from orchards. The land steepened more and their lungs never seemed to fill. I heard that white folks up here don't have much, the youth huffed, but you'd think they'd at least have air. The map showed one more village, Blowing Rock, then a ways farther a stream and soon a plank bridge. An arrow pointed over the bridge. Beyond that, nothing but blank paper, as though no word or mark could convey what the fugitives sought but had never known.

They had crossed the bridge near dusk. At the first cabin they came to, a hound bayed as they approached. They went on. The youth wondered aloud how they were supposed to know which place, which family, to trust. The fugitives passed a two-story farmhouse, prosperous looking. The older man said walk on. As the day waned, a cabin and a barn appeared, light glowing from a front window. Their lantern remained unlit, though now neither of them could see where he stepped. They passed a small orchard and soon after the man tugged his companion's arm and led him off the road and into a pasture.

"Where we going, Viticus?" the youth asked.

"To roost in that barn till morning," the man answered. "No folks want strangers calling in the dark."

They entered the barn, let their hands find the ladder and then climbed into the loft. Through a space between boards the fugitives could see the cabin window's glow.

"I'm hungry," the youth complained. "Gimme that lantern and I'll get us some apples."

"No," his companion said. "You think a man going to help them that stole from him."

"Ain't gonna miss a few apples."

The man ignored him. They settled their bodies into the straw and slept.

A cowbell woke them, the animal ambling into the barn, a man in frayed overalls following with a gallon pail. A scraggly gray beard covered much of his face, some streaks of brown in his lank hair. He was thin and tall, and his neck and back bowed forward as if from years of ducking. As the farmer set his stool beside the cow's flank, a gray cat appeared and positioned itself close by. Milk spurts hissed against the tin. The fugitives peered through the board gaps. The youth's stomach growled audibly. I ain't trying to, he whispered in response to his companion's nudge. When the bucket was filled, the farmer aimed a teat at the cat. The creature's tongue lapped without pause as the milk splashed on its face. As the farmer lifted the pail and stood, the youth shifted to better see. Bits of straw slipped through a board gap and drifted down. The farmer did not look up but his shoulders tensed and his free hand clenched the pail tighter. He quickly left the barn.

"You done it now," the man said.

"He gonna have to see us sometime," the youth replied.

"But now it'll be with a gun aimed our direction," Viticus hissed. "Get your sorry self down that ladder."

They climbed down and saw what they'd missed earlier.

"Don't like the look of that none," the youth said, nodding at the rope dangling from a loft beam.

"Then get out front of this barn," his companion said. "I want that white man looking at empty hands."

Once outside, they could see the farm clearly. Crop rows were weed choked, the orchard unpruned, the cabin itself shabby and small, two rooms at most. They watched the farmer go inside.

"How you know he got a gun when he hardly got a roof over his head?" the youth asked. "The Colonel wouldn't put hogs in such as that."

"He got a gun," the man replied, and set the lantern on the ground with the burlap tote.

A crow cawed as it passed overhead, then settled in the cornfield.

"Don't seem mindful of his crop," the youth said.

"No, he don't," the man said, more to himself than his companion.

The youth went to the barn corner and peeked toward the cabin. The farmer came out of the cabin, a flintlock in his right hand.

"He do have a gun and it already cocked," the youth said. "Hellfire, Viticus, we gotta light out of here."

"Light out where?" his companion answered. "We past where that map can take us."

"Shouldn't never have high tailed off," the youth fretted. "I known better but done it. We go back, I won't be tending that stable no more. No suh, the Colonel will send me out with the rest of you field hands."

"This white man's done nothing yet," the man said softly. "Just keep your hands out so he see the pink."

But the youth turned and ran into the cornfield. Shaking tassels marked his progress. He didn't stop until he was in the field's center. The older fugitive grimaced and stepped farther away from the barn mouth.

The farmer entered the pasture, the flintlock crooked in his arm. Any indication of his humor lay hidden beneath the beard. The older fugitive did not raise his hands, but he turned his palms outward.

The white man approached from the west. The sunrise made his eyes squint.

"I ain't stole nothing, mister," the black man said when the farmer stopped a few yards in front of him.

"That's kindly of you," the farmer replied.

The dawn's slanted brightness made the white man raise a hand to his brow.

"Move back into that barn so I can feature you better."

The black man glanced at the rope.

"Pay that rope no mind," the farmer said. "It ain't me put it up. That was my wife's doing."

The fugitive kept stepping back until both of them stood inside the barn. The cat reappeared, sat on its haunches watching the two men.

"Where might you hail from?" the farmer asked.

The black man's face assumed a guarded blankness.

"I ain't sending you back yonder if that's your fearing," the farmer said. "I've never had any truck with them that would. That's why you're up here, ain't it, knowing that we don't?"

The black man nodded.

"So where you run off from?"

"Down in Wake County, Colonel Barkley's home place."

"Got himself a big house with fancy rugs and what not, I reckon," the farmer said, "and plenty more like you to keep it clean and pretty for him."

"Yes, suh."

The farmer appeared satisfied. He did not uncock the hammer but the barrel now pointed at the ground.

"You know the way over the line to Tennessee?"

"No, suh."

"It ain't a far way but you'll need a map, especially if you lief to stay clear of outliers," the white man said. "You get here last night?"

"Yes, suh."

"Did you help yourself to some of them apples?"

The black man shook his head.

"You got food in your tote there?"

"No, suh."

"You must be hungry then," the farmer said. "Get what apples you want. There's a spring over there too what if your throat's dry. I'll go to the cabin and fix you a map." The white man paused. "Fetch some corn to take if you like, and tell that othern he don't have to hide in there lest he just favors it."

The farmer walked back toward the cabin.

"Come out, boy," Viticus said.

The tassels swayed and the youth reappeared.

"You hear what he say?"

"I heard it," the youth answered, and began walking toward the orchard.

They ate two apples each before going to the spring.

"Never tasted water that cold and it full summer," the youth said when he'd drunk his fill. "The Colonel say it snows here anytime and when it do you won't see no road nor nothing. Marster Helm's houseboy run off last summer, the Colonel say they found him froze stiff as a poker."

"You believing that then you a chucklehead," Viticus said.

"I just telling it," the youth answered.

"Uh, huh," his elder said, but his eyes were not on the youth but something in the far pasture. Two mounds lay side by side, marked with a single creek stone. Upturned earth sprouted a few weeds, but only a few. The youth turned from the spring and looked as well.

"Lord God," he said. "This place don't long allow a body to rest easy."

"Come on," Viticus said.

The fugitives stepped back through the orchard and waited in front of the barn. The farmer was on his way back, a bucket in one hand and the flintlock in the other.

"Why come him to still haul that gun?" the youth asked.

The older man's lips hardly moved as he spoke.

"Cause he ain't fool enough to trust two strangers, specially after you cut and run."

The farmer's eyes were on the youth as he crossed the pasture. He set the bucket before them and studied the youth's face a few more moments, then turned to the older fugitive.

"There's pone and sorghum in there," the farmer said, and nodded at the bucket. "My daughter brung it yesterday. She's nary the cook her momma was, but it'll stash your belly."

"Thank you, suh," the youth said.

"I brung it for him, not you," the farmer said.

The older fugitive did not move.

"Go ahead," the farmer said to him. "Just fetch that pone out the bucket and strap that sorghum on it."

"Thank you, suh," the older fugitive said, but he still did not reach for the pail.

"What?" the white man asked.

"If I be of a mind to share . . . "

The white man grimaced.

"He don't deserve none but it's your stomach to miss it, not mine."

The older fugitive took out a piece of the pone and the cistern of sorghum. He swathed the bread in syrup and offered it to the youth, who took it without a word. Neither sat in the grass to eat but remained standing. When they'd finished, the older fugitive set the cistern carefully in the bucket.

He stepped back and thanked the farmer again but the farmer seemed not to hear. His blue eyes were on the youth.

"You belonged to this Colonel Barkley feller too?"

"Yes, suh," the youth said.

"Been on his place all your life."

"Yes, suh."

"And your momma, she been at the Colonel's awhile before you was born."

"Yes, suh."

The farmer nodded and let his gaze drift toward the barn a moment before resettling on the youth. "The Colonel got red hair, has he?"

"You know the Colonel?" the youth asked.

"Naw, just his sort," the farmer answered. "You call him Colonel. Is he off to the war?"

"Yes, suh."

"And he is a Colonel, I mean rank?"

"Yes, suh," the youth answered. "The Colonel got him up a whole regiment to take north with him."

"A whole regiment, you say."

"Yes, suh."

The white man spat and wiped a shirtsleeve across his mouth.

"I done my damnedest to keep my boy from it," he said. "There's places up here conscripters would nary have found him, but he set out over to Tennessee anyway. You know the last thing I told him?"

The fugitives waited.

"I told him if he got in the thick of it, look for them what hid behind the lines with fancy uniforms and plumes in their hats. Them's the ones to shoot, I said, cause it's them sons of bitches started this thing. That boy could drop a squirrel at fifty yards. I hope he kilt a couple of them."

The older fugitive hesitated, then spoke.

"He fight for Mr. Lincoln, do he?"

"Not no more," the farmer said.

To the west, the land rose blue and jagged. The older fugitive let his gaze settle on the mountains before turning back to the farmer. The youth settled a boot toe into the grass, scuffed a small indentation. They waited as they had always waited for a white man, be it overseer, owner, now this farmer, to finish his say and dismiss them.

"The Colonel," the farmer asked, "he up in Virginia now?"

"Yes suh," the older fugitive said, "least as I know."

"Up near Richmond," the youth added. "That's what the Miss's cook heard."

The farmer nodded.

"Black niggers to do his work and now white niggers to do his fighting," he said.

The sun was full overhead now. Sweat beads glistened on the white man's brow but he did not raise a hand to wipe them away. The youth cleared his throat while staring at the scuff mark he'd made on the ground. The farmer looked only at the older fugitive now.

"I need you to understand something and there's nary a way to understand it without the telling," the farmer said to the other man. "Them days after we got the word, I'd wake of the night and Dorcie wouldn't be next to me. I'd find her sitting on the porch, just staring at the dark. Then one night I woke up and she wasn't on the porch. I found her here in this barn."

The farmer paused, as if to allow some comment, but none came.

"Me and Dorcie got three daughters alive and healthy and their young ones is too. You'd figure that would of been enough for her. You'd think it harder on a father to lose his onliest son, knowing there'd be never a one to carry on the family name after you ain't around no more. But he was the youngest, and womenfolk near always make a fuss over a come-late baby."

"That rope there in the barn," the farmer said, lifting a Barlow knife from his overall pocket. "I've left it dangling all these months 'cause I pondered it for my ownself, but every time I made ready to use it something stopped me."

The farmer nodded at a ball of twine by the stable door and tossed the knife to the older fugitive.

"Cut off a piece of that twine nigh long as your arm."

The fugitive freed the blade from the elk-bone casing. He stepped into the barn's deep shadow and cut the twine. The farmer motioned with the flintlock.

"Tie his hands behind his back."

The other man hesitated.

"If you want to get to Tennessee," the farmer said, "you got to do what I tell you."

"I don't like none of this," the youth muttered, but he did not resist as his companion wrapped the rope twice around his wrists and secured it with a knot.

"Toss me my Barlow," the farmer said.

The older fugitive did and the farmer slipped the knife into his front pocket.

"All right then," the farmer said and nodded at the tote. "You got fire?"

"Got flint," the other man said.

The farmer nodded and removed a thin piece of paper from his pocket.

"Bible paper. It's all I had."

The older fugitive took the proffered paper and unfolded it.

"That X is us here," the farmer said, and pointed at a mountain to the west. "Head cross this ridge and toward that mountain. You hit a trail just before it and head right. There comes a creek soon and you go up it till it peters out. Climb a bit more and you'll see a valley. You made it then. "

"And him?" the man said of the youth.

"Ain't your concern."

"It kindly is," the man said.

"Go on now and you'll be in Tennessee come nightfall."

The youth's shoulders were shaking. He looked at his companion and then at the white man.

"You got no cause to tie me up," the youth said. "I ain't gonna be no trouble. You tell him, Viticus."

"He'd not be much bother to take with me," the older fugitive said. "I promised his momma I'd look after him."

"You make the same promise to his father?" the farmer said and let his eyes settle on the older fugitive's shoulder. "From the looks of that scar I'd notion you to be glad I'm doing it. I'd think every time you looked at that red hair of his you'd want to kill him yourself."

"I didn't mean to hide from you," the youth said, his breathing short and fast now. "I just seen that gun and got rabbity."

"Go on now," the farmer told the older fugitive.

Two hours later he came to the creek. The burlap tote hung over one shoulder and the lantern hung from the other. He began the climb. The angled ground was slick and he grabbed rhododendron branches to keep from tumbling back down.

There was no shingle or handbill proclaiming he'd entered Tennessee, but when he crested the mountain and the valley lay before him, he saw a wooden building below, next to it a pole waving the flag of Lincoln. He stood there in the late-afternoon light, absorbing the valley's sudden expansiveness after days in the mountains. The land rippled out and appeared to reach all the way to where the sun and earth merged. He shifted the twine so it didn't rub the ridge of scar. Something furrowed his brow a few moments. Then he moved on and did not look back.

THE WOMAN AT THE POND

Water has its own archeology, not a layering but a leveling, and thus truer to our sense of the past, because what is memory but near and far events spread and smoothed beneath the present's surface. A green birthday candle that didn't expire with a wish lies next to a green Coleman lantern lit twelve years later. Chalky sun motes in a sixth-grade classroom harbor close to a university library's high window, a song on a staticky radio shoals against the same song at a hastily arranged wedding reception. This is what I think of when James Murray's daughter decides to drain the pond. A fear of lawsuits, she claims, something her late father considered himself exonerated from by posting a sign: *Fish And Swim At Your Own Risk.*

She hired Wallace Rudisell for the job, a task that requires opening the release valve on the standpipe, keeping it clear until what once was a creek will be a creek once more. I grew up with Wallace, and, unlike so many of our classmates, he and I still live in Lattimore. Wallace inherited our town's hardware store, one of the few remaining businesses.

"Bet you're wanting to get some of those lures back you lost in high school," Wallace says when I ask when he'll drain the pond. "There must be a lot of them. For a while you were out there most every evening."

Which is true. I was seventeen and in a town of three hundred, my days spent bagging groceries. Back then there was no internet, no cable TV or VCR, at least in our house. Some evenings that summer I'd listen to the radio or watch television with my parents, or look over college brochures and financial-aid forms the guidance counselor had given me, but I'd usually go down to the pond. Come fall of my senior year, though, Angie and I began dating. We found other things to do in the dark.

A few times Wallace or another friend joined me, but I usually fished alone. After a day at the grocery store, I didn't mind being away from people awhile, and the pond at twilight was a good place. The swimmers and other fishermen were gone, leaving behind beer and cola bottles, tangles of fishing line, gray cinder blocks fisherman used for seats. Later in the night, couples came to the pond, their leavings on the bank as well—rubbers and blankets, once a pair of panties hung on the white oak's limb. But that hour when day and night made their slow exchange, I had the pond to myself.

Over the years James Murray's jon-boat had become communal property. Having wearied of swimming out to retrieve the boat, I'd bought twenty-feet of blue nylon rope to keep it moored. I'd unknot the rope from the white oak, set my fishing gear and Coleman lantern in the bow, and paddle out to the pond's center. I'd fish until it was neither day nor night, but balanced between. There never seemed to be a breeze, pond and shore equally smoothed. Just stillness, as though the world had taken a soft breath, and was holding it in, and even time had leveled out, moving neither forward nor back. Then the frogs and crickets waiting for full dark announced themselves, or a breeze came up and I again heard the slosh of water against land. Or, one night near the end of that summer, a truck rumbling toward the pond.

On Saturday I leave at two o'clock when the other shift manager comes in. I no longer live near the pond, but my mother does, so I pull out of the grocery store's parking lot and turn right, passing under Lattimore's one stoplight. On the left are four boarded-up stores, behind them like an anchored cloud, the mill's water tower, blue paint chipping off the tank. I drive by Glenn's Café where Angie works, soon after that the small clapboard house where she and our daughter, Rose, live. Angie's Ford Escort isn't there, but the truck belonging to Rose's boyfriend is. I don't turn in. It's not my weekend to be in charge, and at least I know Rose is on the pill, because I took her to the clinic myself.

Soon there are only farmhouses, most in disrepair—slumping barns and woodsheds, rusty tractors snared by kudzu and trumpet vines. I make a final right turn and park in front of my mother's house. She comes onto the porch and I know from her disappointed expression that she's gotten the week confused and expects to see Rose. We talk a minute and she goes back inside. I walk down the sloping land, straddle the sagging barbed wire and make my way through brambles and broom sedge, what was once a pasture.

The night the truck came to the pond, an afternoon thunderstorm had rinsed the humidity from the air. The evening felt more like late September than mid-August. After rowing out, I had cast toward the willows on the far bank, where I'd caught bass in the past. The lure I used was a Rapala, my favorite because I could fish it on the surface or submerged. After a dozen tries nothing struck, so I paddled closer to the willows and cast into the cove where the creek ended. A small bass hit and I reeled it in, its red gills flaring as I freed the treble hook and lowered the fish back into the water.

A few minutes later the truck bumped down the dirt road to the water's edge. The headlights slashed across the pond before the vehicle jerked right and halted beside the white oak as the headlights dimmed.

Music came from the truck's open windows and carried over the water with such clarity I recognized the song. The cab light came on and the music stopped. Minutes passed, and stars began filling the sky. As a thick-shouldered moon rimmed up over a ridge, a man and woman got out of the truck. The jon-boat drifted toward the willows and I let it, afraid any movement would give away my presence. The man and woman's voices rose, became angry, then a sound sharp as a rifle shot. The woman fell and the man got back in the cab. The headlights flared and the truck turned around, slinging mud before the tires gained traction. The truck swerved up the dirt road and out of sight.

The woman slowly lifted herself from the ground. She moved closer to the bank and sat on a cinder block. As more stars pierced the sky, and the moon lifted itself above the willow trees, I waited for the truck to return or the woman to leave, though I had no idea where she might go. The jon-boat drifted deeper into the willows, the drooping branches raking at my face. I didn't want to move, but the willows had entangled the boat. The graying wood creaked as it bumped against the bank. I lifted the paddle and pushed away as quietly as possible. As I did, the boat rocked and the metal tackle box banged against its side.

"Who's out there?" the woman asked. "I can see you, I can."

I lit the lantern and paddled to the pond's center.

"I'm fishing," I said, and lifted the rod and reel to prove it. The woman didn't respond. "Are you okay?"

"My face will be bruised," she said after a few moments. "But no teeth knocked out. Bruises fade. I'll be better off tomorrow than he will."

I set the paddle on my knees. In the quiet, it seemed the pond too was listening.

"You mean the man that hit you?"

"Yeah, him."

"Is he coming back?"

"Yeah, he's coming back. The bastard needs me to drive to Charlotte. Another DUI and he'll be pedaling to work on a bicycle. He won't get too drunk to remember that. Anyway, he didn't go far."

The woman pointed up the dirt road where a faint square of light hovered like foxfire.

"He's drinking the rest of his whiskey while some hillbilly whines on the radio about how hard life is. When the bottle's empty, he'll be back."

As the jon-boat drifted closer to the bank, the woman stood and I dug the paddle's wooden blade into the silt to keep some distance between us. The lantern's glow fell on both of us now. She was younger than I'd thought, maybe no more than thirty. A large woman, wide hipped and tall, at least five-eight. Her long blonde hair was clearly dyed. A red welt covered the left side of a face. She wore a man's leather jacket over her yellow blouse and black skirt. Mud grimed the yellow blouse. She raised her hand and fanned at the haze of insects.

"I hope there are fewer gnats and mosquitoes out there," she said. "The damn things are eating me alive."

"Only if I stay in the middle," I answered.

I glanced up at the truck.

"I guess I'll go back out."

I lifted the paddle, thinking if the man didn't come get her in a few minutes I'd beach the boat in the creek cove, work my way through the brush and head home.

"Can I get in the boat with you?" the woman asked.

"I'm just going to make a couple of more casts," I answered. "I need to get back home."

"Just a few minutes," she said, and gave me a small smile, the hardness in her face and voice lessening. "I'm not going to hurt you. Just a few minutes. To get away from the bugs."

"Can you swim?"

"Yes," she said.

"What about that man that hit you?"

"He'll be there a while yet. He drinks his whiskey slow."

The woman brushed some of the drying mud from her skirt, as if to make herself more presentable.

"Just a few minutes."

"Okay," I said, and rowed to the bank.

I steadied the jon-boat while she got in the front, the lantern at her feet. The woman talked while I paddled, not turning her head, as if addressing the pond.

"I finally get away from this county and that son-of-a-bitch drags me back to visit his sister. She's not home so instead he buys a bottle of Wild Turkey and we end up here, with him wanting to lay down on the bank with just a horse blanket beneath us and the mud. When I tell him no way, he gets this jacket from the truck. For your head, he tells me, like that would change my mind. What a prince."

She shifted her body to face me.

"Nothing like coming back home, right?"

"You're from Lattimore?" I asked.

"No, but this county. Lawndale. You know where that is?"

"Yes."

"But our buddy in the truck used to live in Lattimore, so we're having a Cleveland County reunion tonight, assuming you aren't just visiting."

"I live here."

"Still in high school?"

I nodded.

"I'll be a senior."

"We used to kick your asses in football," she said. "That was supposed to be a big deal."

I pulled in the paddle when we reached the pond's center. The rod lay beside me, but I didn't pick it up. The lantern was still on, but we didn't really need it. The moon laid a silvery skim of light on the water.

"When you get back to Charlotte, will you call the police?"

"No, they wouldn't do anything. The bastard will pay though. He left more than his damn jacket on that blanket."

The woman took a wallet from the jacket, opened it to show no bills were inside.

"He got paid today so what he didn't spend on that whiskey is in my pocket now. He'll wake up tomorrow thinking a hangover is the worst thing he'll have to deal with, but he will soon learn different."

"What if he believes you took it?"

"I'll make myself scarce a while. That's easy to do in a town big as Charlotte. Anyway, he'll be back living here before long."

"He tell you that?"

The woman smiled.

"He doesn't need to. Haven't you heard of women's intuition? Plus, he's always talking about this place. Badmouthing it a lot, but it's got its hooks in him. No, he'll move back, probably work at the mill, and he'll still be here when they pack the dirt over his coffin."

She'd paused and looked at me.

"What about you? Already got your job lined up after high school?"

"I'm going to college."

"College," she said, studying me closely. "I'd not have thought that. You've got the look of someone who'd stick around here."

Wallace waves from the opposite bank and makes his way around the pond. His pants and tennis shoes are daubed with mud. Wallace works mostly indoors, so the July sun has reddened his face and unsleeved arms. He nods at the valve.

"Damn thing's clogged up twice, but it's getting there."

174

The pond is a red-clay bowl, one-third full. In what was once the shallows, rusty beer cans and Styrofoam bait containers have emerged along with a ball cap and a flip flop. Farther in, Christmas trees submerged years are now visible, the black branches threaded with red-and-white bobbers and bream hooks, plastic worms and bass plugs, including a six-inch Rapala that I risk the slick mud to pull free. Its hooks are so rusty one breaks off.

"Let me see," Wallace says, and examines the lure.

"I used to fish with one like this," I tell him, "same size and model."

"Probably one of yours then," Wallace says, and offers the lure as if to confirm my ownership. "You want any of these others?"

"No, I don't even want that one."

"I'll take them then," Wallace says, lifting a yellow Jitterbug from a limb. "I hear people collect old plugs nowadays. They might be worth a few dollars, add to the hundred I'm getting to do this. These days I need every bit of money I can get."

We move under the big white oak and sit in its shade, watch the pond's slow contraction. More things emerge—a rod and reel, a metal bait bucket, more lures and hooks and bobbers. There are swirls in the water now, fish vainly searching for the upper levels of their world. A large bass leaps near the valve.

Wallace nods at a burlap sack.

"The bluegill will flush down that drain, but it looks like I'll get some good-sized fish to fry up."

We watch the water, soon a steady dimpling on the surface. Another bass flails upward, shimmers green and silver in the afternoon sun.

"Angie said Rose is trying to get loans so she can go to your alma mater next year," Wallace says.

"It's an alma mater only if you graduate," I reply.

Wallace picks up a stick, scrapes some mud off his shoes. He starts to speak, then hesitates, finally does speak.

"I always admired your taking responsibility like that. Coming back here, I mean." Wallace shakes his head. "We sure live in a different time. Hell, nowadays there's women who don't know or care who their baby's father is, much less expect him to marry her. And the men, they're worse. They act like it's nothing to them, don't even want to be a part of their own child's life."

When I don't reply, Wallace checks his watch.

"This is taking longer than I figured. I'm going to the cafe. I haven't had lunch. Want me to bring you back something?"

"A Coke would be nice," I say.

As Wallace drives away, I think of the woman letting her right hand brush the water as I rowed the jon-boat toward shore.

"It feels warm," she said, "warmer than the air. I bet you could slip in and sink and it would feel cozy as a warm blanket."

"The bottom's cold," I answered.

"If you got that deep," she said, "it wouldn't matter anyway, would it."

After we got out, the woman asked whose boat it was. I told her I didn't know and started to knot the rope to the white oak.

"Leave it untied then," she said. "I may take it back out."

"I don't think you should do that," I told her. "The boat could overturn or something."

"I won't overturn the boat," the woman said, and pulled a ten-dollar bill from her skirt pocket.

"Here's something for taking me out. This too," she said, taking the jacket off. "It's a nice one and he's not getting it back. It looks like a good fit."

"I'd better not," I said, and picked up my fishing equipment and the lantern. I looked at her. "When he comes back, you're not afraid he'll do something else? I mean, I can call the police."

She shook her head.

"Don't do that. Like I said, he needs a driver, so he'll make nice. You go on home."

And so I did, and once there, did not call the police or tell my parents. I had trouble sleeping that night, but the next day at work, as the hours passed, I assured myself that if anything really bad had happened everyone in Lattimore would have known by now.

I went back to the pond, for the last time, that evening after work. The nylon rope was missing but the paddle lay under the front seat. As I got in, I lifted the paddle and found a ten-dollar bill beneath it. I rowed out to the center and tied on the Rapala and threw it at the pond's far bank.

As darkness descended, what had seemed certain earlier seemed less so. When a cast landed in some brush, I cranked the reel fast, hoping to avoid snagging the Rapala, but that also caused the lure to go deeper. The rod bowed and I was hung. Any other time, I'd have rowed to the snag and leaned over the gunwale, let my hand follow the line into the water to find the lure and free the hook. Instead, I tightened the line and gave a hard jerk. The lure stayed where it was.

For a minute I sat there. Something thrashed in the reeds, probably a bass or muskrat. Then the water was still. Moonlight brightened, as if trying to probe the dark water. I took out my pocketknife, cut the line, then rowed to shore and beached the boat. That night I dreamed that I'd let my hand follow the line until my fingers were tangled in hair.

Wallace's truck comes back down the dirt road. He hands me my Coke and opens a white bag containing his drink and hamburger. We sit under the tree.

"It's draining good now," he says.

The fish not inhaled by the drain are more visible, fins sharking the surface. A catfish that easily weighs five pounds wallows onto the bank as if hoping for some sudden evolution. Wallace quickly finishes his hamburger. He takes the burlap sack and walks into what's left of the pond. He hooks a finger through the catfish's gills and drops it into the sack.

In another half hour what thinning water remains boils with bass and catfish. More fish beach themselves and Wallace gathers them like fallen fruit, the sack punching and writhing in his grasp.

"You come over tonight," he says to me. "There'll be plenty."

As evening comes, more snags emerge, fewer lures. A whiskey bottle and another bait bucket, some cans that probably rolled and drifted into the pond's deep center. Then I see the cinderblock, with what looks like a withered arm draped over it. Wallace continues to gather more fish, including a blue cat that will go ten pounds, its whiskers long as nightcrawlers. I walk onto the red slanting mud, moving slowly so I won't slip. I stop when I stand only a fishing rod's length from the cinderblock.

"What do you see?" Walter asks.

I wait for the water to give me an answer, and before long it does. Not an arm but a leather jacket sleeve, tied to the block by a fray of blue nylon. I step into the water and loosen the jacket from the concrete, and as I do I remember the ten-dollar bill left in the boat, her assumption that I'd be the one to find it.

I feel something in the jacket's right pocket and pull out a withered billfold. Inside are two silted shreds of thin plastic, a driver's license, some other card now indiscernible. No bills.

I stand in the pond's center and toss the billfold's remnants into the drain. I drop the jacket and step back as Wallace gills the last fish abandoned by the water. Wallace knots the sack and lifts it. The veins in his bicep and forearm ridge up as he does so.

"That's at least fifty pounds worth," he says, and sets the sack down. "Let me clear this drain one more time. Then I'm going home to cook these up."

Wallace leans over the drain and claws away the clumps of mud and wood. The remaining water gurgles down the pipe.

"I hate to see this pond go," he says. "I guess the older you get the less you like any kind of change."

Wallace lifts the sack of fish and pulls it over his shoulder. We walk out of the pond as dusk comes on.

"You going to come over later?" he asks.

"Not tonight."

"Another time then," Wallace says. "Need a ride up to your mom's house?"

"No," I answer. "I'll walk it."

After Wallace drives off, I sit on the bank. Shadows deepen where the water was, making it appear that the pond has refilled. After awhile I get up. By the time I'm over the barbed wire fence, I can look back and no longer tell what was and what is.

POETRY

From *Eureka Mill* (1998)

INVOCATION

This late night I spread
a fraying Springmaid bedsheet
across the kitchen table.
In the almost silence
of house-creak and time's
persistent tracking of eternity,
I unscrew the mason jar,
pool the lid with moonshine,
    flare the battered cigarette lighter.
A blue trembling rises from liquid
expanding finally to smoke,
all elements merging tonight,
whispering out the window,
curling northward to seep six feet
into the black bony dirt
and guide his spirit across
the declining mountains to this room,
where I sit and sip, await
a tobacco-breathed haint, shadowless shadow,
bloodless blood-kin I have summoned
to hear my measured human prayer:
    Grandfather guide my hand
    to weave with words a thread
    of truth as I write down
    your life and other lives,

close kin but strangers too,
those lives all lived as gears
in Springs' cotton mill
and let me not forget
your lives were more than that.

EUREKA

Here was no place   for illumination
the cotton dust thick   window-strained light.
The metal squall drowned   what could not be shouted
everything geared   warping and filling.

Though surely there were   some times that he paused
my grandfather thinking   *This is my life*
and catching himself   before he was caught
lost wages or fingers   the risk of reflection.

Or another recalled   in those reckoning moments
remembering the mountains   the hardscrabble farm
where a workday as long   bought no guarantee
of money come fall   full bellies in winter.

To earn extra pay   each spring he would climb
the mill's water tower   repaint the one word.
That vowel-heavy word   defined the horizon
a word my grandfather   could not even read.

MILL VILLAGE

Mill houses lined both sides of every road
like boxcars on a track. They were so close
a man could piss off of his own front porch,
hit four houses if he had the wind.

Everytime your neighbors had a fight,
then made up in bed as couples do,
came home drunk, played the radio,
you knew, whether or not you wanted to.

So I bought a dimestore picture, a country scene,
built a frame and nailed it on the wall,
no people in it, just a lot of land,
stretching out behind an empty barn.

Sometimes at night if I was feeling low,
I'd stuff my ears with cotton. Then I'd stare
up at the picture like it was a window,
and I was back home listening to the farm.

But what was done was done. Before too long
the weave room jarred the hearing from my ears,
and I got used to living with a crowd.
Before too long I took the picture down.

BEARINGS

He's scraped manure off his boots a last time,
filled the front room with what he has chosen
to keep on owning. He's alone. His uncle gone,
gearing back through the hills upwinding into
the gasping curves and drops of the mountains.

He stands on the porch, no work until tomorrow,
millhouses planted like corn rows each way he
looks. Eureka's water tower rising above as if
a hard high-legged scarecrow. He steps down on
the strange level road, walks west toward town.

He finds a grill, asks for what he's memorized:
a hamburger and a coke and his change. Outside
in the loud afternoon, he stares into windows
until he sees shoes. The clerk takes his bills
and grins when my grandfather asks for a poke.

He walks out toward Eureka's smoke and rumble,
toward the millhouses crouched and huddled in
the mill's shadow, and soon finds he is lost.
Each house might be his or maybe the next one,
and he walks an hour before he finally asks.

He tells the man he is looking for James Rash,
a friend who's just moved here. The man says
"Tommy Singleton got fired last week. I'd bet
that's where your friend is at" and points to
a house, and so my grandfather found himself.

He stayed inside till the whistle woke him up,
and threw his boots on the roof so they might
guide him back those first evenings and later
the Saturday nights he weaved under moonshine,
searching roof after roof trying to find home.

185

BROWN LUNG

Sometimes I'd spend the whole night coughing up
what I'd been breathing in all day at work.
I'd sleep in a chair or take a good stiff drink,
anything to get a few hours rest.

The doctor called it asthma and suggested
I find a different line of work as if
a man who had no land or education
could find himself another way to live.

For that advice I paid a half-day's wage.
Who said advice is cheap? It got so bad
each time I got a break at work I'd find
the closest window, try to catch a breath.

My foreman was a decent man who knew
I would not last much longer on that job.
He got me transferred out of the card room,
let me load the boxcars in the yard.

But even though I slept more I'd still wake
gasping for air at least one time a night,
and when I dreamed I dreamed of bumper crops
of Carolina cotton in my chest.

JULY, 1949

This is what I cannot remember—
a young woman stooped in a field,
the hoe callousing her hands,
the rows stretching out like hours.
And this woman, my mother, rising
to dust rising half a mile
up the road, the car,
she has waited days for
realized in the trembling heat.

It will rust until spring, the hoe
dropped at the field's edge.
She is running toward the car,
the sandlapper relatives who spill out
coughing mountain air with lint-filled lungs,
running toward the half-filled grip
she will learn to call a suitcase.

She is dreaming another life,
young enough to believe
it can only get better—
indoor plumbing, eight hours shifts, a man
who waits unknowing for her, a man
who cannot hear through the weave room's
roar the world's soft click,
fate's tumblers falling into place,
soft as the sound of my mother's
bare feet as she runs,
runs toward him, toward me.

From *Among the Believers* (2000)

PLOWING ON MOONLIGHT

I rose with the moon, left the drowsy sheets,
my nine months wife singing in her sleep,
left boots on the floor, overalls and hat
scarecrowing a bedpost so I could plant
my seeds with just a plow between
the earth and me, my pale feet sunk deep
in the ridged wake where I labored,
gripped the handles like a divining rod,
my eyes closed to the few stars out
glittering like mica in a creek. All night
I plowed, limbs pebbled, beard budded by frost,
my chest nippled, my breath blooming white,
and knew again the sway of the sea,
the flow of river, the smallest creek,
rain's pelt and soak, the taproot's thrust,
the cicada's winged resurrection.
I opened my eyes to dawnlight,
left my field and lay with my wife,
warming as I pressed against her body,
my hand listening to her waxing belly.

THE EXCHANGE

Between Wytheville, Virginia
and the North Carolina line,
he meets a wagon headed
where he's been, seated beside
her parents a dark-eyed girl
who grips the reins in her fist,
no more than sixteen, he'd guess
as they come closer and she
doesn't look away or blush
but allows his eyes to hold
hers that moment their lives pass.
He rides into Boone at dusk,
stops at an inn where he buys
his supper, a sleepless night
thinking of fallow fields still
miles away, the girl he might
not find the like of again.
When dawn breaks he mounts his roan,
then backtracks, searches three days
hamlets and farms, any smoke
rising above the tree line
before he heads south, toward home,
the French Broad's valley where spring
unclinches the dogwood buds
as he plants the bottomland,
come night by candlelight builds
a butter churn and cradle,
cherry headboard for the bed,
forges a double-eagle
into a wedding ring and then
back to Virginia and spends
five weeks riding and asking
from Elk Creek to Damascas
before he finds the wagon
tethered to the hitching post
of a crossroads store, inside

the girl who smiles as if she'd
known all along his gray eyes
would search until they found her.
She asks one question, his name,
as her eyes study the gold
smoldering there between them,
the offered palm she lightens,
slips the ring on herself so
he knows right then the woman
she will be, bold enough match
for a man rash as his name.

A PREACHER WHO TAKES UP SERPENTS
LAMENTS THE PRESENCE OF SKEPTICS
IN HIS CHURCH

Every Sabbath they come,
gawk like I'm something
in a tent at a county fair.
In the vanity of their unbelief
they will cover an eye with a camera
and believe it will make them see.
They see nothing. I show them Mark: 16
but they believe in the word of man.
They believe death is an end.

And would live like manure maggots,
wallow in the filth of man's creation.
Less than a mile from here
the stench of sulphur rises
like fog off the Pigeon River.
They do not believe it is a sign
of their own wickedness.
They cannot see a river
is a vein in God's arm.

When I open the wire cages
they back away like crayfish
and tell each other I am insane—
terrified I may not be.

Others, my own people, whisper
"He tempts God," and will not join me.
They cannot understand surrender
is humility, not arrogance,
that a man afraid to die cannot live.

Only the serpents sense the truth.
The diamondback's blunted tail is silent,

the moccasins pearl-white mouth closed.
The coral snake coils around
my wrist, a harmless bright bracelet,
in the presence of the Lord.

RETURN

Gaunt and silent, pale,
my uncle seems the ghost
a lower aim would have made
as he steps off the train
into the truck, inside
his father and sister who
slid and braked ten miles
down the mountain to Boone,
snow falling as it has
since noon. The road disappears
before they're halfway home.
My uncle walks point, shoulders
his duffle bag, shadows
Middlefork to the pool
where Holder Branch enters,
follows the creek up the mountain,
through the step-muffling snow,
past church and graveyard. Soon
the last light starts to fade.
The snow blurs blue. He sees
the candle in the window,
unknots the bag, removes
the bullet-nicked helmet, walks
across the pasture to the spring,
breaks the ice and drinks.

THE FOX

Two months before he died my uncle saw
a red fox at the edge of the field he plowed,
watching him, its tongue unpanting though
the August heat-haze waved the air like water.

That night he claimed it was his father, then laughed
as if he wasn't serious, as if
all summer long we hadn't watched his face
grow old too quick, gray-stubbled, sudden-lined.

His wife would try the last days that he lived
to get him to the hospital but he
took to his bed, awaited the approach
of padded feet, coming close, then closer.

AUGUST, 1959: MORNING SERVICE

Beside the open window
on the cemetery side,
I drowsed as Preacher Lusk gripped
his Bible like a bat snagged
from the pentecostal gloom.
In that room where heat clabbered
like churned butter, my eyes closed,
freed my mind into the light
on the window's other side,
followed the dreamy bell-ring
of Randy Ford's cows across
Licklog Creek to a spring pool
where orange salamanders swirled
and scuttled like flames. It was
not muttered words that urged me
back to that church, nor was it
the hard comfort of pews rowed
like the gravestones of my kin,
but the a cappella hymn
sung by my great-aunt, this years
before the Smithsonian
taped her voice as if the song
of some vanishing species,
which it was, which all songs are,
years before the stroke wrenched her
face into a gnarled silence,
this morning before all that
she led us across Jordan,
and the gravestones leaned as if
even the dead were listening.

AMONG THE BELIEVERS

Even the young back then died old.
My great-aunt's brow at twenty-eight
was labored by a hardscrabble world
no final breath could smooth away.
They laid her out in her wedding dress,
the life that killed in her arms, the head
turned to suckle her cold breast
in eternity. A cousin held
a camera above the open casket,
cast a shadow the camera raised
where flesh and wood and darkness met,
a photograph the husband claimed.
Nailed on the wall above his bed,
smudged and traced for five decades,
a cross of shadow, shadowing death,
across an uncomprehending face.

GOOD FRIDAY, 1995: DRIVING WESTWARD

This day I feel I live among strangers.
The old blood ties beckon so I drive west
to Buncombe County, a weedy graveyard
where my rare last name crumbles on stone.

All were hardshell Baptists, farmers
who believed the soul is another seed
that endures when flesh and blood are shed,
that all things planted rise toward the sun.

I dream them shaking dirt off strange new forms.
Gathered for the last harvest, they hold hands,
take their first dazed steps toward heaven.

From *Raising the Dead* (2002)

LAST SERVICE

Though cranes and bulldozers came,
yanked free marble and creek stones
like loose teeth, and then shovels
unearthed coffins and Christ's
stained glass face no longer paned
windows but like the steeple,
piano, bell, and hymnals
followed that rolling graveyard
over the quick-dying streams,
the soon obsolete bridges—
they still congregated there,
wading then crossing in boats
those last Sunday nights, their farms
already lost in the lake,
nothing but that brief island
left of their world as they lit
the church with candles and sang
from memory deep as water
old hymns of resurrection
before leaving that high ground
where the dead had once risen.

UNDER JOCASSEE

One summer morning when
the sky is blue and deep
as the middle of the lake,
rent a boat and shadow
Jocassee's western shoreline
until you reach the cove
that was Horsepasture River.
Now bow your head and soon
you'll see as through a mirror
not a river but a road
flowing underneath you.
Follow that road into
the deeper water where
you'll pass a family graveyard,
then a house and barn.
All's that's changed is time,
so cut the motor and drift
back sixty years and remember
a woman who lived in that house,
remember an August morning
as she walks from the barn,
the milking done, a woman
singing only to herself,
no children yet, her husband
distant in the field.
Suddenly she shivers,
something dark has come
over her although
no cloud shades the sun.
She's no longer singing.
She believes someone
has crossed her grave, although
she will go to her grave,
a grave you've just passed over,
wondering why she looked up.

JOCASSEE: 1916

Dam-break, a flood in drought time,
August sun flashing on tin—
a barn roof, all that's above
as two men pass like a cloud
over pasture, boat bow filled
with crowbar and ax, a rope,
for something in that barn lives,
so anchor, hang on the roof,
peel back tin slats, break through beams
before it comes, a stallion
shedding tin's dazzle like scales
as it rises through the roof
like an image opening
inside the mind, born of fire
and waterborne, alive.

WATAUGA COUNTY: 1803

Night falling, river rising,
into the cabin, a hound
howling on the porch, and then
an unbuckling from bank roots,
no time to lantern children
up to loft or higher ground
as the cabin, current-caught,
filled like a trough before lodged
on a rock, and when dawn brought
neighbors, and kinfolk the hound
still howled on the porch, allowed
no one to enter until
shot dead by a flintlock pressed
against its head so men might
drag out those drowned in the harsh
covenant of that failed ark.

IN DISMAL GORGE

The lost can stay lost down here,
in laurel slicks, false-pathed caves.
Too much too soon disappears.

On creek banks clearings appear,
once homesteads. Nothing remains.
The lost can stay lost down here,

like Tom Clark's child, our worst fears
confirmed as we searched in vain.
Too much too soon disappears.

How often this is made clear
where cliff-shadows pall our days.
The lost can stay lost down here,

stones scattered like a river
in drought, now twice-buried graves.
Too much too soon disappears,

lives slip away like water.
We fill our Bibles with names.
The lost can stay lost down here.
Too much too soon disappears.

BLACK-EYED SUSANS

The hay was belt-buckle high
when rain let up, three days' sun
baked stalks dry, and by midday
all but the far pasture mowed,
raked into windrows, above
June sky still blue as I drove
my tractor up on the ridge
to the far pasture where strands
of sagging barbed wire marked where
my land stopped, church land began,
knowing I'd find some grave-gift,
flowers, flag, styrofoam cross
blown on my land, and so first
walked the boundary, made sure what
belonged on the other side
got returned, soon enough saw
black-eyed susans, the same kind
growing in my yard, a note
tight-folded to a bow.
Always was all that it said,
which said enough for I knew
what grave that note belonged to.
I knew as well who wrote it,
she and him married three months
when he died, now always young,
always their love in full bloom,
too new to life to know life
was no honeymoon. Instead,
she learned that lesson with me
over three decades, what fires
our flesh set early on cooled
by time and just surviving,
and learned why old folks called it
getting hitched, because like mules
so much of life was one long row
you never saw the end of,

and always he was close by,
under a stone you could see
from the porch, wedding picture
she kept hid in her drawer,
his black-and-white flashbulb grin
grinning at me like he knew
he'd made me more of a ghost
to her than he'd ever be.
There at that moment—that word
in my hand, his grave so close,
If I'd had a shovel near
I'd have dug him up right then,
hung his bones up on the fence
like a varmint, made her see
what the real was, for memory
is always the easiest
thing to love, to keep alive
in the heart. After a while
I laid the note and bouquet
where they belonged, never spoke
a word about it to her
then or ever, even when
she was dying, calling his
name with her last words. Sometimes
on a Sunday afternoon
I'll cross the pasture, make sure
her stone's not starting to lean,
if it's early summer bring
black-eyed susans for her grave,
leave a few on his as well,
for soon enough we'll all be
sleeping together, beyond
all things that ever mattered.

From *Raising the Dead*

WOLF LAUREL

Tree branches ice-shackled, ground
hard as an anvil, three sons
and a father leave the blaze
huddled around all morning,
wade snow two miles where they cross
Wolf Laurel Creek, poke rifles
in rock holes, cliff leans hoping
to quarry what's killed five sheep,
but no den found as the ridge
sips away the gray last light
of winter solstice, and they
head back toward home, the trail
falling in blur-dark; and then
the father falls too, eyes locked,
wrist unpulsed, the sons without
lantern, enough lingering light,
know they must leave him or risk
all of them lost, know what waits
for death in that place, so break
a hole in Wolf Laurel's ice,
come back at first light to find
the creek's scab of cold covered
with snow-drift, circling paw prints
brushed away that sons might see
a father's face staring through
the ice as a mirror.

AT REID HARTLEY'S JUNKYARD

To enter we find the gap
between barbed wire and briars,
pass the German Shepherd chained
to an axle, cross the ditch
of oil black as a tar pit,
my aunt compelled to come here
on a Sunday after church,
asking me when her husband
refused to search this island
reefed with past catastrophes.
We make our way to the heart
of the junkyard, cling of rust
and beggarlice on our clothes,
bumpers hot as a skillet
as we squeeze between car husks
to find in this forever
stilled traffic one Ford pickup,
tires stripped, radio yanked out,
driver's door open. My aunt
gets in, stares through glass her son
looked through the last time he knew
the world, as though believing
like others who come here she
might see something to carry
from this wreckage, as I will
when I look past my aunt's ruined
Sunday dress, torn stockings, find
her right foot pressed to the brake.

MADISON COUNTY: JUNE, 1999

Where North Carolina locks
like a final puzzle piece
into eastern Tennessee,
old songs of salvation rise
through static on Sunday night
in this mountain county where
my name echoes on gravestones
dimmed by time like the evening
a kinsman held fire, let it lick
his palm like a pet before
he raised that hand so we might
see providence as his tongue
forged a new language bellowed
into a pentecostal blaze.
That is all I remember:
an unburned hand, those strange words,
what came before or after
on that long ago Sunday
dark as beyond the headlights
as I practice smaller acts
of faith on hill crests, blind curves,
and though my life lies elsewhere
some whisper inside urges
another destination,
as if that unburned hand were
raised in welcome, still might lead
me to another state marked
by no human boundary,
where my inarticulate
heart might finally find voice
in words cured by fire, water.

A HOMESTEAD ON THE HORSEPASTURE

Those last days he stayed to watch
water tug his farm under
one row at a time, so slow
his eyes snagged no memory
of what was lost, no moment
he could say I saw it end.
When little else showed but what
his own hands had raised he soaked
house and barn with kerosene,
shattered a lantern, and as
it burned the taste of ashes
filled his mouth until nothing
remained but what he'd corbeled
out of creek stone he would leave
for the water to reclaim.

From *Waking* (2011)

RESOLUTION

The surge and clatter of whitewater conceals
how shallow underneath is, how quickly gone.
Leave that noise behind. Come here
where the water is slow, and clear.
Watch the crayfish prance across the sand,
the mica flash, the sculpen blend with stone.
It's all beyond your reach though it appears
as near and known as your outstretched hand.

FIRST MEMORY

Dragonflies dip, rise. Their backs
catch light, purple like church glass.
Gray barn planks balance on stilts,
walk toward the pond's deep end.
A green smell simmers shallows,
where tadpoles flow like black tears.
Minnows lengthen their shadows.
Something unseen stirs in the reeds.

From *Waking*

WATAUGA COUNTY: 1959

On Clay Ridge a crescent moon
balanced itself, soon became
an open parenthesis
no father, uncle could close
as we hunched on farmhouse steps,
wore Sunday clothes days early,
what conversation the rasp
of matches. Small blades of flame
rose to faces no tears marked
as I heard silence widen
like fish swirls on a calm pond,
touch the last fence he had strung,
the tractor in the far field
already starting to rust.

SPILLCORN

The road is now a shadow
of a road, overgrown with
scrub pine, blackjack oak. Years back
one of my kinsmen logged here,
a man needing steady work
no hailstorm or August drought
could take away, so followed
Spillcorn Creek into the gorge,
brought with him a mule and sled,
a Colt revolver to kill
the rattlesnakes, and always
tucked in his lunch sack a book:
history, sometimes novel
from the Marshall library,
so come midday he might rest
his spine against bark and read—
what had roughed his hands now smooth
as his fingertips turned
the leaves, each word whispered soft
as the wind reading the trees.

WHITE WINGS

Tucked in each pew's back pocket,
hymnals simmered in mote dust
until Sundays when the soiled
rough hands of farmers lifted
those songbibles, pages spread
like white wings being set free,
but what rose was one voice
woven from many, and heard
by Jason Storey who stood
in a field half an acre
of gravestones away, mute as
a fence post while neighbors sang
inside the church doors he swore
never to pass through after
wife and son died in childbirth,
that long ago Christmas when
three days of snow made the road
to Blowing Rock disappear,
the doctor brought on horseback
arriving too late. Decades
Jason Storey would remain
true to his word, yet was there
in that field come rain or cold,
but came no closer, between
church and field two marble stones,
angel-winged, impassable.

THREE A.M. AND THE STARS WERE OUT

When the phone rings way too late
for good news, just another
farmer wanting me to lose
half a night's sleep and drive some
backcountry wash-out for miles,
fix what he's botched, on such nights
I'm like an old, drowsy god
tired of answering prayers,
so let it ring a while, hope
they might hang up, though of course
they don't, don't because they know
the younger vets shuck off these
dark expeditions to me
thinking it's my job, not theirs,
because I've done it so long
I'm used to such nights, because
old as I am I'll still do
what they refuse to, and soon
I'm driving out of Marshall
headed north, most often toward
Shelton Laurel, toward some barn
where a calf that's been bad-bred
to save stud fees is trying
to be born, or a cow laid
out in a barn stall, dying
of milk fever, easily cured
if a man hadn't wagered
against his own dismal luck,
waited too late, hoping to
save my fee for a salt lick,
roll of barbed wire, and it's not
all his own fault, poor too long
turns the smartest man stupid,
makes him see nothing beyond

a short term gain, which is why
I know more likely than not
I'll be arriving too late,
what's to be done best done with
rifle or shotgun, so make
driving the good part, turn off
my radio, let the dark
close around until I know
a kind of loneliness that
doesn't feel sad as I pass
the homes of folks I don't know,
may never know, but wonder
what they are dreaming, what life
they wake to—thinking such things,
or sometimes just watching for
what stays unseen except on
country roads after midnight,
the copperheads soaking up
what heat the blacktop still holds,
foxes and bobcats, one time
in the forties a panther,
yellow eyes bright as truck beams,
black-tipped tail swishing before
leaping away through the trees,
back into its extinction,
all this thinking and watching
keeping my mind off what waits
on up the road, worst of all
the calves I have to pull one
piece at a time, birthing death.
Though sometimes it all works out.
I turn a calf's head and then
like a safe's combination
the womb unlocks, calf slides free,
or this night when stubborn life
got back on its feet, round eyes
clear and hungry, my I.V.

stuck in its neck, and I take
my time packing up, ask for
a second cup of coffee,
so I can linger awhile
in the barn mouth watching stars
awake in their wide pasture.

THE CODE

The code said any man who asked received
more than food and shelter, safety too,
so when a stranger came out of the night
with bloodstains on his shirt, MacGregor knew
what his obligations were and shared
his hearth and meat and whiskey. Soon enough
a pack of hounds leaped baying at his door,
with them men who wore MacGregor tartan,
kin seeking one who killed one of their own.
The old man turned them back into the dark,
then led his guest across the hills to where
a boat could be procured. Upon that shore
one favor would be asked, a favor granted.
MacGregor dipped the shirt into the loch,
washed his only son's blood from the cloth.

GOOD FRIDAY, 2006: SHELTON LAUREL

Below this knoll a man kneels.
Face close to the earth, he works
soil like a potter works clay,
kneading and shaping until
hands slowly open, reveal
a single green stalk before
he palms himself up the row
as if he hauls on his back
morning's sun-sprawl, a bringer
of light he cannot bring here
where oak trees knit tight shadows
across the marble that marks
the grave of David Shelton.
Thirteen years-old, he had asked
one mercy, not to be shot
like his father—in the face.
He shares this grave with the others
hauled back in the snow that night
by kin so their bodies could
darken Shelton ground. Wind lifts
the leaves, grows still. A man sows
his field the old way. The land
unscrolls like a palimpsest.

NOVEL EXCERPTS

From *One Foot In Eden* (2002)

The High Sheriff

There had been trouble in the upper part of the county at a honky-tonk called The Borderline, and Bobby had come by the house because he didn't want to go up there alone. A rough clientele, young bucks from Salem and Jocassee mixed with young bucks come down from North Carolina. That was usually the trouble, North Carolina boys fighting South Carolina boys.

I had a good book on the Cherokee Indians I'd just started, but when Bobby knocked on the door I knew I wouldn't be reading anymore this night. "Go have you a smoke on the porch," I told Bobby. "It'll take me a minute to get dressed."

Janice didn't open her eyes when I went into the bedroom to get my shoes and uniform. The lamp was still on, a book titled *History of Charleston* beside her. I looked at Janice, the high cheekbones and full lips, the rise of her breasts under the nightgown, and despite everything that had happened, and hadn't happened in our marriage, desire stirred in me like a bad habit I couldn't get shed of. I turned off the lamp.

Bobby and I followed the two-lane blacktop into the mountains. No light shone from the few farmhouse windows, not even a hangnail moon above. Darkness pressed against the car windows, deep and silent, and I couldn't help but think I was seeing into the future when much of this land would be buried deep underwater.

"It's a lonesome-feeling night, Sheriff," Bobby said, like he'd read my mind.

Bobby lit a Chesterfield, his face flaring visible for a moment before sinking back into the dark.

"Haints are bad to stir on a night like this," Bobby said, "leastways that's what my momma always claimed."

221

"So there are more things in heaven and earth than we might dream of?"

"What?" Bobby said.

"Haints. You believe in them?"

"I never said I did. I'm just saying what it was Momma notioned."

The fighting was over by the time Bobby and I got to The Borderline. Casualties were propped up in chairs, though a few still lay amidst shattered beer bottles, cigarette butts, blood, and teeth. It was as close to war as I'd seen since the Pacific. I let them see my badge. Then I stepped through the battle-field to the bar.

"How'd this start?" I asked Bennie Lusk.

Bennie held a mop in his hands, waiting for the last men on the floor to get moved so he could mop up the beer and blood.

"How do you think?" Bennie said.

He nodded toward a corner where Holland Winchester sprawled in a chair like a boxer resting between rounds, a boxer in a fight with Jersey Joe or Marciano. Holland's nose swerved toward his cheek, and a slit in the middle of his forehead opened like a third eye. His clenched fists lay on the table, bruised and puffy. He wore his uniform, and if you hadn't known Holland was sitting in a South Carolina honky-tonk, hadn't seen the Falstaff and Carling Black Label signs glowing on the walls, your next guess would have been he was still in Korea, waiting at a dressing station to be stitched and bandaged.

"What do you reckon the damage?" I asked Bennie.

"Ten ought to cover it."

Bobby and I walked over to Holland.

"Sheriff," he said, his wrecked face looking up at me. "Looks like you got here too late to join the ruckus."

"Looks that way," I said. "But it seems you got your share of it."

"Yeah," Holland said. "Sometimes when a man's hurting on the inside a good bar fight can help him feel some better."

"I don't quite catch your meaning," I said. "All I know is you've caused a good bit of damage to Mr. Lusk's establishment."

"I reckon I did," Holland said, looking around as if he hadn't noticed.

"I know what it's like when you get back from a war," I said. "You need some time to settle back in. You pay Mr. Lusk ten dollars, and we'll leave it at that."

"I ain't got no problem with that, Sheriff," Holland said.

"Next time you'll go to jail," I said. I smiled but I leveled my eyes on his to let him know I was serious.

"We'll see about that," Holland said. He smiled too but his dark-brown eyes had gone flat and cold as mine.

He reached into his pocket and lay a leather pouch and roll of bills on the table.

"There, Deputy," Holland said to Bobby, peeling off a five-dollar bill and five ones. "You run that money over to Bennie."

Bobby's face reddened.

"I don't take my damn orders from you," Bobby said.

For a moment I was tempted to go ahead and cuff him, because it was sure as dust in August that we'd have another run-in with Holland and he wouldn't come quietly. Tonight he was already wore out and wounded. Tonight might be easy as it got.

"Take the money to Bennie," I said.

Bobby didn't like it, but he picked up the money.

Holland stuffed the roll of bills back in his pocket.

"Look here, Sheriff."

Holland opened the leather pouch and shook the pouch's contents onto the table. A Gold Star fell out, then other things.

"Know what they are?" Holland asked, dropping the Gold Star back in the pouch.

I stared at what looked like eight dried-up figs. I knew what they were because I'd seen such things before in the Pacific.

"Yes," I told Holland. "I know what they are."

Holland nodded.

"That's right, Sheriff. You would know. You was in the World War."

Holland held one up to me.

"You reckon them ears can still hear?"

"No," I said.

"You sure about that."

"Yes," I said. "The dead don't hear and they don't speak."

"What do they do, Sheriff?"

"They just disappear."

Holland placed the ear with the others. They lay on the table between us like something wagered in a poker game.

"There was some said it was awful to cut the ear off a dead man," Holland said. "The way I see it, taking his life was a thousand times worse and I got medals for that."

Holland picked the ears up one at a time and placed them in the pouch.

"These here won't let me forget what I did over there. I don't take it lightly killing a man but I ain't afraid to own up to it either. All I did was what they sent me there to do."

Holland stuffed the pouch into his pocket.

"What did you bring back, Sheriff?" Holland asked.

"A sword and a rifle," I said. "Nothing like what you got in that pouch."

Then Holland Winchester said the last words he would ever say to me.

"There's some that gets through it easier than others when the shooting starts, right, Sheriff?"

Those words were what I remembered two weeks later when Bobby interrupted my lunch.

"Holland Winchester's missing," Bobby said. "His momma's got it in her head he's been killed."

Bobby sounded hopeful.

"You don't think we'd be that lucky, do you?" I said.

"Probably not," Bobby said, the hope in his voice giving way to irritation. "Holland's truck is at the farm. It ain't like he would walk to a honkytonk from there. He's probably just laying off drunk somewheres. Probably down at the river. I told her to call if he comes back."

"Let's give him a couple of hours to wander back home," I said "then I'll go up there and have a look-see."

Janice sat at the kitchen table, and she flinched when I said "look-see." Hillbilly talk, Janice called such words, but it was the way most folks still spoke in Oconee County. It put people more at ease when you talked like them, and when you are the high sheriff you spend a lot of time trying to put people at ease.

Janice wore a dark-blue skirt and white blouse. She had another meeting this afternoon. Friends of the Library, DAR—something like that.

"There's a missing person up at Jocassee," I said, "so I might not be back for supper."

"That will be fine," Janice said, not looking up from the table. "I won't be here anyway. Franny Anderson invited me to have dinner with her after our meeting."

I leaned over to kiss her.

"Don't," she said. "You'll smear my lipstick."

I walked back to the office and waited for Holland's mother to telephone. When no call came, I got in my patrol car and headed up Highway 288 toward Jocassee, toward what had once been home. The radio said it was over one hundred degrees downstate in Columbia. Dog days are biting us hard, the announcer said. I had the window down, but the back of my uniform already stuck to my skin as I left the town limits. The road was wavy with heat and humidity, its edges cluttered with campaign signs staked in the ground like tomato plants, some for General Eisenhower or Adlai Stevenson and even one for Strom Thurmond. Most were more local, including a couple with my name on them.

The blacktop steepened and pressure built in my ears until I opened my jaws. The road curved around Stumphouse Mountain, and beyond the silver-painted guard posts the land dropped away like those old European maps of the unknown world. If it were late fall or winter I would have been able to see a white rope of water on the far side of the gorge, a waterfall that had claimed two lives in the last twenty years.

The road leveled out, and suddenly I was in the mountains. It surprised me, as it somehow always did, that so much could change in just a few miles. It was still hot, but the humidity had been rinsed from the air. Pines got scarce, replaced by ash and oak. The soil was different too, no longer red but black. Rockier as well, harder to make a living from.

Dead blacksnakes draped on the fences told me what I already knew from the way corn and tobacco wilted in the fields—it had rained no more up here than it had in Seneca. I wondered how Daddy and my brother's crops were doing, and I reckoned no better.

I pulled off the road when I came to Roy Whitmire's store, parking beside the sign that said *Last Chance For Gas Twenty Miles.* I stepped past men sitting on Cheerwine and Double Cola crates. With their bald heads and wrinkled necks they looked like mud turtles sunning on stumps. The men gave me familiar nods, but the dog days had sapped the talk out of them. I swirled my hand in the drink cooler on the porch, ice and water numbing my fingers before I found a six-ounce bottle. I wasn't thirsty, but it wasn't right not to buy something. I stepped inside, into a big room that was darker than outside but no cooler.

The store was pretty much the way it had always been, the front shelf filled with everything from Eagle Claw fish hooks to Goody headache powders, a big jar on the counter, pickled eggs in the murky brine pressed against the glass like huge eyeballs. Next to the cash register another jar, this one filled with black licorice whips.

"Howdy, stranger," Roy said, grinning as he stepped from around the counter to shake my hand.

We made small talk a few minutes. My eyes adjusted to the dark and I saw the stuffed bobcat on the back wall—paw poised to strike, yellow eyes glaring—still at bay after three decades. Fifty-pound sacks of Dekalb corn seed lay stacked on the floor below it.

"I don't reckon you've seen Holland Winchester the last couple of days?" I finally said, getting to the reason I'd stopped.

"No," Roy said. "Of course I ain't exactly been out searching for him. I got enough trouble that's already found me without looking for more."

Roy lifted the nickel I'd placed on the counter, leaving the penny where it lay.

"Buffalo head," he said, holding the nickel between us. "You don't see many of them anymore. They done got near scarce as real buffalo. You sure you don't want to keep it?"

"No," I said.

Roy closed the register.

"Your daddy and brother, they're seeing a hard time of it, like most every-body with something in the ground. That ain't no good news for them or me."

Roy nodded toward the shelf behind him.

"I got a shoebox full of credit tickets. If it don't come a good rain soon I'd just as well use them to start my fires this winter. But you don't have to worry about such things down in town, do you?"

"No, I guess not."

I lay the Coke bottle on the counter.

"You telephone me if Holland comes by."

"I'll do it," Roy said. "You bring me one of your voting posters next time you're up this way. I'll put it in the window."

Before I got in my car I glanced at the sky. Like it mattered to me, a man with a certain paycheck come rain or drought.

A mile from the North Carolina line I turned off the blacktop and headed into the valley called Jocassee. The word meant "valley of the lost" to the Cherokee, for a princess named Jocassee had once drowned herself here and her body had never been found. The road I followed had once been a trail, a trail De Soto had followed four hundred years ago when he'd searched these mountains for gold. De Soto and his men had found no riches and believed the land worthless for raising corn. Two centuries after De Soto, the French-man Michaux would find something here rarer than gold, a flower that existed nowhere else in the world.

I took another right and passed fields where men once hid horses during what folks up here still spoke of as the Confederate War. A war most folks in Jocassee had tried to stay out of, believing it was the slave owners' war, not theirs. When they'd been forced to choose, many had fought with the Union instead of the Confederacy, including several of my ancestors. Though I'd tried, there weren't enough votes in Jocassee to get the county to pave the road or even dump a few truckloads of gravel. Like almost everything else up here, the road was little different than it had been in the 1860s. But change was coming, a change big enough to swallow this whole valley.

On the road's left side was the land Carolina Power had bought from the timber company last winter, a thousand acres that ran all the way down to Horsepasture River. The power company already had holdings on the other side of the water, and I doubted there was anyone left up here who didn't now know what Carolina Power was going to do to this valley.

It wasn't hard to figure out. All you had to do was look downstate at Santee-Cooper Reservoir. People up here wouldn't like it worth a damn to be run off their land, but when the time came there would be nothing they could do about it.

The road curved and dipped deeper into the valley. I passed my brother Travis's house and then the house I'd grown up in. Daddy worked in the far field, the dust plumes rising behind his tractor telling the whole story of the kind of year it looked to be.

The land leveled out. I smelled the river, but the road swerved left before I saw water. Branches slapped my windshield as I bumped over a road now no better than a logger's skid trail. I stopped at the battered mailbox with *Winchester* painted on its side. I turned in and parked behind a blue Ford truck new as the telephone line that ran out of the woods. Holland was right. He'd done his portion of the killing Uncle Sam had sent him to do. A truck and telephone had been part of his reward.

Mrs. Winchester sat on her front porch. I knew she'd been there a while, waiting for Holland or me to show up. I took off my hat and stepped onto the porch. I remembered seeing her when I was a boy and thinking how pretty she'd been with her long, black hair, her eyes dark as mahogany wood. She couldn't be more than fifty-two or three, but her hair was gray as squirrel fur now, her face furrowed like an overworked field. Only her eyes looked the same, deep brown like her son's.

Those eyes didn't blink when she spoke. Except for her mouth, her face was so rigid it could have been on a daguerreotype.

"He's dead," Mrs. Winchester said. "My boy is dead."

There was such finality in her voice I expected her to get up and lead me to Holland's body.

"How do you know that?" I asked when she didn't say or do anything else.

"I heard the shot. I didn't think nothing of it at first but when Holland didn't come in for his noon-dinner I knew it certain as I'm sitting on this here porch."

Her face didn't change, but for the first time grief and anger tinged her voice.

"Billy Holcombe's done killed my boy."

"Why would Billy Holcombe want to do such a thing?"

She didn't answer that question, didn't even try to. Ten years of experience told me there was more *wouldn't* answer than *couldn't* answer in her silence.

I looked at some corn planted close to the house. A scarecrow leaned like a drunk above the puny stalks. The hat and straw that had shaped the seed-sack face lay on the ground. It didn't matter. The drought had already taken anything the crows would want.

"When's the last time you seen Holland?" I asked, meeting her eyes again.

"This morning. I went out to feed the chickens. I come back and he was gone."

"And nobody came and picked him up?"

"No, I'd a heard it if they'd of done so."

"And Holland didn't say he was off to anywhere?"

"You go see Billy Holcombe," Mrs. Winchester said. "He's the one knows where Holland is."

Her eyes were stern and righteous, but I knew she wasn't telling me everything. For a moment I wondered if maybe she had done something to Holland, but that didn't seem likely. Everything I'd learned as a law man told me a mother who'd killed her grown child would have already confessed. She could have no more carried that burden inside her than I could have carried a baby inside me. What seemed likely was what Bobby had said. Holland was passed out somewhere drunk, someplace pretty close by since he hadn't taken his truck.

"I know the Holcombes is some kin to you," Mrs. Winchester said, and she let that hang in the air between us.

"If he's went and done something against the law that'll make no difference," I said, slipping more and more into the way of speaking I'd grown up with.

I put my hat back on.

"I'm going to have me a look around. I'll walk the river a ways and I'll go see Billy Holcombe, but I ain't accusing nobody of nothing yet. If Holland hasn't showed by morning I'll get a serious search going."

"He ain't coming back," Mrs. Winchester said.

She got up from the chair and went inside.

I walked down to a river that drought had made more dry stones than water. A current that would have knocked a man down in April was now a trickle. I limped across the shore of rocks as I followed the river downstream. I shouted Holland's name every so often, using what wind I had in my one good lung. But even if he wasn't passed out drunk, he'd have a hard time hearing me. Cicadas filled the trees, loud and unceasing as a cotton mill's weave room.

I straddled a barbed wire fence and stepped onto Billy Holcombe's land, land Billy had bought years back from Mrs. Winchester's husband. I wondered if that had something to do with why I was up here—an argument over a boundary line. Plenty of blood had been spilled over such matters in Oconee County. But I was getting way ahead of myself. I didn't even have a body yet.

Billy's tobacco pressed up close to the river. His rows were tight, no more than two feet apart, which meant more yield but the cultivating had to be done by hand. It was a good crop, bright green and tall, nothing like the tobacco in the fields I'd seen earlier. The river had saved him, soaking the soil so well in spring the roots still got moisture. Come fall he might be one of the few farmers in Jocassee with anything to cure in a tobacco barn.

Billy Holcombe hoed at the opposite end of the row where I stood, Cousin Billy, though a good ways back. He was a good bit younger than me, so I hadn't known him growing up, but I'd known his parents and older sister. All I remembered of him was that the first year I'd been down at Clemson College he'd gotten polio.

His being the only person in Jocassee to get polio hadn't been surprising, at least to the Holcombe's neighbors. Bad luck followed his people like some mangy hound they couldn't run off. His granddaddy and uncle had both owned farms at one time but lost them and ended up sharecropping for the Winchesters. They hadn't been trifling men. They'd worked hard and didn't drink, but it seemed the hail always fell hardest on the Holcombe's crops. If lightning hit a barn in Jocassee or blackleg killed a cow, it most always belonged to a Holcombe.

Billy's back was to me. The cicadas sang so loud he probably hadn't heard me calling Holland's name. I waited for him to finish his row, remembering how it felt to hoe tobacco—how the sweat stung your eyes and your back stayed bent so long you felt by day's end you'd need a crowbar to straighten yourself. I remembered how palms got rough as sandpaper and the back of your neck got red as brick and you'd get to the end of one row and keep your head down like a mule wearing blinders because you didn't want to see how many more of those long rows you had left.

But that wasn't the worst of it. The worst was knowing no matter how hard you worked, it might come to nothing. Even if the weather spared your crop, and that was a big if, you still had root knot and blue mold to worry about, not to mention bud worms and tobacco worms. Billy's tobacco looked healthy, but even so he wasn't home free yet. The hardest work came at harvest time. The tobacco gum turned your hands and arms brown as it stuck to your skin like pine resin. You had to string the leaves onto tobacco sticks and hang the sticks in the barn to cure. Even then a lightning strike or cigarette could set the barn on fire, and in five minutes nine months' work would be nothing but smoke and ashes.

Billy Holcombe knew all this better than I did, because it wasn't memory for him. It was as much a part of Billy as his own shadow. But as I watched him finish his row I knew he couldn't allow himself to think about how uncertain his livelihood was. To farm a man did have to act like a mule—keep his eyes and thoughts on the ground straight in front of him. If he didn't he couldn't keep coming out to his fields day after day.

I walked into the field, stepping on clumps of dirt and weeds Billy's hoe had turned up. That hoe rose and fell ahead of me, and despite myself it was like the hoe was in my hands, not his. For a few moments I could feel the worn oak handle smooth against my palms, could feel the hoe blade break the soil. Don't pretend you miss such a life as this, I told myself.

I didn't speak until he'd finished his row. He turned and found me not five feet behind him. For the first time I wondered if Mrs. Winchester might have spoken the gospel truth, because Billy didn't act at all surprised to see me.

"How you doing, Sheriff?" he said, meeting my eyes.

He didn't say *What's the matter?* or *Has something happened?* He spoke as if we'd just bumped into each other in downtown Seneca, not the middle of his tobacco field.

"I'm looking for Holland Winchester," I said, watching his blue eyes. "You seen him?"

"No," Billy said.

The eyes can lie, but eventually they'll tell you the truth. When Billy said no he glanced at his clenched right hand. I knew what that meant because I'd seen many another man do the same thing in such a situation. That right hand of Billy's had helped lift rocks from his field big as watermelons. It had helped fell oak trees you couldn't get your arms around. And maybe, just maybe, that hand had helped hold a shotgun steady enough to kill a man.

Billy Holcombe was looking for strength.

But I wasn't going to press him, not yet.

"Well if you do see him," I said, "tell him he's got his momma worried."

"I'll do that, Sheriff."

Billy wiped his brow with the back of his hand. He was sweating from the hoeing, but I wondered if he had another reason to sweat.

"If he doesn't come home tonight I'll bring some men with me in the morning," I told Mrs. Winchester. "We'll search the woods and river, if we need to."

I wrote down my telephone number.

"Here," I said, handing it to her. "You call if Holland comes in tonight. I don't care if it's three in the morning."

I got in the patrol car and bumped down the dirt road. I thought again about what Holland had said to me two weeks ago about some men being better able to stand things when the shooting starts. I knew he was talking about more than just not getting killed or maimed so bad you wished you'd been killed. Holland was talking about how some men weren't much bothered by the killing. I had been, and I carried with me the glazed eyes of every Japanese soldier I'd taken the life from on Guadalcanal. But I'd fought with men like Holland who seemed bred for fighting the same way gamecocks are. Their eyes lit up when the shooting started. They were utterly fearless, and you thanked God they were on your side instead of the other. Like Holland, they'd wanted souvenirs from their kills, mainly gold teeth carved out with Ka-Bar knives, leaving mouths of dead Japanese gapped-toothed like jack-o'-lanterns.

As I slowed at the mailbox with *Alexander* painted on it, I wondered if Billy Holcombe could kill a man. If Holland Winchester didn't show up by morning I was going to have to give that question some serious thought.

Travis's truck was parked beside Daddy's, and Travis himself was on the roof. He'd heard me drive up but kept hammering until he'd used the half dozen nails clenched in his mouth. Then he stepped down the ladder to where I waited. We'd been born less than two years apart, and though we were both gray-eyed and tall, I'd always been big-boned like Daddy, while Travis favored Momma. But Travis had filled out in the last few years. There was no mistaking we were brothers, at least on the outside.

"What brings you up here," he said, and not in a welcome way. "I know it ain't your family."

His saying that rankled me, mainly because of the truth in it.

"I've been looking for Holland Winchester."

"What's he done now?" Travis asked.

"Disappeared."

"And you're wanting to find him?"

"Not particularly, but that's my job."

"Well he ain't here, Sheriff."

I let the "Sheriff" comment pass. I didn't want this visit to end like the last one.

"I was going to take Daddy over to Salem for supper."

"He's done ate," Travis said. "There was a time you'd have known that."

"Where is he?"

"Mending fence in the pasture."

Travis waved the hammer toward the roof.

"That's why I'm doing this now. Everybody but Daddy knows he's too old to be cat-walking on a roof. If he was here he'd not let me get up there without him helping me."

Travis clamped his mouth shut like it was a spigot he'd let run longer than he meant to. He glanced at the roof. I knew he wanted to get back up there, away from me. A whippoorwill called from the white oak in the back yard, its cry mournful as a funeral dirge.

"How are Will and Carlton?" I asked.

"Come around once in a while and you'd know."

"I been meaning to," and soon as I spoke I knew my words to be the wrong thing to say.

"Been meaning to," Travis said, his words mocking mine.

He stared at me, the same way he'd stare at a stump in his field or anything else bothersome he'd just as soon not have to deal with.

"How long has it been since you seen them or Daddy? Five months? Six? You think if you buy Daddy a cafe meal that's some big thing?"

"I don't need this, Travis," I said.

"No, you don't," Travis said, twisting my meaning. "You ain't needed anything up here for a long time."

Travis raised his hammer. For a second I thought he might throw it at me.

I couldn't have blamed him if he'd tried. Once we'd been close in a way I'd never been with my other brother or sister.

"You boys are ever alike as to share the same shadow," Momma had said when we were growing up. She hadn't been just talking about how we favored one another in our looks. It was something deep inside us—the way we knew what each other was feeling or thinking, the way we didn't argue and fight like most brothers. We had never said it, but we'd always believed no matter who else came into our lives—wives, children—we would always be that close. Travis believed I'd betrayed that pact, and I knew he was right.

"I got to finish this roof," Travis said.

"Tell Daddy I came by," I said, getting back in the car.

232

I drove out of the valley, the sun sinking into the trees. By the time I got on the blacktop, twilight had turned the strange color it always does in August, a pink tinged with green and silver. That color had always made it seem like time had somehow leaked out of the world, past and present blending together. My mind skimmed across time like a water spider crossing a pool, all the way back to 1935 when I was eighteen and Clemson had just offered me a football scholarship.

"I want to do something to help you celebrate," Janice Griffen had told me as we left homeroom. "How about dinner, at my house? My father will grill us steaks."

I had been too flustered to say anything but yes. Not only flustered but surprised by the invitation. Janice was a town kid, a doctor's daughter.

I had parked our family's twelve-year-old truck a quarter mile from Doctor Griffen's house. I wore my church clothes, my dress shoes blistering my heels as I walked past big white houses with front yards green as new money.

Doctor Griffen had met me at the door. He'd placed his arm around my shoulder and led me down a hallway wide as the road that led to my family's house, a burgundy-colored rug cushioning my steps. I followed Doctor Griffen to a den lined with bookshelves. A mahogany writing desk filled one corner, a radio big as a pot-belly stove in the other.

"Have a seat," Doctor Griffen said. "Janice will be down soon."

In a few minutes we gathered around a huge oak dining room table. What struck me at that moment was how everything in that house seemed solid as that table, solid enough to weather a Depression that had caused men once rich to wander the country begging for work and food.

But I had been wrong. Even at that moment the house, the carpet and furniture, the very chair I sat in, was an illusion. Almost all of Doctor Griffen's money had been lost years before in the stock crash of 1929, the rest five years later in a land deal.

"Try your steak, Will," Doctor Griffen said after the prayer. "If it's too rare I'll put it back on the grill."

He spoke in a light-hearted way, as if an undercooked steak was the biggest concern he had. He was doing all he could, as he would the next three years, to keep an illusion alive for his daughter and wife.

I picked up my knife, but two forks lay to the left of my plate. I hesitated.

"This one," Janice had said, handing me the larger fork of the two.

When I drove into Seneca streetlights were on, the movie house marquee as well. *Singing in the Rain Coming Soon,* red letters claimed. There were plenty of farmers praying that marquee was right. The air seemed heavier, as it always did after I'd been in the mountains. I parked the car in front of the courthouse and walked across the street to McSwain's Café.

Darrell McSwain sweated like Satan's own cook as he flipped the liver mush and hamburgers sizzling on his grill. A fan blew right on him, but all it did was keep the smoke out of his face. Couples filled the booths. I nodded at the folks I knew and sat down on a stool. The jukebox played Lefty Frizzell's "Too Few Kisses Too Late."

"So what will you have, Sheriff?" Darrell asked.

"How about some cool weather?"

"Sold all I had to a drummer. Last I seen of him he was high-footing it to the Yukon."

"Then how about some ice tea and a burger."

"I can manage that," Darrell said, and turned toward his grill.

Someone had left a Greenville News on the counter. The Air Force was bombing the hell out of North Korea. Batista had more problems in Cuba. But these events seemed somehow farther away than when I'd read about them this morning. It was as if being in Jocassee had taken me out of the here and now.

"How are they going to do this year?" Darrell McSwain asked when he lay my supper on the counter.

I'd played football three years at Clemson, so Darrell and a lot of other people assumed I had some kind of lifelong loyalty. They seemed to forget what had happened after the spring game my junior year. I'd tore up my knee in that game, and Clemson had found a loophole to take my scholarship away.

"We'll make sure he gets his degree," Coach Barkley had promised Daddy when he recruited me, and that had been important to Daddy and especially my Uncle Thomas, who had the most education of anyone in Jocassee.

"There's nothing more valuable than what is behind this glass," Uncle Thomas had once told me, opening a child-tall bookshelf and handing me a book. "Knowledge is the one thing no one can take away from you."

I'd done my part, good grades in high school and at Clemson, but one hit on the knee and suddenly good grades and a promise made three years earlier no longer mattered.

"I haven't been keeping up with them, Darrell," I said, and he moved on down the counter with his tea pitcher.

I walked over to the office afterward. Mrs. Winchester hadn't called. I told Bobby to go home and get a good night's sleep, because it looked like we might be traipsing through woods and water come morning.

After a while I went home too, or at least what I called home now. Janice was in bed reading her book on Charleston.

"How was your meeting?" I asked.

"Frustrating, as usual. Gladys Williams had her silly suggestions. Anne Lester wouldn't agree to anything."

"I'm sorry to hear that," I said.

I undressed and got into bed. In a few minutes Janice lay the book on the table and turned off the lamp. The window was open, but no breeze fluttered the curtains. It was a night when sleep would come slow and fitfully, a night I would stare at a ceiling I could not see and think about the choices I'd made in my life, the choices my brother had reminded me of.

I pressed my chest against Janice's back, my hand rubbing her hip.

"No," she said, moving away.

The heat lay over me thick and still as a quilt. The only thing stirring was my mind, remembering that first year Janice and I had been married, remembering the nights Janice reached out for me. She would go to bed first because I'd be up to midnight doing my school work, my body bruised and aching from the afternoon's practice. The lights would be off, and I would undress and lie down beside her. Janice would pull me to her, no nightgown or slip, only her warm skin smooth against mine. I would be exhausted and she half asleep, and somehow that made it better, as if our hearts had an energy that went beyond our bodies, like we'd stepped out of time into the sweet everlasting.

I finally got out of bed, walked into the living room and picked up *Red Carolinians,* the book I'd just begun when Bobby had interrupted me that night two weeks ago. The story was one I'd heard about and seen parts of growing up in Jocassee, a story of people living and working land for generations and then vanishing, leaving behind the arrowheads and pieces of pottery I'd turned up while plowing. Leaving behind place names too— Jocassee, Oconee, Chattooga—each pretty, vowel-heavy word an echo of a lost world.

I thought of how the descendants of settlers from Scotland and Wales and Ireland and England—people poor and desperate enough to risk their lives to take that land, as the Cherokees had once taken it from other tribes—would soon vanish from Jocassee as well. Fifteen years, twenty at most, and it'll be all water, at least that was what the people who would know had told me. Reservoir, reservation, the two words sounded so alike. In a dictionary they would be on the same page.

There was a kind of justice in what would happen. But this time the disappearance would be total. There would be no names left, because Alexander

Springs and Boone Creek and Robertson's Ford and Chapman's Bridge would all disappear. Every tombstone with Holcombe or Lusk or Alexander or Nicholson chiseled into it would vanish as well.

I looked at my watch. Past midnight and Mrs. Winchester still hadn't called. As I finished the book's last sentence, I wondered if Holland's body might also vanish under that coming water.

"The Bartram book hasn't come in yet, Sheriff," Mrs. Pipkin said the next morning. "I've unfortunately learned the employees at the state library are never in a hurry. A month ago my husband ordered a book he needed for his shop class. It still hasn't shown up."

Mrs. Pipkin slipped the library card into the book I'd returned, a book that had quoted Bartram. My Uncle Thomas had owned *Bartram's Travels*, and he'd let me borrow it when I was in high school. I wanted to read it again, so I'd asked Mrs. Pipkin to find a copy.

"Maybe it will come in today," Mrs. Pipkin said. "I'll let you know if it does."

Mrs. Pipkin disappeared into the fiction section to re-shelve a book.

Prim, that's how I supposed a novelist would describe Mrs. Pipkin—her hair tight in a bun, her spinster dresses and clipped, precise words. But she was attractive despite her best efforts. Her beauty was like a secret she couldn't conceal. I wondered if she lay down at night with her black hair loose about her shoulders. I wondered if there were nights she reached for the man who lay beside her, understanding that a woman's beauty is sometimes best revealed in darkness.

I walked across the square to the courthouse and telephoned Tom Watson and Leonard Roach while Bobby rounded up a dozen other men. Tom and Leonard rode with me, Leonard's bloodhound Stonewall lying between them on the back seat.

"You picked a good day to get us up in the hills, Sheriff," Tom said. "By noon-dinner time Seneca's going to be hot as a bellyful of wasps."

When we got to Mrs. Winchester's she met us on the porch.

"You'll be needful of this," she said, offering me what she clutched in a hand gnarled into a claw by rheumatism.

I took the shirt I hadn't had to ask for. She knew what we were about.

It was a grim business for her to see, Tom pulling the grappling hooks out of the back of the car in case we needed them, Leonard pressing Holland's shirt to Stonewall's nose as three carloads of men set themselves six feet apart to start their sweep through the woods.

Her expression didn't change as she watched though. She'd already buried a husband and two of her four children. It crossed my mind that a body to bury beside the others was all she hoped for now. I needed to know why she was so certain he was dead, so as Stonewall trotted through the woods toward Billy Holcombe's farm, I stepped up on the porch.

"I've got to know more than you've told me, Mrs. Winchester," I said. "I reckon you know that."

For a few seconds she didn't say or do anything. Then she nodded.

"So what can you tell me?"

"Holland was having relations with her," she said, not even blinking.

"You mean Billy Holcombe's wife?"

"Yes."

"And you heard a shot from over there?"

"I heard it," Mrs. Winchester said. "What Holland went and done wasn't right, but he shouldn't ought to have died for it."

Stonewall bayed closer and closer to Billy Holcombe's farm. What she told me was the truth, all of it, because it all made sense—Billy acting so unsurprised to see me, Holland disappearing but his truck being here, the shot she'd heard.

"He was wearing his soldier uniform," Mrs. Winchester said. "He always wore it when he went over there."

For the first time her voice wavered.

"However is it fair that he could do all that fighting in Korea and not get much more than a briar scratch, then come back home and get shot in his own back yard? Can you answer me that, Sheriff?"

I shook my head. I had no answer, at least none I wanted to tell her. She was an old woman who'd outlived two, maybe three, of her children. Whatever mistakes she'd made raising them she didn't need to be reminded of. I just looked down at the ground between us, knowing she and I had more in common than she probably realized.

I had lost a child too, not like her but in my own way. There had been times as the years passed when I'd wonder what that child would have looked like had it been born alive. I'd imagine a child at five or six or eight or ever how many years had passed since the miscarriage. Sometimes I'd imagine a boy, sometimes a girl. Picking at scabs, that was all I was doing at such times, but I couldn't seem to stop myself.

I put my hat back on.

"I'll do all of what I can to find your son, Mrs. Winchester."

"I thank you for it," she said.

I stepped off the porch and walked into the woods, meeting Leonard and Bobby and Tom on their way back.

"It's like he's done disappeared into thin air, Sheriff," Leonard said. "We got out there in front of Holcombe's house and the trail went colder than grave frost. I figured I'd start Stonewall again out in front of Mrs. Winchester's, see if he can sniff up another trail."

"If Stonewall doesn't, you all start dragging the river," I said. "You speak to anybody over there?"

"No," Bobby said. "I saw Holcombe's wife peeking behind a window but she didn't come out."

"Well, I'm going to talk to the both of them. I'll get up with you later."

I walked on, the cicadas making their racket above me in the trees, calling for rain as Daddy used to say. Doing a pretty poor job of it too, for the pieces of sky I saw through the trees were blue as a jaybird.

I stepped through the barbed wire fence. Down toward the river I saw Billy in his field, but I stepped up on the porch instead. I rapped my knuckles on the door.

When she looked at me through the screen I saw what had brought Holland this way. Amy Holcombe was blue-eyed with yellow hair that fell to her waist, tall and slim but full-breasted. When she opened the screen door, I saw she was pregnant.

I wondered right then and there whose child it was.

"What brings you out this morning, Sheriff?" she asked, trying to act surprised—as if she hadn't noticed the dog and searchers tramping all over her yard.

"Holland Winchester's missing," I said. "His momma says he was over here yesterday."

"I don't know the least thing about that," Amy Holcombe said, and she said it in a flat kind of way, the way someone would say something they'd memorized for a test.

"You mind me visiting with you a minute, Mrs. Holcombe?" I asked and stepped a little closer.

"I've got a bushel of chores to do," she said. "I ain't even cleared breakfast off the table."

"Just for a minute, Mrs. Holcombe. Then I'll be on my way."

She didn't want to let me in, but I could tell she was calculating it would be more trouble not to. She opened the screen door wider.

"The house is ever a mess. Like I said, I got a lot to do."

I smelled the wood smoke as I stepped inside and remembered I hadn't seen a gap in the trees for a power line. A clock that didn't work lay on the mantle above the hearth. Beside it an oil lamp, against the wall a couple of ladder-back chairs. That was enough to know they were poor in a way none of my people had been since the Depression. They got water from a well, and they still used an outhouse. I wasn't even sure they had a truck. There'd been no tire tracks in the weeds and rocks that passed for a driveway.

She didn't ask me to sit down, but I did anyway.

"I can get you some tea to drink," she said, but her tone made it clear she didn't want to get me anything other than out of her house.

"No, thanks."

She sat down in the other chair.

"I just wanted to ask you about Holland Winchester. Like I said, his momma thinks you might know something."

"I didn't know," Amy Holcombe said, and she caught herself, because what she was going to say was either "I didn't know him" or "I didn't know him hardly at all." Either way it was past tense, the tense used to speak of the dead.

"I didn't know him to be missing," she finally said, and that was slick on her part because she didn't have to take back the *I didn't know.*

"I think maybe you and your husband know where he is," I said. "It's going to be easier on everybody if you all just go ahead and admit it."

"I don't know nothing about where Holland Winchester is," she said, getting up from her chair. "I got things to do, Sheriff."

"You won't mind me looking around, will you?"

"Me and Billy, we got nothing to hide," she said. She picked up the broom like she was going to sweep me out if I didn't move toward the door on my own.

I got up from the chair. Nothing to hide but a body, I thought, a body I believed would turn up soon enough.

"Goodbye, Mrs. Holcombe," I said, but she'd already turned her back to me.

The sunlight was bright and startling after being in the house. I checked the barn first and found a truck with two flat tires and a cracked engine block. The only way that truck could have moved was if there'd been a team of horses to drag it. That was good news for me. Holland's body couldn't be too far away. I stepped in the woodshed, and after that I peered down the well. I wasn't seriously searching, just getting a feel for the layout of the farm.

I watched Billy out in his field. He hadn't tried to make a run for it, the way many another man might have. Instead, he was going about his business.

239

I wondered for the first time if I'd underestimated him. I wondered if he might be like those men I'd known in the Pacific, the ones you'd have expected to be the first to cut and run and then in battle they surprised you, surprised themselves.

I had been a man like that, though I was big and stout-looking enough to fool everybody but myself. I hadn't known what I would do in battle, and the morning I waited for the LAV to land on Guadalcanal, I was so afraid I threw up.

"The hillbilly's not used to the ocean," one of the other soldiers said, but it wasn't seasickness. Then we'd waded in, and I heard a thump against the chest of the man beside me. He stopped as if he'd forgotten something on the LAV as a stain blossomed on the front of his uniform. The sand puffed up in front of me from a bullet aimed too low, and I felt in that moment something of what I'd felt in football games after the first hit, the first smear of blood on my jersey. The fear was still there, but it was muted, like the sound of the crowd is once the game starts. Even my bad knee didn't seem to slow me down. I ran for the tree line like a wingback zig-zagging to avoid tacklers. I made it but was still gasping the watery tropical air when a Japanese soldier raised up ten yards in front of me. I aimed for his heart and I found it.

In the three weeks before a bullet pierced my lung and sent me back home, I'd killed at least three other men.

"I'm giving you this deputy's job because you know if it comes to the have-to you can kill a man," Sheriff McLeod had told me after I got back to Seneca.

"Yes sir," I'd answered, glad to have a job outside a mill, a job where I'd get to use my brain some, use it even more when Sheriff McLeod retired two years later.

As I walked down the field edge to where Billy worked, I started a conversation with myself, because there had been times doing such had helped me solve crimes. *O.K., Billy, where would you hide a body? Maybe in the barn loft? Maybe the bottom of the well? It doesn't seem likely. You had to know those were the kinds of places we'd look first. Maybe in the woods, but a fresh dug grave would stick out like a No-Heller in a church full of Hardshell Baptists. Besides, the ground is hard as cement. No, Billy,* I said to myself. *You didn't bury that body.*

The season was against him. It was the time of year when the Dog Star rose with the sun, and while that meant hot weather and little rain, there was more to it than that. The old Romans had considered it an unwholesome season, and it was hard not to agree with them. Ponds and rivers got scummy and stagnant this time of year, the air still and heavy, like a weight pressing down. The cattle got pinkeye and blackleg, and a dog or cat could go mad. Polio got worse too, or so people believed. Children weren't allowed to go swimming or to picture shows.

For Billy it also meant a dead man would bloat and rot twice as fast. If he didn't bury Holland's body, anybody within a half mile would soon enough smell it.

Unless he put it in the river, and that was where I figured the body to be. Low as the river was it could still hide a body, especially if you weighted it down with a creek rock or waterlogged tree.

Billy saw me coming and raised up from topping his tobacco. He stood in the middle of a row. The first stick of dynamite went off and then another, but Billy didn't take his eyes off me. I thought for a moment he might raise his hands over his head and make it easy for all of us, but he didn't.

Then I saw them, drifting down slow as black ashes over the trees across the river. To tell the truth I was disappointed in Billy. He hadn't kept his head about him after all. It was almost funny the way he stood in the field facing me, doing his best to look innocent while right behind him the buzzards in the sky marked a giant X where Holland's body was. Billy's shotgun lay at the end of his row, and I stood between him and it.

"Looks to be something dead over yonder," I said.

I waited for Billy's face to go pale as he looked over his shoulder and saw he'd forgotten about buzzards when he'd hidden Holland's body. I'd seen men piss on themselves at such moments. Others would cry, or fall down, or run though they knew there was nowhere to run to, run like chickens that had just had their heads cut off and their bodies didn't yet know they were doomed.

"It's my plow horse," Billy said, hardly giving the buzzards a glance. "He broke his leg yesterday."

And that set me back, set me back hard as if he'd sucker-punched me in the stomach. He couldn't have come up with a lie that quick and delivered it that matter-of-fact, at least I didn't believe he could.

"That's some hard luck," I told him.

We talked a couple more minutes, but before I could bring up what Mrs. Winchester had told me and Bobby, Tom and Leonard sloshed out of the river, Stonewall loping behind them.

"Bring up anything?" I asked.

Tom opened his pack to show a big trout the dynamite had blown out of the water. I pointed out the buzzards to them.

"Damn," Bobby said. "I guess we been looking down when we should of been looking up."

"You want us to go look?" Tom asked, but I told them I'd take care of that, for them to go on to town for lunch, round up some more men if they could and get back by two o'clock. They started to leave, but I nodded at Bobby to stay a few moments longer.

"What you got the .12 gauge for?" I asked Billy.

"Groundhog been troubling my cabbage," he said, and that was a reasonable enough answer.

"You seen him lately?" I asked.

"Who?" Billy asked.

Smart, Billy, I thought, *but be careful you don't outsmart yourself.*

"The groundhog," I said.

"No, I don't expect I will with you all blasting up the river."

"Then you won't mind Bobby taking your shotgun with him. We might need to check it if a body turns up. Besides, I don't like to be around loaded guns. I'm bad superstitious that way."

"Suit yourself," Billy said, like it was no matter to him.

Bobby picked up the gun and left. I squatted down and wiped my glasses, something to do while I thought about what should come next.

Leonard and Stonewall had come up with nothing. Neither had the men searching the water and woods. We'd search the other side of the river come afternoon, and Tom could take his grappling hook and dynamite farther downstream. Surely Holland's body would show up by dusk.

But maybe I wouldn't have to wait that long, I thought. Maybe if I got under Billy Holcombe's skin he might save me a few hours.

"I'm going to give you the lay of the land, Billy," I said. "Then I'll let you have your say. Mrs. Winchester says Holland was tomcatting around with your Missus. She believe you done shot and killed him for it."

Come on, Billy, I thought. *Get riled up. Tell me what a worthless son of a bitch Holland was. I'll not argue with the truth of that. Tell me how he threatened you or your wife. Tell me how it was self-defense. Confess and we'll get this over with here and now.*

"That's all lies," Billy said, but the lack of heat in his voice argued otherwise.

"She claims she heard the shot."

"She heard me shoot my plow horse."

"She claims the shot was near your house," I said, not giving him much as a second between questions. "Maybe even inside it."

"She's a old woman. She's just addled."

"What about your wife and Holland?" I asked.

"That's a lie."

I looked at the buzzards. I'd have to walk over in a minute and make sure that was a horse they were drawn to. My knee wouldn't enjoy risking a slip in the river, but there was nothing to be done about that.

"So you wouldn't have a problem with me checking inside your house?"

"No," Billy said.

His face showed me little. He was getting more comfortable with his lies, like a card player learning how to bluff.

"Or anywhere else on your land."

"No."

"And you shot that horse yesterday morning as well?"

He caught what I was trying to do.

"I shot my horse yesterday morning, but I didn't shoot nothing else."

"So your horse broke its leg plowing?"

"Yes," Billy said. "I was plowing my cabbage and his hoof got slicked on a rock. I didn't want to smell him so I took him over the river, put him back a ways in the woods."

That made sense but only up to a point. *You may have gotten a bit too clever for your own good, Billy,* I thought.

What I said was, "Let's go have a look at that horse."

I let Billy lead, both of us taking our time as we made our way down the bank. He stepped into the water, but slow and careful, careful beyond worrying about slipping. He was scared, scared because it was clear he couldn't swim. *That would make it harder to sink a body deep where you'd want it, Billy,* I thought. *It could still be done, but you'd have a rougher time of it. Maybe that body is in the woods after all,* I told myself.

I stepped into the water right behind him, close enough to grab him if he slipped, if he tried to run when he got to the far bank. That would have been quite a spectacle, the two of us limping through the woods on our game legs, him trying to get away, me trying to catch up. But though I stayed close I really didn't believe he'd run. Yesterday, that would have been the time for that. It was too late now, too late for a lot of things.

A crime of passion, Billy, that was your defense, I thought as I followed him through the shallows. *You should have come into my office yesterday and turned yourself in, telling it all up front about Holland and your wife. You'd have probably gotten off light, Billy, even if it was a war hero you killed. But you've messed up now. You hid your crime. You made it seem calculated, premeditated.*

The water rose to my knees but no higher.

Press a one-inch piece of curved metal with your index finger and your world changes forever, doesn't it Billy. Just a little thing like the pressing of a bit of metal, or a little thing like a teammate banging his shoulder pads into the side of your knee in a scrimmage—an accident, not even a hard hit, just a little popping sound inside your knee.

"My father will help us" was what Janice had said after Coach Barkley told me I no longer had a scholarship. I was married by then, Janice two months pregnant. What she meant was that her father would give us money to finish my teaching degree, money to help with the baby. But Janice had come back from her parents' house with the news her father was poor as any Jocassee farmer. I dropped out of school to work at Liberty Mill. Then came the miscarriage, and hospital bills made sure not even night classes were a possibility.

"Something's wrong," she'd said that June night.

I'd reached up and turned on the lamp. Blood soaked the bed's center, the blood of our child. We frantically pushed away from the sagging middle of the bed—away from each other. Away from the stain that widened between us.

"Severe tearing and scarring of the cervix," the doctor told Janice and me three days later as we'd prepared to leave the hospital. "I'm sure you know what this means."

Janice and I had a pretty good idea what it meant, but neither of us said a word, as if by not answering we might at least keep something alive.

"You won't be able to have children," the doctor said.

As I'd helped Janice out of her seat she winced in pain. I'd held onto her arm and we'd walked out of the hospital slow and careful, like people who no longer trusted even the ground beneath them.

I smelled death soon as Billy and I struggled up the bank, its odor stronger with each step deeper into the woods. Then I saw it. There were so many buzzards it was hard to tell at first what they huddled over. Every buzzard in Oconee County seemed to have gathered, the trees black with others waiting their turn. I held a handkerchief to my face and waded in among them. I kicked off enough to see Billy had told the truth about at least one thing.

"Let's get the hell out of here," I said.

We waded back across the river before I asked him the question that had made me think he might be lying about what was drawing the buzzards.

"How did you get a horse with a broke leg across a river?" I asked.

I could tell right away that question was one he hadn't expected. His eyes locked on his right hand, the same as they'd done the day before. Looking for strength. I bet he didn't even know he was doing it, but it was good as any lie detector machine.

"I beat hell out of him," he said, but a good ten seconds passed before he thought up that lie.

Billy turned his back to me and started topping his tobacco. I just stood there a minute. Letting him know I didn't need to rush off to look for any more suspects because we were past the suspect stage now.

When did it start to go wrong for you, Billy? I wondered. *Are you like me? Can you remember one thing—a harsh exchange of words, a bad harvest, a morning when she offered her cheek instead of her lips when you kissed her? I know when it went wrong for me,* I thought, *and here's the worst thing, Billy. I believe Janice and I would be different people now, better people. That miscarriage wouldn't have happened. We would have children, and I'd be a teacher, maybe at a college. At night Janice wouldn't turn her back to me, Billy. Something cold wouldn't have locked inside our hearts if I had been one step slower or quicker to that ball carrier, if the coach's whistle had stopped one play a second quicker.*

I left Billy in his tobacco field and walked through the woods to Mrs. Winchester's house. I told her we'd be back that afternoon. Then I headed up the dirt road to see Daddy.

He came out of the barn when I drove up. Daddy had aged a lot the last few years, especially since Momma had died. His heart gave him trouble, and the doctor told him he needed to slow down. He had sold most of his cattle and worked fewer acres.

But Daddy still did more than he should. He wasn't a man who could sit on a porch all day or spend afternoons up at Roy Whitmire's gas station playing checkers and gossiping. I knew Travis would find him one day soon face down in a field or pasture. From what the doctor said it was a miracle it hadn't already happened.

"Travis said you was hunting for Holland. Found him yet?" Daddy asked.

"No, sir, not yet. But we still got some woods and river to cover this afternoon."

"You been upriver to see the Widow?"

"Not yet."

"I reckon you'll have to," Daddy said.

"If nothing doesn't show by late afternoon I expect so."

"You ain't skittish to go up there, are you?"

"No sir."

"Good, for there's a many who are. People always have wanted to believe the worst things about her."

"She's done herself no favors shutting herself up in that hollow by herself," I said. "That's the kind of thing gets people to talking."

"If that suits her I see no reason for it to be anyone else's concerning," Daddy said.

He looked at his watch.

"You ate?"

"No sir. I was thinking you and me could go over to Salem and get a bite."

"No need for that," Daddy said. "Laura brought over some collards and peas the other evening. Fixed me a pone of cornbread too. We'll warm that up."

"I thought you might enjoy cafe food for a change."

"No," Daddy said. "What I got here fits me fine."

I knew if I went to Salem I'd be going by myself, so I went inside and sat at the kitchen table while he warmed the food. The kitchen looked like it always had in some ways—the Black Draught calendar above the stove, the metal tins of sugar and salt on the counter. But Momma's recipe box wasn't on that counter. There was no sifter or rolling pin out. The kitchen didn't have the warm smell it'd had when I was growing up and Momma always seemed to have bread or a pie in the stove.

Memory took me back to a winter evening when Travis and I had walked home after hunting squirrels on Sassafras Mountain. It had started snowing, flakes big as nickels swirling down from a low, gray sky. By the time we stepped out of the woods we couldn't see our feet, but we could see the yellow pane of light across the pasture. That glowing window was like a beacon leading us to a warm, safe place where people who loved us would always be waiting.

Maybe that's the best blessing childhood offers, I thought as Daddy lay my plate before me, believing that things never change.

"That's better than any cafe food," Daddy said.

There had been a time I would have agreed with him. The thick, salty tang of fatback added to the collards and field peas would have made it taste all the better. Laura's crackling cornbread would have tasted sweet and moist as cake. Now the food tasted greasy, sliding down my throat like motor oil.

"Country food," Janice called it. The few times we'd come here for Sunday dinner and a bowl of collards or plate of venison had come to her she'd smiled and said, "No, thank you," and passed the bowl or plate to the next person.

"How's Janice," Daddy asked, as he always did.

"She's just fine, Daddy."

"That's good to hear," he said.

I could hear the cicadas singing in the trees as we tried to think of something else to say. Though we sat five feet apart, it seemed a lake had spread out between us, but it was something wider and harder to get across.

"You need to see them twins," Daddy finally said. "They done growed up on us."

"I mean to do that, Daddy. If we don't find Holland this afternoon I'll try to go by there tomorrow."

"One of them boys carries your name, son," Daddy said, trying to make his tone gentle. "You shouldn't have to already be up here to let him catch sight of his uncle."

Daddy looked at his empty plate. There was nothing for me to say. Like Holland when he'd decided to get involved with another man's wife and Billy when he'd decided to do something about it, I'd made my choice.

"We could use some rain," Daddy said, trying to move us past what he'd said about my nephews. I knew he'd make small talk the rest of my visit. He would have said the same words to a stranger, and I wondered if that was what I had become to him, and stranger who had once been a son.

"Yes sir," I said, and drank the last of my tea.

"You want some more?" he asked.

"No. I need to get back over to Billy Holcombe's farm."

"You think he had something to do with Holland disappearing?" Daddy asked.

"I think he killed Holland."

"I just can't notion Billy doing something such as that."

I got up from the table.

"People can disappoint you sometimes, Daddy. I reckon you know that as well as anybody."

Daddy knew what I was talking about.

"Come back when you can," Daddy said.

I walked on out to the car. Daddy stood in the doorway and watched me back down the drive to the county road. As a young man he'd been a legendary hell-raiser, like Holland a man bad to drink and fight. After he'd married Momma he'd settled down, working dawn to dusk to make sure we had clothes and shoes and never went hungry. We never had, even in the leanest of times during the Depression. He'd held onto this land too, land that had been in his family for one hundred and eighty years.

He had held onto it not only for those who'd come before him but for his children and grandchildren. I knew his greatest satisfaction was being able to look in the fields and see his son and grandsons working the same land he'd worked all his life. He'd heard the talk about Carolina Power flooding the valley, but I knew he couldn't have believed there'd be a time when Alexanders didn't farm this land. I hoped he was dead before Carolina Power had the chance to take that belief from him.

He'd prepared Travis and me to carry on what Alexanders had done here for six generations. Daddy had been a stout, rough-looking man, a man not to be trifled with. But he'd taught us in a patient, caring way, his hand always light on our shoulders. When I went off to Clemson, he'd believed it was only for a few years, that I would come back to Jocassee.

Now he was an old man with a bad heart and a farm that would one day vanish completely as a dream. A man whose oldest son had become little more than a stranger. I stared through the windshield at his lean, craggy face like I'd watch something about to be swept away by a current, for I realized this could well be the last time I saw him alive.

Right then I decided I wouldn't run for re-election. I'd serve out my term and then come back here and live with him. I'd farm this land until Carolina Power ran us all out and drowned these fields and creeks and the river itself. However long that was, it would give me some time to be a son and a brother again, maybe even learn how to be an uncle.

I backed out of Daddy's driveway and headed toward Billy Holcombe's farm, but it was like the car was driving itself. My mind was busy mapping the future.

I'd ask Janice to come with me, but I knew she wouldn't. I'd pack up a few clothes and leave the savings and house and car. It sounded so easy, but it wouldn't be. I would carry fifteen years of being part of another person's life away with me as well. I wouldn't be able to shuck a marriage the way I could a house or job.

I checked my watch. One-thirty. Janice was probably at a tea or playing bridge. She'd be wearing a hat and hose despite the weather, still playing the role of the wealthy doctor's daughter.

"Where's Mrs. White Gloves?" a town councilman has asked his wife at a Christmas party when he didn't know we were behind him.

"Probably still at home teaching the sheriff the proper way to unfold a napkin," the councilman's wife had said.

You want to think the worst of her, I told myself as the road curved with the river. *It's easier than the truth—that sometimes what goes wrong between two people is nobody's fault.*

I remembered what else the councilman had said that night, what Janice had heard as clearly as I had.

"Thank God she and the sheriff don't have any children. Can you imagine what kind of mother she'd be?"

"Please don't," Janice said when she stopped me from grabbing the council-man by the collar. "Their snippy comments don't mean a thing."

But the hurt in Janice's eyes had argued otherwise.

By two o'clock, forty men had gathered in front of Billy Holcombe's house. Besides more dynamite, Tom Watson had brought another grappling hook and some bamboo poles to poke undercuts with. I gave him five more men and sent him on his way. Leonard led the rest across the river to search the Carolina Power land.

"Keep your noses and eyes open," I said as they walked away. "I know there's a dead horse over there. There might could be a dead man as well."

I turned to Bobby.

"Anything I need to know of back in town?"

"Mrs. Pipkin brought over a book, said it was the one you'd asked her to get from the state library. That's about it. It's too hot for people to get into much meanness."

"I reckon so."

I nodded toward Billy Holcombe's house.

"Let's go have us a look-see."

"We've come to search," I told Amy Holcombe when she came to the door.

She didn't say a word, just stepped out of our way. I went straight to the back room. I wasn't looking for a body. I was looking for a murder scene. Bobby and I stripped the sheets off the mattress, but there was no bloodstain and none on the floor. We checked the closet and under the house. There was no bloody sheet, no fresh packed dirt. Bobby climbed into the well and poked the bottom with a hoe handle. Then we searched the barn and shed, but we knew soon as we stepped inside there was no body in either, because in the dog days there's no holding the smell of death.

"I'm about convinced that son of a bitch is off somewhere still alive and having a good laugh at us," Bobby said.

"No," I said. "Holland's dead and he's within a mile of where we're standing."

"You're sure of that?" Bobby said.

"Yes," I said.

I needed to get inside Billy's head, a head that held a lot more smarts than I'd earlier imagined. I needed to think the way he did to figure out what had been done. That had worked in the past when I'd searched for a runaway from a chain gang or for a lost child or a whiskey still. Once you locked in on how a person saw the world, the hiding place could become no harder to find than a lightning bug on a July night. But that wasn't the only reason I wanted to live Billy's life awhile, sorry as it was. I was weary of living my own, glad to take my mind off a decision I was telling myself I'd already made.

"Get a couple of men and go check his fields," I told Bobby. "Maybe he's done some late planting this year."

"That's a good idea," Bobby said. "I'd not thought of that."

"Be careful not to trample his crops," I said.

I sat down on a chopping block outside the woodshed and looked out over the dying beans and corn to where Billy worked. I knew the why and the how, and I pretty much knew the where. Like I'd told Bobby, that body was within a mile of where I sat. There was no way it couldn't be. I knew the plow horse had hauled the body, because Holland was too big for Billy to carry.

Suddenly I realized something, not the answer but what would lead to the answer—the horse hadn't broke its leg in the field but while carrying Holland's body across the river. Its hoof had slipped on a slick-rock, just like Billy had said, but that rock had been in the river. The weight on its back had done the rest.

What happened then, Billy? I thought. *You probably did what you said. You beat the hell out of that horse and got it up the bank, and into the woods and then shot it. But you got Holland's body off first. You left it there in the river or on the bank. You came back and tied a creek rock to the body and wedged it in an under-cut or sank it deep in a pool. You didn't bury it in the ground, Billy. You were smart enough to know better. Your best chance was the river, your only real chance, because water can keep things covered up, even in a time of drought.*

I checked my watch. Almost five-thirty. I'd heard the dynamite blasts off and on for the last three hours, but Tom would have let me know if something had come up. The same with Leonard. I watched the men out in the field, moving slow through the tobacco as though wading through a pond. Billy worked out there among them, doing his best to act like he didn't even notice all the commotion around him.

"I know the Holcombes is some kin to you," Mrs. Winchester had said. I didn't want her or anyone else saying I hadn't done everything possible to find out what had happened to Holland. So there was one other thing to be done, a visit I'd put off long as I could.

She lived a good mile upriver. My scarred lung and knee begged me to send Bobby, for it was an up-and-down mile. But I knew how superstitious Bobby was. He'd grown up in Long Creek but had kin who'd lived in this valley, including his Uncle Luke who'd been the Widow's neighbor for a while. Bobby would know the stories about her. He'd no more make a visit to that old woman than he'd spend the night in a graveyard. No, I'd have to be the one to call on Widow Glendower.

I followed the river up past the old Chapman place to where Wolf Creek flowed into the river.

Once when Travis and I had been kids we'd fished Wolf Creek. It had been October, the time of year when brown trout swim into creeks to spawn. We'd started at the river where the creek entered and caught two trout right off, big males with hooked jaws, the spots on their sides big and bright as holly berries. Travis and I had worked our way on up the creek, dragging our heavy stringers behind us. One more pool and we'll turn back we kept telling each other, because we knew who lived at the head of that creek. But the fishing was too good. We'd kept on going.

Then we came to where the creek forked. Between the two forks stood Widow Glendower, like she'd been expecting Travis and me. She was dressed in her black widow's weeds. That made her white hair and white skin more unsettling. She couldn't have been more than fifty, but to Travis and me she looked older than the mountains themselves. We had managed to hold onto our rods and reels, but we dropped the stringers of trout at her feet and took off down the creek, splashing and tripping and not daring to look back till we made the river. We'd never fished Wolf Creek again.

When Widow Glendower came to the cabin door she didn't look much different than she'd looked a quarter century before when I'd last seen her.

"You look to be an Alexander," she said.

"Yes," I said, but there was nothing to her knowing that. Anybody in Jocassee would recognize Alexander features.

"You ain't got need for a granny-woman, have you?"

"No," I said. "I'm the high sheriff and I'm looking for Holland Winchester. I was wondering if you'd seen him?"

"Oh I've seen him," Widow Glendower said. "I seen him twenty-odd years ago when I brung him into this world."

"Have you seen him the last two days?"

"No," she said, saying the word slow as if she was mulling my question over in her head.

"Does he ever come up this way hunting or fishing?"

"No. I'd recall it if I seen him doing such."

I stepped off the porch, knowing I'd wasted my time coming here. Widow Glendower grinned at me.

"Come back and visit anytime, Sheriff," she said. "And be sure you let me know if you have need of a granny-woman."

I was short-breathed and my knee needed a rest, but I didn't stop walking until I reached the river. I sat down on a log where I had a good view of the bank and finally saw what I was looking for, the plant Andre Michaux had found in the valley in 1788. The Cherokee called it shee-show. Because it grew close to water, they had believed it could end a drought.

I walked over and kneeled beside the plant whose flowers looked like tiny white bells. I touched the leathery green leaves. De Soto's secretary Rodrigo Rangel had not mentioned the flower in his writings. Neither had Bartram. Michaux had been the first European to see the plant for what it was, something rare and beautiful, submerged from the rest of the world in the valley of the lost.

Most of the men had gathered in Billy Holcombe's yard by the time I got back. Stonewall hadn't caught a scent. Tom Watson had brought nothing out of the river but a snapping turtle and a few more trout.

Billy soon called it a day as well. I watched him limp out of his field toward the house where his supper waited. *You don't seem a man luck has found often in his life, Billy,* I thought. *Maybe now that you need it most though, it has finally come. Currents can tug a body out of the deepest undercut. You've read your Bible, Billy,* I thought. *You know the dead can rise on the third day.*

When the last man finally straggled in, I told Leonard and the others who'd walked the woods that I wouldn't be needing them anymore. I told Tom and his men to be back at 9:00 in the morning.

"That body's got to be in the river," I told Bobby as we got in the car.

"Well I don't see how we missed it," Bobby said. "We poked every undercut and dynamited every blue hole a damn mile upstream and down. You think it to be farther away than that?"

"No," I said as we bounced down Billy's drive. "That body can't be too far from that horse," and soon as I said that I realized what Billy Holcombe had done. I laughed out loud at the sheer smarts of it.

"What's tickled your funny bone?" Bobby asked.

"I'll show you."

I turned the car around and headed back up the drive.

"Get a shovel and a rope from the trunk," I told Bobby as we got out.

Bobby did as I told him while I stepped up on the porch.

"Come on," I told Billy when he came to the door. "And bring a lantern. We need to go back over to where your plow horse is."

Billy was worried. I could tell that right away. Lucas Bridges, the county coroner, claimed a dying man or woman had a certain smell about them. I believed a scared man did too, and what I smelled coming off Billy Holcombe was more than sweat from field work.

"Step ahead of us and be the bell-cow," I told Billy as we left the yard. "I'd rather see a snake before I put my foot down on him."

Though rattlesnakes were bad to crawl on hot nights, I was more concerned with Billy trying to slip off into the dark. I wanted him out in front where I could watch him.

"What you got on your mind?" Bobby asked.

"Maybe just a snipe hunt, but I don't think so," I said.

We made our way across the river, the same river De Soto had crossed. De Soto hadn't found what he'd been looking for in Jocassee, but, as Michaux had discovered, things could be found in the valley of the lost. All you had to do was look with a careful eye. That and know where to look.

The moon wasn't out, and it took me a moment to realize what that meant. Then a breeze rustled the trees. If the horse hadn't been close by I'd have smelled the sharpness in the air that comes before rain. I wondered if Billy knew the rain was coming. If he did I wondered if he saw it as more good luck. Or did he believe it no longer mattered since I knew now what he'd done with Holland's body? *Yes, Billy, the eyes can lie, but eventually they'll tell the truth. If I could see your eyes they would tell me, Billy. But I'll know soon enough,* I thought as we stepped onto the far bank. Soon enough.

"We got to move that horse," I told Bobby. "Do you think if we put a rope around its neck we could drag it a few yards?"

"We can try," Bobby said.

The buzzards had flown up in the trees to roost for the night, so all Bobby had to scare off was a possum. Bobby tied the rope on, doing his best not to breathe, for the horse was plenty rank after two days under a dog-day sun.

"You help too," I told Billy. We dragged the horse until I said stop. The lantern made the ground shadowy, but there was enough light to see there was no body. I picked up the shovel and stepped closer. Two jabs and I knew that ground hadn't been dug.

"Let's go," I said, "and leave the damn rope, Bobby. I don't feel like smelling dead horse all the way to Seneca."

For a few minutes I had been so certain. But I'd been dead wrong. Now it was as if I was back at the beginning, with nothing certain at all, not even if there had been a murder. Maybe he's not even dead, I thought. Maybe Holland had gotten Amy Holcombe pregnant and taken off to Texas or California. Maybe Bobby was right and Holland was having a good laugh at our expense, that this was Holland's way of getting back at me for what happened at The Borderline—have me come out here and make a fool of myself searching for someone who was alive half a country away.

But I couldn't believe Holland was alive. Billy Holcombe had been expecting me when I stepped into his field. Mrs. Winchester's grief was real. As we recrossed I could smell the coming rain. A real chunk washer, I hoped, enough to raise the dead.

"I'll see you tomorrow," I told Billy as he stepped up on his porch. "Who knows what might turn up, especially after a good rain." Billy said nothing to that. He just went on inside to finish his supper.

"You mind driving?" I asked Bobby.

"Not at all," Bobby said, so I handed him the keys. I closed my eyes as we bumped down toward the river.

"Radio bother you?" Bobby asked.

"No," I said.

Hank Williams' voice rose out of the static, singing about his loneliness. He was a young man, still in his twenties but already rich and famous. I wondered if what he sang was just words to him. His voice argued otherwise. That old, weary voice knew what the high lonesome was. I'd heard Williams was bad to drink. There was something deep inside him that money and fame couldn't cure. I reckoned it must be in a lot of us since his records were so popular. Loneliness was a word you could give it, but it was something beyond words. It was a kind of yearning, a sense that part of your heart was unfilled.

A preacher would say it was a man's condition since leaving Eden, and so many of the old hymns were about how in another life we'd be with God. But we lived in the here and now. You tried to find something to fill that absence. Maybe a marriage could cure that yearning, though mine hadn't. Drink did it for many a man besides Williams. Maybe children filled it for some, or maybe like Daddy even the love of a place that connected you to generations of your family.

"Wake up, Sheriff. We're back," Bobby said.

I opened my eyes.

"You go on home, Bobby. I'll meet you here at 8:30."

I went into the office, walking past the cell I thought for a few minutes this evening I was going to fill. The book Mrs. Pipkin had brought lay on my desk. A damp cellar smell rose off the old paper when I opened it. *Travels through North and South Carolina, Georgia, East and West Florida*, the cover page said. Below the title, *By William Bartram*.

The first splats of rain streaked the windows, and though I hadn't even a tomato plant in the ground, memory made my heart lift. I knew Daddy heard that rain, and Travis did too. They would sleep better tonight than they'd slept in weeks.

I knew I should call Janice, but I couldn't make my hands pick up the telephone. Sometime tomorrow I would have to figure out the words I would say to her and then say them, as the first time I'd left.

"I'd end up getting drafted anyhow," I'd told her when I joined the Marines in 1941. But I'd wanted to go. I'd wanted to get away from her, away from a life that had been something so different from what had seemed promised, away from my dead-end job in a cotton mill, away from that miscarriage and a marriage that we both knew was a failure. How could it not be when all our union had brought into the world was death.

But I had come back to Seneca and Janice. Maybe it had been a sense of obligation, of knowing that Janice had chosen me when there were plenty of other men from wealthy families she could have had. I now believed it was more than that though. I believed that our lost child had bonded us in ways that outlasted even love.

I opened the brittle pages to Part II, the section where Bartram left Charleston for what would be called for a few more years the Cherokee Nation. I followed his words the way he'd followed the Savannah River upstream to where the land became hills and then mountains. I turned the page, and Bartram was describing the place where my grandfather's great-grandfather had settled twelve years before Bartram passed through the valley.

I continued on again three or four miles, keeping on the trading path which led me over uneven rocky land, and crossing rivulets and brooks, rapidly descending over rocky precipices, when I came into a charming vale, embellished with a delightful glittering river, which meandered through it.

He had been from Scotland, that first Alexander, a man who had fought with Prince Charlie at the battle of Culloden. He'd come down the Shenandoah Valley. Ian Alexander found his wife in southwest Virginia, a woman named Mary Thomas, who being Welsh would have shared his hatred of the English. He stayed there five years, then came farther south, stopping in this place that surely reminded him of the Scottish midlands where he'd been born. Most of his neighbors were Cherokee, and his oldest son would marry a Cherokee. But soon Colonel Williamson would push the Indians into the high mountains of North Carolina.

My Uncle Thomas had not known which side that first Alexander had supported. He must have seen what the British were doing to the Cherokee was the same thing they'd done to the Scots, but with the Indians gone there would be more land for whites like him. More interesting, what had his son done? Did he fight with his wife's people or against them? Something had happened, but it was lost now in the valley's past.

Bartram did not mention meeting anyone as he'd passed through Jocassee that spring day. But I wondered if Ian Alexander had stood in a field and watched Bartram as he rode his horse along the trading path. Perhaps Old Ian acknowledged the white stranger with a wave, perhaps a meal offered and accepted.

I read on, following Bartram as he moved northwest and crossed what would someday be a state line. He'd stopped and rested at the top of Oconee Mountain. Turning to look back on the land he'd traversed that day, Bartram had described what he saw. *The mountainous wilderness appearing undulated as the great ocean after a tempest,* he'd written, as if he'd witnessed the valley under a huge, watery silence two centuries before it would happen.

Like Michaux, Bartram was a naturalist. He understood that things disappeared. Maybe that was why he'd felt compelled to preserve with sketches and words everything he saw, from Cherokee council-houses to buffalo bones. He wanted to get it all down. He wanted things to be remembered.

I lay the book down. The rain drummed against the roof and the town was quiet and still. I was tired, tireder than I'd been in a long time. I went into the cell and lay down on the cot.

I dreamed of water deep as time.

Sunlight streaked through the bars when I woke. The telephone was ringing, so I stumbled out of the cell to my desk.

"Daddy's had another heart attack," Travis said.

"Where is he?"

"Over here at the hospital."

"I'll be there in five minutes," I said.

I wrote a note telling Bobby to go on up to Jocassee and start dragging the river, that I'd join them as soon as I could.

At the hospital I found Travis and Laura slouched in plastic chairs. The twins lay on the couches.

"How bad is it?" I asked Travis.

"The doctor says he might live a day or two, but he ain't going to leave here alive."

"What happened?"

256

"Shank of the evening I went over to work some more on his roof. I figured he was mending fence so I didn't start no searching till near dark. I found him in the far pasture."

Travis looked at the floor.

"I thought he was dead. It'd be better if he had been."

"Did you try to call me last night?"

"No," Travis said, still looking at the floor.

"Why the hell not?"

Travis looked up, his gray eyes meeting mine.

"You ain't given a damn about him for so long I didn't think you'd want your sleep bothered."

I grabbed the front of his shirt, lifting him out of the chair. My knuckles pressed against his breast bone.

"You don't know a thing of what I feel."

"You're right," Travis said, his eyes still looking straight into mine. "I knew once but not anymore."

The room seemed to close in around us. Whatever my life had been and was to be had come to this moment when I held my fist against Travis's chest.

"No, Will," Travis said, his eyes no longer looking into mine but looking behind me.

I turned and saw my nephew, my namesake, with a pocketknife sprouting from his fist, the other twin beside him, hands clenched.

"Put it down, son," Travis said.

"Not till he lets you go," Will said.

I opened my fist, stepped back. The room's white walls widened again. We all stood there for a minute, sharing nothing but the same name.

"Will they let me see him?"

"Yeah," Travis said, rubbing his chest. "They'll let you."

"You might need this," Laura said, and handed me a hospital pass.

I showed the pass to the nurse on the second floor and she led me to the room. Daddy lay stretched out on the bed, his eyes staring at the ceiling, tubes taped to both arms. His skin was tinged blue, each breath an effort. Travis was right. It would have been better if he'd died in his fields, feeling the land against his body, seeing trees and crops and a sky that promised rain.

"We're trying to make him comfortable," the nurse said.

"Does he know I'm here?"

"I don't know. Maybe."

The nurse left the room.

I held Daddy's hand, and I knew it for a dead man's hand. It was that cold. A hand that did not acknowledge mine. His eyes stayed fixed on the ceiling. His body was nothing more than a husk now. I prayed for his soul, but he didn't need my prayers. He'd lived a good life and treated people a lot better than they'd sometimes treated him.

"I'm sorry, Daddy," I said aloud.

And I was, but it was too late to matter. He was gone from me now and never coming back. I held his hand until the nurse came back in to change his sheets.

"I'll be back this evening," I told Travis. "Leave a message with Janice if something happens."

Travis nodded. He knew my meaning.

I drove on up into the mountains, a blue sky overhead, but plenty of rain had fallen. The creeks ran quick and muddy. The fields were no longer dust. It had been a soaking rain, the answer to prayers and dead black snakes and shee-show and whatever else people had found to believe in.

Billy wasn't in his fields, but I hadn't expected him to be since it was too muddy to get much done anyway. *You might get some corn and beans after all, Billy,* I thought as I followed the other men's muddy footprints down the field edge to the river. Already the corn stalks seemed to be standing taller, the beans greener.

The river was high, fast and muddy like the creeks. Crossing was a lot trickier than yesterday. I found a limb to use as a staff and took my time. I gave a shout, and Bobby answered downstream. The water was too high to use the grappling hooks. All Bobby and the rest of the men were doing was hoping to find what water had already brought up on its own.

By eleven the river crested. Tom and Leonard cast the grappling hooks into blue holes as the rest of us walked the banks. The river had washed up tree limbs and a tractor tire and even a rod and reel. But it still hid Holland. We stopped at noon and ate donuts and drank Cheerwines Bobby had brought.

"If that storm didn't bring that body up I don't know what the hell will," Bobby said as we sat on the bank.

"It sure enough brought up most everything else," Tom said.

We watched the river flow past, almost as clear now as it had been the day before and not much higher.

It was the river I'd been baptized in.

"Washed in the blood of the lamb," Preacher Robertson had said as the blue sky fell away and water rushed over me. It seemed Preacher Robertson held me there forever, but I hadn't been afraid. I was ten years old. I had felt the power of that river and believed it nothing less than God Himself swirling around me.

After we ate, Tom and Leonard worked the blue holes while Bobby and me waded in and poked bamboo poles under banks and between big rocks. All we found was snakes and muskrats.

"Let's go," I said at four o'clock. We recrossed the river and slogged our way back up the field edge.

"You go on back with Tom and the others," I told Bobby when we got to the cars. "I'll be along directly."

I watched Tom's car disappear around a bend, then stepped into Billy Holcombe's yard. I heard a rasping sound coming from the woodshed and walked over and peered inside. At first I saw nothing, but my eyes began to adjust to the dark. Billy slowly took his form behind what looked like prison bars. Like a haint shape-shifting, my older kin would have said. But I was the ghost, haunting a valley where I no longer belonged.

Soon I saw the bars he worked on were wood, not steel. He hummed to himself, so soft it sounded no louder than a wasp's drone. I could smell the wood, wild cherry, and I knew the crib was as much for his wife as for the child. Whatever happened between Holland and her, the crib was a sign she and Billy had gotten past it. She had stuck by him the last few days, lied for him. Whatever had happened that morning, she'd had to make a choice between Holland and Billy and she'd chosen Billy.

Billy kept on humming, and I bet he didn't even know he was doing it. I listened to a man who believed his future was going to be better than his past, a man who'd woke up to rain-soaked fields and the knowledge come fall he'd have a bumper crop. A man about to learn he'd gotten away with murder.

I wondered what would happen when Carolina Power ran him off his land. Billy's parents had been sharecroppers. This land didn't connect Billy to his family the way Daddy's land connected him to ours. Billy's land signaled a break from his past, from what his family had been. Maybe land to Billy was just something to be used, like a truck or plow horse.

Billy might think his ship had come in when Carolina Power bought his place for a few dollars an acre more than he'd paid for it, at least until he saw the price of a farm like his in another part of the country. Maybe he'd take that money to Seneca or Anderson and buy a house with an indoor toilet and electricity and think he'd found paradise. He'd work in a mill where he'd get a paycheck at the end of every week and not have to worry anymore about drought and hail and tobacco worms.

Other changes he wouldn't like as much, things that would make him miss being behind a horse and plow. He'd have to ask permission to get a drink of water or take a piss. The work would be the same thing day after day, week after week, the mill hot and humid as dog days all year round. He'd breathe an unending drizzle of lint he'd spend half his nights coughing back up. His work would give him no satisfaction, but he'd have a wife and child to go home to when the mill whistle freed him at day's end. There were men who would envy that about him if nothing else.

As for my life, it was in Seneca. My morning telephone call had woke me up in more than one way. It had been a reminder of something I had already known despite what I'd been able to pretend for a few hours—I had chosen my life long ago when I had picked up a fork, picked it up in a house I had believed to be solid and permanent as anything on earth.

But nothing is solid and permanent. Our lives are raised on the shakiest foundations. You don't need to read history books to know that. You only have to know the history of your own life.

I watched Billy through the bars, knowing in a few minutes I'd drive out of this valley. I'd look in my rearview mirror and watch the land disappear as if sinking into water.

When I had become a deputy I had made out my will and stipulated that I was to be buried here in Jocassee with the other Alexanders. I hoped I would be in that grave before they built the reservoir so when the water rose it would rise over me and Daddy and Momma and over Old Ian Alexander and his wife Mary and over the lost body of the princess name Jocassee and the Cherokee mounds and the trails De Soto and Bartram and Michaux had followed and the meadows and streams and forests they had described and all would forever vanish and our faces and names and deeds and misdeeds would be forgotten as if we and Jocassee had never been.

I wish you well, Billy, I thought. I stepped closer and blotted out most of his light.

"You got away with it," I said and left him there, his hands shaping the future.

From *Saints at the River* (2004)

PROLOGUE

She follows the river's trail downstream, leaving behind her parents and younger brother who still eat their picnic lunch. She is twelve years old and it is her school's Easter break. Her father has taken time off from his job and they have followed the Appalachian Mountains south, stopping first in Gatlinburg, then the Smokies, and finally this river. She finds a place above a falls where the water looks shallow and slow. The river is a boundary between South Carolina and Georgia, and she wants to wade into the middle and place one foot in South Carolina and one in Georgia so she can tell her friends back in Minnesota she has been in two states at the same time.

She kicks off her sandals and enters, the water so much colder than she imagined, and quickly deeper, up to her kneecaps, the current surging under the smooth surface. She shivers. Fifty yards downstream a granite cliff rises two hundred feet into the air to cast this section of river into shadow. She glances back to where her parents and brother sit on the blanket. It is warmer there, the sun full upon them. She thinks about going back but is almost halfway now.

She takes a step, and the water rises higher on her knees. Four more steps she tells herself. Just four more and I'll turn back. She takes another step and the bottom she tries to set her foot on is no longer there and she is being shoved downstream and she does not panic because she has passed all of her Red Cross courses. The water shallows and her face breaks the surface and she breathes deep. She tries to turn her body so she won't hit her head on a rock and as she thinks this she's afraid for the first time and she's suddenly back underwater and hears the rush of water against her ears. She tries to hold her breath but her knee smashes against a boulder and she gasps in pain and water pours into her mouth. Then for a few moments the water pools and slows. She rises coughing up water, gasping air, her feet dragging the bottom like an anchor trying to snag waterlogged wood or rock jut and as the current quickens

261

again she sees her family running along the shore and she knows they are shouting her name though she cannot hear them and as the current turns her she hears the falls and knows there is nothing that will keep her from it as the current quickens and quickens and another rock smashes against her knee but she hardly feels it as she snatches another breath before the river pulls her under and she feels the river fall and she falls with it as water whitens around her and she falls deep into the darkness and as she rises her head scrapes against a rock ceiling and all is black and silent and she tells herself don't breathe but the need grows inside her beginning in the upper stomach then up through the chest and throat and as that need rises her mouth and nose open and the lungs explode in pain and then the pain is gone with the dark as bright colors shatter around her like glass shards, and she remembers her sixth grade science class, the gurgle of the aquarium at the back of the room that morning the teacher held a prism out the window so it might fill with color, and she has a final, beautiful thought—that she is now inside that prism and knows something even the teacher does not know, that the prism's colors are voices, voices that swirl around her head like a crown, and at that moment her arms and legs she did not even know were flailing cease and she becomes part of the river.

CHAPTER ONE

Ghosts.

That's what I thought of on an early-May morning as I stared at the blank computer screen, imagined this newsroom forty or fifty years ago. Certainly there would have been more noise: the steady clacking of teletypes and typewriters, the whole room hot and sweating and loud-voiced. *Bustling* would have been the word to describe it, like a giant beehive, a fumigated one, for there would be cigarette and cigar smoke bluing the air overhead like a stalled cloud. Everywhere would be men, white men, wearing rumpled suits and ties and suspenders. No bottled water or granola bars on these guys' desks.

If their ghosts ever wandered back here, they probably assumed the place had been renovated into a hospital wing, for in the second year of a new millennium the fluorescent bulbs spread an antiseptic glow. Faces were shuttered inside cubicles, and the air was smoke-free and 72 degrees year-round. Perhaps most surprising to those men would be the fact that an equal number of women, and of varying skin tones, filled the desks.

A few things had not changed. Thanks to *The Messenger*'s skinflint owner, Thomas Hudson, salaries were still low, the hours awful, and, as always, looming deadlines provided chronic doses of stress.

My managing editor, Lee Gervais, interrupted my thoughts.

"I do believe Miss Maggie Glenn is daydreaming about me," he said.

Lee leaned over my shoulder, his eyes rheumy and red-veined as they took in my blank computer screen. He was thirty-eight, ten years my senior, but he looked older, the flesh on his pasty and puffy, what hair he had retreating to the sides and back of his head. Lee wore a white short-sleeved dress shirt. The skin on the undersides of his arms was loose like an old woman's. He came from a wealthy family, and part of his softness was the result of never using his muscles for lifting anything heavier than a tennis racket or pitching wedge. The rest came from lifting too many gin and tonics.

"Yes," I almost said, because I knew Lee would have preferred the newsroom of fifty years ago, a place where he could have told dirty jokes between drags on his cigarette and sips from a whiskey bottle kept in the top desk drawer.

"No, Lee. I'm just trying to get myself motivated on a Thursday morning when I'd rather be sleeping.

"I think I can help," Lee said. "How would you like a photographer's dream assignment?"

"George Clooney coming to town," I asked.

"Better than that. A chance to work with Allen Hemphill on a sure front-page feature."

"What's the catch?"

Lee shook his head. "How did an Oconee farm girl get so cynical?"

Lee's low country accent made *girl* and *gull* indistinguishable. It was an accent I knew he had refined the way another man might perfect some convoluted Masonic handshake. And in a way that was what his accent was: a sign of belonging. It spoke of old money and old houses, of Porter-Gaud Academy and Charleston cotillions.

"A year of working for you," I said.

"So are you interested or not?"

"I'm interested. But why not Phil or Julian?"

"The assignment's in Oconee County. Since you know the natives, you can translate mountain speech into Standard English for Hemphill."

So there is a catch, I thought.

"Contrary to what you may have heard, Lee, Oconee County's not the heart of darkness. It's four hours away not four centuries."

I tried to smile but I'd heard such comments too many times since I'd moved to Columbia.

"Sounds about right to me," Lee said. "That part of the state used to be called Dark Corner. I suspect there's a reason."

263

"I can tell you the reason. Your ancestors down in Charleston were ticked off because mountain people wouldn't help fight to keep slaves."

Lee nodded. "Mountain people. Is that the correct term now? I guess the PC ayatollahs would give me twenty lashes if I said *hillbilly.*"

"They should," I said, my tone no longer playful. "It's an offensive term."

Lee's act got old quickly, but he had given me good assignments in the twelve months I'd worked with him. He'd also talked Thomas Hudson into giving me a raise at Christmas. Lee wasn't a bad man, just the kind who mistook insensitivity for masculinity. He had been in Kappa Alpha at the University of Georgia, and behind his desk he'd hung a picture of his fraternity brothers on the porch of their antebellum two-story house. They were dressed as Confederate soldiers. Not mere foot soldiers, of course, but officers with swords and plumed hats. He'd always be a frat boy.

"Hey, I'm just joking," Lee said.

I smiled at him, the same way I'd smile at an eight year-old boy.

"What will Hemphill and I be doing in Oconee County?"

"Something on the girl who drowned up there three weeks ago."

"They finally got her out?"

"No," Lee said, "and that's the story. Her father is starting to raise hell, saying the locals aren't doing enough. He's trying to get some portable dam company involved, but the tree huggers want to stop that. They're swearing on their humpback whale CDs it's against some federal law."

"The Wild and Scenic Rivers Act. It prohibits anyone from disturbing the river's natural state."

"So you already know about all this?"

"If you mean the girl, just what I've read in the paper. But I know about the Tamassee, and I probably know most of the people involved."

"Good. That's even better. I get the feeling this story is going to break national. The *Atlanta Constitution* has done a long article, and the *Charlotte Observer* has someone up there now. I've heard CNN may do something as well."

Lee glanced at the wall clock. I wondered if he was checking how long before lunchtime and a chance to down a couple of Heinekens at the Capital Grill. I occasionally joined him there, and I'd seen how his eyes closed when he raised the green bottle for his first long swallow. I knew that was probably the high point of his working day, that he must have felt like a climber at altitude getting a hit of bottled oxygen.

"The story's getting national play—is that how you were able to convince Hemphill to take it?"

"Hudson chose the assignment," Lee said, "and pushed Hemphill hard. Hudson's evidently getting tired of his highest-paid reporter covering chitlin struts and peach festivals."

"So you wanted him on it as well?"

"I'm only doing what the boss wants, following the party line. But just because he's won some hotshot awards," Lee said, frustration in his voice, "it's not like he's earned the right to take a good salary and do nothing. If he was seventy and had been doing this fifty years, okay, but Hemphill's thirty-nine for God's sake. He hasn't put in twenty years yet."

More than just frustration, I thought, when Lee finished. Perhaps professional jealousy. Perhaps resentment that someone of a lower caste had surpassed him in status.

Lee glanced at the clock again. "Give Hudson credit. If he can get Hemphill off his ass, get him to write to his capability, this could be one hell of a story. Just pray they don't get her out before that dam's built, because you'll get some good pictures, something UPI or Reuters might pick up."

"I think I'll save my prayers for a worthier cause."

"Suit yourself," Lee said, "but that girl can't get any deader than she already is. If we get a good story out of what's happening now, that's not so terrible. It's not hurting her."

He laid his hand on my shoulder.

"I need to know by twelve if you want this. Otherwise, I'll send Julian."

"Okay," I said. "I'll let you know by twelve."

His grip tightened. My Uncle Mark once told me that a man's hands reveal a lot about him. Lee's were smoother and softer than any woman's I'd grown up with.

Lee let go of my shoulder and stepped out of my cubicle.

"If you don't go, you're disappointing not just me but Hemphill."

"How so?" I asked. The question was directed at his back.

"Hemphill was the one who suggested you," Lee said, pausing before he walked away. "Since I knew you were from Oconee County it seemed perfect, so I convinced Hudson you were the best choice."

I had a shoot at the University in the afternoon, but I couldn't remember if it was at two or two-thirty, so I checked my calendar, a calendar that had no visits to Oconee County marked on it. I hadn't been back since Christmas and had no plans to return until Aunt Margaret's birthday in July, but the office party I'd attended two weeks earlier now made me reconsider. Allen and I were the only singles, so it wasn't surprising we ended up in a corner together, leaning against a wall and sipping cheap white wine from styrofoam coffee cups. We had talked about our backgrounds, which were in many ways similar—both of us growing up in the rural South, both of us the first in our families to go to college. Yet I did most of the talking. It was clear that this was a man who'd spent much of his life letting people reveal themselves to him, not vice versa.

And I was a woman who spent much of her life focusing on surfaces to reveal deeper meanings. Allen wore a wedding band, although I'd overheard Hudson's secretary say SINGLE had been checked on his insurance application. I'd glanced at that wedding ring several times, wondering if it symbolized some lingering attachment to an ex-wife. Or was it merely a prop to keep women such as myself at bay, let us know he wasn't interested?

But he was interested, at least had seemed so at the time. As the days passed and I hadn't heard from him I'd begun to second-guess my instincts. Now, however, Lee had confirmed them.

"Good girl," Lee said when I stopped by his office on my way out to lunch. "I wouldn't send you up there if I didn't know you'd do a great job."

"When do we leave?"

"Two o'clock tomorrow. That gives you plenty of time to make the meeting the Forest Service has set up."

"Tomorrow afternoon I'm supposed to photograph a Confederate flag rally."

"We getting ready to secede again?" Lee quipped. "I'd better go home and dust off my uniform."

"Why bother, Lee? You'd just lose again."

"You think so?"

I tried to imagine Lee on a battlefield in Virginia, shoeless and surviving on ditch water and hardtack. But I knew he'd have dropped dead of a heart attack before he marched across Bull Street, much less across the Georgia and Virginia state lines.

"So what about the rally?" I asked.

"I'll send Phil," Lee smiled. "This will be like a paid vacation. Just take a few photos and we'll pick up the tab. You'll even have a Pulitzer Prize finalist for a chauffeur."

I went back to my cubicle and stared at a blank computer screen. The only sounds in the surrounding cubicles were fingertips tapping keyboards, a mouse clicking like a telegraph key. Ten people in the room and not one talking. You would have thought human speech had become obsolete as smoke signals. I wondered how the old newspaper men would react to this muted environment. Would they be able to work without the shouting traffic of typesetters and galley boys, the background roar of presses, the smell and smear of ink?

I unsealed my coffee. Moist heat rose from the styrofoam, carrying with it the rich, dark odor that always reminded me of fresh-dug earth, not the sandy loam of the piedmont but the black mountain soil flung off shovels to open my mother's grave.

Ghosts, I told myself, more ghosts.

From *The World Made Straight* (2006)

CHAPTER ONE

Travis came upon the marijuana plants while fishing Caney Creek. It was a Saturday, the first week of August, and after helping his father sucker tobacco all morning he'd had the rest of the day for himself. He'd changed into his fishing clothes and driven three miles of dirt road to the French Broad. Travis drove fast, the rod and reel clattering in the truck bed, red dust rising in his wake. The Marlin .22 slid on its makeshift gun rack with each hard curve. He had the windows down, and if the radio worked he would have had it blasting. The truck was a '66 Ford, battered from a dozen years of farm use. Travis had paid a neighbor five hundred dollars for it three months earlier.

He parked by the bridge and walked upriver toward where Caney Creek entered. Afternoon light slanted over Divide Mountain and tinged the water the deep gold of curing tobacco. A fish leaped in the shallows, but Travis's spinning rod was broken down and even if it hadn't been he wouldn't have bothered to cast. Nothing swam in the French Broad he could sell, only hatchery-bred rainbows and browns, some small-mouth, and catfish. The old men who fished the river stayed in one place for hours, motionless as the stumps and rocks they sat on. Travis liked to keep moving, and he fished where even the younger fishermen wouldn't go.

In forty minutes he was half a mile up Caney Creek, the rod still in two pieces. There were trout in this lower section, browns and rainbows that had worked their way up from the river, but Old Man Jenkins would not buy them. The gorge narrowed to a thirty-foot wall of water and rock, below it the creek's deepest pool. This was the place where everyone else turned back, but Travis waded through waist-high water to reach the waterfall's right side. Then he began climbing, the rod clasped in his left palm as his fingers used juts and fissures for leverage and resting places. When he got to the top he

268

fitted the rod sections together and threaded monofilament through the guides. He was about to tie on the silver Panther Martin spinner when a tapping began above him. Travis spotted the yellowhammer thirty feet up in the hickory and immediately wished he had his .22 with him. He scanned the woods for a dead tree or old fence post where the bird's next might be. A flytier in Marshall paid two dollars if you brought him a yellowhammer or wood duck, a nickel for a single good feather, and Travis needed every dollar and nickel he could get if he was going to get his truck insurance paid this month.

The only fish this far up were what fishing books and magazines called brook trout, though Travis had never heard Old Man Jenkins or anyone else call them a name other than speckled trout. Jenkins swore they tasted better than any brown or rainbow and paid Travis fifty cents apiece no matter how small. Old Man Jenkins ate them head and all, like sardines.

Mountain laurel slapped his face and arms, and he scraped his hands and elbows climbing rocks there was no other way around. Water was the only path now. Travis thought of his daddy back at the farmhouse and smiled. The old man had told him never to fish places like this alone, because a broken leg or rattlesnake bite could get a body graveyard dead before someone found you. That was about the only kind of talk he'd ever heard from the old man, Travis thought as he tested his knot, always being put down about something—how fast he drove, who he hung out with. Nothing but a bother from the day he was born. Puny and sickly as a baby and nothing but trouble since. That's what his father had said to his junior high principal, like it was Travis's fault he wasn't stout as his daddy, and like the old man hadn't raised all sorts of hell when he himself was young.

The only places with enough water to hold fish were the pools, some no bigger than a washtub. Travis flicked the spinner into the front of each pool and reeled soon as it hit the surface, the spinner moving through the water like a slow bright bullet. In every third or fourth pool a small orange-finned trout came flopping onto the bank, treble hook snagged in its mouth. Travis slapped the speckleds' heads against a rock and felt the fish shudder in his hand and die. If he missed a strike, he cast again in the same pool. Unlike brown and rainbows, speckleds would hit twice, sometimes even three times. Old Man Jenkins had said when he was a boy most every stream in Madison County was thick as gnats with speckleds, but they'd been too easy caught and soon fished out, which was why now you had to go to the back of the beyond to find them.

Eight trout weighted the back of his fishing vest when Travis passed the NO TRESPASSING sign nailed aslant a pin oak tree. The sign was as scabbed with rust as the decade-old car tag nailed on his family's barn, and he paid it no more heed now than when he'd first seen it a month ago. He knew he was on Toomey land, and he knew the stores. How Carlton Toomey once used his thumb to gouge a man's eye out in a bar fight and another time opened a man's face from ear to mouth with a broken beer bottle. Stories about events Travis's daddy had witnessed before he'd got right with the Lord. But Travis had heard other things. About how Carlton Toomey and his son were too lazy and hard-drinking to hold steady jobs. Travis's daddy claimed the Toomeys poached bears on national forest land. They cut off the paws and gutted out the gallbladders because folks in China paid good money to make potions from them. The Toomeys left the meat to rot, too sorry even to cut a few hams off the bears' flanks. Anybody that trifling wouldn't bother walking the hundred yards between farmhouse and creek to watch for trespassers.

Travis waded on upstream, going farther than he'd ever been before. He caught more speckleds, and soon seven dollars' worth bulged the back of his fishing vest. Enough money for gas and to help pay his insurance, and though it wasn't near the money he'd been making at Pay-Lo bagging groceries, at least he could do this alone, not fussed at by some old hag of a store manager with nothing better to do than watch his every move, then fire him just because he was late a few times.

He came to where the creek forked and it was there he saw a sudden high greening a few yards above him on the left. He stepped from the water and climbed the bank to make sure it was what he thought. The plants were staked like tomatoes and set in rows like tobacco or corn. They were worth money, a lot of money, because Travis knew how much his friend Shank paid for an ounce of good pot and this wasn't ounces but pounds.

He heard something behind him and turned, ready to drop the rod and reel and make a run for it. On the other side of the creek a gray squirrel scrambled up the thick bark of a black-jack oak. Travis told himself there was no reason to get all feather-legged, that nobody would have seen him coming up the creek.

He let his eyes scan what lay beyond the plants. A woodshed concealed the marijuana from anyone at the farmhouse or the dirt drive that petered out at the porch steps. Animal hides stalled mid-climb on the shed's graying boards. Coon and fox, in the center a bear, their limbs spread as though even in death they were still trying to escape. Nailed up there like a warning, Travis thought.

He looked past the shed and didn't see anything moving, not even a cow or chicken. Nothing but some open ground and then a stand of tulip poplar. He rubbed a pot leaf between his finger and thumb, and it felt like money, a

270

lot more money than he'd ever make at a grocery store. He looked around one more time before taking out his pocketknife and cutting down five plants. The stalks had a twiney toughness like rope.

That was the easy part. Dragging them a mile down the creek was a chore, especially while trying to keep the leaves and buds from being stripped off. When he got to the river he hid the marijuana in the underbrush and walked the trail to make sure no one was fishing. Then he carried the plants to the road edge, stashed them in the gully, and got the truck.

When the last plants lay in the truck bed, he wiped his face with his hand. Blood and sweat wet his palm. Travis looked in the side mirror and saw a thin red line where mountain laurel had slapped his cheek. The cut made him look tougher, more dangerous, and he wished it had slashed him deeper, enough to leave a scar. He dumped his catch into the ditch, the trout stiff and glaze-eyed. He wouldn't be delivering Old Man Jenkins any speckleds this evening.

Travis drove home with the plants hidden under willow branches and feed sacks. He planned to stay only long enough to get a shower and put on clean clothes, but as he was about to leave his father stopped him.

"We haven't ate yet."

"I'll get something in town," Travis replied.

"No. Your momma's fixing supper right now, and she's got the table set for three."

"I ain't got time. Shank's expecting me."

"You'll make time, boy," his father said. "Else you and that truck can stay in for the evening."

It was six-thirty before Travis turned into the abandoned Gulf station and parked window to window beside Shank's Plymouth Wildebeast.

"You won't believe what I got in the back of this truck."

Shank grinned.

"It's not the old prune-faced bitch that fired you, is it?"

"No, this here is worth something. Get out and I'll show you."

They walked around to the truck bed and Shank peered in.

"I didn't know there to be a big market for willow branches and feed sacks."

Travis looked around to see if anyone was watching, then pulled back enough of a sack so Travis could see some leaves.

"I got five of them," Travis said.

"Holy shit. Where'd that come from?"

"Found it when I was fishing."

Travis pulled the sack back over the plant.

"Reckon I better start doing my fishing with you," Shank said. "It's for sure I been going to the wrong places." Shank leaned against the tailgate. "What are you going to do with it? I know you ain't about to smoke it yourself."

"Sell it, if I can figure out who'll buy it."

"I bet Leonard Shuler would," Shank said. "Probably give you good money for it too."

"He don't know me though. I'm not one of his potheads like you."

"Well, we'll just have to go and get you all introduced," Shank said. "Let me lock my car and me and you will go pay him a visit."

"How about we go over to Dink Shackleford's first and get some beer."

"Leonard's got beer," Shank said, "and his ain't piss-warm like what we got last time at Dink's."

They drove out of Marshall, following 25 North. A pink, dreamy glow tinged the air. Rose-light evenings, Travis's mother had called them. The carburetor coughed and gasped as the pickup struggled up High Rock Ridge. Travis figured soon enough he'd have money for a carburetor kit, maybe even get the whole damn engine rebuilt.

"You're in for a treat, meeting Leonard," Shank said. "There's not another like him, leastways in this county."

"Wasn't he a teacher somewhere up north?"

"Yeah, but they kicked his ass out."

"What for," Travis asked, "taking money during homeroom for dope instead of lunch?"

Shank laughed.

"I wouldn't put it past him, but the way I heard it he shot some fellow."

"Kill him?"

"No, but he wasn't trying to. If he had that man would have been dead before he hit the ground."

"I heard tell he's a good shot."

"He's way beyond good," Shank said. "He can hit a chigger's ass with that pistol of his."

After a mile they turned off the blacktop and onto a dirt road. On both sides what had once been pasture sprouted with scrub pine and broom sedge. They passed a deserted farmhouse, and the road withered to no better than a logger's skid trail. Trees thickened, a few silver-trunked river birch like slats of caught light among the darker hardwoods. The land made a deep seesaw and the woods opened into a small meadow, at the center a battered green and white trailer, its back windows painted black. Parked beside the trailer was a

Buick LeSabre, front fender crumpled, rusty tailpipe held in place with a clothes hanger. Two large big-shouldered dogs scrambled out from under the trailer, barking furiously, brindle hair hackled behind their necks.

"Those damn dogs are Plott hounds," Travis said, rolling his window up higher.

Shank laughed.

"They're all bark and bristle," Shank said. "Them two wouldn't fight a tomcat, much less a bear."

The trailer door opened and a man wearing nothing but a frayed pair of khaki shorts stepped out, his brown eyes blinking like some creature unused to light. He yelled at the dogs and they slunk back under the trailer.

The man was no taller than Travis. Blond, stringy hair touched his shoulders, something not quite a beard and not quite stubble on his face. Older than Travis had figured, at least in his mid-thirties. But it was more than the creases in the brow that told Travis this. It was the way the man's shoulders drooped and arms hung—like taut, invisible ropes were attached to both his wrists and pulling toward the ground.

"That's Leonard?"

"Yeah," Shank said. "The one and only."

"He don't look like much."

"Well, he'll fool you that way. There's a lot more to him than you'd think. Like I said, you ought to see that son-of-a-bitch shoot a gun. He shot both that yankee's shoulders in the exact same place. They say you could of put a level on those two holes and the bubble would of stayed plumb."

"That sounds like a crock of shit to me," Travis said. He lit a cigarette, felt the warm smoke fill his lungs. Smoking cigarettes was the one thing his old man didn't nag him about. Afraid it would cut into his sales profits, Travis figured.

"If you'd seen him shooting at the fair last year you'd not think so," Shank said.

Leonard walked over to Travis's window, but he spoke to Shank.

"Who's this you got with you?"

"Travis Shelton."

"Shelton," Leonard said, pronouncing the name slowly as he looked at Travis. "You from the Laurel?"

Leonard's eyes were a deep gray, the same color as the birds old folks called mountain witch doves. Travis had once heard the best marksmen most always had gray eyes and wondered why that might be so.

"No," Travis said. "But my daddy grew up there."

Leonard nodded in a manner that seemed to say he'd figured as much. He stared at Travis a few moments before speaking, as though he'd seen Travis before and was trying to haul up in his mind exactly where.

"You vouch for this guy?" Leonard asked Shank.

"Hell, yeah," Shank said. "Me and Travis been best buddies since first grade."

Leonard stepped back from the car.

"I got beer and pills but just a few nickel bags if you've come for pot," Leonard said. "Supplies are low until people start to harvest."

"Well, we come at a good time then," Shank turned to Travis. "Let's show Leonard what you brought him."

Travis and Shank got out. Travis pulled back the branches and feed sacks.

"Where'd you get that?" Leonard asked.

"Found it," Travis said.

"Found it, did you. And you figured finders keepers."

"Yeah," said Travis.

"Looks like you dragged it through every briar patch and laurel slick between here and the county line," Leonard said.

"There's plenty of buds left," Shank said, lifting one of the stalks so Leonard could see it better.

"What you give me for it?" Travis asked.

Leonard lifted a stalk himself, rubbed the leaves the same way Travis had seen tobacco buyers do before the market's opening bell rang.

"Fifty dollars."

"You're trying to cheat me," Travis said. "I'll find somebody else to buy it."

As soon as he spoke he wished he hadn't. Travis was about to say that he reckoned fifty dollars would be fine but Leonard spoke first.

"I'll give you sixty dollars, and I'll give you even more if you bring me some that doesn't look like it's been run through a hay bine."

"OK," Travis said, surprised at Leonard but more surprised at himself, how tough he'd sounded. He tried not to smile as he thought of telling guys back in Marshall that he'd called Leonard Shuler a cheater to his face and Leonard hadn't done a damn thing about it but offer more money.

Leonard pulled a roll of bills from his pocket, peeled off three twenties, and handed them to Travis.

"I was figuring you might add a couple of beers, maybe some quaaludes or a joint," Shank said.

Leonard nodded toward the meadow's far corner.

"Put them over there in those tall weeds next to my tomatoes. Then come inside if you've got a notion to."

Travis and Shank lifted the plants from the truck bed and laid them where Leonard said. As they approached the door Travis watched where the Plotts had vanished under the trailer. He didn't lift his eyes until he reached the steps. Inside, it took Travis's vision a few moments to adjust, because the only light came from the TV screen. Strings of unlit Christmas lights ran across the walls and over door eaves like bad wiring. A dusty couch slouched against the back wall. In the corner Leonard sat in a fake-leather recliner patched with black electrician's tape. A stereo system filled a cabinet and the music coming from the speakers didn't have guitars or words. Beside it stood two shoddily built bookshelves teetering with albums and books. What held Travis's attention lay on a cherrywood gun rack above the couch.

Travis had seen a Model 70 Winchester only in catalogs. The checkering was done by hand, the walnut so polished and smooth it seemed to Travis he looked deep into the wood, almost through the wood, as he might look through a jar filled with sourwood honey. Shank saw him staring at the rifle and grinned.

"That's nothing like the peashooter you got, is it?" Shank said. "That's a real rifle, a Winchester Seventy."

Shank turned to Leonard.

"Let him have a look at that pistol."

Shank nodded at a small table next to Leonard's chair. Behind the lamp Travis saw the tip of a barrel.

"Let him hold that sweetheart in his hand," Shank said.

"I don't think so," Leonard said.

"Come on, Leonard. Just let him hold it. We're not talking about shooting."

Leonard looked put out with them both. He lifted the pistol from the table and emptied bullets from the cylinder into his palm, then handed it to Shank.

Shank held the pistol a few moments and passed it to Travis. Travis knew the gun was composed of springs and screws and sheet metal, but it felt more solid than that, as if smithed from a single piece of case-hardened steel. The white grips had a rich blueing to them that looked, like the Winchester's stock, almost liquid. The Colt of the company's name was etched on the receiver.

"It's a forty-five," Shank said. "There's no better pistol a man can buy, is there Leonard?"

"Show-and-tell is over for today," Leonard said, and held his hand out for the pistol. He took the weapon and placed it back behind the lamp. Travis stepped closer to the gun rack, his eyes not on the Winchester but what lay beneath it, a long-handled piece of metal with a dinner-plate-sized disk on one end.

"What's that thing?" Travis asked.

"A metal detector," Leonard said.

"You looking for buried treasure?"

"No," Leonard said. "A guy wanted some dope and came up a few bucks short. It was collateral."

"What do you do with it?"

"He used it to hunt Civil War relics."

Travis looked more closely at the machine. He thought it might be fun to try, kind of like fishing in the ground instead of water.

"You use it much?"

"I've found some dimes and quarters on the riverbank."

Leonard sat back down in the recliner. He nodded at the couch. "You can stand there like fence posts if you like, but if not that couch ought to hold both of you."

A woman came from the back room and stood in the foyer between the living room and kitchen. She wore cut-off jeans and a halter top, her legs and arms thin but cantaloupe-sized bulges beneath the halter. Her hair was blond but Travis could see the dark roots. She was sunburned and splotches of pink underskin made her look wormy and mangy. Like some stray dog around a garbage dump, Travis thought. Except for her face. Hard-looking, as if the sun had dried up any softness there once was, but pretty—high cheekbones and full lips, dark-brown eyes. If she wasn't all scabbed up she'd be near beautiful, Travis figured.

"How about getting Shank and his buddy here a couple of beers, Dena," Leonard said.

"Get them your ownself," the woman said. She took a Coke from the refrigerator and disappeared again into the back room.

Leonard shook his head but said nothing as he got up. He brought back two cans of Budweiser and a sandwich bag filled with pot and rolling papers. He handed the beers to Travis and Shank and sat down in the chair. Travis was thirsty and drank quickly as he watched Leonard carefully shake pot out of the baggie and onto the paper. Leonard licked the paper and twisted both ends.

"Here," he said, and handed the marijuana to Shank.

Shank lit the joint, the orange tip brightening as he inhaled. Shank offered the joint back but Leonard declined.

"All these times I've been out here I never seen you mellow out and take a toke," Shank said. "Why is that?"

"I'm not a very mellow guy," Leonard nodded at Travis. "Looks like your buddy isn't either."

"He's just scared his daddy would find out."

"That ain't so," Travis said. "I just like a beer buzz better."

He lifted the beer to his lips and drank until the can was empty, then squeezed the can's middle. The cool metal popped and creaked as it folded inward.

"I'd like me another one."

"Quite the drinker, aren't you," Leonard said. "Just make sure you don't overdo it. I don't want you passed out and pissing my couch."

Travis stood and for a moment felt off plumb, maybe because he'd drunk the beer so fast. When the world steadied he got the beer from the refrigerator and sat back down. He looked at the TV, some kind of Western, but without the sound he couldn't tell what was happening. He drank the second beer quick as the first.

Shank had his eyes closed.

"Man, I'm feeling so good," Shank said. "If we had us some real music on that stereo things would be perfect."

"Real music," Leonard said, and smiled, but Travis knew he was only smiling to himself.

Travis studied the man who sat in the recliner, trying to figure out what it was that made Leonard Shuler a man you didn't want to mess with. Leonard looked soft, Travis thought, pale and soft like bread dough. Just because a man had a couple of bear dogs and a hotshot pistol didn't make him such a badass. He thought about his own daddy and Carlton Toomey, big men who didn't need to talk loud because they could clear out a room with just a hard look. Travis wondered if anyone would ever call him a badass and wished again that he didn't take after his mother, so thin-boned.

"So what is this shit you're listening to, Leonard?" Shank asked.

"It's called *Appalachian Spring*. It's by Copland."

"Never heard of them," Shank said.

Leonard looked amused.

"Are you sure? They used to be the warm-up act for Lynyrd Skynyrd."

"Well, it still sucks," Shank said.

"That's probably because you fail to empathize with his view of the region," Leonard said.

"Empa what?" Shank said.

"Empathize," Leonard said.

"I don't know what you're talking about," Shank said. "All I know is I'd rather tie a bunch of cats together by their tails and hear them squall."

Travis knew Leonard was putting down not just Shank but him also, talking over him like he was stupid. It made Travis think of his teachers at the high school, teachers who used sentences with big words against him when he gave them trouble, trying to tangle him up in a laurel slick of language. Figuring he hadn't read nothing but what they made him read, never used a dictionary to look up a word he didn't know.

Travis got up and made his way to the refrigerator, damned if he was going to ask permission. He pulled the metal tab off the beer but didn't go back to the couch. He went down the hallway to find the bathroom.

He almost had to walk slantways because of the makeshift shelves lining the narrow hallway. They were tall as Travis and each shelf sagged under the weight of books of various sizes and shapes, more books than Travis had seen anywhere outside a library. There was a bookshelf in the bathroom as well. He read the titles as he pissed, all unfamiliar to him. But some looked interesting. When he stepped back into the hallway, he saw the bedroom door was open. The woman sat up in the bed reading a magazine. Travis walked into the room.

The woman laid down the magazine.

"What the hell do you want?"

Travis grinned.

"What you offering?"

Even buzzed on beer he knew it was a stupid thing to say. Ever since he'd got to Leonard's his mouth had been like a faucet he couldn't shut off.

The woman's brown eyes stared at him like he was nothing more than a sack of manure somebody had dumped on the floor.

"I ain't offering you anything," she said. "Even if I was, a little peckerhead like you wouldn't know what to do with it."

The woman looked toward the open door.

"Leonard," she shouted.

Leonard appeared at the doorway.

"It's past time to get your Cub Scout meeting over," she said.

Leonard nodded at Travis.

"I believe you boys have overstayed your welcome."

"I was getting ready to leave anyhow," Travis said. He turned toward the door and the can slipped from his hand, spilling beer on the bed.

"Nothing but a little peckerhead," the woman repeated.

In a few moments he and Shank were outside. The last rind of sun embered on Brushy Mountain. Cicadas had started their racket in the trees and lightning bugs rode an invisible current over the grass. Travis tried to catch one, but when he opened his hand it held nothing but air. He tried again and felt a soft tickling in his palm.

"You get more plants, come again," Leonard said from the steps.

"I was hoping you'd show us some of that fancy shooting of yours," Shank said.

"Not this evening," Leonard said.

Travis loosened his fingers. The lightning bug seemed not so much to fly as float out of his hand. In a few moments it was one tiny flicker among many, like a star returned to its constellation.

"Good night," Leonard said, turning to go back inside the trailer.

"Empathy means you can feel what other people are feeling," Travis said.

Leonard's hand was on the door handle but he paused and looked at Travis. He nodded and went inside.

"Boy, you're in high cotton now," Shank said as they drove toward Marshall. "Sixty damn dollars. That'll pay your truck insurance for two months."

"I figured to give you ten," Travis said, "for hooking me up with Leonard."

"No, I got a good buzz. That's payment enough."

Travis drifted onto the shoulder and for a moment one tire was on asphalt and the other on dirt and grass. He swerved back onto the road.

"You better let me drive," Shank said. "I was hoping to stay out of the emergency room tonight."

"I'm all right," Travis said, but he slowed down, thinking about what the old man would do if he wrecked or got stopped for drunk driving. Better off if I got killed outright, he figured.

"Are you going to get some more plants?" Shank asked.

"I expect I will."

"Well, if you do, be careful. Whoever planted it's not likely to appreciate you thinning their crop out for them."

Travis went back the next Saturday, two flat-woven cabbage sacks stuffed into his belt. After he'd been fired from the Pay-Lo, he'd about given up on paying the insurance on his truck, but now things had changed. He had what was pretty damn near a money tree and all he had to do was get its leaves to Leonard Shuler. An honest-to-god money tree if there was ever such a thing, he kept thinking to himself when he got a little scared.

He climbed the waterfall, the trip up easier without a rod and reel. Once he passed the NO TRESPASSING sign, he moved slower, quieter. From the far bank's underbrush a warbler sang a refrain of three slow notes and three quick ones, the song echoing into the scattering of tamarack trees rising there. Travis's mother had once told him the bird was saying *pleased pleased pleased to meetcha.*

Soon cinnamon ferns brushed like huge green feathers against his legs, thick enough to hide a copperhead or satinback. But he kept his eyes raised, watching upstream for the glimpse of a shirt, a movement on a bank. I bet Carlton Toomey didn't even plant it, Travis told himself, probably somebody who figured the Toomeys were too sorry to notice pot growing on their land.

When he came to where the plants were, he got on all fours and crawled up the bank, raising his head like a soldier in a trench. A Confederate flag brightened his tee-shirt, and he wished he'd had the good sense to wear something less visible. Might as well have a damn bull's-eye on his chest. He scanned the tree line across the field and saw no one. Travis told himself even if someone hid in the tulip poplars they could never get to him before he was long gone down the creek.

Travis cut the stalks just below the last leaves. Six plants filled up the sacks. He thought about cutting more, taking what he had to the truck and coming back to get the rest, but figured that was too risky. On his return Travis didn't see anyone on the river trail. If he had and they'd asked what was in the sacks, he'd have said galax.

When Travis pulled up to the trailer, Leonard was watering the tomatoes. He unlatched the tailgate and waited for Leonard to finish. Less than a mile away, the granite north face of Price Mountain jutted up beyond the pasture. Afternoon heat haze made the mountain appear to expand and contract as if breathing. *God's like these hills,* Preacher Caldwell had said one Sunday, *high enough up to see everything that goes on.* It ain't like stealing a cash crop like tobacco where a man's shed some real sweat, Travis reminded himself, for marijuana was little more bother than a few seeds dropped in the ground. Taking pot plants was just the same as picking up windfall apples—less so because those that grew it had broken the law themselves. That was the way to think about it, Travis decided.

"How come you grow your own tomatoes but not your own pot?" Travis asked when Leonard laid down his hose and came over.

"Because I'm a low-risk kind of guy. It's getting too chancy unless you have a place way back in some hollow."

One of the Plotts nudged Leonard's leg and Leonard scratched the dog's head. The dog closed its watery brown eyes, seemed about to fall asleep. Not very fierce for a bear dog, Travis thought.

"Where's Shank?" Leonard said. "I thought you two were partners."

"I don't need a partner," Travis said. He lifted the first sack from the truck bed, pulled out each stalk carefully so as not to tear off any leaves and buds. He placed the plants on the ground between them. It was a good feeling, knowing everything on his end was done. A lot like when he and the old man unloaded tobacco at the auction barn. Even his daddy would be in a good mood as they laid their crop on the worn market-house floor.

As Travis emptied the second sack he imagined the old man's reaction if he knew what Travis was doing. Probably have a fit, Travis figured, though some part of his daddy, the part that had been near an outlaw when he was Travis's age, would surely admire the pluck of what his boy had done, even if he never said so. Travis nodded at his harvest.

"That's one hundred and twenty dollars' worth at the least," he said.

Leonard stepped closer and studied the plants a few moments. He pulled the billfold from his pocket and handed Travis five twenty-dollar bills. Leonard hesitated, then added four fives.

Travis stuffed the bills into his pocket but did not get back in the truck.

"What?" Leonard finally said.

"I figured you to ask me in for a beer."

"I don't think so. I don't much want to play host this afternoon."

"You don't think I'm good enough to set foot in that roachy old trailer of yours."

Leonard settled his eyes on Travis.

"You get your hackles up pretty quick, don't you?"

Travis did his best to match Leonard's steady gaze.

"I'm not afraid of you," Travis said.

Leonard shifted his gaze lower and to the right as though someone sat in a chair beside Travis. Someone who took Travis's words no more seriously than Leonard did.

"After the world has its way with you a few years, it'll knock some of the strut out of you," Leonard said, no longer smiling. "If you live that long."

A part of Travis wanted to clamp a hand over his own mouth, keep it there till he was back in Marshall. He had the uneasy feeling that Leonard knew things about him, things so deep inside that Travis himself hadn't figured them out, and every time he opened his mouth Leonard knew more.

"I ain't wanting your advice," Travis said. "I just want some beer."

"One beer," Leonard said, and they walked into the trailer. While Leonard got the beers Travis went down the hall to the bathroom. The bedroom door was shut and he hoped it stayed so. If the woman came out she'd surely have some more sass words for him. When he came back Leonard sat in the leather recliner, a beer in each hand. He handed one to Travis. Travis sat on the couch and pulled the tab. He still didn't much care for the taste, but the beer was cold and felt good as it slid down his throat.

"You got a lot of books," Travis said, nodding toward the shelves.

"Keeps me from being ignorant," Leonard said.

"I've known plenty of teachers without any sense," Travis said. "They didn't even know how to change their own car tire."

Leonard leaned back a little deeper in the chair.

"Stupidity and ignorance aren't the same thing. You can't cure someone of stupidity. Somebody like yourself that's merely ignorant there might be hope for."

"What reason you got to say I'm ignorant?"

"That tee-shirt you're wearing, for one thing. If you'd worn it up here in the 1860s it could have gotten you killed, and by your own blood kin."

Travis had drunk only half his beer but Leonard's words were as hard to grasp as wisps of ground fog.

"You trying to say my family was yankees?"

"No, at least not in the geographical sense. They just didn't see any reason to side with the slave owners."

"So they weren't on either side?"

"They had a side. Nobody had the luxury of staying out of it up here. Most places they'd fight a battle and move on, but once war came it didn't leave Madison County."

Travis took a last swallow and set the empty can at his feet. He wondered if the older man was just messing with him, like when Shank had asked about the music. But it didn't seem that way. Leonard looked to be serious.

"You go out to Shelton Laurel much?" Leonard asked.

"Just for family reunions when I was a kid."

"And your kin never talked about what happened in 1863 or said anything about Bloody Madison?"

"What's Bloody Madison?"

"The name this county went by during the Civil War."

Travis thought back to church homecomings and family reunions in the Laurel. Most of the talk, at least among the men, had been about tobacco. But not all of it.

"Sometimes my daddy and uncle talked about kin that got killed in Shelton Laurel during the war, but I always figured the yankees had done it."

The Plotts began barking, and a few moments later Travis saw a red Camaro rumble up to the trailer, its back wheels jacked up, white racing stripe on the hood. Two men with long black hair got out. One threw a cigarette butt on the ground and didn't bother to grind it out with his boot heel. They stood beside the car, both doors open, the engine catching and coughing. When Leonard didn't come out, the driver leaned into the car and blew the horn. Both dogs barked furiously but stayed near the trailer.

Leonard lifted himself wearily from the chair. He went to the kitchen and came back with two plastic baggies filled with pills. The car horn blew again.

"The worst thing the nineteen sixties did to this country was introduce drugs to rednecks," Leonard said. He laid the baggies on the coffee table and went to the refrigerator.

"You don't seem to much mind taking their money," Travis said.

Leonard's lips creased into a tight smile.

"True enough," he said, taking another beer from the refrigerator. "Here," he said, holding the can out to Travis. "A farewell present. It's best if you don't come around here anymore."

"What if I get you some more plants?"

"I don't think you better try to do that," Leonard said. "Whoever's pot that is will be harvesting in the next few days. You better not be anywhere near when they're doing it either."

Travis left the couch and stepped into the kitchen. The first faint buzz from the alcohol made his scalp tingle.

"I ain't scared," Travis said.

"Well, maybe you should be in this instance."

Leonard's words were soft, barely audible over the roar of the Camaro. He wasn't talking down to him the way the teachers or his father might. For a moment Travis thought he saw something like concern flicker in Leonard's eyes. Then it was gone.

"But what if I do get more?" Travis asked as he reached for the beer. Leonard did not release his grip on the can.

"Same price, but if you want any beer you'll have to pay bootleg price like your buddies."

The next day after lunch, Travis took off his church clothes and put on a green tee-shirt and a pair of cutoffs instead of regular jeans. That meant more scrapes and scratches but he'd be able to run faster if needed. The day was hot and humid, and when he parked by the bridge the only people on the river were a man and two boys swimming near the far bank. By the time Travis reached the creek, his tee-shirt was soggy and sweat stung his eyes.

Upstream, trees blocked most of the sun and the water he waded cooled him off. At the waterfall, an otter slid into the pool. Travis watched his body surge through the water as straight and sleek as a torpedo before disappearing under the bank. He wondered how much otter pelts brought and figured come winter it might be worth finding out, maybe set out a rabbit gum and bait it with a dead trout. He knelt and cupped his hand to drink, the pool's water so cold it hurt his teeth.

He climbed the left side of the falls, then made his way upstream to the sign. If someone waited for him, Travis believed that by now the person would have figured out he came up the creek, so he left it and climbed the ridge into the woods. He followed the sound of water until he'd gone far enough and came down the slope deliberate and quiet, stopping every few yards to listen.

He was almost to the creek when something rustled to his left in the underbrush. Travis did not move until he heard *pleased pleased pleased to meet-cha* rising from the web of sweetbrier and scrub oak. When he stepped onto the sandy bank, he looked upstream and down before crossing.

The marijuana was still there, every bit as tall as the corn Travis and his daddy had planted in early April. He pulled the sacks from his belt and walked toward the closest plant, his eyes on the trees across the field. The ground gave slightly beneath his right foot. He heard a click, then the sound of metal striking bone. Pain flamed up his leg like a quick fuse, consumed his whole body. The sun slid sideways and the ground tilted as well and slapped up against the side of his face.

When he came to, his head lay inches from a pot plant. This ain't nothing but a bad dream, he told himself, thinking if he believed hard enough that might make it true. He used his forearm to lift his head and look at the leg. The leg twisted slightly and pain slugged him like a tire iron. The world darkened for a few moments before slowly lighting back up. He looked at his foot and immediately wished he hadn't. The trap's jaws clenched his leg just above the ankle. Blood soaked his tennis shoe and Travis feared if he looked too long he'd see the white nakedness of bone. Don't look at it anymore until you have to, he told himself, and laid his head back on the ground.

His face was turned toward the west now, and he guessed midafternoon from the sun's angle. Maybe it ain't that bad, he thought. Maybe if I just lay here awhile, it'll ease up some and I can get the trap off. He kept still as possible, taking shallow breaths. A soft humming rose inside his head, like a mud dauber had crawled deep into his ear and gotten stuck. But it wasn't a bad sound. It reminded Travis of when his mother sang him to sleep when he was a child. He could hear the creek and its sound merged with the sound inside his head. Did trout hear water? he wondered. That was a crazy sort of thought and he tried to think of something that made sense.

He remembered what Old Man Jenkins had said about how just one man could pretty much fish out a stream of speckled trout if he took a notion to. Travis wondered how many speckled trout he'd be able to catch out of Caney Creek before they were all gone. He wondered if after he did he'd be able to find another way-back trickle of water that held them. He tried to imagine that stream, imagine he was there right now fishing it.

He must have passed out again, because when he opened his eyes the sun hovered just above the tree line. The humming in his head was gone and when he tested the leg, pain flamed up every bit as fierce as before. He wondered how long it would be until his parents got worried and how long it would take after that before someone found his truck and folks began searching. Tomorrow at the earliest, he figured, and even then they'd search the river before looking anywhere else.

Travis lifted his head a few inches and shouted toward the woods. No one called back. Being so close to the ground muffled his voice, so he used a forearm to raise himself a little higher and shout again.

I'm going to have to sit up, he told himself, and just the thought of doing so made bile rise into his throat. He took deliberate breaths and used both arms to lift himself. Pain smashed against his body and the world drained of color until all of what surrounded him was shaded a deep blue. He leaned back on the ground, sweat popping out on his face and arms like blisters. Everything was moving farther away, the sky and trees and plants, as though he were being slowly lowered into a well. He shivered and wondered why he hadn't brought a sweatshirt or jacket with him.

Two men came out of the woods, and seeing them somehow cleared his head for a few moments, brought the world's color and proximity back. They walked toward him with no more hurry than men come to check their plants for cutworms. Travis knew the big man in front was Carlton Toomey and the man trailing him his son. He couldn't remember the son's name but had seen him in town. What he remembered was the son had been away from the county for nearly a decade, and some said he'd been in the Marines and others said prison and some said both, though you wouldn't know it from his long brown hair, the bright bead necklace around his neck. The younger man wore a dirty white tee-shirt and jeans, the older man blue coveralls with no shirt underneath. Grease coated their hands and arms.

They stood above him but did not speak or look at him. Carlton Toomey jerked a red rag from his back pocket and rubbed his hands and wrists. The son stared at the woods across the creek. Travis wondered if they weren't there at all, were just some imagining in his head.

"My leg's hurt," Travis said, figuring if they spoke back they must be real.

"I reckon it is," Carlton Toomey said, looking at him now. "I reckon it's near about cut clear off."

The younger man spoke.

"What we going to do?"

Carlton Toomey did not answer, instead eased himself onto the ground beside the boy. They were almost eye level now.

"Who's your people?"

"My daddy's Harvey Shelton."

"You ain't much more than ass and elbows, boy. I'd have thought what Harvey Shelton sired to be stouter. You must favor your mother." Carlton Toomey nodded his head and smiled. "Me and your daddy used to drink some together, but that was back when he was sowing his wild oats. He still farming tobacco?"

"Yes sir."

"The best days of tobacco men is behind them. I planted my share of burley, made decent money for a while. But that tit has done gone dry. How much your daddy make last year, six—seven thousand?"

Travis tried to remember, but the numbers would not line up in his head. His brain seemed tangled in cobwebs.

"He'd make as much sitting on his ass and collecting welfare. If you're going to make a go of it in these mountains today you got to find another way."

Carlton Toomey stuffed the rag in his back pocket.

"I've done that, but your daddy's too stubborn to change. Always has been. Stubborn as a white oak stump. But you've figured it out, else you'd not have stole my plants in the first place."

"I reckon I need me a doctor," Travis said. He was feeling better, knowing the older man was there beside him. His leg didn't hurt nearly as much now as before, and he told himself he could probably walk on it if he had to once the Toomeys got the trap off.

"The best thing to do is put him there below the falls," the son said. "They'll figure him to fallen and drowned himself."

Carlton Toomey looked up.

"I think we done used up our allotment of accidental drownings around here. It'd likely be more than just Crockett nosing around if there was another."

Toomey looked back at Travis. He spoke slowly, his voice soft.

"Coming back up here a second time took some guts. Even if I'd figured out you was the one I'd have let it go, just for the feistiness of your doing it. But coming a third time was downright stupid, and greedy. It ain't like you're some shit-britches young'un. You're old enough to know better."

"I'm sorry," Travis said.

Carlton Toomey reached out his hand and gently brushed some of the dirt off Travis's face.

"I know you are, son, just like every other poor son-of-a-bitch that's got his ass in a sling he can't get out of."

Travis knew he was forgetting something, something important he needed to tell Carlton Toomey. He squeezed his eyes shut a few moments to think harder. It finally came to him.

"I reckon you better get me to the doctor," Travis said.

"We got to harvest these plants first," the older Toomey replied. "What if we was to take you down to the hospital and folks started wondering why we'd set a bear trap. They might figure there's something up here we wanted to keep folks from poking around and finding."

Carlton Toomey's words started to blur and swirl in Travis' mind. They were hard to hold in place long enough to make sense. He tried to remember what had brought him this far up the creek. Travis finally thought of something he could say in just a few words.

"Could you get that trap off my foot?"

"Sure," Toomey said. He slid over a few feet to reach the trap, then looked up at his son.

"Step on that lever, Hubert, and I'll get his leg out."

The younger man stepped closer. Travis stared hard at the beads. They were red and yellow and black, a dime-sized silver peace sign clipped on the necklace as well. Hubert raised his head as he pressed and afternoon sun glanced the silver, momentarily blinding Travis. The pain rose up his leg again but it seemed less a part of him now, the way an aching tooth he'd had last fall felt after a needle of Novocain. Travis kept staring at the beads, because they were the only thing now that hadn't been drained of color. There was a name for those beads. He almost remembered but then the name slipped free like a balloon let go, rising steadily farther and farther away.

"That's got it," Carlton Toomey said and slowly raised Travis's leg, placed it on the ground beside the trap. Toomey used spit and his rag to wipe blood from the wound.

"What's your given name, son?" he asked.

"Travis."

"This ain't near bad as it looks, Travis," Toomey said. "I don't think that trap even put a gouge in the leg bone. Probably didn't tear up any ligaments or tendons either. You're just a pint low in the blood department. That's the thing what's making you foggyheaded."

"Now what?" the son said.

"Go call Dooley and tell him we'll be bringing him plants sooner than we thought. Bring back them machetes and we'll get this done." He paused. "Give me that hawkbill of yours."

Hubert took the knife from his pocket and handed it to his father.

"What you going to do to him?" Hubert asked.

"What's got to be done," the elder Toomey said. "Now go on and get those damn machetes."

Hubert started walking toward the farmhouse.

"I'm sorry I have to do this, son," Carlton said.

The knife blade made a clicking sound as it locked into place. Travis squeezed his eyes shut. For a few moments the only sound was the gurgle of the creek, and he remembered how it was the speckled trout that had brought him here. He remembered how you could not see the orange fins and red flank spots but only the dark backs in the rippling water. And how it was only when they lay gasping on the green bank moss that you realized how bright and pretty they were.

From *Serena* (2009)

PART ONE, CHAPTER 1—SUMMER 1929

When Pemberton returned to the North Carolina mountains after three months in Boston settling his father's estate, among those waiting on the train platform was a woman pregnant with Pemberton's child. She was accompanied by her father, who carried beneath his shabby frock coat a bowie knife sharpened with great attentiveness earlier that morning so it would plunge as deep as possible into Pemberton's heart.

The conductor shouted "Waynesville" as the train shuddered to a halt. Pemberton looked out the window and saw his partners on the platform, both dressed in suits to meet his bride of two days, an unexpected bonus from his time in Boston. Buchanan, ever the dandy, had waxed his mustache and oiled his hair. His polished bluchers gleamed, the white cotton dress shirt fresh-pressed. Wilkie wore a gray fedora, as he often did to protect his bald pate from the sun. A Princeton Phi Beta Kappa key glinted on the older man's watch fob, a blue silk handkerchief tucked in his breast pocket.

Pemberton opened the gold shell of his watch and found the train on time to the exact minute. He turned to his bride, who'd been napping. Serena's dreams had been especially troubling last night. Twice he'd been waked by her thrashing, her fierce latching onto him until she'd fallen back asleep. He kissed her lightly on the lips and she awoke.

"Not the best place for a honeymoon."

"It will suit us well enough," Serena said, leaning into his shoulder. "We're here together, which is all that matters."

Pemberton inhaled the bright aroma of Tre Jur talcum and remembered how he'd not just smelled but tasted that vividness on her skin earlier that morning. A porter came up the aisle, whistling a song Pemberton didn't recognize. His gaze returned to the window.

Next to the ticket booth Harmon and his daughter waited, Harmon slouching against the chestnut board wall. It struck Pemberton that males in these mountains rarely stood upright. Instead, they leaned into some tree or wall whenever possible. If none were available they squatted, buttocks flank against the backs of their heels. Harmon held a pint jar in his hand, what remained of its contents barely covering the bottom. The daughter sat on the bench, her posture upright to better reveal her condition. Pemberton could not recall her first name. He wasn't surprised to see them or that the girl was with child. *His child,* Pemberton had learned the night before he and Serena left Boston. Abe Harmon is down here saying he has business to settle with you, business about his daughter, Buchanan had said when he called. It could just be a drunken bluster, but I thought you ought to know.

"Our welcoming party includes some of the locals," Pemberton said to his bride.

"As we were led to expect," Serena said.

She placed her right hand on his wrist for a moment, and Pemberton felt the calluses on her upper palm, the plain gold wedding band she wore in lieu of a diamond. The ring was like his in every detail except width. Pemberton stood and retrieved two grips from the overhead compartment. He handed them to the porter, who stepped back and followed as Pemberton led his bride down the aisle and the steps to the platform. There was a gap of two feet between the steel and wood. Serena did not reach for his hand as she stepped onto the planks.

Buchanan caught Pemberton's eye first, gave him a warning nod toward Harmon and his daughter before acknowledging Serena with a stiff formal bow. Wilkie took off his fedora. At five-nine, Serena stood taller than either man, but Pemberton knew other aspects of Serena's appearance helped foster Buchanan and Wilkie's obvious surprise—pants and boots instead of a dress and cloche hat, sun-bronzed skin that belied Serena's social class, lips and cheeks untinted by rouge, hair blonde and thick but cut short in a bob, distinctly feminine yet also austere.

Serena went up to the older man and held out her hand. Though he was, at seventy, over twice her age, Wilkie stared at Serena like a smitten schoolboy, the fedora pressed against his sternum as if to conceal a heart already captured.

"Wilkie, I assume."

"Yes, yes, I am," Wilkie stammered.

"Serena Pemberton," she said, her hand still extended.

Wilkie fumbled with his hat a moment before freeing his right hand and shaking Serena's.

"And Buchanan," Serena said, turning to the other partner. "Correct?"

"Yes."

Buchanan took her proffered hand and cupped it awkwardly in his.

Serena smiled. "Don't you know how to properly shake hands, Mr. Buchanan?"

Pemberton watched with amusement as Buchanan blushed and corrected his grip and quickly withdrew his hand. In the year that Boston Lumber Company had operated in these mountains, Buchanan's wife had come only once, arriving in a taffeta gown that was soiled before she'd crossed Waynesville's one street and entered her husband's house. She'd spent one night and left on the morning train. Now Buchanan and his wife met once a month for a weekend in Richmond, as far south as Mrs. Buchanan would travel. Wilkie's wife had never left Boston.

Pemberton's partners appeared incapable of further speech. Their eyes shifted to the leather jodhpurs Serena wore, the beige oxford shirt and black boots. Serena's proper diction and erect carriage confirmed that she'd attended finishing school in New England, as had their wives. But Serena had been born in Colorado and lived there until sixteen, child of a timber man who'd taught his daughter to shake hands firmly and look men in the eye as well as ride and shoot. She'd come east only after her parents' deaths.

The porter laid the grips on the platform and walked back toward the baggage car that held Serena's Saratoga trunk and Pemberton's smaller steamer trunk.

"I assume Campbell got the Arabian to camp," Pemberton said.

"Yes," Buchanan replied, "though it nearly killed young Vaughn. That horse isn't just big but quite spirited, 'cut proud,' as they say."

"What news of the camp?" Pemberton asked.

"No serious problems," Buchanan said. "A worker found bobcat tracks on Laurel Creek and thought they were a mountain lion's. A couple of crews refused to go back up there until Galloway checked it out."

"Mountain lions," Serena said, "are they common here?"

"Not at all, Mrs. Pemberton," Wilkie answered reassuringly. "The last one killed in this state was in 1920, I'm glad to say."

"Yet the locals persist in believing one remains," Buchanan said. "There's quite a bit of lore about it, which all the workers are aware of, not only about its great size but its color, which evolves from tawny to jet-black. I'm quite content to have it remain folklore, but your husband desires otherwise. He's hoping the creature is real so he can hunt it."

"That was before his nuptials," Wilkie noted. "Now that Pemberton's a married man I'm sure he'll give up hunting panthers for less dangerous diversions."

"I hope he'll pursue this panther and would be disappointed if he were to do otherwise," Serena said, turning so she addressed Pemberton as much as his partners. "Pemberton's a man unafraid of challenges, which is why I married him."

Serena paused, a slight smile creasing her face.

"And why he married me."

The porter set the second trunk on the platform. Pemberton gave the man a quarter and dismissed him. Serena looked over at the father and daughter, who now sat on the bench together, watchful and silent as actors awaiting their cues.

"I don't know you," Serena said.

The daughter continued to stare sullenly at Serena. It was the father who spoke, his voice slurred.

"My business ain't with you. It's with him standing there beside you."

"His business is mine," Serena said, "just as mine is his."

Harmon nodded at his daughter's belly, then turned back to Serena.

"Not this business. It was done before you got here."

"You're implying she's carrying my husband's child."

"I ain't *implying* nothing," Harmon said.

"You're a lucky man then," Serena said to Harmon. "You'll not find a better sire to breed her with. The size of her belly attests to that."

Serena turned her gaze and words to the daughter.

"But that's the only one you'll have of his. I'm here now. Any other children he has will be with me."

Harmon pushed himself fully upright, and Pemberton glimpsed the white-pearl handle of a bowie knife before the coat settled over it. He wondered how a man like Harmon could possess such a fine weapon. Perhaps booty in a poker game or an heirloom passed down from a more prosperous ancestor. The depot master's face appeared behind the glass partition, lingered a moment, and vanished. A group of gangly mountaineers, all Boston Lumber employees, watched expressionless from an adjacent livestock barn.

Among them was an overseer named Campbell, whose many duties included serving as a liason between the workers and owners. Campbell always wore gray chambray shirts and corduroy pants at camp, but this afternoon he wore overalls same as the other men. *It's Sunday,* Pemberton realized, and felt momentarily disoriented. He couldn't recall the last time he'd glanced at a calendar. In Boston with Serena, time had seemed caught within the sweeping circle of watch and clock hands—passing hours and minutes unable to break free to become passing days. But the days and months had passed, as the Harmon girl's swelling belly made clear.

Harmon's large freckled hands grasped the bench edge, and he leaned slightly forward. His blue eyes glared at Pemberton.

"Let's go home, Daddy," Harmon's daughter said, and placed her hand on his.

He swatted the hand away as if a bothersome fly and stood up, wavered a moment.

"God damn the both of you," Harmon said, taking a step toward the Pembertons.

He opened the frock coat and freed the bowie knife from its leather sheath. The blade caught the late-afternoon sun, and for a brief moment it appeared Harmon held a glistening flame in his hand. Pemberton looked at Harmon's daughter, her hands covering her stomach as if to shield the unborn child from what was occurring.

"Take your father home," Pemberton told her.

"Daddy, please," the daughter said.

"Go get Sheriff McDowell," Buchanan yelled at the men watching from the livestock barn.

A crew foreman named Snipes did as commanded, walking rapidly not toward the courthouse but to the boarding house where the sheriff resided. The other men stayed where they were. Buchanan moved to step between the two men, but Harmon waved him away with the knife.

"We're settling this now," Harmon shouted.

"He's right," Serena said. "Get your knife and settle it now, Pemberton."

Harmon stepped forward, wavering slightly as he narrowed the distance between them.

"You best listen to her," Harmon said, taking another step forward, "because one of us is leaving with his toes pointed up."

Pemberton leaned and unclasped his calfskin grip, grabbled among its contents for the wedding present Serena had given him. He slipped the hunting knife from its sheath and settled the elk-bone handle deeper in his palm, its roughness all the better for clasping. For a lingering moment, Pemberton allowed himself to appreciate the feel of a weapon well made, the knife's balance and solidity, its blade, hilt and handle precisely calibrated as the epees he'd fenced with at Harvard. He took off his coat and laid it across the grip.

Harmon took another step forward, and they were less than a yard apart. He kept the knife held high and pointed toward the sky, and Pemberton knew that Harmon, drunk or sober, had done little fighting with a blade. Pemberton took a step closer and Harmon slashed the air between them. The man's tobacco-yellowed teeth were clenched, the veins in his neck taut as guy wires. Pemberton kept his knife low and close to his side. He smelled the moonshine on Harmon's breath, a harsh greasy odor, like coal-oil.

Harmon lunged forward and Pemberton raised his left arm. The bowie knife swept the air but its arc stopped when Harmon's forearm hit Pemberton's. Harmon jerked down and the bowie knife raked across Pemberton's flesh. Pemberton took one final step, the hunting knife's blade flat as he slipped it inside Harmon's coat and plunged the steel through shirt cloth and into the soft flesh above the older man's left hip bone. He grabbed Harmon's shoulder with his free hand for leverage and quickly opened a thin smile across the man's stomach. A cedarwood button popped free from Harmon's soiled white shirt, hit the plank floor, spun a moment and settled. Then a soft sucking sound as Pemberton withdrew the blade. For a few moments there was no blood.

Harmon's knife fell clattering onto the platform. Like a man attempting to rescind the steps that had led to this outcome, the highlander placed both hands to his stomach and slowly walked backward, then sagged onto the bench. He lifted his hands to assess the damage and his intestines spilled onto his lap in loose gray ropes. Harmon studied the inner workings of his body as if for some further verification of his fate. He raised his head a last time and leaned it back against the depot's boards. Pemberton looked away as Harmon's blue eyes dimmed.

Serena stood beside him now.

"Your arm," she said.

Pemberton saw that his poplin shirt was slashed below the elbow, the blue cloth darkened by blood. Serena unclasped a silver cuff link and rolled up the shirtsleeve, examined the cut across his forearm.

"It won't need stitches," she said, "just iodine and a dressing."

Pemberton nodded. Adrenaline surged through him and when Buchanan's concerned face loomed closer his partner's features—the clipped black hedge of moustache between the pointed narrow nose and small mouth, the round pale-green eyes that always looked slightly surprised—seemed at once both vivid and remote. Pemberton took deep measured breaths, wanting to compose himself before speaking to anyone.

Serena picked up the bowie knife and carried it to Harmon's daughter, who leaned over her father, hands cradling the blank face close to hers as if something might yet be conveyed to him. Tears flowed down the young woman's cheeks, but she made no sound.

"Here," Serena said, holding the knife by the blade. "By all rights it belongs to my husband. It's a fine knife, and you can get a good price for it if you demand one. And I would," she added. "Sell it, I mean. That money will help when the child is born. It's all you'll ever get from my husband and me."

Harmon's daughter looked at her now, but she did not raise a hand to take the knife. Serena set the bowie knife on the bench and walked across the platform to stand beside Pemberton. Except for Campbell, who was walking toward the platform, the men leaning against the livestock barn's railing had not moved. Pemberton was glad they were there, because at least some good might come from what had happened. The workers already understood Pemberton was as physically strong as any of them, had learned that last spring when they'd put down the train tracks. Now they knew he could kill a man, had seen it with their own eyes. They'd respect him, and Serena, even more. He turned and met Serena's gray eyes.

"Let's go to the camp," Pemberton said.

He placed his hand on Serena's elbow, turning her toward the steps Campbell had just ascended. Campbell's long angular face was typically enigmatic, and he altered his path so as not to walk directly by the Pembertons—done so casually someone watching would assume it wasn't deliberate.

Pemberton and Serena stepped off the platform and followed the track to where Wilkie and Buchanan waited. Cinders crunched under their feet, made gray wisps like snuffed matches. Pemberton gave a backward glance and saw Campbell leaning over Harmon's daughter, his hand on her shoulder as he spoke to her. Sheriff McDowell, dressed in his Sunday finery, stood beside the bench as well. He and Campbell helped the girl to her feet and led her into the depot.

"Is my Packard here?" Pemberton asked Buchanan.

Buchanan nodded and Pemberton addressed the baggage boy, who was still on the platform.

"Get the grips and put them in the back seat, then tie the smaller trunk onto the rack. The train can bring the bigger one later."

"Don't you think you'd better speak to the sheriff?" Buchanan asked after he handed Pemberton the Packard's key.

"Why should I explain anything to that son-of-a-bitch," Pemberton said. "You saw what happened."

He and Serena were getting in the Packard when McDowell walked up briskly behind them. When he turned, Pemberton saw that despite the Sunday finery the sheriff wore his holster. Like that of so many of the highlanders, the sheriff's age was hard to estimate. Pemberton supposed near fifty, though the jet-black hair and taut body befitted a younger man.

"We're going to my office," McDowell said.

"Why?" Pemberton asked. "It was self-defense. A dozen men will verify that."

"I'm charging you with disorderly conduct. That's a ten-dollar fine or a week in jail."

Pemberton pulled out his billfold and handed McDowell two fives.

"We're still going to my office," McDowell said. "You're not leaving Waynesville until you write out a statement attesting you acted in self-defense."

They stood less than a yard apart, neither man stepping back. Pemberton decided a fight wasn't worth it.

"Do you need a statement from me as well?" Serena said.

McDowell looked at Serena as if he hadn't noticed her until now.

"No."

"I would offer you my hand, Sheriff," Serena said, "but from what my husband has told me you probably wouldn't take it."

"He's right," McDowell replied.

"I'll wait for you in the car," Serena told Pemberton.

When Pemberton returned, he got in the Packard and turned the key. He pressed the starter button and released the hand brake, and they began the six-mile drive to the camp. Outside Waynesville, Pemberton slowed as they approached the saw mill's five-acre splash pond, its surface hidden by logs bunched and intertwined like kindling. Pemberton braked and slipped the Packard out of gear but kept the engine running.

"Wilkie wanted the saw mill close to town," Pemberton said. "It wouldn't have been my choice, but it's worked out well enough."

They looked past the splash pond's stalled flotilla of logs awaiting dawn when they'd be untangled and poled onto the log buggy and sawn. Serena gave the mill a cursory look as well as the small A-frame building Wilkie and Buchanan used as an office. Pemberton pointed to an immense tree rising out of the woods behind the saw mill. An orange growth furred the bark, and the upper branches were withered, unleafed.

"Chestnut-blight."

"Good it takes them years to die completely," Serena said. "That gives us all the time we need, but also a reason to prefer mahogany."

Pemberton let his hand settle on the hard rubber ball topping the gear shift. He put the car into gear and they drove on.

"I'm surprised the roads are paved," Serena said.

"Not many are. This one is, at least for a few miles. The road to Asheville as well. The train would get us to camp quicker, even at fifteen miles an hour, but I can show you our holdings this way."

They were soon out of Waynesville, the land increasingly mountainous and less inhabited, the occasional slant of pasture like green felt woven to a rougher fabric. Almost full summer now, Pemberton realized, the dogwood's white blossoms withered on the ground, the hardwood's branches thickened green. They passed a cabin, in the side yard a woman drawing water from a well. She wore no shoes and the towheaded child beside her wore pants cinched tight by twine.

"These highlanders," Serena said as she looked out the window. "I've read they've been so isolated that their speech harks back to Elizabethan times."

"Buchanan believes so," Pemberton said. "He keeps a journal of such words and phrases."

The land began a steep ascent and soon there were no more farms. Pressure built in Pemberton's ears and he swallowed. He turned off the blacktop onto a dirt road that curved upward almost a mile before making a final sharp rise. Pemberton stopped the car and they got out. A granite outcrop leaned over the road's right side, water trickling down the rock face. To the left only a long falling away, that and a pale round moon impatient for the night.

Pemberton reached for Serena's hand and they walked to the drop-off's edge. Below, Cove Creek Valley pressed back the mountains, opening a square mile of level land. At the valley's center was the camp, surrounded by a wasteland of stumps and branches. To the left, Half Acre Ridge had been cut bare as well. On the right, the razed lower quarter of Noland Mountain. As it crossed the valley, the railroad track appeared sewn into the lowland like stitches.

"Twelve months' work," Pemberton said.

"We'd have done this much in nine months out west," Serena replied.

"We get four times the amount of rain here. Plus we had to lay down track into the valley."

"That would make a difference," Serena said. "How far do our holdings go?"

Pemberton pointed north. "The mountain beyond where we're logging now."

"And west."

"Balsam Mountain," Pemberton said, pointing it out as well. "Horse Pen Ridge to the south, and you can see where we quit cutting to the east."

"Thirty-four thousand acres."

"There were seven thousand more east of Waynesville that we've already logged."

"And to the west, Champion Paper owns that?"

297

"All the way to the Tennessee line," Pemberton said.

"That's the land they're after for the park?"

Pemberton nodded. "And if Champion sells, they'll be coming after our land next."

"But we'll not let them have it," Serena said.

"No, at least not until we're done with it. Harris, our local copper and kaolin magnate, was at the meeting I told you about, and he made clear he's against this national park scheme as much as we are. Not a bad thing to have the wealthiest man in the county on our side."

"Or as a future partner," Serena added.

"You'll like him," Pemberton said. "He's shrewd and he doesn't suffer fools."

Serena touched his shoulder above the wound.

"We need to go and dress your arm."

"A kiss first," Pemberton said, moving their joined hands to the small of Serena's back and pulling her closer.

Serena raised her lips to Pemberton's and pressed them firm against his. Her free hand clutched the back of his head to bring him nearer, a soft exaltation of her breath into his mouth as she unpursed her lips and kissed fiercer, her teeth and tongue touching his. Serena pressed her body fully into his. Incapable of coyness, as always, even the first time they'd met. Pemberton felt again what he'd never known with another woman—a sense of being unshackled into some limitless possibility, limitless though at the same time somehow contained within the two of them.

They got in the Packard and descended into the valley. The road became rockier, the gullies and washouts more pronounced. They drove through a creek clogged with silt, then more woods until the woods were gone and they were driving across the valley floor. There was no road now, just a wide sprawl of mud and dirt. They passed a stable and a shotgun frame building whose front room served as the payroll office, the back room a bar and dining area. To the right were the workers' dining hall and the commissary. They crossed over the railroad track, passing the line of flatcars waiting for morning. A caboose that served as the doctor's office sat next to the track, its rusting wheels sunk into the valley floor.

They passed a row of three dozen stringhouses set precariously on Bent Knob Ridge, their foundations propped by ragged locust poles. The stringhouses resembled cheap wooden boxcars, not just in size and appearance but also in the way cable connected each in the line to the other. On top of every one was an iron rung. Axes had gouged splintery holes through the wood to serve as windows.

"The workers' housing, I assume," Serena said.

"Yes, as soon as we're finished here we can put them on flat cars and haul them to our new site. The workers don't even have to move their belongings."

Serena nodded, her eyes on the stringhouses.

"Very efficient," Serena said, nodding as she spoke. "How much is the rent?"

"Eight dollars a month."

"And their pay."

"Two dollars a day right now, but Buchanan wants to raise it to two-ten."

"Why?"

"He claims we'll lose good men to other camps," Pemberton said as he pulled up to the front of their house. "I say these government land grabs mean a surplus of workers, especially if Champion sells out."

"What does Wilkie think?"

"Wilkie agrees with me," Pemberton said. "He says the one good thing about this stock market crash is cheaper labor."

"I agree with you and Wilkie," Serena said.

A youth named Joel Vaughn waited on the front steps, beside him a cardboard box, in it meat and bread and cheese, a bottle of red wine. As Pemberton and Serena got out of the Packard, Vaughn stood and doffed his wool golf cap, revealing a thatch of carrot-colored hair. A mind equally bright, Campbell had quickly realized, and trusted Vaughn with responsibilities usually given to much older workers, including, as evidenced by the scraped forearms and purple swelling on his freckled left cheekbone, tussles with a horse as spirited as it was valuable. Vaughn retrieved the grips from the car and followed Pemberton and his bride onto the porch. Pemberton unlocked the door and nodded for the young man to enter first.

"I'd carry you over the threshold," Pemberton said, "but for the arm."

Serena smiled. "Don't worry, Pemberton. I can manage."

Serena stepped inside and he followed. Serena examined the light switch a moment as if skeptical it would work. Then she turned it on.

In the front room were two Coxwell chairs set in front of the fireplace, off to the left a small kitchen with its Homestead stove and ice box. A poplar table with four cane-bottom chairs stood beside the front room's one window. Serena nodded and walked down the hall, glanced at the bathroom before entering the back room. She turned on the bedside lamp and sat down on the wrought iron bed, tested the mattress's firmness and seemed satisfied. Vaughn appeared at the doorway with the steamer trunk, which had belonged to Pemberton's father.

"Put it in the hall closet," Pemberton said.

Vaughn did as he was told and went out. He came back with the food and wine.

"Mr. Buchanan thought you might be needful of something to eat."

"Put it on the table," Pemberton said. "Then go get iodine and gauze from the caboose."

The youth paused, his eyes on Pemberton's blood-soaked sleeve.

"You wanting me to get Doctor Cheney?"

"No," Serena said. "I'll dress it for him."

After Vaughn left, Serena stepped closer to the bedroom window and peered out at the stringhouses.

"Do the workers have electricity?"

"Just in the dining hall."

"It's best that way," Serena said, stepping back into the room's center. "Not just money saved but for the men. They'll work harder if they live like Spartans."

Pemberton raised an open palm toward the room's bare rough-board walls.

"This is rather Spartan as well."

"Money freed to buy more timber tracts," Serena said. "If we'd wished our wealth spent otherwise we'd have stayed in Boston."

"True enough."

"Who lives next door?"

"Campbell. He's as valuable as any man in this camp. He can book keep, repair anything, and uses a Gunter's chain as well as any of the surveyors. I like having him close by."

"And the last house?"

"Doctor Cheney."

"The wag from Wild Hog Gap."

"The only doctor we could get to live out here. Even to get him we had to offer a house and an automobile."

Serena opened the room's chifforobe and looked inside, perused the closet as well.

"And what of my wedding present, Pemberton?"

"In the stable."

"I've never seen a white Arabian."

"It's an impressive horse," Pemberton said.

"I'll take him for a ride first thing tomorrow."

When Vaughn had delivered the iodine and gauze, Serena sat on the bed and unbuttoned Pemberton's shirt, removed the weapon wedged behind his belt. She took the knife from the sheath and examined the dried blood on the blade before placing it on the bedside table. Serena opened the bottle of iodine.

"How does it feel, fighting a man like that? With a knife I mean. Is it like fencing or . . . more intimate?"

Pemberton tried to think of how what he'd felt could be put in words.

"I don't know," he finally said, "except it feels utterly real and utterly unreal at the same time."

Serena gripped his arm harder but her voice softened.

"This will sting," she said, and slowly poured the auburn-colored liquid into the wound. "The cause of your notoriety in Boston, did that knife fight feel the same as the one today?"

"Actually, it was a beer stein in Boston," Pemberton replied. "More of an accident during a barroom brawl."

"The story I heard involved a knife," Serena said, "and made the victim's demise sound anything but accidental."

As Serena paused to dab iodine leaking from the wound, Pemberton wondered if he detected a slight disappointment in Serena's tone or only imagined it.

"But this one, hardly an accident," Serena noted. "*Myself will grip the sword—yea, though I die.*"

"I'm afraid I don't recognize the quote," Pemberton said. "I'm not the scholar you are."

"No matter. It's a maxim better learned the way you did, not from a book."

As Serena loosed gauze from its wooden spool, Pemberton smiled.

"Who knows?" he said lightly. "In a place this primitive I suspect knife-wielding is not the purview of one sex. You may do battle with some snuff-breathed harridan and learn the same way I have."

"I would do it," Serena said, her voice measured as she spoke, "if for no other reason than to share what you felt today. That's what I want, everything a part of you also a part of me."

Pemberton watched the cloth thicken as Serena wrapped it around his forearm, iodine soaking through the first layers, then blotted by the dressing. He remembered the Back Bay dinner party of a month ago when Mrs. Lowell, the hostess, came up to him. *There's a woman here who wishes to be introduced to you, Mr. Pemberton,* the matron had said. *I should caution you, though. She has frightened off every other bachelor in Boston.* Pemberton recalled how he'd assured the matron he was not a man easily frightened, that perhaps the woman in question might need to be cautioned about him as well. Mrs.

Lowell had noted the justness of Pemberton's comment, matching his smile as she took his forearm. *Let us go meet her then. Just remember you were warned, just as I've warned her.*

"There," Serena said when she'd finished. "Three days and it should be healed."

Serena picked up the knife and took it into the kitchen, cleaned the blade with water and a cloth. She dried the knife and returned to the back room.

"I'll take a whetstone to the blade tomorrow," Serena said, setting the knife on the bedside table. "It's a weapon worthy of a man like you, and built to last a lifetime."

"To extend a lifetime as well," Pemberton noted, "as it has so fortuitously shown."

Serena laid the knife on the bedside table.

"And perhaps it will again, so keep it close."

"I'll keep it in the office," Pemberton promised.

Serena sat down in a ladderback chair opposite the bed and pulled off her jodhpurs. She undressed, not looking at what she unfastened and let fall to the floor. All the while her eyes fixed upon Pemberton. She took off her underclothing and stood before him. The women he'd known before Serena had been shy with their bodies, waiting for a room to darken or sheets to be pulled up, but that wasn't Serena's way.

Except for her eyes and hair, she was not conventionally beautiful, her breast and hips small and legs long for her torso. Serena's narrow shoulders, thin nose and high cheekbones honed her body to a severe keenness. Her feet were small, and considering all other aspects of her features, oddly delicate, vulnerable looking. Their bodies were well matched, Serena's lithe form fitting his larger frame and more muscular build. Sometimes at night they cleaved so fiercely the bed buckled and leaped beneath them. Pemberton would hear their quick breaths and not know which were Serena's and which his. *A kind of annihilation,* that was what Serena called their coupling, and though Pemberton would never have thought to describe it that way, he knew her words had named the thing exactly.

Serena did not come to him immediately, and a sensual languor settled over Pemberton. He gazed at her body, into the eyes that had entranced him the first time he'd met her, irises the color of burnished pewter. Hard and dense like pewter too, the gold flecks not so much within the gray as floating motelike on the surface. Eyes that did not close when their flesh came together, pulling him inside her with her gaze as much as her body.

Serena opened the curtains so the moon spread its cold light across the bed. She turned from the window and looked around the room, as if for a few moments she'd forgotten where she was.

"This will do fine for us," she finally said, returning her gaze to Pemberton as she stepped toward the bed.

CHAPTER TWO

The following morning Pemberton introduced his bride to the camp's hundred workers. As he spoke, Serena stood beside him, dressed in black riding breeches and a blue denim shirt. Her jodhpurs were different from the ones the day before, European made, the leather scuffed and worn, toes rimmed with tarnished silver. Serena held the gelding's reins, the Arabian's whiteness so intense as to appear almost translucent in the day's first light. The saddle weighting the stallion's back was made of German leather with wool-flocked gusseted panels, its cost more than a logger earned in a year. Several men made soft-spoken observations about the stirrups, which weren't paired on the left side.

Wilkie and Buchanan stood on the porch, cups of coffee in their hands. Both were dressed in suits and ties, their one concession to the environment knee-high leather boots, pants cuffs tucked inside so as not to get muddied. It was clothing Pemberton, whose gray tiger cloth pants and plaid work shirts differed little from the workers' attire, found faintly ridiculous in such an environment, now even more so in light of Serena's attire.

"Mrs. Pemberton's father owned the Vulcan Lumber Company in Colorado," Pemberton said. "He taught her well. She's the equal of any man here, and you'll soon find the truth of it. Her orders are to be followed the same as you'd follow mine."

Among the gathered loggers was a thick-bearded cutting crew foreman named Bilded. He hocked audibly and spit a gob of yellow phlegm on the ground. At six-two and two hundred pounds, Hartley was one of the few men in camp big as Pemberton.

Serena opened the saddlebag and removed a Waterman pen and a leather-bound notepad. She spoke to the horse quietly, then handed the reins to Pemberton and walked over to Bilded and stood exactly where he'd spit. She pointed beside the office at a cane ash tree that had been left standing for its shade.

"I'll make a wager with you," Serena said to Bilded. "We both estimate total board feet of that cane ash. Then we'll write our estimates on a piece of paper and see who's closest."

Bilded stared at Serena a few moments, then at the tree as if already measuring its height and width. He looked not at Serena but at the cane ash when he spoke.

"How we going to know who's closest?"

"I'll have it cut down and taken to the saw mill," Pemberton said. "We'll know who won by this evening."

Doctor Cheney had now come on the porch to watch as well. He raked a match head across the railing to light his after-breakfast cigar, the sound audible enough that several workers turned to find its source. Pemberton looked also, and noted how morning accentuated the doctor's unhealthy pallor, making the corpulent face appear gray and malleable, like dirty bread dough. An effect the wattled neck and pouchy cheeks further emphasized.

"How much we wagering?" Bilded asked.

"Two weeks' pay."

The amount gave Bilded pause.

"There ain't no trick to it? I win I get two weeks' extra pay."

"Yes" Serena said, "and if you lose you work two weeks free."

She offered the pad and pen to Bilded, but he did not raise a hand to take it. A worker behind him snickered.

"Perhaps you want me to go first then?" Serena said.

"Yeah," Bilded answered after a few moments.

Serena turned toward the tree and studied it a full minute before she raised the pen in her left hand and wrote a number. She tore the page from the pad and folded it.

"Your turn," she said and handed the notepad and pen to Bilded.

Bilded walked up to the cane ash to better judge its girth, then came back and examined the tree a while longer before writing his own number.

Serena turned to Pemberton.

"Who's a man we and the workers both trust to hold our estimates?"

"Campbell," Pemberton said, nodding toward the overseer, who watched from the office doorway. "You all right with that, Bilded?"

"Yeah," Bilded said.

Serena rode out behind the cutting crews as they followed the train tracks toward the south face of Noland Mountain, passing through acres of stumps that, from a distance, resembled grave markers in a recently vacated battlefield. The loggers soon left the main train line that went over the right side of the mountain and followed the spur, their lunches in tote sacks and paper bags, metal milk pails and metal boxes shaped like bread loaves. Some of the men wore bib overalls, others flannel shirts and pants. Most wore Chippawah boots and a few wore shoes of canvas or leather. The signal boys went barefoot. The loggers passed the Shay train engine they called a sidewinder and the two coach cars that brought and returned workers who lived in Waynesville, then the six flat cars and the McGiffert loader and finally at the spur's end the hi-lead skidder already hissing and smoking, the boom's long steel cables spooling off the drums and stretching a half mile upward to where the tail block looped around a massive hickory stump. The boom angled toward the mountain, and the cables were so taut it looked as if the whole mountain was hooked and ready to be dragged down the tracks to Waynesville. Logs cut late on Saturday yet dangled from the cables, and men passed heedlessly under them as they might clouds packed with dynamite. All the while, the air grew thinner as the workers made their way up the steep incline toward tools hidden under leaves, hung on tree branches like the harps of the old Hebrews. Not just axes but eight-foot cross-cut saws and steel wedges and blocks and pike poles, the nine-pound hammers called go-devils and the six-pound hammers called grab skips. Some of these implements had initials burned in their handles, and some were given names as might be allowed a horse or rifle. All but the newest had their handles worn smooth by flesh much in the manner of stones rubbed by water.

As the men made their way through the stumps and brush they called slash, their eyes considered where they stepped, for though snakes rarely stirred until the sun fell full on the slopes, the yellow jackets and hornets offered no such respite. Nor did the mountain itself, which could send a man tumbling, especially on a day such as this when recent rains made the ground slick and yielding to feet and grasping hands. Most of the loggers were still exhausted from last week's six eleven-hour shifts. Some were hung over and some were injured. As they made their way up the mountain, these men had already drunk four or five cups of coffee, and all carried with them cigarettes and chewing tobacco. Some used cocaine to keep going and stay alert, because once the cutting began a man had to watch for axe blades glancing off trees and saw teeth grabbing a knee and the tongs on the cable swinging free or the cables snapping. Most of all the sharded limbs called widow makers that waited minutes or hours or even days before falling earthward like javelins.

Pemberton stood on the porch as Serena followed the crews into the woods. Even at a distance he could see the sway of her hips and arched back. Though they'd coupled that morning as well as last night, Pemberton felt desire quicken his pulse, summon the image of the first time he'd watched her ride at the New England Hunt Club. That morning he'd sat on the clubhouse veranda and watched Serena and her horse leap the hedges and railings. He'd never been a man easily awed, but that was the only word for what he'd felt as Serena and the horse lifted and then hung aloft for what seemed seconds before falling on the barriers' far sides. He'd felt incredibly lucky they'd found one another, though Serena had already told him their meeting wasn't mere good fortune but inevitability.

That morning at the club two women had come out on the veranda and sat nearby, dressed, unlike Serena, in red swallowtail hunting blazers and black derbies, hot tea set before them to ward against the morning's chill. *I suppose she imagines riding without a coat and cap de rigeur,* the younger of the women had said, to which the other replied that it probably was in Colorado. *My brother's wife attended Miss Porter's with her,* the older woman said. *She just showed up one day, an orphan from the western hinterlands. Albeit a wealthy woman, better educated than you'd imagine, but even Sarah Porter had no luck teaching her any social graces. Rather too proud, my sister-in-law claims, even for that haughty bunch. A couple of the girls pitied her enough to invite her home with them for the holidays and she not only refused but in a very ungracious manner. She stayed there with those old school marms instead.* The younger woman had blushed, but her companion had turned to Pemberton with a smile. *Well,* she'd said frostily, *she at least deems you worthy of her company.*

Except for Mrs. Lowell's brief comment about previous suitors, that morning had been the only time he'd heard Serena's past spoken of by anyone besides Serena. She'd volunteered little herself. When Pemberton asked about her time in Colorado or New England, Serena's answers were almost always cursory, telling him that she and Pemberton needed the past no more than it needed them.

Yet Serena's bad dreams continued. She never spoke of them, even when Pemberton asked, even in those moments he pulled her thrashing body out of them as if pulling her from a treacherous surf. Something to do with what had happened to her family back in Colorado, he was sure of that. Sure also that others who knew her would have been astonished at how childlike Serena appeared in those moments, the way she clung so fiercely to him until she whimpered back into sleep.

The kitchen door slammed as a worker came out and hurled a washtub of gray dishwater into a ditch reeking of grease and food scraps. The last logger had disappeared into the woods. Soon Pemberton heard the axes as the lead choppers began notching trees, a sound like rifle shots ricocheting across the valley as workers sawed and chopped another few acres of wilderness out of Haywood County.

By this time the crew chosen to fell the cane ash had returned to camp with their tools. The three men squatted before the tree as they would a campfire, talking among themselves about how best to commence. Campbell joined them, answering the loggers' questions with words arranged to sound more like suggestions than orders. After a few minutes Campbell rose. He turned toward the porch, giving Pemberton a nod, allowing his gaze to linger long enough to confirm nothing more was required of him. Campbell's hazel eyes were almond-shaped, like a cat's. Pemberton had found their wideness appropriate for a man so aware of things on the periphery, aware and also cautious, reasons Campbell had lasted into his late thirties in an occupation where inattentiveness was rarely forgiven. Pemberton nodded and Campbell walked up the track to talk to the train's engineer. Pemberton watched him go, noting that even a man cautious as Campbell had a missing ring finger. If you could gather up all the severed body parts and sew them together, you'd gain an extra worker every month, Doctor Cheney had once joked.

The cutting crew quickly showed why Campbell picked them. The lead chopper took up his ax and with two expert strokes made an undercut a foot from the ground. The two sawyers got down on one knee and gripped the hickory handles with both hands and began, wedges of bark crackling and breaking against the steel teeth. The men gained their rhythm, and soon saw-dust mounded at their feet like time sieving through an hourglass. Pemberton knew the workers who used them called the cross-cut saws "misery whips" because of the effort demanded, but watching these men it appeared effort-less, as if they slid the blade between two smooth-sanded planks. When the saw began to pinch, the lead chopper used the go-devil to drive in a wedge. In fifteen minutes the tree lay on the ground.

Pemberton went inside and worked on invoices, occasionally looking out the window toward Noland Mountain. He and Serena hadn't been apart for more than an a few minutes since the marriage ceremony. Her absence made the paperwork more tedious, the room emptier. Pemberton remembered how she'd waked him that morning with a kiss on his eyelids, a hand settled lightly on his shoulder. Serena had been drowsy as well, and when she'd brought Pemberton ever so languidly into her arms, it was as if he'd left his own dream and together they'd entered a better, richer one.

Serena was gone all morning, getting familiar with the landscape, learning the names of workers and ridges and creeks.

The Franklin clock on the credenza chimed noon when Harris' Stude-baker pulled up beside the office. Pemberton set the invoices on the desk and walked out to meet him. Like Pemberton, Harris dressed little better than the workers, the only sign of his wealth a thick gold ring on his right hand, in the setting a sapphire sharp and bright blue as its owner's eyes. Seventy years old,

Pemberton knew, but the vigorous silver hair and shiny gold tooth fillings were congruent for a man anything but rusty.

"So where is she?" Harris asked as he stepped onto the office porch. "A woman as impressive as you claim shouldn't be hidden away."

Harris paused and smiled as he turned his head slightly, his right eye focused on Pemberton as if to better sight a target.

"Though on second thought, maybe you should hide her away. If she is all you say."

"You'll see," Pemberton said. "She's over on Noland. We can get horses and ride up there."

"I don't have time for that," Harris answered. "Much as I'd enjoy meeting your bride, this park nonsense takes precedent. Our esteemed Secretary of the Interior got Rockefeller to donate five million. Now Albright is sure he can buy out Champion."

"Do you think they'll sell?"

"I don't know," Harris said, "but just the fact Champion's listening to offers encourages not only Secretary Albright but the rest of them, here and in Washington. They're already starting to run farmers off their land in Tennessee."

"This needs to be settled once and for all," Pemberton said.

"Goddamn right it needs to be settled. I'm tired as you are of lining the pockets of those Raleigh pettifoggers."

Harris pulled a watch from his pocket and checked the time.

"Later than I thought," he said.

"Have you had a chance to look at the Glencoe Ridge tract?" Pemberton asked.

"Come by the office Saturday morning and we'll go see it together. Bring your bride along too," Harris said, and paused to nod approvingly at the valley's stumps and slash. "You've done well here, even with those two fops you have for partners."

Pemberton did not go back into the office after Harris left but instead rode out to Nolan Mountain. He found Serena eating lunch with two foremen. Between bites of sandwiches, they discussed whether buying a second hi-lead skidder would be worth the extra cost. Pemberton got off his horse and joined them.

"The cane ash is at the saw mill," Pemberton said as he sat down beside her, "so Campbell will definitely have the board feet by five-thirty."

"Any of the other men make side bets with you?"

"No."

"Would either of you care to wager?" Serena said to the foremen.

"No ma'am," the older worker replied. "I don't have a hankering to bet against you on anything concerning lumber. I might have before this morning, but not now, especially after you showed us that trick with the choker."

The younger worker merely shook his head.

The two men finished eating and gathered their crews. Soon the sounds of axes and cross-cut saws filled the nearby woods. The Arabian snorted and Serena walked over and placed her hand on the horse's mane. She spoke to the horse and the gelding calmed.

"Harris came by," Pemberton said. "He wants the three of us to go look at the Glencoe Ridge tract Saturday."

"Will he be looking for anything other than kaolin and copper?"

"I doubt it," Pemberton said, "though some gold has been panned from creeks in the county. There are ruby and sapphire mines near Franklin, but that's forty miles from here."

"I hope he finds something," Serena said, stepping closer to take Pemberton's hand. "It will be another beginning for us, our first real partnership."

Pemberton smiled. "Plus Harris."

"For now," Serena said.

As Pemberton rode back to camp, he thought of an afternoon back in Boston when he and Serena were lying in bed, the sheets damp and tangled. The third, maybe the fourth day he'd been with her. Serena's head lain on his shoulder, her left hand on his chest, as she spoke.

"After Carolina, where to next?"

"I haven't thought that far ahead," Pemberton had replied.

"I?" she'd said. "Why not 'we'?"

"Well, since it's 'we,'" Pemberton had replied playfully, "I'll defer to you."

Serena had lifted her head and met his eyes.

"Brazil. I've researched it. Virgin forests of mahogany and no law but nature's law."

"Very well," Pemberton had said. "Now the only decision 'we' have to worry about is where to have dinner. Since you decided everything else for us, am I allowed to choose?"

Serena had not answered his question. Instead, she'd pressed her hand more firmly against his chest, let her palm stay there as she measured the beat of his blood.

"I'd heard you had a strong heart, fearless," she'd said, "and so it is."

"So you research men as well as potential logging sights?" Pemberton had asked.

"Of course," Serena had said.

At six, every worker in camp gathered in front of the office. Though most cutting crews consisted of three men, a crew that lost a man often attached to another, an arrangement that wasn't always temporary. A man named Snipes acted as leader for such a crew since the other foreman, Stewart, was a diligent worker but an uninspiring helmsman. Stewart was relieved as anyone by this arrangement.

Among Snipes' crew was an illiterate lay preacher named McIntyre, who was much given to vigorous and lengthy pronouncements on the imminent apocalypse. McIntyre sought any opportunity to espouse his views, especially to Reverend Bolick, a Presbyterian cleric who held services at the camp on Wednesday nights and Sunday mornings. Reverend Bolick considered his fellow theologian not only obnoxious but demented and went out of his way to avoid him, as did most men at the camp. McIntyre had been absent all morning with a bout of the flux but had come to work at noon. When he saw Serena standing on the office porch in pants, he almost choked on the peppermint he sucked to ease his stomach.

"There she is," McIntyre sputtered, "the whore of Babylon in the very flesh."

Dunbar, the youngest member of the crew at nineteen, looked toward the porch incomprehensively. He turned to McIntyre, who was dressed in the black preacher's hat and frayed black dress coat he wore even on the hottest days as a sign of his true calling.

"Where?" Dunbar asked.

"Right on that porch, standing there brazen as Jezebel."

Stewart, who along with McIntyre's wife and sister-in-law made up the whole of the lay preacher's congregation, turned to his minister and spoke.

"Why are you of a mind to say such a thing as that, Preacher?"

"Them pants," McIntyre proclaimed. "It's in the Revelations. Says the whore of Babylon will come forth in the last days wearing pants."

Ross, a dour man not kindly disposed to McIntyre's rants, stared at the lay preacher as he might a chimpanzee that had wandered into camp and begun chattering.

"I've read Revelation many a time, McIntyre," Ross said, "and I've somehow missed that verse."

"It ain't in the King James," McIntyre said. "It's in the original Greek."

"Read Greek, do you?" Ross said. "That's ever amazing for a man who can't even read English."

"Well, no," McIntyre said slowly. "I don't read Greek, but I've heard from them what does."

"Them what does," Ross said, and shook his head.

Snipes removed a briar pipe from his mouth to speak. His overalls were so worn and patched the original denim seemed an afterthought, but there'd been no attempt to blend new colors with old. Instead, the crew foreman's overalls were mended with a conflagration of yellow, green, red, and orange cloth. Snipes considered himself a learned man and argued that, since colors bright and various were known in nature to warn other creatures of danger, such patches would deter not only varmints both large and small but might in the same manner also deter falling limbs and lightning strikes. Snipes held the pipe out before him, contemplated it a moment, then raised his head and spoke.

"They's differences in every language in the world," Snipes said sagely, and appeared ready to expound on this point when Ross raised an open palm.

"Here comes the tally," Ross said. "Get ready to have your pockets lightened, Dunbar."

Campbell stood on the ash tree's stump and took a pad from his coat pocket. The men grew silent. Campbell looked at neither the men nor the owners. His gaze remained on the pad as he spoke, as if to belie any favoritism even as he rendered the verdict.

"Mrs. Pemberton the winner by thirty board feet," Campbell said and he stepped down without further comment.

The men began to disperse, those who had bet and won, such as Ross, stepping more lightly than the losers. Soon only those on the porch remained.

"Cause for a celebratory drink of our best scotch," Buchanan announced.

He and Wilkie followed Doctor Cheney and the Pembertons into the office. They passed through the front room and entered a smaller room with a bar on one wall and a fourteen-foot dining table in the center, around it a dozen well-padded captain's chairs. The room had a creekstone fireplace and a single window. Buchanan stepped behind the bar and set a bottle of Glenlivet and soda water on the lacquered wood. He lifted five Steuben goblets from under the bar and filled a silver canister with chips from the ice box.

"I call this the Recovery Room," Doctor Cheney said to Serena. "You see it is well stocked with all manner of alcohol. I find it quite sufficient for my medicinal needs."

"Doctor Cheney has no need for a recovery room elsewhere, because the good doctor's patients rarely recover," Buchanan said from behind the bar. "I know these other rogues' preferences, but what is yours, Mrs. Pemberton?"

"The same."

Everyone sat except Buchanan. Serena studied the table, let the fingers of her left hand trail across its surface.

"A single piece of chestnut," Serena said appreciatively. "Was the tree cut nearby?"

"In this very valley," Buchanan said. "It measured one-hundred-and-twelve feet. We've yet to find a bigger one."

Serena raised her eyes from the table, looked around the room.

"I'm afraid this room is quite austere, Mrs. Pemberton," Wilkie said, "but comfortable, even cozy in its way, especially during winter. We hope you'll take your evening meals here, as the four of us have done before the pleasure of your arrival."

Still appraising the room, Serena nodded.

"Excellent," Doctor Cheney said. "A woman's beauty would do much to brighten these drab surroundings."

Buchanan spoke as he handed Serena her drink.

"Pemberton has told me of your parents' unfortunate demise in the 1918 flu epidemic, but do you have siblings?"

"I had a brother and two sisters. They died as well."

"In the epidemic?" Wilkie asked.

"Yes."

Wilkie's moustache quivered slightly, and his rheumy eyes saddened.

"How old were you, my dear?"

"Sixteen."

"I lost a sibling as well in that epidemic, my youngest sister," Wilkie said to Serena, "but to lose your whole family, and at such a young age. I just can't imagine."

"I too am sorry for you losses, but your good fortune is now our good fortune," Dr. Cheney quipped.

"It was more than good fortune," Serena said. "The doctor said so himself."

"What then did my fellow healer ascribe your survival to?"

Serena looked steadily at Cheney, her eyes as inexpressive as her tone.

"He said I simply refused to die."

Doctor Cheney slowly tilted his head, as if peering around a corner. The physician stared at Serena curiously, his thick eyebrows raised a few moments, then relaxed. Buchanan brought the other drinks to the table and sat down. Pemberton raised his drink, offered a smile as well to lighten the moment.

"A toast to another victory for management over labor," he said.

"I toast you as well, Mrs. Pemberton," Doctor Cheney said. "The nature of the fairer sex is to lack the male's analytical skills, but, at least in this instance, you have somehow compensated for that weakness."

Serena's features tightened, but the irritation vanished as quickly at it had appeared, swept clear from her face like a lock of unruly hair.

"My husband tells me that you are from these very mountains, a place called Wild Hog Gap," Serena said to Cheney. "Obviously, your views on my sex were formed by the slatterns you grew up with, but I assure you the natures of women are more various than your limited experience allows."

As if tugged upward by fishhooks, the sides of Doctor Cheney's mouth creased into a mirthless smile.

"By God you married a saucy one," Wilkie chortled, raising his tumbler to Pemberton. "The camp is going to be lively now."

Buchanan retrieved the bottle of scotch and placed it on the table.

"Have you ever been to these parts before, Mrs. Pemberton?" he asked.

"No, I haven't."

"As you've seen, we are somewhat isolated here."

"Somewhat?" Wilkie exclaimed. "At times I feel I've been banished to the moon."

"Asheville is only fifty miles away," Buchanan said. "It has its village charms."

"Indeed," Doctor Cheney interjected, "including several T. B. sanatoriums."

"Yet you've no doubt heard of George Vanderbilt's estate," Buchanan continued, "which is there as well."

Biltmore is indeed impressive," Wilkie conceded, "an actual French castle, Mrs. Pemberton. Olmstead himself came down from Brookline to design the grounds. Vanderbilt's daughter Cornelia lives there now, with a Brit named Cecil. I've been their guest on occasion. Very gracious people."

Wilkie paused to empty his tumbler and set it on the table. His cheeks were rosy from the alcohol, but Pemberton knew it was Serena's presence that made him even more loquacious than usual.

"I heard a phrase today worthy of your journal, Buchanan," Wilkie continued. "Two workers at the splash pond were discussing a fight and spoke of how one combatant 'feathered into' the other. It apparently means to inflict great damage."

Buchanan retrieved a fountain pen and black leather notebook from his coat's inner pocket. Buchanan placed the pen on the notebook's rag paper and wrote *feathered into,* behind it a question mark. He blew on the ink and closed the notebook.

"I doubt that it goes back to the British Isles," Buchanan said. "Perhaps instead a colloquialism to do with cock-fighting."

"Kephart would no doubt know," Wilkie said. "Have you heard of him, Mrs. Pemberton, our local Thoreau? Buchanan here is quite an admirer of his work, despite Kephart's being behind this national park nonsense."

"I've seen his books in the window at Grolier's," Serena said. "As you may imagine, they were quite taken with a Harvard man turned Natty Bumppo."

"As well as a former librarian in Saint Louis," Wilkie noted.

"A librarian and an author," Serena said, "yet he'd stop us from harvesting the very thing books are made of."

Pemberton drained his second dram of scotch and felt the alcohol's smooth slide down his throat, its warm glow deepening his contentment. He felt like an overwhelming wonder that this woman, whom he'd not even known existed when he'd left this valley three months earlier, was now his wife. Pemberton settled his right hand on Serena's knee, unsurprised when her left hand settled on his knee as well. She leaned toward him and for a few seconds let her head nestle in the space between his neck and shoulder. Pemberton tried to imagine how this moment could be better. He could think of nothing, other than that he and Serena were alone.

At seven o'clock, two kitchen workers set the table with Spode bone china and silver cutlery and linen napkins. They left and returned pushing a cart laden with wicker baskets of buttered biscuits and a silver platter draped with beef, large bowls of Steuben crystal brimming with potatoes and carrots and squash, various jams and relishes.

They were midway through their meal when Campbell, who'd been bent over the adding machine in the front room, appeared at the door.

"I need to know if you and Mrs. Pemberton are holding Bilded to the bet," Campbell said. "For the payroll."

"Is there a reason we shouldn't?" Pemberton asked.

"He has a wife and three children."

The words were delivered with no inflection, and Campbell's face was an absolute blank. Pemberton wondered, not for the first time, what it would be like to play poker with this man.

"All for the better," Serena said. "It will make a more effective lesson for the other workers."

"Will he still be a foreman?" Campbell asked.

"Yes, for the next two weeks," Serena said, looking not at Campbell but Pemberton.

"And then?"

"He'll be fired," Pemberton told the overseer. "Another lesson for the men."

Campbell nodded and stepped back into the office, closing the door behind him. The clacking, ratchet and pause of the adding machine resumed.

Buchanan appeared about to speak, but didn't.

"A problem, Buchanan?" Pemberton asked.

"No," Buchanan said after a few moments. "The wager did not involve me."

"Did you note how Campbell attempted to sway you, Pemberton," Doctor Cheney said, "yet without doing so outright. He's quite intelligent that way, don't you think?"

"Yes," Pemberton agreed. "Had his circumstances been such, he could have matriculated at Harvard. Perhaps, unlike me, he would have graduated."

"Yet without your experiences in the taverns of Boston," Wilkie said, "you would have fallen prey to Abe Harmon and his bowie knife."

"True enough," said Pemberton, "but my year of fencing at Harvard contributed to that education as well."

Serena raised her hand to Pemberton's face and let her index finger trace the thin white scar on his cheek.

"A *Fechtwunde* is more impressive than a piece of sheepskin," she said.

The kitchen workers came in with raspberries and cream. Beside Wilkie's bowl, one of the women placed a water glass and bottles containing bitters and iron tonics, a tin of sulphur lozenges. Potions for Wilkie's contrary stomach and tired blood. The workers poured cups of coffee and departed.

"Yet you are a woman of obvious learning, Mrs. Pemberton," Wilkie said. "Your husband says you are exceedingly well read in the arts and philosophy."

"My father brought tutors to the camp. They were all British, Oxford educated."

"Which explains the British inflection in your speech," Wilkie noted approvingly.

"And no doubt also explains a certain coldness in the tone,' Doctor Cheney added as he stirred cream in his coffee, "which only the unenlightened would view as a lack of feeling toward others, even your own family."

Wilkie's nose twitched in annoyance.

"Worse than unenlightened to think such a thing," Wilkie said, "cruel as well."

"Surely," Doctor Cheney said, his plump lips rounding contemplatively, "I speak only as one who hasn't had the advantages of British tutors."

"Your father sounds like a man of remarkable temperament," Wilkie said, returning his gaze to Serena. "I would enjoy hearing more about him."

"Why?" Serena said, as if puzzled. "He's dead now and of no use to any of us."

CHAPTER THREE

Dew darkened the hem of her gingham dress as Rachel Harmon walked out of the yard, the grass cool and slick against her bare feet and ankles. Jacob nestled in the crook of her left arm, in her right hand the tote sack. He'd grown so much in only six weeks. His features were transformed as well, the hair not just thicker but darker, the eyes that had been blue at birth now brown as chestnuts. She'd not known an infant's eyes could do such a thing and it unsettled her, a reminder of eyes last seen at the train depot. Rachel looked down the road to where Widow Jenkins' farmhouse stood, found the purl of smoke rising from the chimney that confirmed the old woman was up and about. The child squirmed inside the blanket she'd covered him in against the morning chill.

"You've got a full belly and fresh swaddlings," she whispered, "so you've no cause to be fussy."

Rachel tucked the blanket tighter. She ran her index finger across the ridge of his gums, Jacob's mouth closing around the finger to suckle. She wondered when his teeth would be coming in, something else to ask the Widow.

Rachel followed the road as it began its long curve toward the river. On the edges Queen Anne's lace still held beaded blossoms of dew. A big yellow and black writing spider hung in its web's center, and Rachel remembered how her father claimed seeing your initial sewn into the web meant you'd soon die. She did not look closely at the web, instead glanced at the sky to make sure no clouds gathered in the west over Clingman's Dome. She stepped onto the Widow's porch and knocked.

"It ain't bolted," the old woman said, and Rachel stepped inside. A greasy odor of fry pan lard filled the cabin, a scrim of smoke eddying around the room's borders. Widow Jenkins rose slowly from a caneback chair pulled close to the hearth.

"Let me hold that chap."

Rachel bent her knees and laid down the tote sack. She shifted the child in her arms and handed him over.

"He's acting fussy this morning," Rachel said. "I'm of a mind he might be starting to teeth."

"Child, a baby don't teeth till six months," Widow Jenkins scoffed. "It could be the colic or the rash or the ragweed. There's many a thing to make a young one like this to feel out of sorts, but it ain't his teeth."

The Widow raised Jacob with her arms and peered into the child's face. Gold-wire spectacles made her eyes bulge as if loosed from their sockets.

"I told your daddy he needed to marry again so you'd have a momma, but he wouldn't listen," Widow Jenkins said to Rachel. "If he had you'd know some things about babies, maybe enough to where you'd not have let the first man who gave you a wink and a smile lead you into a fool's paradise. You're still a child and don't know nothing of the world yet, girl."

Rachel stared at the puncheon floor and listened, the way it seemed she'd done for two months now. Folks at her daddy's funeral had told her much the same, as had the granny women who'd delivered Jacob and women in town who'd never given Rachel any notice before. Telling her for her own good, they all claimed, because they cared about her. Some of them like Widow Jenkins did care, but Rachel knew some just did it for spite. She'd watch their lips turn downward, trying to look sad and serious, but a mean kind of smile would be in their eyes.

Widow Jenkins sat back down in her chair and laid Jacob on her lap.

"A child ought to carry his daddy's name," she said, still speaking like Rachel was five instead of almost seventeen. "That way he'll have a last name and not have to go through his life explaining why he don't."

"He's got a last name," Rachel said, lifting her gaze from the floor to meet the older woman's eyes, "and Harmon is as a good a one as I know."

For a few moments there was no sound but the fire. A hiss and crackle, then the gray shell of a log collapsing in on itself, spilling a slush of spark and ash beneath the andirons. When Widow Jenkins spoke again, her voice was softer, kinder.

"You're right. Harmon is a good name, and an old woman ought not have to be reminded of that."

Rachel took the sugar teat and fresh swaddlings from the tote sack, the glass bottle of milk she'd drawn earlier. She laid them on the table.

"I'll be back soon as I can."

"You having to sell that horse and cow just to get by, and him that's the cause of it richer than a king," Widow Jenkins said sadly. "It's a hard place this world can be. No wonder a baby cries coming into it. Tears from the very start."

Rachel walked back up the road to the barn and took a step just inside. She paused and let her gaze scan the loft and rafters, remembering, as she always did, the bat that had so frightened her years ago. She heard the chickens in the far back clucking in their nesting boxes and reminded herself to gather the eggs soon as she returned. Her eyes adjusted to the barn's darkness, and objects slowly gained form and solidity—a rusting milk can, the sack of lice powder to dust the chickens with, a rotting wagon wheel. She looked up a final time and stepped all the way inside, lifted the saddle and its pad off the rack and walked to the middle stall. The draft horse was asleep, his weight shifted so the right hoof was at an angle. Rachel patted his rear haunches to let him know she was there, before placing the cabbage sack in the pack. She tethered the mattock to the saddle as well.

"We got us a trip to make, Dan," she told the horse.

Rachel didn't take the road past Widow Jenkins' house but instead followed Rudisell Creek down the mountain to where it entered the Pigeon River, the path narrowed by tall sprawling poke stalks that drooped under the weight of their purple berries, goldenrod bright as caught sunshine. Rachel knew in the deeper woods the ginseng leaves would soon begin to show their brightness as well. The prettiest time of year, she'd always believed, prettier than fall or even spring when the dogwood branches swayed and sparkled as if harboring clouds of white butterflies.

Dan moved with care down the trail, gentle and watchful with Rachel as he'd always been. Her father had bought the horse a year before Rachel was born. Even when he'd been at his drunkest or angriest, her father never mistreated the animal, never kicked or cursed it, never forgotten to give it food or water. Selling the horse was another lost link to her father.

She and Dan came to the dirt road and followed the river south toward Waynesville, the sun rising over her right shoulder. A few minutes later Rachel heard an automobile in the distance, her heart stammering when she glanced up and saw the vehicle coming toward her was green. It wasn't the Packard, and she felt ashamed that a part of herself, even now, could have wished it was Mr. Pemberton coming to Colt Ridge to somehow set things right. The same as when she'd gone to the camp's church service the last two Sundays, dawdling outside the dining hall with Jacob in her arms, hoping Mr. Pemberton would walk by.

The automobile sputtered past, leaving its wake of gray dust. Soon she passed a stone farmhouse, hearth smoke wisping from the chimney, in the fields plump heads of cabbage and corn taller than she was, closer to the road pumpkins and squash brightening a smother of weeds. All of which promised

the kind of harvest they might have had on Colt Ridge this fall if her father
had lived long enough to tend his crops. A wagon came from the other direction, two children dangling their legs off the back. They stared at Rachel
gravely, as if sensing all that had befallen her in the last months. The road
leveled and nudged close to the Pigeon River. In the morning's slanted light,
the river gleamed like a vein of flowing gold. Fool's gold, she thought.

Rachel remembered the previous August, how at noon-dinner time she'd
take a meal to Mr. Pemberton's house and Joel Vaughn, who'd grown up with
her on Colt Ridge, would be waiting on the porch. Joel's job was to make sure
no one interrupted her and Mr. Pemberton, and though Joel never said a
word there'd always be a troubled look on his face when he opened the front
door. Mr. Pemberton was always in the back room, and as Rachel walked
through the house she looked around at the electric lights and the ice box and
fancy table and cushioned chairs. Being in a place so wondrous, even for just
a half hour, made her feel the same way as when she pored over the Sears wish
book. Only better, because it wasn't a picture or description but the very
things themselves. But that wasn't what had brought her to Mr. Pemberton's
bed. He'd made notice of her, chosen Rachel over the other girls in the camp,
including her friends Bonny and Rebecca, who were young like her. Rachel
had believed she was in love, though since he'd been the first man she'd ever
kissed, much less lain down with, how could she know. Rachel thought how
maybe the Widow was right. If she'd had a mother who'd not left when Rachel
was five, maybe she would have known better.

But maybe not, Rachel told herself. After all, she'd ignored the warning
looks of not only Joel but also Mr. Campbell, who'd shook his head *No* at
Rachel when he saw her going to the house with the tray one noon. Rachel
had just smiled back at the hard stares the older women in the kitchen gave
her each time she returned. When one of the men who cooked said something smart to her like *Don't look like he had much of an appetite today, for food
at least,* she'd blush and lower her eyes, but even then a part of her felt proud
all the same. It was no different than when Bonny or Rebecca whispered *Your
hair's mussed up,* and the three of them giggled like they were back in grammar school and a boy had tried to kiss one of them.

One day Mr. Pemberton had fallen asleep before she left his bed. Rachel
had gotten up slowly so as not to wake him, then walked room by room
through the house, touching what she had passed—the bedroom's gold-
gilded oval mirror, a silver pitcher and basin in the bathroom, the Marvel
water heater in the hallway, the ice box and oak-front shelf clock. What had
struck her most was how such wonders appeared placed around the rooms

with so little thought. That was the amazing thing, Rachel had thought, how what seemed treasures to her could be hardly noticed by someone else. She'd sat in one of the Coxwell chairs and settled the plush velvet against her hips and back. It had been like sitting on a cloud.

When her flow stopped, she'd kept believing it was something else, not telling Mr. Pemberton or Bonny or Rebecca, even when one month became three months and then four. It'll come any day now, she'd told herself, even after the mornings she'd thrown up, and her dress began tightening at the waist. By the sixth month, Mr. Pemberton had gone back to Boston. Soon enough she didn't have to tell anyone because despite the loose apron her belly showed the truth of it, not only to everyone in the camp but also to her father.

Outside of Waynesville the dirt road merged with the old Asheville Toll Road. Rachel dismounted. She took the horse by the reins and led it into town. As she passed the courthouse, two women stood outside Scott's General Store. They stopped talking and watched Rachel, their eyes stern and disapproving. She tethered Dan in front of Donaldson's Feed and Seed and went in to tell the storekeeper she'd take his offer for the horse and cow.

"And you won't pick them up till this weekend, right?"

The storekeeper nodded but didn't open his cash register.

"I was hoping you could pay me now," Rachel said.

Mr. Donaldson took three ten-dollar bills from his cash register and handed them to her.

"Just make sure you don't lame that horse before I get up there."

Rachel took a snap purse from her dress pocket and placed the money in it. "You want to buy the saddle?"

"I've got no need for a saddle," the storekeeper said brusquely.

Rachel walked across the street to Mr. Scott's store. When he produced the bill, it was more than she expected, though what exactly Rachel expected she could not say. She placed the remaining two-dollar bills and two dimes in her snap purse and went next door to Merritt's Apothecary. When Rachel came out, she had only the dimes left.

Rachel untethered Dan and she and the horse walked on by Dodson's Café and then two smaller storefronts. She was passing the courthouse when someone called her name. Sheriff McDowell stepped out of his office door, not dressed in Sunday finery like three months ago but in his uniform, a silver badge pinned to his khaki shirt. As he walked toward her, Rachel remembered how he'd put his arm around her that day and helped her off the bench and into the depot, how later he'd driven her back up to Colt Ridge and though the day wasn't cold, he'd built a small fire in the hearth. They'd sat there together by the fire, not talking, until Widow Jenkins arrived to spend the night with her.

The sheriff tipped his hat when he caught up with her.

"I don't mean to hold you up," he said. "Just wanted to check and see how you and your child were doing."

Rachel met the sheriff's eyes, noting again their unusual hue. Honey-colored, but not glowy like that of bees fed on clover, but instead the dark amber of basswood honey. A warm comforting color. She looked for the least hint of judgment in the sheriff's gaze and saw none.

"We're doing okay," Rachel said, though there being only two dimes in her snap purse argued otherwise.

A Model-T rattled past, causing the horse to shy toward the sidewalk. The sheriff and Rachel stood together in the street a few moments more, neither speaking until McDowell touched the brim of his hat again.

"Well, like I said, I just wanted to see how you're doing. If I can help you, in any way, you let me know."

"Thank you," Rachel said, and paused for a moment. "That day Daddy was killed, I appreciate what you did, especially staying with me."

Sheriff McDowell nodded. "I was glad to do it."

The sheriff walked back toward his office as Rachel tugged Dan's reins and led him on past the courthouse.

At the end of the street Rachel came to a wooden frame building, in its narrow yard a dozen marble tombstones of varying sizes and hues. Inside she heard the *tap tap tap* of a hammer and chisel. Rachel tethered the horse to the closest hitching post and crossed the marble-stobbed yard. She paused at the open door above which was written *Ludlow Surratt—Stone Mason.*

An air presser and air hammer lay next to the entrance, in the room's center a workbench, on it mallets and chisels, a compass saw and a slate board chalked with words and numbers. Some of the stones lining the four walls had names and dates. Others were blank but for lambs and crosses and volutes. The air smelled chalky, the room's earthen floor whitened as if with a fine snow. Surratt sat in a low wooden chair, a stone leaning against the workbench before him. He wore a hat and an apron and as he worked he leaned close to the marble, the hammer and chisel inches from his face.

Rachel knocked and he turned, his clothes and hands and eyelashes whitened by the marble dust. He laid the hammer and chisel on the bench and without a word went to the back of the shop. He lifted the sixteen-by-fourteen inch marble tablet Rachel had commissioned the week after her father had died. Before she could say anything, he'd set it beside the doorway. Surratt stepped back and stood beside Rachel. They looked at the tablet, the name Abraham Harmon etched in the marble, above it the fylfot Rachel had chosen from the sketch pad.

"I think it came out all right," the stone mason said. "You satisfied?"

"Yes sir. It looks fine," Rachel said, then hesitated. "The rest of your money. I thought I'd have it, but I don't."

Surratt did not look especially surprised at this news, and Rachel supposed there were others who had come to him with similar stories.

"That saddle," Rachel said, nodding to the horse. "You could have it for what I owe."

"I knew your daddy. Some found him too bristly but I liked him," Surratt said. "We'll work something else out. You'll need that saddle."

"No sir, I won't. I just sold my horse to Mr. Donaldson. After this weekend I'll not need it."

"This weekend?"

"Yes sir," Rachel said. "That's when he's coming to pick up my horse and cow both."

The stonemason mulled this information over.

"I'll take the saddle then, and we'll call it square between us. Have Donaldson bring it back with him," Surratt said, pausing as another Model T sputtered past. "Who have you hired to haul the stone up there?"

Rachel lifted the burlap cabbage sack from the saddle pack.

"I figured to do it."

"That stone weighs more than it looks, near thirty pounds," Surratt said. "It'll bust right through a sack that thin. Besides, once you get up there you still have to plant it."

"I got a mattock with me," Rachel said. "If you can help me tie the stone to the saddle horn I can manage."

Surratt took a red handkerchief from his back pocket, winced and rubbed the cloth across his forehead. He stuffed the handkerchief back in his pocket as he eyes resettled on Rachel.

"How old are you?"

"Almost seventeen."

"Almost."

"Yes sir."

Rachel expected the stone mason to tell her what Widow Jenkins had said, how she was just a girl and knew nothing. He'd be right to tell her so, Rachel supposed. How could she argue otherwise when all morning she'd figured wrong on everything from a baby's teething time to what things cost.

Surratt leaned over the tombstone and blew a limn of white dust from one of the chiseled letters. He let his hand linger on the stone a moment, as if to verify its solidity a final time. He stood up and untied his leather apron.

"I ain't that busy," he said. "I'll put the stone in my truck and take it on up there right now. I'll plant it for you too."

"Thank you," Rachel said. "That's a considerable kindness."

She rode back through Waynesville and north on the old toll road, but quickly left it for a different trail than the one she'd come on. The land soon turned steeper, rockier, the mattock's steel head clanking against the stirrup. The horse breathed harder as the air thinned, its soft nostrils rising with each pull of air. They sloshed through a creek, the water low and clear. Leathery rhododendron leaves rubbed against Rachel's dress.

She traveled another half hour, moving up the highest ridge. The woods drew back briefly and revealed an abandoned homestead. The front door yawned open, on the porch a spill of pans and plates and moldering quilts that bespoke a hasty exodus. Above the farmhouses' front door a rusty horse-shoe upturned to catch what good luck might fall the occupant's way. Clearly not enough, Rachel thought, knowing before too long her place might look the same if she didn't make a good harvest of ginseng.

The mountains and woods quickly reclosed around her. The trees were all hardwoods now. Light seeped wanly through their foliage as through layers of gauze. No birds sang and no deer or rabbit bolted in front of her. The only things growing along the trail were mushrooms and toadstools, the only sound acorns crackling and popping beneath Dan's iron hooves. The woods smelled like it had just rained.

The trail rose a last time and ended at the road. On the other side stood a deserted white clapboard church. The wide front door had a padlock on it, and the white paint had grayed and begun peeling. So many people lived in the timber camp now that Reverend Bolick held his services in the camp's dining hall instead of the church. Mr. Surratt's truck was not parked by the cemetery gate, but Rachel saw the stone was set in the ground. She tied Dan to the gate and walked inside. She moved through the grave markers, some just creek rocks with no names or dates, others soapstone and granite, a few marble. What names there were were familiar—Jenkins and Candler and McDowell and Pressley, Harmon. She was almost to her father's grave when she heard howling down the ridge below the cemetery, a lonesome sound like a whippoorwill or a far-off train. A pack of wild dogs made their way across a clearing, the one who'd raised his throat to the sky now running to catch up with the others. Rachel remembered the mattock strapped to the saddle and thought about getting it in case the dogs veered up the ridge, but they soon disappeared into the woods. Then there was only silence.

She stood by the tombstone, dirt the stonemason had displaced darkening the grave. Her father had been a hard man to live with, awkward in his affection, never saying much. His temper like a kitchen match waiting to be struck, especially if he'd been drinking. One of Rachel's clearest memories of her mother was lying on her parents' bed on a hot day. She'd told her mother that the blue bedspread felt cool and smooth despite the summer heat, like it'd feel if you could sleep on top of a creek pool. *Because it's satin,* her mother said, and Rachel had thought even the word was cool and smooth, whispery like the sound of a creek. She remembered the day her father took the bedspread and threw it into the hearth. It was the morning after her mother left, and as her father stuffed the satin bedspread deeper into the flames, he'd told Rachel to never mention her mother again, if Rachel did he'd slap her mouth. Whether he would have or not, she had never risked finding out. Rachel heard an older woman at the funeral claim her father had been a different man before her mother left, less prone to anger and bitterness. Never bad to drink. Rachel couldn't remember that man.

Yet he'd raised a child by himself, a girl child, and Rachel figured he'd done it as well as any man could have alone. She'd never gone wanting for food and clothing. There were plenty of things he hadn't taught her, maybe couldn't teach her, but she'd learned about crops and plants and animals, how to mend a fence and chink a cabin. He'd had her do these things herself while he watched. Making sure she knew how, Rachel now realized, when he'd not be around to do it for her. What was that if not a kind of love.

She touched the tombstone and felt its sturdiness and solidity. It made her think of the cradle her father had built two weeks before he'd died. He'd brought it in and set it by her bed, not speaking a single word of acknowledging he'd made it for the child. But she could see the care in the making of it, how he'd chosen hickory, the hardest wood and most lasting wood there was. Made not just to last but to look pretty too, for he'd sanded the cradle and then varnished it with linseed oil.

Rachel removed her hand from the stone she knew would outlast her lifetime, and that meant it would outlast her grief. I've gotten him buried in godly ground and I've burned the clothes he died in, Rachel told herself. I've signed the death certificate and now his grave stone's up. I've done all I can do. As she told herself this, Rachel felt the grief inside grow so wide and deep it felt like some dark fathomless pool she'd never emerge from. Because there was nothing left to do now, nothing except endure it.

Think of something happy, she told herself, something he did for you. A small thing. For a few moments nothing came. Then something did, something that had happened about this time of year. After supper her father had gone to the barn while Rachel went to the garden. In the waning light she'd gathered ripe pole beans whose dark pods nestled up to the rows of sweet corn she'd planted as trellis. Her father called from the barn mouth, and she'd set the wash pan between two rows, thinking he needed her to carry the milk pail to the springhouse.

"Pretty, isn't it," he'd said as she entered the barn.

Her father pointed to a large silver-green moth. For a few minutes the chores were put off as the two of them just stood there. The barn's stripes of light grew dimmer, and the moth seemed to brighten, as if the slow open and close of its wings gathered up the evening's last light. Then the creature rose. As the moth fluttered out into the night, her father had lifted his large strong hand and settled it on Rachel's shoulder a moment, not turning to her as he did so. A moth at twilight, the touch of a hand. Something, Rachel thought.

As she rode back down the trail, she remembered the days after the funeral, how the house's silence was a palpable thing and she couldn't endure a day without visiting Widow Jenkins for something borrowed or returned. Then one morning she'd begun to feel her sorrow easing, like something jagged that had cut into her so long it had finally dulled its edges, worn itself down. That same day Rachel couldn't remember which side her father had parted his hair on, and she'd realized again what she'd learned at five when her mother left—that what made losing someone you loved bearable was not remembering but forgetting. Forgetting small things first, the smell of the soap her mother had bathed with, the color of the dress she'd worn to church, then after a while the sound of her mother's voice, the color of her hair. It amazed Rachel how much you could forget, and everything you forgot made that person less alive inside you until you could finally endure it. After more time passed you could let yourself remember, even want to remember. But even then what you felt those first days could return and remind you the grief was still there, like old barbed wire embedded in a tree's heartwood.

And now this brown-eyed child. Don't love it, Rachel told herself. Don't love anything that can be taken away.

From *The Cove* (2012)

CHAPTER ONE

At first Laurel thought it was a warbler or thrush, though unlike any she had heard before—its song more sustained, as if so pure no breath need carry it into the world. Laurel raised her hands from the creek and stood. She remembered the bird Miss Calicut had shown the class. A Carolina Parakeet, Miss Calicut had said, and unfolded a handkerchief to reveal the green body and red and yellow head. Most parakeets live in tropical places like Brazil, Miss Calicut explained, but not this one. She'd let the students pass the bird around the room, telling them to look closely and not forget what it looked like, because soon there'd be none left, not just in these mountains but probably in the whole world.

Sixteen years since then, but Laurel remembered the long tail and thick beak, how the green and red and yellow were so bright they seemed to glow. Most of all she remembered how light the bird felt inside the handkerchief's cool silk, as if even in death retaining the weightlessness of flight. Laurel couldn't remember if Miss Calicut described the parakeet's song, but what she heard now seemed a fitting match, pretty as the parakeets themselves.

As Laurel rinsed the last soap from her wash, the song merged with the water's rhythms and the soothing smell of rose pink and bee balm. She lifted Hank's army shirt from the pool and went to where the granite outcrop leaned out like a huge anvil. Emerging from the mountain's vast shadows was, as always, like stepping from behind a curtain. She winced from the sunlight, and her bare feet felt the strangeness of treading a surface not aslant. The granite was warm and dry except on the far side where the water flowed, but even there the creek slowed and thinned, as if it too savored the light and was reluctant to enter the cove's darkness.

Laurel laid Hank's shirt near the ledge and stretched out the longer right sleeve first, then the other. She looked around the bedraped granite, her wash like leavings from the stream's recent flooding. Laurel raised her chin and closed her eyes, not to hear the bird but to let the sun immerse her face in a warm waterless bath. The only place in the cove she could do this, because the outcrop wasn't dimmed by ridges and trees. Instead, the granite caught and held the sunlight. Laurel could be warm here even with her feet numbed by the creek water. Hank had built a clothesline in the side yard but she didn't use it, even in winter. Clothes dried quicker in the sunlight and they smelled and felt cleaner, unlike the cove's depths where clothes hung a whole day retained a mildewed dampness.

They'll dry just as quick if I ain't watching, Laurel told herself, and set down the wicker basket. She remembered how Becky Dobbins, a store owner's daughter, asked why the farmer killed such a pretty bird. Because they'll eat your apples and cherries, Riley Watkins had answered from the back row. Anyway, they're the stupidest things you ever seen, Riley added, and told how his daddy fired into a flock and the unharmed parakeets didn't fly away but kept circling until not one was left alive. Miss Calicut had shaken her head. It's not because they're stupid, Riley.

Laurel followed the creek's ascent, stepping around waterfalls and rocks and felled trees when she had to, otherwise keeping her feet in water and away from any prowling copperhead or satinback. The land steepened and the water blurred white. Oaks and tulip poplars dimmed the sun and the rhododendron squeezed the banks tighter. Laurel paused and listened, the bird's call rising over the water's rush. They never desert the flock, Miss Calicut had told them, and Laurel had never known it to be otherwise. On the rarer and rarer occasions the parakeets passed over the cove, they always flew close together. Sometimes they called to one another, a sharp cry of *we we we*. A cry but not a song, because birds didn't sing while flying. The one time a flock lit in her family's orchard, the parakeets had no chance to sing.

But this parakeet, if that's what it was, did sing, and it sang alone. Laurel sidled around another waterfall. The song became louder, clearer, coming not from the creek but near the ridge crest. As quietly as possible, Laurel left the water and made her way through trees twined with virgin's bower, then into a thicket of rhododendron. Close now, the song's source only a few yards away. On the thicket's other side, sunlight fell through a breech in the canopy. Laurel crouched and moved nearer, pulled aside a last thick-leaved rhododendron branch. A flash of silvery flame caused her to scuttle back into the thicket, brightness pulsing on the back of her eyelids.

The song did not pause. She blinked until the brightness went away and again moved closer, no longer crouching but on her knees. Through a gap in the leaves she saw a haversack, then shoes and pants. Laurel lifted her gaze, her eyelids squinched to shutter the brightness.

A man sat with his back against a tree, eyes closed as his fingers skipped across a silver flute. All the while his cheeks pursed and puffed, nostrils flaring for air. The man's blond hair was a greasy tangle, his whiskers not yet a full beard but enough of one to, like his hair, snare dirt and twigs. Laurel let her gaze take in a blue chambray shirt torn and frayed and missing buttons, the corduroy pants ragged as the shirt, and shoes whose true color was lost in a lathering of dried mud. Sunday shoes, not brogans or top overs. Except for the flute, whatever else the man possessed looked to be in the haversack. A circle of black ground and charred wood argued he'd been on the ridge at least a day.

The song ended and the man opened his eyes. He set the flute across his raised knees and tilted his head, as though awaiting a response to the song. Perhaps one he would not welcome, because he appeared suddenly tense. His eyes swept past Laurel and she saw that no crow's feet crinkled the eyes, the brow and cheeks were briar scratched but unlined. The eyes were the same blue as water in a deep river pool, the face long and thin, features more hewn than kneaded. Laurel tugged the muslin on her left shoulder closer to her neck. Then he closed his eyes again and pressed his lower lip to the metal, played something more clearly a human song.

Up this high, the rhododendron blossoms hadn't fully wilted. Their rich perfume and the vanilla smell of the virgin's bower made Laurel light-headed as minutes passed and one song blended into another. The sun leaned west and what light the gap in the trees allowed sifted away. The flute's sparkling silver muted to gray but the music retained its airy brightness.

It felt like she'd listened only a few minutes, but when Laurel got back to the outcrop Hank's shirt was almost dry. She gathered the socks and step-ins, her other muslin work dress, and Hank's overalls. A purple butterfly lit on the stream edge to sip water. A pretty hue, most anyone would say, the same way they'd speak of church glass or bull thistle as pretty. Just not pretty on white skin, though she hadn't known the difference until first grade. When she was eight, the taunts had gotten so bad that she'd scrubbed the birthmark with lye soap until the skin blistered and bled. With that memory came another, of Jubel Parton. Laurel placed the one-wristed army shirt in the basket last, its damp shadow lingering on the granite. Up on the ridge, the music stopped.

He could be coming down the creek, Laurel realized, maybe glimpsed her through the trees. For the first time, she felt a shiver of fear. As beautiful as the music had been, the man's scratched face and tattered clothes argues trouble, perhaps a tramp looking for a farmhouse to rob. Maybe do worse than just

steal, she thought. Laurel looked toward the ridge and listened for the crunch
of leaves. The only sound was the murmur of the stream. The music resumed,
coming from the same place on the ridge.

She pressed the wicker basket against her belly and made her way down
the trail. The air grew dank and dark and even darker as she passed through a
stand of hemlocks. Toadstools and witch hazel sprouted on the trail edge,
farther down, nightshade and then baneberry whose poisonous fruit looked
like a doll's eyes. Two days' rain had made the woods poxy with mushrooms.
The gray ones with the slimy feel of slugs were harmless, Laurel knew, but the
larger pale mushrooms could kill you, as could the brown-hooded kind that
clumped on rotting wood. Chestnut wood, because that was what filled the
understory, more and more with each passing season. As Laurel approached
her parents' graves, she thought of what she'd asked Slidell to do, what he said
he'd do, though adding that at his age such a vow was like snow promising to
outlast spring.

Laurel set the basket down and stood in front of the graves. One was fifteen years old, the other less than a year, but the names etched on the soapstone had been lichened to a similar gray-green smoothness. Laurel knew
those who avoided this cove would see some further portent in such vanishing. But the barbed wire and colt and calves were portents too, good portents,
though the best was Hank surviving the war when most people believed this
place marked him for sure death. But Hank hadn't died. Missing a hand, but
other men from outside the cove had fared much worse. Paul Clayton had
been in a Washington hospital for two months and Vince Ford and Wesley
Ellenburg had come home in flag-draped coffins. Soon Hank was going to get
married, another good thing.

It would be an adjustment deciding who cooked or who cleaned, who
swept the floors or drew the water. There'd be times when she and Carolyn
might get huffy with each other, but they'd figure it out. They'd become like
sisters after a while. Carolyn was a reader, Hank had said, everything from her
daddy's newspaper to books, so they'd have that in common. As Laurel left
the woods, she saw Hank and Slidell stretching barbed wire in the upper
pasture. Eighty-one, but Slidell tried to help Hank an hour or two each day.
With so many men conscripted, hired hands were scarce, those few around
unwilling to work in the cove. Only Slidell would, and he refused money,
only took an occasional favor in return. She watched as Hank set the wire in
the crowbar's claw and pulled against the brace, enough strength garnered in
that one arm and hand to stretch the strand tight as a fiddle string. Hank's
right bicep was twice as big as the left, the forearm thick and ropy with blue

veins that bulged with each pull. He was so much stronger than when he'd first returned from Europe. Strong enough that even one-armed, no one, including Jubel Parton, would want to cross him.

Laurel stopped at the springhouse and set a quart jar of sweet milk and a cake of butter atop the clothes. Past time to start supper, but once on the porch she lingered and watched the men work. The pasture fence was nearly a quarter done, the wire strung and the locust posts deep rooted and straight, more proof to Carolyn's father, who sometimes watched from the notch head, that even with one hand Hank could support a wife and children. Hank remained tight-lipped about his exact plans, the way he was about a lot of things, but last month Laurel had passed his room and seen him studying what their mother had called the wish book, a pencil in his hand. Later she'd taken the thick catalogue off of Hank's bureau and found the pages he'd cornered-folded. Penciled stars marked a Provider six-hole cast iron range, Golden Oak chiffonier, and Franklin sewing machine. She'd been about to close the wish book when she saw another fold. This page showed a three-quarter-carat diamond ring. Beside the words *must include ring size* Hank had written 6.

Laurel went inside. She took the dough tray off its peg and set it on the cook table. As she opened the meal gum and scooped out flour with the straight cup, Laurel debated whether to tell Hank and Slidell about the man with the flute, decided not to.

CHAPTER TWO

When Laurel awoke on Saturday, she busied herself with the morning chores, cleaning out the ash grate, fetching milk and butter from the springhouse, water from the well. Hank had laid wood and kindling in the firebox last night, so she stuffed a page from last year's wish book inside and raked a kitchen match across the black iron. The fire caught and Laurel clanged the door shut. The warm smell of coffee filled the room as she fried the eggs and slid them on the plates, took cornbread from the pie safe and placed it on the table by the blackberry jam and butter, milk for the coffee. Last month Hank had wondered aloud if they should buy a shoat to raise for breakfast meat. He'd shown no surprise when Laurel argued against it.

Even before the parakeets had come to the cove, the chore Laurel hated most growing up was feeding the hogs. There had been three in the pen, one a shoat but the others thick and hairy and tall as calves. Each time Laurel fed them, she'd approached with shaking hands, moving quietly so she could pour the slops before the hogs rushed the trough. But they always knew.

When she leaned the pail over the top board, the hogs squealed and grunted, clambered into the wooden trough and crashed their swollen bodies against the board slats. The gray wood bowed and the rusty nails creaked and each time Laurel believed the boards and nails would give and the hogs would tear her apart like a poppet doll.

Hank cursed and Laurel knew some button or snap frustrated him, that or a bootlace. Things he wouldn't let her help him with. He came out wearing the shirt she'd washed yesterday, the left sleeve cut off at the elbow so he'd not have to bother pinning it. She poured the coffee and they sat down to eat. There was a fairness in not telling about the man with the flute, Laurel thought, because Hank kept so much to himself, especially about Carolyn Weatherbee. He was all but betrothed, if not betrothed, but Laurel knew nothing about the wedding plans.

Her daddy's a superstitious old fool and I got to humor him since he's already tallied my gone hand against me. That was how Hank explained never asking Laurel along on Sunday mornings when he borrowed Slidell's horse and wagon and made the three-mile trip to the Weatherbees. That'll soon change, she reminded herself. What the old man believed wouldn't matter once Hank and Carolyn were married and living in the cove.

They didn't speak until only smears of jam remained on their plates.

"I'll go feed the colt and calves," Hank said as he pushed back his chair.

"Slidell helping you today?"

"Probably not. It sounded like he's got a full portion doing his own chores, especially since we're off to town come afternoon."

After Hank left, Laurel washed the cups and dishes and flatware, filled the gray berlin kettle with pole beans and set it on the stove to simmer. She went to the sink, sifted soda powder on her toothbrush and brushed her teeth before she tied her hair back with a crimped hairpin. Dew soaked her bare feet as she walked toward the cornfield. A crow cawed once and lifted from amid the tasseled stalks, passed over the two nailed boards and the tattered remnants of a shirt. She'd need to get another from the bottom drawer, maybe set a straw hat atop the seedsack face. Might at least keep them from roosting on it, Laurel figured.

The cliff loomed over her and though her eyes were cast downward she felt its presence. Even inside the cabin she could feel it, as though the cliff's shadow was so dense it soaked through the wood. Nothing but shadow land, her mother had told Laurel, and claimed there wasn't a gloamier place in the whole Blue Ridge. A cursed place as well, most people in the county believed, cursed long before Laurel's father bought the land. The Cherokee had stayed away from the cove, and the first white family to settle here had all died of smallpox. There were stories of hunters who'd come into the cove and never been seen again, a place where ghosts and fetches wandered. But Laurel's parents didn't know these things the spring her father crossed the state line separating Cocke County and Madison in search of cheap land, found a hundred acres for the price of twenty in Tennessee.

Laurel was eight when her father collapsed in the field. Doctor Carter had told him there was nothing to be done except not exert himself. Then Laurel's mother had died and after that hardly anyone except Slidell entered the cove. Even Preacher Goins, who'd bibled her mother's funeral, made sure he left before dark. He hadn't taken Laurel's hand or hugged her and Laurel knew the why of that too. At school her classmates echoed what their parents believed—that her father's heart gave out after rocking Laurel with the birthmark touching his chest, that her mother's poisoned limb had turned the color of Laurel's stained skin, that the cove itself had marked Laurel as its own. Superstitions are just coincidence or ignorance. That was what Miss Calicut always told the class when a student said an owl's hoot meant someone would die or killing black snakes could end a drought. But her saying so didn't do much good, especially when parents complained that Miss Calicut needed to stick to reading and ciphering—things a schoolmarm understood.

Laurel laid the hoe at a row end. Hank was in the high pasture, his back to her as he planted another fence post. I'll just go as far as the wash pool, she told herself. As she passed the barn, she saw a praying mantis long as a pencil clinging to a board. At the wood's edge, dark berries sagged the poke stalks and the joepye weed was level with her eyes. All sure signs summer would soon be over.

Laurel followed the path through dead chestnuts whose peeling bark revealed wood the color of bone. Cleared four hundred dollars on the deal and we'll be able to live off the chestnuts alone, her father bragged when he bought the land, but red dots sinister as those on black widows had already appeared on the tree trunks. Then as their first summer here passed, more and more dark patches scoured the once-green ridges. One more calamity, because blue mold had rotted the tobacco and the light-starved orchard had yielded only a sprinkling of shriveled fruit. Her father had sworn a blind man would be more fortunate, because he'd at least not have to watch it happen.

When Laurel got to the outcrop, she sat and listened to sounds usually no more noticeable than her own breath. But she heard them now, water swiveling around rocks, the wind stirring leaves, the farther-off pecking of a yellowhammer. All of these she heard first, because the music was quieter today, a mournful song played softly.

Coincidence and ignorance, Miss Calicut said, but there had been times in the last year, especially after her father died, that Laurel felt she herself might be a ghost. Did a ghost even know it was a ghost? Days would pass and Laurel wouldn't see a single living soul. She'd left the cove only on the Saturdays she went to town with Slidell or to the monthly victory jubilees. Both places people avoided her, crossing the street, moving to another barn corner. Wasn't that what a ghost was, a thing cut off from the living? Those nights in the cove Laurel had waked to sounds and silences never noticed when Hank or her father had been around—the emptiness of every other room, the creak of the well's rope and pulley, the cabin resettling some part of itself—the loneliest sorts of sounds and silences. There had been mornings she'd looked in the mirror and wondered if what she saw wasn't a reflection but instead a floating weightless thing. After a while she quit changing the month on the Black Draught calendar. If Slidell showed up in his brogans and overalls to help with chores Laurel couldn't do alone, it was Wednesday. If he wore a white linen shirt and corduroy pants, it was the weekend. Laurel remembered how once she'd lean close just to see her breath condense on the mirror's glass.

Once night at a victory jubilee Jubel Parton asked her to go outside, winking at his friends as he did so. Reeking of whiskey, he kissed her sloppily on the mouth. Doing it because he's drunk, Laurel had believed, but let him do it anyway, because if his hands and lips could touch her, she was yet flesh and blood. Jubel's daddy owned Parton's Outdoor Goods, so the next Saturday when she and Slidell were in Mars Hill, Laurel had walked down an aisle of steel traps and cane poles to the counter. Jubel told another clerk to take the register and led Laurel to the cellar where they lay on burlap feed bags that chafed her arms and legs. She'd have let him have her right then, but after a few minutes he stopped. Need us a rubber so there won't be no woods colt, Jubel had said, and told her he'd bring one to the next jubilee. Three weeks later Jubel was waiting outside. He'd taken a last swallow from a whiskey bottle and handed it to Ray Janson, who snickered as Jubel took Laurel's hand, grabbed a horse blanket from a wagon, and walked to the pasture's edge. There was enough light from the barn mouth to risk being seen and Laurel asked to go into the woods. Better here, Jubel had answered. After they'd finished, Jubel gave her a checkered handkerchief to wash the blood off her legs. It was only when she got up that Laurel saw the others. Jubel walked toward Ray Janson and held out his hand for the wagered gold coin.

As the flute began another song, Laurel thought of how in six months they'd have a horse big enough to haul the wagon. They could start selling milk and eggs, if not in Mars Hill then Marshall, and each year there'd be more livestock. She'd even seen the parakeets last week. A small flock, no more than a half dozen, but they had swooped low enough to show their red and yellow heads before crossing the ridge toward the Ledbetter farm. And this music, another pretty thing that had found its way into the cove. Laurel dipped her hand and felt the shock of cold as she palmed the water and drank. Go on up there or go on home, she told herself, you've got too many chores to dawdle. She stepped into the water and followed the flute's song up the ridge and into the rhododendron.

The stranger was exactly as he'd been yesterday, back against the tree and eyes closed as he balanced the flute. His not moving gave her a chill. Having to eat or drink or stretch your legs was a human thing. Laurel looked for mushrooms in a fairy ring or some other sign. Expecting the worst of him same as folks do to you, Laurel chided herself. Scabs and scratches proved that the stranger bled. Eating too, for nubbed corncobs lay in the campfire's ashes. Laurel eased herself onto the ground. The song was wistful as the ballads Slidell and the Clayton brothers played, except words weren't needed to feel the yearning. That made the music all the more sorrowful, because this song wasn't about one lost love or one dead child or parent. It was as if the music was about every loss that had ever been.

The man stopped midsong and peered intently down the ridge, then seemed to relax. He placed the flute in the leather case and sat a few minutes, thinking about something. She couldn't tell if what he pondered pleased or vexed him, but Laurel suddenly wished she could know. It would be, like the music, something secretly shared. The man stood and stretched, walked up to the ridge crest and gazed toward the Ledbetter farm. Laurel lifted a rhododendron branch to see his campsite better. A tree branch shaped like a club lay beside the leaf pallet. One end wasn't much thicker than a tobacco stick, but a burl knot on the other bulged big as a yarn ball. He could have seen a copperhead or heard a panther. It could be for nothing more than that, Laurel told herself, but crept farther back into the rhododendron.

The stranger came down the ridge and took an apple from the haversack. Green and hard, but he bit right into it, his mouth pruning with its sourness. Laurel's stomach grumbled because it was near noon-dinner time for her too, but if she moved he'd hear her. The man finished the apple and threw the core into the woods, picked up the flute. This time the notes were hesitant, more like birdsong. His eyes closed and the notes blended into each other and it wasn't the song of a warbler or peewee but a thrush, the kind with black spots and a reddish tail. Go, Laurel told herself, before he stops again.

As she walked into the yard, Hank checked the pocket watch he'd brought back from France.

"We need to soon get going or Slidell will leave without us," Hank said.

Laurel hurriedly fixed their food and left the dishes for later. She and Hank walked toward the notch, passing through more dead chestnuts. The blight that killed them was first found in New York City, Miss Calicut had told them, but there were people who swore that, in these mountains at least, it had started here in the cove. The land began to slant upward and the cliff's shadow deepened. As the trail thinned, Hank stepped ahead of her. The trail curled around the cliff face and the sky spread out wide and blue as if leveled by a rolling pin.

At the trail notch, an ash tree narrowed the passage. Glass bottles had been knotted to the limb with leather strips, hung so close so they could clink against each other, on the wood itself an *X* painted in red. Pieces of glass, some blue and some clear, cluttered the ground like spills of rock candy.

Put there as a warning. Hank cursed and kicked the glass shards off the path, raised wisps of salt as he did so. His shoulders pulled inward and his hand clenched. When he'd first come back from the war, Hank had torn bottles and cans off the branch, but they always reappeared. He paused and Laurel thought he might strip the tree again. Instead, Hank went on and Laurel followed.

"Hope we didn't hold you up," Hank said as they came into the yard.

"Naw," Slidell said.

He raised himself from the porch steps, picked up his shotgun, and began walking toward the barn. Slidell's face was chapped and deep furrowed, but he moved with the gait of a man decades younger. Shoulders unhunched, belly taut and hazel eyes clear. Even the white hair was spry, thick and bristly. Hank followed Slidell to the barn to help harness Ginny to the wagon. Laurel waited in the side yard by the bee box. A drowsy hum came from inside the white wood. One day soon Slidell would smoke the bees, take out the super, and pour the honey into quart mason jars. He'd bring Hank and Laurel more than he'd keep for himself. Laurel would hear him coming, the jars clanking inside a tote sack swung over his shoulder.

She joined the men on the buckboard and Slidell gathered the checkreins in his gnarly hands. They bumped down a wide path, passing the small grave-yard and the pasture, once a cornfield, where Slidell's father and brother had been killed by outliers during the Confederate War. *Folks will step on my land and not fret that a man and a fourteen-year-old boy was murdered here* with less conscience than killing two snakes, Slidell had once told her. This is a place folks ought to be scared of, not some gloamy cove.

Soon the path spread its weedy shoulders and became a dirt wayfare. The land slanted downward and trees thickened. Ginny was old and swaybacked, her gait slow and measured. Slidell gave the checkreins an occasional half-hearted shake, more out of habit than expectation in the horse's pace would quicken.

Hank nodded at the double-barreled shotgun in the wagon bed.

"That boar hog vexing you again?"

"No, but last week he was standing bold as Jehoshaphat at the end of this wayfare. He didn't look to be trifled with, especially with those tusks jutting off his face like hay hooks."

"But you haven't seen him near the notch?" Laurel asked.

"Not yet, but come near harvest time I figure him to make his way up to my cabbage patch like he done last year, unless that shotgun curbs his appetite once and for all."

"I hope you kill it," Laurel said.

"Help me be on the lookout and maybe I'll satisfy the both of us," Slidell said. He jostled the checkreins again and turned to Hank. "You buying more wire today?"

"That and staples," Hank answered. "I might price a pulley for the new well, in case I ever get the damn thing done."

"I wish I could help you," Slidell said, "but well digging is a young man's game, at least far deep as you are now. This war will end soon and there'll be more young men around. They'll have been out in the world and be less obliged to listen to tall tales and nonsense."

"Maybe," Hank said.

They came to the old Marshall toll pike and turned left. Wheel tracks from wagons and automobiles braided the dust and chert. The trees were not as close or numerous. They passed several cabins, then a two-story farmhouse whose tin roof shimmered. More homes appeared and fewer fields and pastures. Laurel could see the college now, first the clock tower and then the brick and wood buildings. The pike crested a last time and they descended, first passing the granite arch and brick drive that led up to the college, then coming into town.

As always, Laurel felt her stomach tense. Since it was Saturday, wagons and horses were tethered to every hitching post, a few automobiles nosed up to the boardwalks as well. The wagon made a halting progress amid farm families and town folk, a few college students. Laurel looked for Marcie Bettingfield's wagon, hoping to hear how she and her baby were doing. They passed Lusk's Barbershop and Feith Savings and Loan, across from them what had been a tailor's shop but now had UNITED STATES RECRUITING OFFICE painted on the window. Chauncey Feith stood outside the doorway in his uniform. Laurel glanced over to see if Hank noticed him, but his eyes were fixed straight ahead, as were hers when they passed Parton's Outdoor Goods.

Two women in bonnets came out of the post office. One nudged the other at the wagon's approach. They hurriedly crossed the street, heads turned so the bonnets concealed their faces. Slidell found an empty hitching post in front of the spinning red-and-white pole advertising Lusk's Barbershop.

"You all take your time," Slidell said as they got off the buckboard. "After I get my trading done, I'll be at the Turkey Trot. Just come get me when you're ready."

"What do you need to buy, sister?" Hank asked after Slidell left.

"Just knitting and sewing doings, and maybe look at some cloth."

"Dawdle awhile if you got a mind to," Hank said as they stepped onto the boardwalk. "After I get my wire and staples I'm going to talk to Neil Lingefelt about that pulley."

A farm woman in a flour-cloth dress came up the boardwalk. When she stepped into the street so as not to pass near them, Hank's face tightened.

"I need to go," he said.

"I'll help you carry stuff to the wagon," Laurel said, "before I go to the cloth shop."

"No," Hank said quickly. "Erwin's boy will help me."

She watched Hank walk up the boardwalk. He paused to shake hands with Marvin Alexander and was greeted with a nod and smile by a passing couple. In those two years they'd been in school together, it had been hard for both of them but worse for Laurel because of the birthmark. Yet she and Hank had never allowed any difference. At school, he'd fight boys older and bigger because of remarks just aimed at Laurel. Once something started, she'd done the same for him, clawing and biting anyone who took on Hank. Then Ellie Anthony, who sat near them, came down with polio. Her parents claimed Laurel and Hank the cause. Other parents vowed to keep their children out of school until Laurel and Hank were gone.

On trips to town after that, they'd been treated even worse. Besides the snubs and glares they'd grown used to, some people spat as she and Hank went by. A man threatened to horsewhip Slidell if he kept bringing them to town and one Saturday she and Hank had been hit by rotten eggs. Bad as it was, they'd at least endured it together, but since Hank's return from Europe, most of the meanness had been directed only at Laurel. More than a hand had been left behind in Europe, people seemed to believe.

Laurel walked across the street to the cloth shop. The bell above the door jingled as Laurel entered. Becky Dobbins's mother, Cordelia, raised her eyes and frowned before turning back to writing in a ledger. Laurel picked up a buying basket and put in three spools of sewing thread and a pack of fish-eye buttons. The muslin she wanted to price was next to the counter, but Laurel slowly made her way amid the various bolts of cloth, the reds and blues and yellows and colors missed and between, a whole school globe's worth of color. Laurel thought of the stranger's shabby clothes and paused before a thick bolt of denim. She wondered if he was playing the silver flute right now.

Laurel went over to the window where dress cloth hung from wood rods like bright flags. She lingered among the linen and serge, the tussah silk that was always cool to the touch. She raised cloth ends to better see the prettiness of the checks and stripes and solids.

"Appreciate it if you don't handle that cloth," Mrs. Dobbins said, "unless you're of a mind to buy it."

Laurel paid for the thread and buttons and went back outside, her eyes blinking as they adjusted to the light. Hank had loaded the last of the thorny wheels of barbed wire in the wagon and was in front of the barbershop talking to Ben Lusk. All the times Laurel had been in town, the barber had never acknowledged her with a word or even a nod. Ben laughed at something Hank said and playfully slapped him on the shoulder. She stepped onto the boardwalk and caught Hank's eye.

"What is it?" Hank asked, coming over to her.

"There's something I've been needing to tell you," Laurel said.

"Why the hell didn't you tell me this before?" Hank seethed when she'd finished.

Laurel didn't answer, just watched as Hank's face seemed to waver between anger and resignation. Slidell came up the boardwalk with a tote sack in his hand. He was about to set it in the wagon when he saw Hank's face.

"What's the matter?" Slidell asked, but Hank was already stepping off the boardwalk and headed toward Parton's Outdoor Goods.

Slidell looked at Laurel.

"What is it?"

"There's going to be a fight," Laurel said.

"I need to stop this," Slidell said, but it was too late.

Jubel came reeling out of the store's front door, Hank right behind. The men clinched and hit the boardwalk together and rolled over twice. Hank came up on top and drove a fist into Jubel's face. Blood spouted from Jubel's nose as Hank cocked his elbow to swing again, but bystanders were already untangling them, ensuring the men were well apart before helping each to his feet. Jubel wiped a forearm over his nose and upper lip, gauged the blood on his shirt.

"I reckon it's still worth a gold quarter eagle," he said.

Hank broke free and swung again, nicking Jubel's chin. Slidell and Tillman Estep pulled Hank away and Chauncey Feith stepped between the two combatants.

"We can't be tussling amongst ourselves when we have Huns to fight," Chauncey admonished.

"What would you know about fighting Huns, Feith?" Hank answered.

Chauncey Feith raised a hand and ever so slowly adjusted the bill of his army cap, but it did not hide his flushed face as the boardwalk filled with more gawkers. A woman Laurel did not know gave Jubel a damp handkerchief.

"You want me to send someone for Doctor Carter?" Feith asked.

"Hell, no," Jubel replied, nodding at his sleeve. "This ain't nothing."

"Okay then," Chauncey Feith said, and turned to the gawkers. "We've got this settled so let's all be about our business."

Jubel was escorted back into the store.

"Time for us to go," Slidell said.

She and Hank followed Slidell across the street to the wagon. As they passed back through town, a man in overalls muttered at Laurel and spat.

"Why didn't you tell me sooner?" Hank asked once they were passed the college.

"I was shameful of it," Laurel said.

"Yeah, I guess you would be," Hank said, no warmth in his voice. "You know about this, Slidell?"

"No."

Slidell lifted a rein to wipe a dribble of tobacco off his mouth, looking straight ahead as he spoke.

"But it's something you'll have to get past, the both of you."

"I'm tired of having to get past stuff," Hank answered. "I've been doing that all my life."

"But you ain't the only one who's had to," Slidell said.

"I ain't forgot what happened to you," Hank said.

"I wasn't talking about me," Slidell answered.

For a few moments the only sounds were the squeak of the springs and axle, the soft clap of iron horseshoes on dirt.

"I know that too," Hank said, not looking at Laurel or Slidell but straight ahead.

CHAPTER THREE

Every evening for a week the old man had walked down the path to the river. A tin bait bucket swayed in his hand and a stringer was tied loosely around his neck. The rest of his gear lay hidden in the high grass a few yards from the wooden rowboat. He would set the oars in the bow, then place the lantern and the hooks and ball of string on the boat's planking and push off. Once in the river, the old man checked lines he had hung from willow branches. Hand over fist, he pulled straight up as if drawing water from a well. Sometimes trout and carp thrashed to the surface, but more often what emerged were blunt-headed fish whose dark bodies tapered like comets. The fisherman sewed the stringer through a gill and pulled the loop tight before dropping his catch back in the river. He would rebait the hooks and paddle to the next line. This evening, as was his habit, the old man was back ashore by dusk. He trudged up the path, his body keeled rightward by the stringer's heft, fishtails thickening with dust.

Walter watched until the fisherman passed the guard tower, then turned from the fence and went inside the barracks, making his way past men playing cards and pinochle, others smoking or writing letters. He lay on his bunk and waited, remembering what the guards had said—that the easy part would be getting over the fence. Finding the way out of these wild mountains would be the challenge. But with the fisherman's boat, he would not be wandering dense forests but following a current that went exactly where he needed to go, and with no trail for dogs to follow.

It was after midnight when Walter stepped out of the barrack's door. In his right hand was a haversack that held the case and flute, a box of matches, the medallion and chain. Tucked in his pocket, the note and the money. Floodlights cast a thick white light over the stockade but no face peered from the guard tower. He waited in the barrack's shadow until the outside guard passed, then scurried to the mesh-wire fence and began to climb. At the top barbed wire snared his pants. He ripped the cloth free and jumped, hit the ground and dared not look back. As the stockade's lights shallowed behind him, the moon and stars revealed the boat. He shoved off and rowed as fast as he could toward the river's center.

Once in the main current, he pointed the bow downstream toward a place called Asheville. The biggest town in the region, the guards claimed. He would steal some clothes and then find the depot and buy his ticket. Two nights from now he could be back in New York.

Walter rowed rapidly until the stockade lights faded into darkness. Heavy armed and gasping, he eased his pace, allowed himself to savor the river's vastness after so long in confinement. The river made a leisurely curve, then became wider, shallower, rocks sprouting midriver. The dark water gurgled, slapped softly against the largest obstructions. Then the banks tucked themselves closer together and the river deepened. For a while there was no light except what leaked from the sky, then a square of yellow from a farmhouse window, farther on a fisherman's lantern tingeing the shallows. A dog barked. He passed other habitations whose occupants slept, houses unseen though he drifted only a few oar lengths from their doors.

Rested, he began to row harder. The river widened and then narrowed again. A black panel slid over the sky, locked into place a moment, then slid back, the moon and stars above once more. He turned and saw a bridge's silhouette, high and solid as a ship's hull. The river ran straight for a long while and no lanterns glowed from shore or window, the world absent but for water. He was near exhaustion but did not slacken his pace. The river shallowed, more scrapes and grabs against the planks. He struggled free from the obstructions, angled the bow into seams and squeezed through, bumping and swaying. When he finally came to deeper water, he let go of the oars and leaned forward, head on folded arms and knees. Just for a moment.

Willow branches brushed him awake, the boat's stern shoaled on the bank. The branches were damp with dew, the stars paling and the moon already gone. He rowed back into the current with quick slapping strokes. The river curved and he passed under another bridge, in the distance the flicker of lights. Silhouettes emerged on the shore—outlines of trees, bulky squares of buildings and houses. He passed a brick edifice with an electric light illuminating the words *Marshall Coal Company.* The water's purling music dimmed amid the crow of a rooster, the cough of an automobile engine. Dawnlight unshackled high branches from the dark.

Walter scanned the bank for a white bedsheet semaphoring a clothesline, saw one, and beached the boat. Mostly children's clothes dangled from the wooden pins, but he found a man's cotton shirt and pair of corduroy pants. Just as he finished changing, a dog began barking inside the house. Lights came on and a face appeared in the window. If Walter could have spoken, he would have offered to pay for the clothes, but because that was not possible, he scrambled down to the water, was adrift before a man wielding a shotgun appeared on the bank. Gray smoke blossomed from the gun barrel. Walter ducked and a hail of pellets landed in the boat's wake. The river curved and he lost sight of the man, for good he thought, but the river straightened. An iron railroad trestle appeared and the man with the shotgun was on it. Walter veered the boat toward the far bank as another downpour of lead hit close by.

He beached the boat and grabbed his haversack, but the bank was nothing but a slant of slick mud. By the time he'd climbed it, the man was thrashing through the undergrowth. A hefty piece of driftwood lay on the bank and Walter picked it up, hit the man flush in the chest when he emerged. The man staggered leftward and slid down the bank and into the river. There was a narrow river trail, but Walter picked up the haversack and plunged through a tangle of briars before making his way across a ridge.

All day he wandered without once hearing or seeing anything human. Rain fell that afternoon and fog rolled over the ground like cold smoke. The trees thickened and the woods became as forlorn as those in a sinister fairy tale, a place where guards claimed lions and bears and wolves roamed. All manner of poisonous serpents and plants thrived here and no step was safe. Immense watery caverns lay just beneath seemingly firm ground. They could give way and a man fall a hundred feet and then into water so utterly dark that the trout living in it were sightless. Walter wasted three matches trying to light the soggy wood, drank water from puddles but was afraid to eat what berries and mushrooms he saw. Night came and he shivered beneath a rock ledge.

The next afternoon Walter came to a brook and followed it. By then he had begun to feel feverish. A music he'd never heard before rose from the stream. The notes had colors as well as sounds, bright threads woven into the water's flow. Some of that bright water splashed up on the bank. It was green and shimmering and he scooped it up into his palm and it became a feather. Wind rustled the branches and he imagined an armada of zeppelins rubbing the treetops.

He heard a dog bark and thought it might be yet another hallucination, but he staggered up to a ridge crest to be sure. On one side was a farmhouse surrounded by fields and an orchard. On the other, no angled rise but a gray wall suspended over a cove like an iceberg, the cliff's looming presence muting the afternoon sunlight. In the cove's deepest section, directly under the cliff face, a purl of smoke drifted above the trees, but that was at least a furlong away. A dreary place, but a fire couldn't be smelled or seen. He stayed three days and three nights, each dawn stealing apples and corn from the farm, gaining his strength back and allowing his blistered feet to heal. On the fourth morning he decided to leave after breakfast, but as he searched for tinder he slipped on the slantland and tumbled. Black and yellow insects boiled out of the ground. Only when he reached the ridge crest was he free of the swarm.

He lay on his leaf pallet but the ground fell away and he was adrift. A ship came toward him, one he had seen before. The woman in the green dress stood at the railing, looking out expectantly. She was searching for him.

SELECTED NONFICTION

(2006–2013)

The Gift of Silence

When readers ask how I came to be a writer, I usually mention several influences: my parents' teaching by example the importance of reading; a grandfather who, though illiterate, was a wonderful storyteller; and, as I grew older, an awareness that my region had produced an inordinate number of excellent writers and that I might find a place in that tradition. Nevertheless, I believe what most made me a writer was my early difficulty with language.

My mother tells me that certain words were impossible for me to pronounce, especially those with j's and g's. Those hard consonants were like tripwires in my mouth, causing me to stumble over words such as "jungle" and "generous." My parents hoped I would grow out of this problem, but by the time I was five, I'd made no improvement. There was no speech therapist in the county, but one did drive in from the closest city once a week.

That once a week was a Saturday morning at the local high school. For an hour the therapist worked with me. I don't remember much of what we did in those sessions, except that several times she held my hands to her face as she pronounced a word. I do remember how large and empty the classroom seemed with just the two of us in it, and how small I felt sitting in a desk made for teenagers. I improved, enough so that by summer's end the therapist said I needed no further sessions. I still had trouble with certain words (one that bedevils me even today is "gesture"), but not enough that when I entered first grade my classmates and teacher appeared to notice. Nevertheless, certain habits of silence had taken hold. It was not just self-consciousness. Even before my sessions with the speech therapist, I had convinced myself that if I listened attentively enough to others my own tongue would be able to mimic their words. So I listened more than I spoke. I became comfortable with silence, and, not surprisingly, spent a lot of time alone wandering nearby woods and creeks. I entertained myself with stories I made up, transporting

347

myself into different places, different selves. I was in training to be a writer, though of course at that time I had yet to write more than my name.

Yet my most vivid memory of that summer is not the Saturday morning sessions at the high school but one night at my grandmother's farmhouse. After dinner, my parents, grandmother and several other older relatives gathered on the front porch. I sat on the steps as the night slowly enveloped us, listening intently as their tongues set free words I could not master. Then it appeared. A bright-green moth big as an adult's hand fluttered over my head and onto the porch, drawn by the light filtering through the screen door. The grown-ups quit talking as it brushed against the screen, circled overhead, and disappeared back into the night. It was a luna moth, I learned later, but in my mind that night it became indelibly connected to the way I viewed language—something magical that I grasped at but that was just out of reach.

In first grade, I began learning that loops and lines made from lead and ink could be as communicative as sound. Now, almost five decades later, language, spoken or written, is no longer out of reach, but it remains just as magical as that bright-green moth. What writer would wish it otherwise.

Lost Moments in Basketball History

David Thompson, Dynamite, and a Summer Night
in Carolina Where Only the Spring Didn't Boil

I knew he was good. As a 14-year-old sophomore, David dominated the cocky senior who starred for our archrival and who was supposed to be the conference's best player. In pickup games around our one-stoplight town of Boiling Springs, no one, usually no two, players could stop him. Only his older brother Vallie came close, his brotherly gift of goading forcing David into an occasional bad shot. I had seen him dunk the ball from a standing start—doing it despite being just 6-foot-3 and with hands so small he couldn't palm the ball. Yes, I knew he was good, already better than any of us would ever be, ever could be, but it wasn't until David played a late-night pickup game at our town's small college that I had my Road to Damascus or, I should say, Road to the Final Four moment.

A few years ago I mentioned to a colleague that both Earl Scruggs and David Thompson grew up in Boiling Springs. There must be something special in that spring water, he'd said, and quipped that the way Thompson jumped it must have included some rocket fuel. I told him it was more likely dynamite.

If you read local histories of Boiling Springs and then-Gardner-Webb College, you will find no mention of the ill-advised use of dynamite. Even today, seven decades later, older residents are reluctant to talk about what occurred. The exact details are sketchy, but the essence is that during the 1940s, the town fathers wanted to promote the "boiling spring" (there was actually only one) as a major tourist attraction, a Southern version of Yellowstone's Old Faithful. The only problem, a rather significant one, was that while Yellowstone's geyser boiled up 50 feet, the town's spring topped out at 24 inches—on a good day. Enter Boiling Springs High School's chemistry teacher. The novelist in me loves to imagine this scene: The town elders gather in a classroom as the eccentric teacher begins to clutter a chalkboard with formulas and symbols. His listeners are skeptical at first, but slowly they are won over by the periodic table's arcane vocabulary. After finishing at the board, the teacher corroborates the future spring's height and velocity with his slide rule. Then he lets the town fathers pass the slide rule around so they can see for themselves that what is being proposed is not a theory but a mathematical fact.

Whatever was said or shown that day, the plan passed. A time was set, the required materials gathered. Most of the town fathers were storeowners or landowners, so surely visions of crowded stores and land booms filled their heads when, days later, the chemistry teacher planted dynamite sticks in and around the spring. I'd like to think that shortly before pushing the detonator, the mayor made a speech about the necessity of progress. After the smoke cleared, the boiling spring, now not even a gurgle, lay flat and calm as water in a sauce pan. It has remained that way ever since.

The stilled spring was only 30 yards from the college gym where, in 1970, hubris was punished yet again. During the summers, Gardner-Webb, a perennial NAIA power, held two weeklong basketball camps. Kids from 8 to 18 came from around the Carolinas, getting instruction from college coaches and players and, occasionally, pros. This particular year it was Skeeter Swift, a guard for the ABA's New Orleans Bucs. Every evening after dinner, these players chose up for 5-on-5 games. Anyone from town could watch, and my brother and I often did. This night David showed up, too, wearing blue jeans, a white T-shirt, and canvas basketball shoes. Gardner-Webb's coach was already recruiting David, and he or someone on his staff wanted to see how this 16-year-old competed against seasoned college talent. There was no air-conditioning in the packed gym, only huge fans that whirred above like hovering helicopters. The July heat and humidity had even the spectators sweating, but David was on the court in long pants, outplaying the collegians attempting to guard him. Pouring sweat, he still made it look not so much easy as inevitable. It was simply whether David wanted to go above or around the other player to score. Perhaps it was also inevitable that Skeeter Swift switched over to guard David. It may or may not have been Skeeter's idea to do this, but regardless, David found himself facing a professional basketball player. Skeeter, as he notes in his autobiography, was a trash-talker on the court and always supremely confident.

If the idea was to teach a lesson in humility, one was given, but not to David. Skeeter talked to David, bumped him, grabbed him, did everything

350

but stop him. Just as with the college players, David had his way. How good? This good, was the answer. In fairness to Skeeter, he may have been torching David on the other end of the court. He was an amazing shooter, his free throw percentage among the best in the ABA's history. But my focus was on David nailing jump shots or gliding in for layups (no dunking allowed in 1970), making it look effortless, even glorious. By the end of the game, there was no doubt who the best player in the gym was. There would be many other times when David showed me how good. His sophomore year at NC State, he scored 37 points in a nationally televised game against a Maryland team led by Tom McMillen, John Lucas, and Len Elmore. The next year, NC State beat one of John Wooden's greatest UCLA teams in the Final Four. David had 28 points, though what I remember most about that game was his rocketing upward to block Bill Walton's shot. NC State went on to beat Al McGuire's Marquette team for the NCAA championship. Other times came in the NBA, especially the last game of the 1978 season, when he scored 73 points, including 32 in the second quarter, losing the NBA scoring title by a fraction of a point. In 1978, he re-signed with Denver for a five-year, $4 million deal, at that time the largest contract in basketball history.

Another later, less sanguine moment, however, came in 1983 when David played for his last team, the Seattle SuperSonics. Even on a 14-inch black-and-white TV, I could see something had gone wrong. His play was lethargic and he had clearly lost weight. Rumors about alcohol and cocaine were soon verified, addictions leading to a career-ending injury suffered not on the court but in a Studio 54 stairwell. By the late 1980s, David was out of the league and broke.

In the past few years he has made a comeback. The man Bill Walton describes as once being "Michael Jordan, Kobe Bryant, Tracy McGrady, and LeBron James rolled into one" now lives in Charlotte, just a few counties east of where he grew up. He's off drugs and alcohol, and is a popular motivational speaker along with doing events with the Denver Nuggets and the Charlotte Bobcats.

Although he's not often mentioned with players such as Oscar Robertson, Michael Jordan, Larry Bird, or Magic Johnson, David's impact on the game places him in their company. Michael Jordan himself notes that "the whole meaning of vertical leap began with David Thompson." The ultimate accolade may have come in 2009 when Michael Jordan, the game's greatest player, chose David to introduce him at his Basketball Hall of Fame induction. I haven't seen a lot of David since high school, but we occasionally cross paths, including at a book festival where he was signing and promoting his autobiography, *Skywalker*, and I a new novel. Although David was a better student than I, neither of us had won any academic awards, so it amused us that we'd ended up being the only authors in our graduating class. We also spoke of how driven we had both been as high school athletes, and how that sense of purpose had continued through the years and into different pursuits.

I have one more memory, my favorite, though it took place on cinders instead of hardwood. I was never good enough to play on a basketball team with David, but we did run track together, both members of a 4x4 relay team good enough to place in the state meet. This, too, was a humid evening, but two weeks before our high school graduation, and not in Boiling Springs but nearer to the state's center. David ran the third leg and I ran the fourth. Here's the way I will remember it: David is out of the last turn and coming toward me, the hollow metal baton in his right hand. As he nears, I start running and reach my hand behind me. The baton settles in my palm, and for a moment we both hold it — two small-town kids who cannot imagine what they will achieve and what they will lose, but headed into that future, for a moment, together.

Coal Miner's Son

In 1981, I saw Gary Stewart perform at a honky tonk outside Charlotte, North Carolina. Thirty or so people showed up, largely because on Tuesday nights beer was half-price. After some initial confusion on Stewart's part about his geographical location (he thought Houston), Stewart and his drummer and bass player picked up their instruments and played three one-hour sets. Stewart was a small man, five-eight, and so skinny that, as my uncle used to say, he'd have to jump up and down to make a shadow. Among his fans that night were two immense women wearing orange T-shirts with GARY STEWART written in black magic marker on the front. When the first set concluded, they jumped on the stage and for a moment Stewart completely disappeared inside their embrace.

I've seen the Rolling Stones and Bruce Springsteen and the E Street Band, and neither ensemble matched the energy Stewart and his two cohorts had that night. Stewart looked like an antic scarecrow as he strutted, gyrated, howled, and moaned on a stage not much bigger than the beat-up Cadillac he and his band arrived in. Stewart played a searing slide guitar on one of his greatest songs, "Flat Natural Born Good-timin' Man," but what I remember most about that night was Stewart's voice, a vibrato tenor fueled by two-hundred years of pent-up Appalachian soul. It's a voice hard to describe—something Hank Williams and Jimmie Rodgers in its yearning, Jerry Lee Lewis in its strut, but most akin to the high-decibel bluegrass wail I heard years ago in my mother's home church in the North Carolina mountains.

By midnight, when Stewart began his third set, he played for fewer than a dozen people. Which didn't seem to matter. He and his band concluded with a raucous "Your place or Mine," and soon after Stewart headed next door to a motel, the two orange-T-shirted women in tow. It was, after all, only 1 a.m., and the evening had hardly begun for a self-described honky-tonk tomcat.

Many of Stewart's songs, whether covers or originals, are about what you'd
expect from a honky-tonk performer: drinking, cheating, and the joy and
pain of both, as reflected in such titles as "She's Actin' Single (I'm Drinkin'
Doubles)," "I See the Want To in Your Eyes," and "Single Again." Yet these
songs are also morality plays about longing for the bliss of heaven while too
often falling towards hell. Like Flannery O'Connor's Misfit, Stewart's lyrics
and voice argue that at any moment you're either going whole hog toward
God or Satan. There is no middle ground, and seemingly few guarantees
either, for Stewart's more overtly religious songs are not joyous. "I've Just Seen
the Rock of Ages" is a gospel tune about an old woman claiming in her dying
moments that she's seen Jacob's ladder and crossed the River Jordan. She
leaves this world whispering that she is heaven-bound, but the music is omi-
nous, especially a tambourine that shivers like a death rattle. Stewart's vocal is
filled with dread, part cry and part moan, and is anything but reassuring.
Stewart's religion is a dark, brooding Calvinism formed by his Appalachian
childhood in Letcher County, Kentucky, where he was born in 1945.

Stewart was one of nine children, the son of a coal miner. In 1957, the
family moved to Florida after a mining accident disabled his father. Stewart
had been given his first guitar as a child, and by age fourteen, he spent weekends playing in honky tonks and soon thereafter dropped out of school. He
married Mary Lou Taylor shortly after his seventeenth birthday. Four years
his senior, Mary Lou would be Stewart's one stabilizing influence during the
next four decades.

Success first came as a songwriter. Teaming with a Fort Pierce cop named
Bill Ethridge, Stewart cowrote hits for Nat Stuckey, Hank Snow, and Del
Reeves. Then a Nashville producer named Roy Dea heard a Stewart demo
tape. Dea would later claim no one, not even Elvis or Hank Williams, had
impressed him more than Stewart. Dea was the perfect producer for Stewart.
He believed Stewart's talent to not only transcend the "Nashville Sound" but
also pretty much any sound ever put on vinyl.

It was three hit singles in the mid '70s, collected on Stewart's RCA album
Out of Hand, that gave Stewart his brief moment of fame. "She's Actin' Single
(I'm Drinkin' Doubles)," "Out of Hand," and "Drinkin' Thing," all hit Number One on the country charts, but his second album, *Steppin' Out*, which
opened with Stewart playing a scorching Duane Allman-influenced slide guitar, was a commercial disappointment, placing Stewart in no man's land
between rock and country similar to what Steve Earle would encounter two
decades later. Had he been born earlier, Stewart would have been a perfect fit
for Sam Phillips and Sun Records. But in the 1970s no one knew what to do

with him. RCA thought they knew, however, and tried to wedge him into a definable niche, switching producers and adding strings, before finally, and most disastrously, pairing him up with another singer, Dean Dillon. Not surprisingly, Stewart's albums are uneven, but all the solo efforts have at least two or three great songs. *Out of Hand* and *Your Place or Mine* have a good half dozen each.

Stewart self-destructed in the late '70s and early '80s. His intake of cocaine and alcohol was legendary even among his hard-living fellow musicians, and he became increasingly difficult to work with. RCA dropped him in 1983.

By the mid '80s, Stewart was back in Florida, living in a trailer whose windows had been painted black. He was plagued by financial problems, a chronic back injury caused by a car wreck, alcohol and drug addictions, the suicide of his son, and, though not diagnosed, what was surely clinical depression. In 1987 journalist Jimmy McDonough interviewed Stewart and claimed it was like being in a production of *Waiting for Godot.* Days passed as McDonough and Mary Lou waited for Stewart to emerge from the trailer's darkened back bedroom. McDonough later published a long article in the *Village Voice* about his visit with Stewart. It's an inspired piece of writing, capturing Stewart's complexity and extraordinary talent, but the article did little to gain Stewart a wider audience.

Through the '90s and into the new century, Stewart continued to perform at honky tonks such as Billy Bob's in Texas in Ft. Worth and appeared to be keeping his demons at bay. He put out several new albums, the best of these, *Brand New,* a HighTune release on which he reunited with Roy Dea. But Mary Lou, who had stood by him through it all, died suddenly in November 2003. A month later he took his own life.

Stewart's death was a harrowing act that had the same symbolic resonance as Vincent Van Gogh's attempt to kill himself by swallowing his own paint. Stewart was more successful with a gun aimed at his throat, making sure that the voice that propelled him to a brief rise and long fall was stilled forever.

Stewart continues to have a cult following, particularly among Southern Appalachians, Texans, and Native Americans. His albums and CDs are still available for anyone willing to make the effort to track them down, including *The Essential Gary Stewart,* a good introduction to his career. There are also dozens of recorded songs that have never been released. Whether these songs will ever be available is hard to know, but those who've heard them live or on demos claim they are some of Stewart's best work.

William Carlos Williams wrote that "the pure products of America go crazy." That's probably a little too easy in Stewart's case. Much of the pain and trouble in his life was as self-inflicted as the bullet that killed him, but he certainly had his battles trying to be true to his artistic vision. He won enough of them to leave behind some of the most original and best music of his era with songs such as "Harlan County Highway," "Dancing Eyes," "Roarin'," "Single Again," and "Drinkin' Thing."

Last fall I saw Big & Rich being interviewed by Joan Rivers before the Country Music Awards. Big & Rich were, like their music, as tame as two neutered housecats, which is exactly why Nashville and Joan Rivers are completely at ease with them. One of Gary Stewart's early songs was "You Can't Housebreak a Tomcat." Nashville tried to housebreak Stewart but never quite did.

In the Beginning

What makes a short story work? That is a question a younger writer asked me recently. I gave my usual answer, and the truest about any piece of art—it just does. The answer didn't satisfy the questioner so I went on to say that the stories that I admired most used poetry's attentiveness to each word to fulfill the novel's sense of a narrative fully told. Language works overtime to fill in spaces a novel can attend to in a more leisurely fashion. In such stories, a phrase or sentence can dazzle us immediately but often seemingly mundane sentences turn out to be, within the context of the story, just as brilliant. Everything word is in service of the story.

On the first page of Flannery O'Connor's "A Good Man Is Hard to Find," for instance, the mother is described as having a face "as broad and innocent as a cabbage." The comparison is unexpected yet apt in regard to a head's size and shape. But it also does much more by pulling the reader deeper into the story's southern setting, thus deeper into the story itself. What I find most impressive, however, is that everything we need to know about the mother is revealed in the simile. What could be more bland and forgettable than a head of cabbage, and amid this story's squabbling family of strong personalities, she is no more memorable than a cabbage, not just to the reader, but more importantly, to the rest of the family. Neither her mother-in-law, husband, nor two children consider that she might have an opinion on the family's ill-fated choices. She is, to her misfortune, only along for the ride.

My favorite living short story writers are Alice Munro and Edna O'Brien. Both are, like O'Connor, capable of dazzling language, including memorable similes (For instance, the narrator of O'Brien's story "Epitaph" speaks of "chestnuts shiny as admiral's boots,") but what I admire most about Munro and O'Brien's stories is how every word is in service of the story. Again and again, seemingly mundane comments or observations are later revealed to have huge import within the story. When I read Munro and O'Brien, a conceit or turn of phrase never feels forced into the story.

Nothing Gold Can Stay is my fifth collection of stories. Like my earlier collection, almost all of the stories are set in western North Carolina. Part of what I want to do in my work is preserve a disappearing idiom, one that has a richness and complexity rarely acknowledged outside the region. In the title story, I have a character remark that a man is "deader than a tarred stump." I've never heard that actual phrase but I have heard many like it in the region. Within the story, the metaphor evokes a rural setting and the speaker's background, as well as revealing something about the speaker's psychology. But the metaphor is most important to the story because it reveals the speaker's intelligence at a moment when his intelligence, his humanness, is most in doubt. Instead of relying on a cliché such as deader than a doornail, his mind is supple enough to find similarity, even in degree of deadness, between two seemingly unalike objects.

I've written four books of poetry and five novels, but I continue to find short stories the most challenging genre. I go back to O'Connor often and the appearance of a new collection by O'Brien or Munro is the literary highlight of my year. I read their stories and when I sit down to write my own, I hope that something of the pleasure their work gives me might be found by those who read my work.

UNCOLLECTED STORIES

(1998–2013)

Outlaws

When I was sixteen, my summer job was robbing trains. I'd mask my lower face with a black bandanna, then, six-shooter in hand, board the train with two older bandits and demand loot. Fourteen times a day I'd get shot by Sheriff Masterson, stagger off the metal steps, and fall into the drainage ditch beside the tracks. Afterwards, we'd wait thirty minutes for the next train, which was the same train, to come hooting up the tracks. Years later I would publish a short story about that summer, and one of my fellow bandits would read it. But that was later.

My aunt, who worked as a cashier at Frontier Village, had gotten me the job. Despite my being sixteen, she'd cajoled Mr. Watkins, who preferred college students, into hiring me. He can play Billy the Kid, she'd told him. Anyway, with a mask on who can tell how old he is? So it was that on a Saturday morning in June I changed into my all-black outlaw duds in the Stagecoach Saloon's basement. The Levi's and cowboy shirt hung loose on my hips and shoulders, and I had to gouge another notch in my gun belt. My hat sank so low my neck looked like a pale stalk on a black mushroom. I found a smaller one in the gift shop. The boots were my own.

My fellow outlaws, both from Charlotte, were Matt, a junior premed major at UNC Asheville, and Jason, who'd just graduated from there. His major was theater arts. After stashing our clothes in the lockers, we walked over to the depot where Donald, a paunchy, silver-haired man who claimed he'd been John Wayne's stunt double in *Rio Bravo,* went over the whats and whens a last time. He sent us on our way with advice gleaned from eight summers' experience. There will always be smart alecks onboard and any acknowledgment just egged them on, and be prepared for anything: kids jabbing at your eyes with gift shop spears, teenagers kicking your shins, adults setting you on fire with cigarettes. They even do that to me, Donald said, and I'm the guy wearing the white hat.

So nine to five, five days a week with Mondays and Tuesdays off, the three of us waited for the train whistle to signal it was time for our hold-up. We had no horses, so we ran out of the woods firing pistols at the sky until the locomotive and its three passenger cars halted. We entered separate compartments and Sheriff Masterson took us on one at a time. Clutching our gut-shot bellies, we'd stagger to the metal steps, roll into the ditch and lie there until the train crossed the trestle and curved back toward the depot.

Getting shot and dying was the easy part. By July, all of us had plenty of wounds besides scrapes and bruises from falling. We'd been burned, poked, tripped, and pierced by weaponry that ranged from knitting needles to slingshot marbles. After each failed robbery, we'd retreat to a hideout with its cache of extra blanks and pistols, three lawn chairs, toilet paper, and Styrofoam cooler filled with sandwiches and soft drinks. Stretched out above it all, a green camouflage tarp kept everything dry when it rained. Our contributions to the hideout were some paperbacks and Jason's transistor radio, which was always tuned to the college station.

One morning in mid-July Jason nodded toward the radio.

"You don't even know what they're saying, do you kid?" Jason asked as he rolled a joint.

"Everybody look what's going down," I said, after a few moments.

"But what's it *about*?" Jason asked.

"I don't know," I answered.

"It's about not wanting to get your ass shot off in Vietnam," Jason said.

Matt looked up from a copy of *Stranger in a Strange Land.*

"I didn't hear anything about Vietnam."

"When you graduate and your deferment's up you'll hear it," Jason said, "especially when they send you one of these."

He took a letter from his pocket and gave it to Matt.

"You gonna try to get out of going?" Matt asked as he handed it back.

"I have gotten out, for four years, but yeah, I plan on keeping an ocean between me and that war." Jason grimaced. "I never got picked for anything good in my life, varsity baseball, homecoming king, class president. Hell, I didn't even get picked for glee club, but I fucking get picked for this."

"So what will you do?" Matt asked.

"I'll convince them I'm nuts. Acting's what I'm trained for, man. I'll speak in tongues while I do handstands if I have to. Maybe shit my britches right before I go in. I've heard that works. They'll 4F me in a heartbeat."

"Don't bet on it," Matt said. "The army's on to that dirty diaper scam. A buddy of mine tried it. He walked in with shit gluing his pants to his bare ass. The army doc told him not to worry, that he'd probably shit himself even worse when the VC started shooting at him."

"I'll come up with something else then," Jason said. "Like I said, I'm an actor."

"Oh yeah," Matt said. "Sure you will."

"So you don't think I can pull it off?"

"Well, it's not like you've been giving Academy Award performances this summer," Matt said. "The kid here does a better death scene than you do."

"Maybe I'm saving up for a more challenging audience than those dipshits on the train," Jason said.

"You better be saving up for a bus ticket to Toronto."

Jason lit the joint and inhaled deeply, then offered it to me as he always did before passing it to Matt.

"Bob Dylan's right, kid," Jason said. "Don't trust anybody over thirty about anything, but especially Vietnam. There's nothing good about being over there."

"I heard they got great dope," Matt said as he passed back the joint.

"Yeah, it's called morphine," Jason answered. "Medics give it to you while they're trying to stitch you back together."

"Some cool animals, too," Matt deadpanned. "Cobras and pythons. Leeches, tigers, and bears, oh my."

"Fuck you," Jason said.

"Just trying a little levity," Matt said.

"We'll see how funny you think it is when you get your letter."

"If I get in med school they can't touch my ass."

"If," Jason said. "From what you said about your GPA that's a big if."

"I've got a year to pull it up," Matt said.

Jason turned to me.

"Growing up around here, you probably believe all that shit about the evil commies, right?"

"I don't know," I said.

"What about your parents?"

"My cousin's over there and Daddy says he ought not be, him or any other American."

"Might be some hope for you hicks after all," Jason said, and held out what was left of the joint to me. "Don't you want to try it just once?"

I shook my head and he threw the remnants down, ground them into the dirt with his boot toe. The train whistle blew.

"Time to get shot," Matt grinned. "In honor of that letter, the kid and I will let you lead us into battle."

"Keep joking about it, asshole," Jason said. "They may get you yet. But me, I'll figure a way out. You'll see."

Frontier Village didn't shut down until after Labor Day, but Matt and I went back to school the last Monday in August. After that Jason would work solo. All through August, Jason talked about ways of getting a deferment, but it wasn't until our last weekend together that he'd figured out what to do.

That Saturday I'd never seen him so animated. He paced manically in front of us, grinning.

"It's radical, boys," he said, "but one-hundred-percent foolproof."

"Enlighten us," Matt said.

"One of my buddies in Charlotte called last night. He ran into a guy we went to high school with, a real dumbass who sawed off his fingers in shop class. Not all of each finger, just the top joints. The thing is, it wasn't that big a deal. You hardly noticed after a while. I mean, it wasn't like girls wanted to throw up when they looked at his hand. Hell, I think it made him *more* popular with girls. They felt so sorry for him they voted the fucker homecoming king. He even played on the baseball team. Here's the kicker, though. He's so dumb he *volunteers* to go, but they don't let him because he won't be able to handle a rifle well enough. All I've got to do is slice off some finger joints and I'm 4F the rest of my life."

"Don't even talk this bullshit," Matt said, and nodded at me. "Look at the kid here, he's already about to faint."

"If you want something to faint about, kid," Jason said, "let me tell you about my cousin who got killed in Nam last winter, though killed is putting it nicely. He took a direct mortar hit. All the king's horses and all the king's men couldn't put him back together again, so they kept the casket closed at the viewing. Anyway, the next morning before the funeral, my uncle gets it into his head he has to see the body and my father goes to the funeral home to stop him. He takes me with him, maybe figures he'll need me to help wrestle my uncle out of there. When we get there the undertaker comes jabbering that he couldn't stop him, that my uncle has jimmied the coffin open. So we go in the back room where the coffin is and my uncle is holding something up, or I guess I should say part of something . . ."

"Don't tell anymore," Matt said. "The kid's got his own cousin over there."

"You don't want to hear it?" Jason asked me.

I shook my head.

"Still think I'm bullshitting about doing it?" Jason asked. "Or having cause to?"

"No, man," Matt said. "I've joked with you some. You know, it's a way of dealing with bad shit like this. You're right, they may come after my ass in a year, but fucking maiming yourself, that's not acting crazy, it is crazy. Even if you could actually do it, what if they found out it was on purpose? Hell, they might take you anyway, or put you in Leavenworth."

"You think I'm going to chop them off in front of those assholes?" Jason said. "It will look like an accident, but I may need you to help me, Mr. Pre-Med."

"Sure thing," Matt said. "I can see it on my application. Medical Experience: Chopped off fingers for draft dodger. Yeah, that'll get me into Bowman Gray."

"I'm just talking about afterward, so I won't bleed to death," Jason said. "The whole point of not serving is so I *won't* die."

"Stop talking this bullshit," Matt said.

"I'm going to do it tomorrow," Jason said. "You boys just wait and see."

I didn't sleep well that night, waking before dawn. In the dark, even the worst things seemed possible. I thought of what I'd seen on TV, soldiers and civilians on stretchers, some missing limbs, some blind, some dead, worst of all the monks who sat perfectly still as they transformed into pyramids of fire. I could report Jason to Mr. Watkins, or even ask my parents what to do, but this seemed to be something they had no part in. Or just stay home. Yet that seemed wrong as well. But then the morning sun revealed the same window that had always been there, the same bureau and mirror. Revealed my world and what was possible in it. He won't do it, I told myself, it's just talk. When my aunt came by at 8:15, I was ready.

I went down the Stagecoach Saloon steps, Jason and Matt already undressing. As we changed into our outfits, I noticed a blue backpack beside Jason's locker.

"What's in there?" I asked.

"What would you do if I said a hatchet?" Jason asked.

When I didn't respond he grinned.

"Courage is what's in there," he answered. "At least half a bottle of it still is."

We walked down the tracks to our hideout, the backpack dangling from Jason's shoulder. Things I'd paid no mind to other mornings, the smell of creosote on the wooden crossties, how sun and dew created bright shivers on the steel rails, I noticed now. I was lagging behind. Matt waited for me while Jason walked on.

"Don't worry, kid," Matt said softly. "Even if he was serious, he'll chicken out."

"You sure?" I asked.

"He's just trying to mess with our heads."

Once we were in the woods, Jason opened the backpack and took out the half-filled bottle, *Beefeater* on the label.

"We'll have one successful robbery this summer," Jason said, "rob Uncle Sam of a soldier to zip up in a body bag."

He unscrewed the cap and lifted two white pills from his front pocket. He shoved them in his mouth and drank until bubbles rose inside the glass. Jason shuddered and lowered the bottle. For a few minutes he just stood there. Then he set the bottle down, took out a pocketknife, and cut the rawhide strips tethering the holsters to his legs.

"Keep them in your pocket for tourniquets," he said, offering the strips to Matt. "Once the wheel rim takes the fingers off, I'll need them on my wrists."

"No way," Matt said.

"What about you, kid?" Jason asked, his voice slurring. "You too chicken-shit to help me?"

I nodded and looked at Matt's watch. Five minutes until the train would be here. Jason lifted the bottle and didn't stop drinking until it was empty. He held his stomach a few moments like he might throw up but he didn't. He raked his right index finger across the left palm.

"That quick and it's done," Jason said, and pulled his pistols from their holsters, flung them to the ground. "Won't be using my trigger fingers anymore, here or anywhere else."

"You're drunk and crazy," Matt said.

"Yeah, I guess I am drunk and that acid, man, it just detonated. 'Scuse me while I kiss the sky."

Jason looked upward, then twirled around and lost his balance. He tumbled onto the ground, rose to his knees and saluted us, before keeling back over.

"What are we going to do?" I asked.

"I'll stay with him," Matt said. "I don't think he'll be moving for a while, but just in case you'd better stop the train before it gets near here."

I left the woods and stepped onto the track. As the train came into view, wood and steel vibrated under my feet. The whistle blew. I jogged up the track waving for the train to stop, but I was just an outlaw taking his cue too soon. Mack, the engineer, blew the whistle again. I was close enough to see his face leaning out the cab window. He looked pissed off and he wasn't slowing down. I jumped into the ditch and the engine rumbled past.

I looked ahead and saw Jason running out of the woods, Matt trailing. Jason lay down by the tracks and stretched his arms, clamping both hands on the rail. Mack grabbed the handbrake but it was too late.

Jason's hands clung to the rail when the left front wheel rolled over them.

That's how I wrote the scene's conclusion years later, then added a couple of paragraphs about an older narrator recalling the event. A standard initiation story, nothing especially new but done well enough for *Esquire* to publish.

What actually occurred was that I didn't see Jason's hands, just that his arms stretched toward the track. Then he was rolling into the ditch, forearms tucked inside the curl of his body. Matt and I scrambled into the ditch beside him. Jason screamed for a few moments until he slowly uncoiled and began laughing hysterically.

"You dumb fuckers thought I'd really do it," he gasped.

"Asshole," Matt said, and walked back into the woods.

Jason turned toward the train and raised his hands and open palms.

"Don't shoot I'm unarmed," he shouted, and started laughing again.

Mack shouted back that Jason was good as fired. Passengers gawked out windows as the train wheels began turning again. Donald stood sad-faced on a top step, white hat held against his leg as though mourning our perfidy.

Back at the hideout, Matt lifted the empty bottle.

"Water?"

"Yep," Jason answered.

"And the acid?"

"Two aspirin," Jason said. "Water and two aspirin, boys. That's all the props I needed. Now what do you say about my acting ability?"

"The stuff about your cousin and uncle," Matt said. "That part of the performance too?"

"Of course," Jason nodded. "You have to create a believable scenario."

"The draft notice?" I asked.

"No, kid, that's all too real, but I figure if I can convince you two that I'm crazy I can convince them. This was my rehearsal."

"You're an asshole," Matt said again. "One of us could have gotten hurt because of your prank. We could lose a day's pay too."

"Don't worry," Jason said. "I'm going to turn myself in right now, tell them all of it was my doing. They won't do anything to you when they know that."

Jason stuffed the pistols back in his holsters and picked up his backpack.

"Hey, I was just having a little fun," he said.

"I hope I never see that son of a bitch again," Matt said when Jason had left. "How about you?"

"That would suit me fine."

But four decades later in Denver I did see Jason again, the cowboy hat replaced by a VFW ball cap.

"Remember me?" he asked. "We used to be outlaws together."

I didn't at first, but as he continued to talk a younger, recognizable face emerged from the folds and creases.

"It's a good story," Jason said, nodding at the *Esquire* he clutched. "You got the details right."

"Thanks," I said. "You exaggerate, of course, make characters better or worse than in real life."

"Don't worry," he said. "I know I was an asshole."

I pointed at the hat.

"You end up over there?"

"Yeah, you guys were easier to fool than the Army," Jason said. "Of course, the induction center didn't provide me a train to freak them out with."

"Well, at least you came back."

"I did that," Jason said.

"My cousin, he didn't."

"I'm sorry to hear that, I truly am," Jason said, and after a few moments, "What about Matt? You ever see him after that summer?"

"No."

"I always wondered if he got sent over there. I looked for him on the wall. His name wasn't there so maybe he got into med school. I guess I could find out on the Internet. When you were writing that story, did you ever do a search on us?"

"I couldn't remember your last names," I answered. "But I don't think I would have anyway. Like I said, it's fiction."

Jason had rolled up the magazine. It resembled a runner's baton as he tapped it against his leg. The bookstore was almost empty now, just the owner and two teenagers browsing the sci-fi section.

"When I dream it isn't fiction," Jason said, "for me or for them."

"Them?"

"Yeah, them," Jason said, stashing the magazine in his back pocket. "You remember who Lieutenant Calley was?"

"I remember."

"Come with me," he said. "There's something I want to show you."

From a shelf marked MILITARY, Jason took down a book and opened it to a page of black-and-white photographs. The top two photos were of Calley, but below was one of eight nameless soldiers, helmets off, arms draped around each other.

Jason pointed at the second soldier to the left.

"Recognize me?"

Except for shorter hair, he looked the same as he had at Frontier Village. Jason stared at the photograph a few more moments.

"Three of these guys were dead within a month," he said. "The Vietnamese say the ghosts of American soldiers who got killed are still over there. They hear them at night entering their villages, even villages that were Viet Cong during the war. They leave food and water out for them." Jason looked up from the page. "Their doing that, I think it matters."

Jason leafed farther into the book, stopped on a page with no photographs. His index finger slid down a few lines and stopped. I read the paragraph.

"You know my last name now," Jason said, reshelving the book.

The teenagers walked toward the checkout, a graphic novel in hand as the owner placed a CLOSED sign on the door.

"After I came back to the states, I told myself that if the people around me had been through what I'd been through—three of your buddies killed and scared shitless you're next, then being in a village where any woman or child could have a grenade and all the while your superior ordering you to do it—they would have acted no differently. To see it that way allows you to move on. You got unlucky in a lottery and put in some shit most people are spared. You just followed the script you'd been given."

"Here's the thing," Jason said after a pause. "It's always been okay when I am awake. I've held down a good job at a radio station for forty years, and though my wife and I got divorced a while back, we raised two great kids. Both college grads, employed, responsible, I'm blessed that way, even have a grandchild coming. So I handle the daylight fine. But night, it used to be different, because in my dreams I'd be back there. Everything was the same, the same villagers in the same places they'd been before. In the dreams I'd already know what was going to happen, not just that day, but what would happen afterwards—the accounts and testimonies, the hearings, Calley's court-martial, the newspaper articles and TV reports. But even knowing all that, when the order was given, *I would do it again*. I didn't have one dream where I didn't.

Until one day I was in the vet affairs office and I read your story. That night, I dreamed I was there again, but I had no hands, which meant I couldn't hold a rifle. I walked among them, even into their huts, and they weren't afraid, and I wasn't afraid either because I knew I had no hands to hurt them. And then, as the months passed, I'd dream that though I had no hands, I balanced a bowl of rice between my wrists. I'd go into the huts and crouch, set the bowl carefully on the floor and after they'd each taken a handful of rice, I'd lift it back up and go to the next hut."

Jason paused and took the rolled-up magazine from his pocket, held it out between us.

"I went to the newsstand and bought this copy. I read the story every night for a while, then just a few pages, and then only a few paragraphs. It wasn't long until I had those paragraphs memorized. I'd lie there in the dark and speak them out loud. Now two, three nights a week I'm back there, but always without my hands."

Jason nodded at the magazine.

"You can have this if you want."

"No," I said. "You keep it."

"Afraid I might forget?"

His smile did not conceal the challenge in his eyes.

"No," I answered.

"Okay. I'll keep it then," Jason said. "Thank you for writing the story the way you did. That's why I came, to thank you, to tell you it's helped. I want to believe it's helped more than just me. I mean, if ghosts enter villages, maybe they enter dreams too."

He held out his hand and we shook.

"If Matt ever shows up at one of your signings, wish him well for me."

After Jason left, I talked to the bookstore owner for a few minutes, then walked back to my hotel. It was only five blocks but I wasn't used to Denver's altitude, so I was out of breath when I got there. I had a couple of drinks at the bar, then took the elevator to my room. The curtains were pulled back and Denver sparkled below. Jason's home was down there and I wondered if he was already asleep. In the darkness beyond the city, jagged mountains rose. On the flight back to Carolina the next morning, I saw them from the passenger window. They were so different from the mountains back home. Young, treeless, no hollowed out coves. Snow settled on summits, yet to be softened by time.

The Far and the Near

My grandfather was seventy-one years old when he manifested an artistic talent no one in our family, including himself, realized he possessed. That July he had suffered a stroke while stretching barbed wire in his pasture. My Aunt Florence was bringing him lunch and found him draped on the fence like something hung out to dry. The worst thing, my aunt said, had been pulling him free from the wire, for the metal thorns were embedded in his flesh as well as his flannel shirt.

The doctors told his two daughters—my mother and my aunt—that months might pass before he came home, but he recovered more quickly than the doctors anticipated. Within two weeks he was in the rehabilitation wing of the hospital, walking the black rubber street of the treadmill, lifting small hand weights. And painting.

"He's knows how to *see,*" the art therapist told my mother and me when we visited one Saturday. "And it's not just being able to look at something and make a copy. He makes us see the world through his eyes. It's amazing."

My mother looked across the room where my grandfather sat before an easel, brush and palette in hand.

"All I've ever seen him paint was his house and some farm equipment," my mother said, her voice a mixture of humor and something close to alarm. "Could this be caused by the stroke?"

"No," the therapist said. "It's something he's always had, something he was born with, a gift. He's just finally gotten the chance to show it."

The therapist nodded toward my grandfather.

"He's going to need this, because he won't be able to do a lot of the things he's used to doing."

As we drove out of the hospital parking lot my mother looked at me and shook her head.

"My goodness, Chad. If your grandmother was alive she'd have a fit seeing him spend a whole afternoon painting. He always looked for a reason not to paint, said he hated doing it worse than anything, even cutting tobacco."

My grandfather left the hospital the next week. An orderly placed the suitcase and paintings in the trunk of my mother's car, then an easel and cardboard box filled with art books and supplies beside it.

"That's from Mrs. Watkins, his therapist," the orderly said. "It's kind of a farewell present."

He had been back home less than an hour when my grandfather set up the easel in the front room. While my mother went and cooked supper, my grandfather had me drag an old trunk from the corner to lay his paints and brushes on. He set up his easel, then sat down in a ladderback chair and began to work on a painting he'd begun at the hospital. I stood behind him and watched as he completed a river scene. I was impressed, because soon I knew not only that the river was the French Broad but I knew exactly what specific section——a shoals above Hot Springs.

"How can you do that without even a picture?" I asked.

"I do have a picture," my grandfather said, not turning from the painting as he spoke. "But it's inside my head, not outside."

Even at fourteen I understood that he was saying the same thing the therapist had said, because as familiar as the scene was, there were some things unfamiliar as well—the way a patch of morning sunlight spread over the river's surface like a gold quilt, willow oak leaves so bright-green they sparkled. It was like seeing a place I had seen many times before, but this time with a pair of glasses belonging to someone else, and that someone else was my grandfather.

Because it was summer, and my grandfather insisted he stay at his farmhouse instead of one of his daughters, my first cousin Jarred and I stayed with him those first few weeks. Jarred was sixteen and I fourteen. I stayed with him during the day and Jarred at night, so I was with him the afternoon my father and uncle loaded up the cattle to sell at the livestock barn in Asheville. We watched from the front porch as the last two cows were taken out of the pasture. After my uncle drove the livestock truck through, my father jumped out of the cab and closed the gate.

"No reason for your daddy to close the gate," my grandfather said as we watched the truck disappear up the road. "There's nothing left to keep in."

Each weekday morning my father let me off at seven-fifteen on his way to work in Asheville. Jarred would be in the kitchen. He had a construction job that summer, helping to build second homes for wealthy Floridians, but he didn't have to be at work until eight-thirty. As soon as I got to the farm-house, Jarred crossed the pasture to get the breakfast Aunt Florence had cooked. He ate with us, then sipped coffee until he had to leave, then cranked up the decade-old Plymouth Fury he and my uncle had taken out a loan for the week school let out. The car sputtered and rattled to life, the rotting muffler Jarred couldn't yet afford to replace coughing plumes of black smoke. He would work all day, then come straight back to the farm-house after he got off at five.

Jarred was the oldest grandchild, and because he had grown up on land adjacent to my grandfather's farm, he'd spent much more time with my grandfather than I had. Jarred had been named after my grandfather as well. Though my grandfather tried his best not to show it, his bond with Jarred was, inevitably, deeper. My grandfather did not leave the kitchen table until Jarred left for work.

Only then would he move into the front room and sit before his easel. He would paint all morning, at first Madison County landscapes——barns and fields, streams and mountains. After a month he began to do portraits as well, first one of Jarred standing alone in the pasture, then one of me leaning against the barn. While he painted I straightened up the house as best I could then went outside and did what he, at least for a while longer, could not do——mow the grass, prune the apple trees, hoe the half-acre of corn and beans he'd planted two months before his stroke.

Afternoons we sat on the front porch. My grandfather read the art books or closed his eyes and napped while I listened to the radio or read musty *Field and Streams* I'd hauled down from the attic. At a few minutes after five he would start looking down the road for Jarred's Plymouth.

"I've seen milking trails wider than that road down to Mars Hill," my grandfather would say. "I wish some of them state politicians would look at a map and realize there's a lot of North Carolina west of Raleigh. If they did we might get some decent roads up here."

By the time I went back to school in late August, my grandfather was able to take care of himself. Despite my mother and Aunt Florence's protests, he was again driving his rust-scabbed '57 Ford pick-up to Gus Boyd's store, sometimes going all the way to Hot Springs or Mars Hill. He hoed the corn and beans and cut the grass himself. It was all they could do to keep him from buying some cattle for his pasture.

It was during this time that one Sunday after church Reverend Luckadoo approached my grandfather about painting a mural for the baptistry. Reverend

Luckadoo had seen several of my grandfather's paintings, including one of the church that now hung in the preacher's living room.

"God has given you a gift, Deacon Hampton" Reverend Luckadoo said, "and this would be a chance to use it to benefit the church."

That my grandfather agreed to do the mural did not surprise me. He'd always been an active member of the church, not only serving as a deacon but also anything else that a small church such as ours might need. He frequently offered the morning prayer and every other Sunday he served as our music director, choosing hymns for the service and then leading the singing.

Reverend Luckadoo looked at my mother and aunt. "But only if we're all in agreement you're healthy enough to do this. It wasn't but two months ago I was visiting you in the hospital."

"I'm not sure this is such a good idea," my mother said.

"What if he had to get on a ladder and fell?" Aunt Florence asked.

"I wouldn't need a ladder," my grandfather said. "Maybe a footstool but not a ladder."

"Well, a footstool then," Aunt Florence said. "If you fell off a footstool you could still get hurt."

"Maybe it could be done on weekends," Reverend Luckadoo suggested. He nodded toward me. "That way Jarred or Chad could go as well."

Jarred can't do it," Aunt Florence said. "He works construction all day Saturday, Sundays afternoons he helps at Billy Nelson's gas station as well."

Reverend Luckadoo looked at me.

"It would be a way of contributing to your church, Chad," he said. "I don't mind doing it," I said, but my lack of enthusiasm was evident.

"It'll just take a weekend," my grandfather said.

"Gus Boyd says he'll donate the paint and brushes," Reverend Luckadoo said. "You just tell him what you need."

So it was that the following Saturday morning my grandfather and I drove toward the church, paint cans and brushes bumping and rattling in the truck bed. We spread old bed sheets over the baptistry. My grandfather handed me a screwdriver.

"Just open the blue paint," he said as he taped a bed sheet to the wall edge, "then bring that piano bench over here. I'm going to start with the sky."

He did not speak loudly but his voice reverberated from the back pews. I had never been in the church when it was so vacant and I found the emptiness strange and unsettling. The building felt not so much unoccupied as abandoned. Though all the lights were on, the church seemed somehow darker, as though it was the congregation as much as the hundred-watt bulbs that filled the building with light.

"You'll need to hold the paint can for me," my grandfather said. "This bench will flip over for sure if I'm bending down to douse my brush."

So I stood beside the piano bench, lifting the blue paint bucket each time the paint thinned on his three-inch brush.

"This isn't going to do," my grandfather said after a few minutes. He handed me the brush, then laid his hand on my shoulder as he stepped down from the piano bench. He took a rag from the back pocket of his coveralls and wiped paint off his thumb and index finger.

"The color isn't thick enough," he said. "There's no texture. I want it to look like the person getting baptized is stepping right into that river."

My grandfather nodded at the cans of paint at our feet. "That paint won't work, but I know some that will," he said and began to reseal the open cans. "Let's load this back on the truck, except for the white and brown. Then we'll go trade this for what we need."

"So what are going to use instead?" I asked as we drove toward Gus Boyd's store.

"Tractor paint," my grandfather said. "They only make three colors but that ought to be enough."

Gus Boyd had five cans of the red tractor paint that Massey-Ferguson made as well as four cans of Ford's blue, but we had to drive down to the John Deere dealership in Mars Hill to get our green.

"I reckon I can count this as part of my tithe," my grandfather said as he pulled several worn five-dollar bills from his billfold. He adjusted the new John Deere hat the clerk had given him. "Well, at least I got me a new hat."

We were back in the church in forty-five minutes, my grandfather on the piano stool making a sky out of Ford tractor paint.

"This is more like it," he said. "See how it makes things look thicker. Now that's a sky you could disappear into."

My grandfather did not want to break for lunch until he finished the upper sky, the part that required he stand on the piano bench, so we worked past noon. I switched the can from my left to right hand more and more often as the hours passed. By the time we finished the muscles in my wrists and arms ached as though I'd spent the morning lifting dumbbells. The curved wire handles had left bloodless slashes in my palms.

We ate the sandwiches my mother had made and sipped from mason jars filled with tea and ice. When we'd finished we sat down on the front pew to rest, or so I thought. For a few minutes my grandfather was motionless. I thought he might have fallen asleep, but when I looked more closely I saw his eyes were open and staring intently at the wall.

"I see it now," he finally said, as much to himself as to me. He got up then. I helped him open paint cans and placed the brushes used earlier in kerosene while my grandfather mixed green tractor paint and white house paint to make the color he wanted. He added more white until the paint lightened to a green, silver-tinged pastel. It was a color I had seen before, but I couldn't remember where. My grandfather no longer needed the piano bench, so I carried it back. Then I sat down on the front row and watched.

My grandfather worked from the bottom up now, kneeling inside the baptistry pool as his green, silver tinged river slowly rose inside the glass. He applied the paint in sweeping horizontal swathes, some overlapping, some not, creating the appearance of currents moving behind the glass. He continued to kneel even when he had to raise the brush over his head. From my vantage point on the front pew, my grandfather looked like a man mid-river waving to someone on shore, or perhaps signaling for help.

When the paint on the wall was level with the baptistry glass, he stood up, his left hand pressing the small of his back as he slowly rose to his full height.

"Time to mix some more paints," he said, opening the cardboard box that contained pint canning jars, jars my mother called jelly glasses. I was like an alchemist's assistant as I helped mix red and blue to make a deep purple, white and brown to make a manila color like August wheat, other hues to match the palette he'd already created in his mind.

"Don't let him overdo it," my mother had warned me before I left the house that morning. "No matter what he thinks he's still over seventy and recovering from a stroke." As we filled the jelly jars I checked my grandfather's face for signs of fatigue.

"Don't you think you ought to rest a few minutes?" I asked.

"No," my grandfather said. "I'm fine."

"You look tired," I said.

My grandfather looked up from the paint he was mixing.

"That doesn't matter. You can't do something like this in bits and pieces. It's like taking a picture with a camera. If you get what you want in the frame, you take the picture right then, whatever you're seeing might not be there the next time."

When my grandfather returned to the baptistry, he lined up a dozen different hued jelly glasses before him like colorful, unlit candles. But it was a carpenter's pencil, not a paint brush, that he worked with first. Between sky and water he outlined a human head and torso the same way someone at a crime scene might outline a victim. One arm lifted toward the sky while the other entered the water at the wrist. My grandfather drew outlines of eyes, nose and mouth. Only then did he dip a one-inch brush into the manila-covered paint. He worked more deliberately now, holding the brush aloft like a dart as he pondered his next brushstroke. The face began to take on details—lips slightly open as though about to speak, a dark-brown beard that gathered under the chin like something woven, the long, angular nose. But the most striking feature was the heaven-searching eyes. They were the same color as the river. I had seen pictures of brown-eyed Jesus's and blue-eyed Jesus's, but never with eyes of green.

After he finished the face, my grandfather lifted the jar with purple paint and colored the robe, then the manila color for the lifted palm spread out in blessing.

The stained-glass windows offered no light and darkness pooled in the sanctuary's corners before my grandfather lay down his brush.

"So what do you think?" he asked.

"It's good," I said, "especially the eyes. I never thought of Jesus having green eyes, but somehow it seems to fit."

"Seems that way to me too," my grandfather said.

"I think you better stop now," I said.

"I hate to but I reckon you're right," he said. "If I get too tired I'll get sloppy. Anyway, all we got left now is background. I reckon that can wait till tomorrow afternoon."

My grandfather turned away from the mural. His eyes were red-veined and rheumy, as though the effort to transfer the vision inside his head onto the wall had strained them.

"I don't think Preacher Luckadoo will mind us leaving this stuff in the baptistry," he said, "but we do need to soak those brushes. I wish we could cover the wall with a couple of bed sheets so people couldn't see it till it was finished, but I'm afraid it'll smear some of the paint."

"We could come in tomorrow before church starts and cover it," I said.

My grandfather nodded.

"That's a first-rate idea. We'll do that very thing."

The next morning my grandfather stood at the right side of the pulpit as he led our singing of "Will There Be Any Stars in My Crown." The makeshift curtain we'd taped up earlier covered the wall behind him, its bottom draping into the empty baptistry pool.

After the service my grandfather ate Sunday lunch with my parents and me. He was a man who liked to linger at the dinner table on Sundays, but on this day he did not sip a cup of coffee after dessert or discuss the week's news. He quickly finished his banana pudding and gave me a nod.

"Go get your work duds on," he told me. "I'll do the same and we'll get on back to the church."

We were inside the church by one-thirty, and for the next few hours I watched my grandfather reroute the Jordan River through Madison County, North Carolina. He began with a red tobacco barn, a barn he was just completing when the front door shut behind us.

"I don't believe they had tobacco barns in Israel two thousand years ago, Deacon Hampton," Preacher Luckadoo said. "I believe that's what they'd call an anachronism."

My grandfather paused but did not lay his brush down.

"I know that," my grandfather said. "But the way I see it people best understand something far away by showing it with something close by."

"I'm not so sure of that," Preacher Luckadoo said. "Tell me how you'd argue that."

"Do you believe we're in the presence of Christ, right here in Madison County, right now in 1986," my grandfather said.

"Yes, I do," Preacher Luckadoo said.

"Well, that's what I'm saying in this here mural."

Preacher Luckadoo's looked skeptical as he studied the painting a few more moments.

"I suppose I see your point," he finally said, "but I'm not sure this is the best way to show it. I still think a stone temple would be better than a tobacco barn. And I'd suggest those eyes be brown. After all, Jesus was a Hebrew."

My grandfather listened politely. As soon as Preacher Luckadoo left he turned back to the mural to put the finishing touches on the tobacco barn.

"I should have told him what happened to the church man that pestered Michelangelo," my grandfather said. "Have you ever heard that story?"

I shook my head.

"Michelangelo was laying on his back dawn to dusk painting the Sistine Chapel. Most every day this church man named Cesena came around, complaining that Michelangelo wasn't working fast enough, not doing such and such the way Cesena wanted it done."

My grandfather set down his brush and turned to me.

"Care to guess what happened?"

"I don't have any idea," I said.

"Well, when Michelangelo painted his scene of hell he stuck Cesena right down there in the middle of it. Of course Cesena got all bent out of shape about that. He went running to the Pope complaining about what Michelangelo had done and telling the Pope that he, the pope, had to do something about it."

My grandfather paused to chuckle.

"The Pope told Cesena that even a pope couldn't get a man out of hell. You can go to the Sistine Chapel today and you'll still see Cesena there with the other lost souls."

By the time we had another visitor it was six o'clock, and all my grandfather had left to do was climb up on the piano bench a last time and fill in some final sections of blue sky.

"I hope that isn't Preacher Luckadoo with some more suggestions," my grandfather said when he heard a car door slam. My grandfather looked warily toward the door. He stepped away from the mural and stood beside the pulpit, allowing me my first unimpeded look at the painting in hours.

On the riverbank behind Christ's shoulders, deep-green rows of corn-stalks sprouted in a patch of dark bottomland. At the field's center a scarecrow spread its arms as though about to embrace someone. A mourning dove perched on the scarecrow's right shoulder. On a hill in the farther distance the red tobacco barn rose into an uncompleted sky.

"What do you think?" my grandfather asked, but he was not speaking to me but to Jarred, who stood in the doorway with a cardboard box filling his arms.

"I like it a lot," Jarred said. He shifted the box deeper into his arms and walked down the aisle towards us. He laid the box on one of the bed sheets and lifted from it three foil-wrapped plates, some silverware and napkins, and three sealed quart jars of iced tea.

"You haven't eaten?" my grandfather asked.

"No," Jarred said. "Momma wanted me to, but I figured I'd eat with you all."

"Well, we're more than glad to have your company," my grandfather said.

Jarred and I sat cross legged on the floor, our grandfather in front of us on the piano bench. We lifted the tin foil from our plates and a warm steam rose to our faces. The smell of fried chicken, boiled okra and biscuits filled the sanctuary.

"Your Momma could always cook," my grandfather said to Jarred after a few bites, "even when she was no more than a child."

The front door opened again, and my father entered.

"Looks like we're going to have a family reunion before it's all over and done with," my grandfather said. He waved my father toward the front.

"You've got school tomorrow and according to your momma you've got homework yet to do," my father said to me. "She sent me to get you."

"But we'll be through in two hours," I pleaded. "We're almost done."

"Is that right?" my father asked my grandfather.

"Probably less with Jarred helping," my grandfather said.

"Alright," my father said, sitting down beside me. "I reckon your momma and your homework can wait. I'll help so that'll speed it up too."

My grandfather held a drumstick out to my father.

"I'm near about full," he said. "You eat it."

"I've never been known to turn down a piece of Florence's chicken," my father said.

As the stained-glass windows deepened from purple to black I ate with my grandfather, father, and first cousin beneath the raised, blessing hand of Christ.

When the plates and jars and silverware were back in the cardboard box, my grandfather picked up a fresh brush to complete his sky while Jarred and my father and I cleaned the brushes. When that was done we wiped paint off the outside of cans and jars before carrying them out to the pick-up, then checked beneath bed sheets for paint drops we scraped from the oak flooring with razor blades.

We were done by eight-thirty. I bundled the last bed sheet into my arms as my grandfather looked over the mural a final time. He nodded, then followed Jarred, my father and me up the aisle toward the door. Jarred suddenly bent down in front of my father and lifted something from the foyer's floor.

"Look," he said, turning to us. "It must have got in when we were carrying stuff out to the truck."

He held his cupped hands toward us and slowly opened them a couple of inches. A Luna moth filled his palm, its green, silver-tinged wings rising and falling steady as a heartbeat. This was the exact color of the river and Christ's eyes, the color I had seen before but only now could place. It was as though a piece of the mural had flecked off and come alive.

"I better let it go before I hurt it," Jarred said and stepped to the doorway. He opened his hands and the moth fluttered into the darkness. Jarred stepped back into the foyer and held his right palm under the ceiling light's glow.

"Well, what do make of that?" he asked. A fine green powder spread across my cousin's palm like some rare, beautiful dust.

The next Sunday the whole congregation saw my grandfather's mural, and the reaction was positive, so much so that two weeks later our church's other deacon, Barry Truesdale, suggested before his prayer that my grandfather consider adding another mural on the church's back wall. Preacher Luckadoo seemed also to have dropped any qualms he had about anachronisms, for that same morning he gave a sermon that recast Simon Peter and Andrew as good old boys running trout-lines on the French Broad.

Perhaps if events had turned out differently, my grandfather might have indeed painted that mural for the back wall. He may well have painted other sections as well, turning Ivy Creek Baptist Church into his own Sistine Chapel. But on a February morning four months later a number of lives, including my grandfather's, were suddenly and irrevocably altered. It was a Saturday, and the curvy mountain road Jarred drove to work was slick from an ice storm the night before. The Plymouth had plunged off the road and tumbled fifty yards into a ravine, catching fire when it hit a large white oak. When he saw Sheriff Watson drive up to my aunt and uncle's house, my grandfather had hurriedly crossed the fifty yards of pasture between the houses. He had stepped onto the porch just as my Uncle Jesse opened the door. My grandfather spoke before Sheriff Watson could say a word.

"Something's happened to Jarred," he said, and Sheriff Ponder Watson.

The night of the visitation I sat in a metal folding chair in the parlor of Hendricks Funeral Home in Mars Hill. Sitting with me were my parents and brother and sister, my aunt and uncle, and my great-aunt Edna. Jarred's closed casket lay in the corner, a coffin I would, come morning, help carry. My grandfather was not sitting with us, was not even in the building. He was supposed to come with my aunt and uncle, but when they had gone to pick him up, my grandfather and the truck were gone.

"He shouldn't have gone off like that," Aunt Edna said to my father. "What are people going to think?"

"There isn't nobody that matters who could have a doubt how much that old man loves Jarred," my father replied. "That's what matters most, Edna. A man has to grieve in his own way."

"Maybe you're right," my great-aunt replied. "Anyway, I ought not to judge. Such a thing as this is so far beyond any person's understanding it's near impossible to know how to act."

The visitation ended at eight o'clock and my grandfather had still not shown up. A light rain began to fall and my father turned on his wipers as we drove back up the mountain. My mother insisted we go by my grandfather's house to see if he was back, but when our headlights splashed across the front of the farmhouse the lights were off, the dirt pull-off where he parked his pick-up empty.

My Uncle Jesse stepped off the front porch. Perhaps because of his black suit we had not seen him.

"He's not in there," my Uncle Jesse said.

"I'm worried about him," my mother said.

"I'll take you and the kids home, then go look for him," my father said.

"No," my mother said. "The kids and me will stay with Florence and Jesse until he comes back on his own or you bring him back." My mother turned to us in the back seat. "You all get out," she said. "We'll walk over with Jesse."

My sisters got out of the car, but I did not move.

"I want to go with you," I told my father.

"Why?" he asked.

"Because I think I know where he is."

It took us ten minutes to get to the church. The pick-up was parked out front, and inside the lights were on. My father and I opened the door and stood in the foyer for a few moments, transfixed. Bed sheets bunched and spread across the sanctuary floor. On top of the sheets were paint cans, the lids beside them, one can overturned. Brushes lay on the sheets as well, paint still on them as though dropped by accident or thrown down in frustration. My grandfather sat on the front pew, his eyes raised to the mural.

But these things were not what my father and I saw first. What we saw first was the mural. The figure in the river no longer bore Christ's face but my grandfather's, and in his arms he carried Jarred's body. The river was red now. In the distance orange flames consumed the barn like crownfire. Christ as well was in the distance, hanging with his arms stretched, head bowed on the wood planks that had held the scarecrow.

"We can't let people see this," my father said. "I'm going back to Jesse and Florence's house and tell your mama we're going to be a while, take her and your sisters home. Then I'll go wake up Gus Boyd and get us some cans of white paint."

We worked until past midnight that evening, turning the wall into a white blank while my grandfather slumped on the front pew. He occasionally raised his face, but his eyes seemed to register nothing. They were blank as the white wall we were replacing his mural with. When we finally finished, my father insisted my grandfather ride with us back to his farmhouse.

"You can stay with us tonight," my father offered.

"No, I'll be better off here," my grandfather replied, so I walked him to the door, went in first to turn on the lights.

"It's been a long night," I told my father as we finally pulled into our drive.

"You'll likely have few longer," my father said. "At least that's my hope."

The next morning I helped carry Jarred's body into the church and then to the cemetery behind the church. I watched my grandfather carefully. He was exhausted, that was clear, and like my aunt and uncle, he mourned fiercely, tears streaming down his face steady as October rain. But that was better than the blank stare of the night before when he'd gone into some stark, wintry void before even grief. On that night I believe my cousin's death caused my grandfather a crisis of faith, but I also believe it was not the final arrival point in his spiritual journey. He would live three more years and during that time he continued to go to church. My grandfather led us in song and prayer with the same enthusiasm as he had before. But the wall behind the sanctuary remained blank, and the paints and brushes and easel in his front room were stored away in the attic. He was, as the therapist had told my mother and me, a man who had the ability to *see* the world in a way most of us couldn't, and not only see it himself but make others see it as well. Perhaps he felt he had shown us enough, especially of the vision we all shared that bleak February night before Jarred's funeral. Perhaps he had taken us, as well as himself, far as any of us could bear.

The Gatsons

It was two weeks after I graduated from elementary school that a big yellow moving van backed slowly toward the front porch of the house next door. My best friend John Grier had lived in that house, and the wide, treeless front yard had been our recreation complex, complete with baseball diamond and ramp for our skateboards. We had been classmates since kindergarten and the only thing that had convinced me I might survive junior high was knowing John would be at my side. But Mr. Grier had been offered a better-paying job in South Carolina, and the day after John and I strode across the elementary school's gym to receive our diplomas, he and the rest of the family were gone.

When the Gatsons arrived, I could not help but see them as usurpers, for I had believed that as long as the house was vacant the Griers might find South Carolina not to their liking and return. But that option was no longer possible when the *For Sale* sign planted beside our pitcher's mound came down. My younger brother Tom and I lay on our stomachs, sharing a pair of dime store binoculars as we peered through the hedge at the Grier's old house.

"That must be the daddy on the porch," Tom said, pointing to a heavy-set man wearing black-rimmed glasses and, despite the midday June heat, a suit and tie. "He looks like that man on TV running against President Johnson."

A green Oldsmobile with white-wall tires pulled in the driveway.

"I bet that's the rest of them," I said and yanked away the binoculars. A woman sat behind the steering wheel. The back seat was empty, but someone, someone child-sized, was in the front seat.

"Is it a boy or girl?" Tom asked.

"Can't tell yet," I said, "but they're getting out."

The mother opened her door, a black dress covering her thin frame. Like her husband she wore glasses, though hers were pink-framed and sparkled in the sun like mica. Her lips were bright red and her black hair rose a foot above

384

her head like a huge, gravity-defying swirl of licorice cotton candy. She closed the car door but made no move toward the porch. Instead, she let her eyes sweep across the house and then take in our house and yard as well. What she saw did not appear to impress her very much.

The passenger door shut.

"It's a girl," I said, the last word coming out of my mouth like the last air in a deflating balloon. "Looks to be about my age."

"Maybe she's a tomboy," my brother said.

"I don't think so," I said, for the girl wore a blue skirt and a white blouse. There were no tennis shoes on her feet or scabs on her knees and a pink bow was tied around her long, brown hair. Like her mother, she wore pink-framed glasses, though hers didn't glitter. She carried a large, white, nub-tailed cat in her arms. The cat wore pink glasses as well, though they wrapped around its head more like goggles.

"They've got a cat that wears glasses," I said, trying to sound matter-of-fact, playing the role of the worldly older brother.

Tom grabbed the binoculars.

"That thing's scary looking," Tom whispered. "Like something on *Shock Theatre* those mad scientists make in their labs. We'd better have as little to do with these folks as possible." Tom lifted himself to his knees. "Let's go play with my army men in the sandbox."

For a moment I didn't speak. As a rising seventh grader I was supposedly too old to be playing with army soldiers in a sandbox, especially with an eight-year old. But becoming a seventh grader was a source of growing trauma for me. For months I'd been hearing about eighth and ninth graders whose major motivation for attending school was to slam seventh graders like me into lockers as they extorted lunch money. I'd heard about teachers who assigned so much homework it could be weighed on a bathroom scale.

But that wasn't the worst of it. The night of my sixth-grade graduation my parents had presented me with a book called *The Adolescent Male*. "Read it and if you have any questions I'll try to answer them," my father had said, his nervous tone making it clear he hoped there wouldn't be. I spent the remaining hours of my graduation night reading with a fascinated horror what hormones were about to do me—everything from acne and blackheads and hair erupting on my face to liking girls to growth spurts and "nocturnal emissions"—and despite the book's claim otherwise, none of this seemed the least bit normal to me.

"All right," I said, glad to revert back to childhood a few hours.

We stood and brushed the dirt off our shirts and shorts. I wedged the binoculars into my pocket.

My brother glanced through the hedge a last time and shook his head. "Where do people like that come from?" Tom asked.

That was a question I could not answer, but next morning at breakfast my mother did.

"They are from Tallahassee, Florida," she said. "Dr. Gatson is an optician and inventor. Mrs. Gatson is the former president of a DAR chapter in Florida. Instead of a wedding ring, she has glasses with tiny diamonds in the frames. They have one daughter, Della Ann, who's twelve."

My father peered over the sports section of the paper. "How did you find out all that? It sounds like something you'd read off a post office bulletin board."

"Mable called me yesterday. She thought I'd want to know. She feels it's her professional duty as a realtor to make the neighbors aware who is in the houses she sells."

My father's face disappeared into the paper again as he spoke.

"The neighborly thing to do would be to go over there and find out about them yourself, instead of depending on Mable Abernathy's gossip."

"That's exactly what I plan to do," my mother said, "now that they've at least got the movers out of the house. I'm going to make an apple pie and the boys and I will take it to them this very morning."

Tom and I stared at each other as if our mother had announced an unexpected trip to the dentist's office.

"Don't give me that look, you two," she said. "You're going and you will be friendly and polite. If they invite us in, as I'm sure they'll do, don't touch anything and if they offer us something to drink don't slurp."

"But Dad doesn't have to go," Tom whined.

"I was thinking this might be a good morning to go to work with Dad," I said. "I've always wondered what he does all day."

"I've been wondering that too," Tom said.

But my mother quickly made clear that what my father did all day at work would be kept from his sons a while longer. Two hours and one pie later we were on the Gatsons' front porch.

"Don't slouch," our mother said, using her free hand to ring the doorbell.

The daughter answered the door, the white cat cradled against her chest exactly as it had been yesterday.

"Well," my mother said, "I believe you're Della Ann. I'm Mrs. Hampton, your next-door neighbor, and these are my boys Vincent and Tom."

Della Ann said nothing. She and the cat just stared at us through their pink eyeglasses.

"Who is it, Della Ann," a female voice asked from the back of the house.

"It's the neighbors, mother," Della Ann shouted. "They've got some kind of pie they want to sell us."

"No, no," my mother said as we heard footsteps come toward us. "I'm giving it to you, dear. To you and your family as a way of welcoming you."

"What kind is it?" Della Ann asked.

"Blackberry," my mother said.

"Yum," Della Ann replied. She looked at the cat. "Kittymus Angel and I love blackberries."

My mother did not have a chance to respond to this comment before Mrs. Gatson appeared at the door. She took the pie from my mother's outstretched arms, and after a few awkward seconds, asked us if we'd like to come in.

"I'm still unpacking in the kitchen, but we could talk while I'm doing that," Mrs. Gatson told my mother. Then she turned to Tom and me. "You children have a seat in the living room," Mrs. Gatson said. "You'll just be in the way in the kitchen."

"Yes," my mother echoed. "You boys talk to Della Ann."

If I had known at the time this would be the only chance I'd ever have to see the inside of the Gatsons' house, I might have been more observant, but my main memory is of sitting beside my brother on a couch and wondering if the girl and cat in the chair opposite us were somehow conjoined in the same manner as siamese twins. Della Ann said nothing. I said nothing. The cat said nothing. It was my brother who finally spoke.

"How come your cat wears glasses?"

Della Ann looked at my brother as if he were feeble-minded.

"The same reason people do. To see better. Princess Kittymus has the best eyesight of any cat in the world."

My brother considered Della Ann's comment a few seconds before he replied.

"Well, if he can see so great how come a dog could catch him and bite his tail off."

"Princess Kittymus is a manx," Della Ann said indignantly, "and manxes don't have tails."

"My brother didn't mean anything by it," I said to Della Ann. "He's eight years old. He doesn't know much about cats or anything else."

And that was the extent of our conversation. The rest of the time we simply sat, my brother and I in one corner, Della Ann and Kittymus in the other.

A few minutes later my mother came out of the kitchen, her lips pressed in a grimace unsuccessfully trying to be a smile.

"It's time to go, boys," she said.

In the next few days the details of my mother's kitchen conversation with Mrs. Gatson emerged in comments meant for my father but overheard by me as I eavesdropped. Evidently, much of the talk between my mother and Mrs. Gatson had been an extensive list of what our family should do to be suitable neighbors. The list included a better job of trimming the hedge on our side, no noise after eight p.m., and, most important of all, going to Doctor Gatson for all our optical needs. My mother informed Tom and me as well that Mrs. Gatson had requested we not play in her yard unless invited.

"There goes our baseball field," I told Tom. "Now what are we going to do the rest of the summer. Our yard's too small and John took the skateboard ramp with him."

"Play with our army men in the sandbox, I guess," Tom said.

"Wow," I said. "What a great summer this is turning out to be, playing in a sand box with my eight-year-old brother."

Within a week Dr. Gatson had opened his optometrist's shop downtown in an abandoned Shell service station. Because he was the only optometrist within twenty miles, he quickly developed a clientele, and just as quickly people began to notice a pattern—everybody who went to Dr. Gatson had a vision problem. People who read every letter on the chart were assured this meant nothing, that glasses were needed and needed as soon as he could grind them in what had been the oil change pit but was now his "lab." And it was always glasses, never contacts, for Dr. Gaston told his patients that extensive research had proven to him that contact lenses actually peeled off part of the eyeball each time they were taken out.

If patients already had a vision problem, they were diagnosed with a second, hitherto uncaught, eye problem, usually requiring extensive use of eye drops Dr.Gatson also made in his lab. He urged his patients to bring in their pets, telling them that in Florida animals wearing glasses was considered no more unusual than people wearing glasses.

"The man's a quack," my father said one night at the dinner table. The Gatsons were now the primary topic of my parents' dinner conversations, and they no longer seemed to care if Tom and me heard their comments or not.

"Someone's going to call the Better Business Bureau on him before long, or maybe the FBI to come shut him down. The old folks don't know any better than to believe him. Seems like every time I see someone over sixty they've got their heads tilted up so they can squirt Gatson's medicine into their eyes. He could be using acid out of some of those old car batteries dumped behind his office for all they know."

"It won't be too soon for me," my mother said. "She called me today. She doesn't approve of where our garbage cans are. I almost asked her if she'd like to have one put over her head."

"I may make that call myself," my father said, "because this thing is getting out of control in this town. It's like something out of *Invasion of the Body Snatchers*. People I thought were everyday, normal people are turning into nut cases. Just today I saw three cats, two dogs and a mule wearing those supposed "animal glasses." Tom Jenkins told me at the post office that Mildred Humphries had a pair made for her cockatoo."

My father shook his head and stared at his empty plate.

"It's scary," he said. "There's no other word for it."

Meanwhile, Tom and I had our own problems with the Gatsons, specifically with Princess Kittymus, who had proven that she was, despite my earlier theory, not attached to Della Ann after all. Every morning and evening the cat appeared alone, the pink goggle-glasses making her look like she had just stepped out of a Saturday morning cartoon instead of the Gatsons' back door. Princess Kittymus would slowly place one paw on the ground, then raise and shake it as though indignant that mere grass and not a plush red carpet lay beneath. It wasn't long before Tom and I noticed our sandbox, which was placed right next to the hedge, had a sour reek to it, and when we dug foxholes and caves for our soldiers we often scooped up more than sand.

"Your cat is peeing and pooping in our sandbox," Tom shouted over the hedge when he spotted Della Ann in her back yard one morning. "You keep that mangy old thing out of our yard."

Della Ann, who had been twirling a baton, let it drop to the ground and glared at Tom.

"Princess Kittymus is doing nothing of the sort," Della Ann replied. "I bet you're doing it yourself. You must not be able to see well enough to know the difference between a sandbox and a bathroom. You need to see my father and get some glasses."

Della Ann reached down to pick up the baton and her glasses slipped off. She raised up, the glasses and baton in her hand. It was as if she had been wearing a hood on her face instead of glasses, because for the first time I saw how blue her eyes were, how high her cheekbones, and the light spray of freckles across the bridge of her nose.

"So are you going to do anything about it or not, Della Ann," Tom shouted as she placed the glasses back on her face.

"Princess Kittymus wouldn't go into a yard nasty and grown-up as yours," Della Ann said. "She's very particular about her surroundings."

"So why does she live with you?" Tom shouted back.

Della Ann raised her baton as if she contemplated throwing it.

"You're an obnoxious little brat. You ought to act more like your brother," she said, pointing the baton at me. "He at least tries to be nice."

That said, Della Ann turned her back to us and resumed twirling the baton.

"Why are you looking at her like that," Tom said after a few seconds

"Like what," I said, my eyes still fixed on Della Ann.

"All googly-eyed. Like you actually like her."

At that moment the opening sentence of the second chapter of *The Male Adolescent* rose in my mind like a newspaper headline: *One of the first signs of entering adolescence is a new appreciation of the opposite sex.* I felt a sudden urge to check my face for acne and stubble and the front of my pants for emissions.

"I can't stand her," I said, trying to convince myself as much as Tom. "And if she won't do anything to keep that cat out of the sandbox, you and me will."

And in the next few days that is what we tried to do. Whenever we saw Princess Kittymus near the sandbox we tried to nail her with a rock, but as soon as we showed ourselves and began to rear back our arms, the cat vanished into a hole in the hedge. Nevertheless, it was clear from the ever-thickening reek in the sandbox that the animal was staying away only until Tom and I were out of sight.

Each time I missed the cat with a rock, each time I caught a whiff of Princess Kittymus' emissions, I became more and more frustrated—frustrated beyond reason, because the cat quickly came to represent to me everything new and unwelcome in my life. To make matters worse, one Saturday afternoon *I Was A Teenage Werewolf* was shown on Shock Theatre. I watched as, through no fault of his own, an adolescent awoke one day transformed into something snarling and hideous.

"That guy scares me," Tom said, and quickly left the room, but I stared transfixed at the body sprouting hair like kudzu from every pore, the suddenly bowed upper legs no doubt sticky with nocturnal emissions. At an especially dramatic moment, the werewolf suddenly turned, his face filling our black-and-white Zenith's screen. I could not help but believe I was looking at a face I would soon see again, not on a TV screen but in a mirror. The creature's face conveyed such a profound and utter misery that I too wanted to howl. "I'm going to have to think this thing out and come up with a plan," I told Tom, and that's exactly what I did, a plan incorporating every bit of meanness and ingenuity a twelve-year-old boy was capable of.

The first thing I did was barter on the pre-teen black market. My classmate David Ross had several shoeboxes filled with fireworks his truck-driver uncle had smuggled across the South Carolina border. Besides strings of firecrackers and sissy stuff like sparklers and bottle rockets, David's uncle had brought him a dozen of the heavy artillery of fireworks—M-80's. I entered David's room with three dollars, a 1960 mint-condition Roger Maris baseball card, and Tom's Duncan yoyo. I left with two five-foot-long strings of Black Cat firecrackers and three M-80's.

Getting the materials was easy enough, but having them work the way I hoped was much more probable. The main challenge was the fuse. There was no way Princess Kittymus was going to let us get close enough to light fuses that were even shorter than her tail. I got a magnifying glass out of my old science kit and climbed up in a dogwood tree across the yard from the sandbox. I placed a firecracker in the sand and tried to angle the sun to light the fuse, but I couldn't even get a wisp of smoke.

What I needed was a much longer fuse that would light the firecrackers and the M-80's at virtually the same time. After several failed experiments with sewing thread, I found the answer with fifty feet of kite string soaked in gasoline and peppered with black powder before left to dry. Taping the firecrackers to the sandbox's inside boards would be easy enough, as would be gluing four empty toilet paper rolls together to make an angled tunnel into the sand. Once the fuse lit the firecrackers it would continue through the toilet paper rolls to detonate the M-80's placed in the last roll.

All the while Tom and I had been studying Princess Kittymus' daily routine from our hiding place in the ditch behind the dogwood. Mrs. Gatson let the cat out as soon as her husband left for work, which was ten minutes before nine o'clock. If it saw no one in our backyard, the cat immediately made its way through the hedge and into our sandbox. It then proceeded to pace the sand on the outer rim, making a narrowing circle until near the sandbox's center. After a minute of scratching and sniffing, Princess Kittymus then relieved herself.

It was the first morning of August before I felt enough preparation had been made. Tom and I were in the yard by eight-thirty, placing the firecrackers and M-80's in the sandbox and carefully laying the string across the grass to the ditch. I held the box of matches I'd taken out of my father's shirt pocket in my hand as we waited for the Gatsons' back door to open.

For many of us, there is that defining moment when the world and the planets and stars all align with our lives in one perfect moment of cosmic harmony. It may be a game-winning jump shot that swishes through a net as the buzzer sounds. For others it may be the flawless rendition of a piano piece one has butchered for years, or perhaps the perfect final line in a poem. For me this moment occurred on the first day of August in 1963.

As soon as Princess Kittymus entered the sandbox, I lit the fuse and watched its slow sizzle across the yard to where the cat sniffed and scratched, seemingly oblivious to the firecrackers that laced the inner boards, the toilet roll sticking up like an angled periscope, and, most important of all, the burning string coming closer with each passing second.

I kept expecting the fuse to sputter and go out or Princess Kittymus to see or hear the fuse and scamper away, but as the distance between the sandbox and the lit fuse lessened, the theoretical became possible and then inevitable as the fuse reached the sandbox just as Princess Kittymus lifted her nubbed manx tail and squatted.

"I reckon we're going to get into a lot of trouble for doing this," Tom said, evidently, like me, never quite believing our plan could actually work until this moment.

"Yes, I believe we might," I said and fixed the binoculars on Princess Kittymus.

When the fuse lit the firecrackers it was like exploding dominoes. The outer rims of the sandbox threw up spurts of sand amid a machine-gun clatter. Princess Kittymus sprang from a squat to a spread-feet-apart stance in about one billionth of a second. The hair on her horseshoe-arched back stuck out like porcupine quills, the legs straight and rigid as the legs on our kitchen table. With the sandbox erupting all around her, the cat was as stiff and motionless as she would have been after a visit to a taxidermist, unable or unwilling to seek an escape route through the din and thickening smoke.

Even at fifty feet there is a slight lag between sight and sound. A geyser of sand erupted underneath Princess Kittymus followed by a muffled explosion like an underwater depth charge. The cat sailed six feet into the air above the sand box, then seemed to hang between the earth and sky for several seconds—its white fur singed with black powder, the goggle-glasses blown off to reveal green eyes bulging as if on stalks—before Princess Kittymus emitted a long, mournful wail and began her descent.

Then Princess Kittymus was gone, but not before making a new hole in the hedge. I stood so I could see over onto the Gatsons' property. Through the binoculars I watched the cat run two circles around the back yard before leaping onto the back porch's screen door. Princess Kittymus hung there by the claws, spread flat against the screen like some kind of bizarre door decoration, yowling frantically until Mrs. Gatson let her inside.

I swung the binoculars toward the living room window, and through the glass I saw Della Ann's blue eyes looking right back at me. I knew from the look on her face that she had seen at least part of what had happened, and I was instantly scalded by remorse. Acne and nocturnal emissions be damned, I liked Della Ann Gatson and wanted her to like me.

I lowered the binoculars and stepped through the hedge. I walked up to the living room window, my lips only inches and a plate of glass away from Della Ann's lips, lips I suddenly realized I wanted to kiss. "I'm sorry," I said, exaggerating my facial gestures so she would better understand my words through the glass.

That was the first but not the last time I would say those words to a member of the opposite sex; and all too often over the years Della Ann's response has been more or less their response. Della Ann nodded that she understood what I had said. Then she raised a fist between her face and mine. Her middle finger sprang free, was held rigid a few seconds, and then vanished back into her fist. She turned from the window and disappeared into the kitchen.

Tom and I were sent to bed without supper that night, a punishment so ridiculously light we had trouble looking properly remorseful.

"And I don't want you boys ever doing anything like this again," our father said as he led us to our room. "The Gatsons may not be the best neighbors, but we still need to be civil. Besides, I don't think they'll be around much longer. Dr. Gatson had a visit from the Better Business Bureau this morning. It seems they've done some research. Dr. Gatson has been run out of five different states in the last three years."

Our father smiled.

"I'd say it's about to be six."

A week before school started a *For Sale* sign sprouted on the Gatsons' front lawn, and a big yellow moving van backed slowly toward the front porch as it had two months earlier. I watched through the binoculars. I hoped not only to catch a glimpse of Princess Kittymus, who had refused to leave the

Gatsons' house since her levitation act in our backyard, but, more importantly, Della Ann, who had ignored my waves and hellos since the sandbox incident.

But only Dr. Gatson and Mrs. Gatson came onto the front porch as the movers worked. At twelve o'clock the movers took a lunch break, and Mr. and Mrs. Gatson went inside. I crawled a few feet to a small break in the hedge that allowed me to focus the binoculars on the Gatsons' dining room window. The table and chairs had been taken away by the movers. The Gatsons' sat on the floor in a tight circle, a platter filled with sandwiches and soft drinks in front of them. Princess Kittymus lay in Della Ann's lap, a new pair of goggle-glasses strapped to her head. There were a few gaps in her fur, but otherwise the cat appeared to be at least physically if not psychologically recovered. Dr. Gatson lifted one of the soft drinks from the platter, smiling as he raised it toward his wife and daughter as if to toast something, though what—his family, the house, new beginnings—I had no idea. Mrs. Gatson and Della Ann also picked up bottles and made similar gestures, the three bottles finally coming together and touching in the small space they sat around. They then took a drink and began to eat their last meal in that room, in that house, maybe even in North Carolina. And what struck me most was how brave they suddenly seemed, particularly Della Ann, who was about to be whisked away to parts unknown not only to me but probably her as well.

I lowered the binoculars and walked past the sandbox where Tom played and on into the house. I lay down on my bed, my eyes looking up at the ceiling, but what I saw was Della Ann Gatson picking up her baton and pink glasses, and I knew that if I lived a thousand years I would never forget what she looked like at that moment. I would remember it all—the color of her eyes, her hair, her cheekbones and lips. I hoped somehow we would meet again, maybe when I too had to leave this place in the world, as she and John had done before me.

I would miss the Gatsons.

White Trash Fishing

When the tie around my neck strangles like a noose, and I'm weary of air-conditioning and fluorescent lights and people who never say "He don't" or "Co-Cola; when I find myself in agreement with my NASCAR-obsessed cousin who claims if it ain't got wheels it ain't a sport; when Pabst Blue Ribbon tastes better than Guiness and I'm tempted to drink it in cinderblock death-traps with names like "Betty's Lounge" and "The Last Chance"; when I hanker for pork rinds and those deviled eggs you barehand out of a gallon jar; when I tire of eating animals, and (yes, my dear vegetarian friends) plants someone else has done the messy business of killing for me; when my wife says what's got into you and makes clear whatever "it" is is no good thing; when I long for muddy water and fish with poisonous fins and faces like nightmares, I know there is only one thing to do: I haul a rusty tacklebox and two Zebco 404 rods and reels out of the basement and go white trash fishing.

What I'm talking is nothing like trout fishing on the Beaverkill, or Henry's Fork, or in the Smokies, or the spring creeks of Pennsylvania or any of the other meccas of the sport where men and women with fly rods pose midstream as if on the cover of an L.L. Bean catalog and would no more harm their catch than their dogs or children.

What I'm talking about is not largemouth bass fishing either, especially its current manifestation as symbol of the New South: a high-tech sport requiring sonar and radar equipment as sophisticated as a nuclear submarine's installed on boats swift as some airplanes so the angler can zig zag across the monstrous reservoirs that fuel the New South and thus compete with hundreds of other fishermen similarly equipped in championships where fish are kept in a livewell until weighed, photographed, psychoanalyzed and who knows what else before being tossed back or mounted on a wall.

No, what I'm talking about is more primal, the antithesis of sport fishing. What I'm talking about is killing what you catch and eating it right there on the riverbank. And I'm talking about a river, not some gin-clear stream or reservoir, because that's where white trash fishing is best done, a river where the water's the color of coffee with cream and a trout or bass would go belly up before it swam five feet. I'm not talking aesthetics here, because there are none. What I'm talking about is sitting on a riverbank littered with empty beer cans, empty bait containers, empty potato chip bags, used diapers, used condoms, rotting newspapers, rotting blankets and just about anything else you'd care (or not care) to imagine.

Besides, it really doesn't matter what the place looks like because I'm talking night fishing and even if the place looked like the Yellowstone River I wouldn't be able to see it anyway. The only reason I'll even be here while the sun's still up is to stake a claim to a spot and get the rods and reels rigged up and the Coleman lantern and stove set up, fueled, and primed for later.

And this is what else I bring: frying pan, corn meal, Crisco, and onions, a mess kit, a cooler filled with ice and PBR, bug spray (though it doesn't do much good), a sleeping bag, a plastic tarp in case it rains, a pistol, the bait, and, of course, what I'm wearing.

And this is what I wear: a cap that says *Catfish Fisherman Do It All Night* or *I Don't Care How They Do It Up North* and the rankest jeans and shirt I can scrounge up out of the attic or bottom drawer, because even if I don't catch a fish the bait will leave a permanent reek on my clothes. Because what I'm talking about is that I'm after catfish, the aquatic equivalent to a possum in that they will eat anything they can grub up off the river bottom. There is no concern about "matching the hatch" or whether to use a green or a white skirt on a spinnerbait. If a catfish finds it, it'll eat it. The problem is it's moving blind down there, especially in the middle of the night, so I've got to help the fish out by giving him something he can smell. What I'm talking about is purple nightcrawlers threaded on a hook like shish kebab. What I'm talking about are doughballs textured with anything from motor oil to ketchup. I'm talking about whatever will get the job done.

When the sun finally goes down it's time to bait the rigs and cast into the dark and listen for a splash to know I didn't snag a willow. Then I sit down on the bank or maybe a stump or a lawnchair someone left, take a beer from the cooler, and wait.

It might be a while, but when I feel tugs from the dark more insistent than the current, I tighten the line and jerk for all I'm worth. I'm not talking finesse here. The object is not giving the fish "a sporting chance." What I'm talking about is setting the hook hard enough to drive the barb into the fish's brain and settle it once and for all right then. I don't "play" the catfish until it tires: I've got thirty pound test line and unless the fish wraps it around a junk car or refrigerator (and yes, there are cars and refrigerators down there along with anything else someone could throw or push into a river) it's not going to break the line, so I reel it in quick as I can and heave it onto the bank. I'm not talking about second chances when a fish flops back into the water when the hook is taken out—I'm talking rocks, tire irons, anything that can whack the fish into a limp silence.

And after I've caught enough I skin and clean the fish then put the frying pan on the stove and roll some chopped-up onions and corn meal into something that looks a lot like what I've been fishing with to make hushpuppies and then I lay the catfish in the pan. I get another beer from the cooler and when the last fish is fried I sit there and eat and sip the beer and listen to the frogs and the crickets and the river itself as it rubs against the bank. And when I finish I unroll the sleeping bag. I take out the pistol and fire off a round at the sky to keep anybody else on the river at a distance. Then I snuff out the candle and sleep so deep it's like I'm under the river, not beside it.

Come mid-morning the sun filters through the trees and I'll wake up. I'll be cotton-mouthed and swollen with mosquito and chigger bites. I'll be sweaty and smelly, my hands and clothes sticky with bait and fish slime, but I will feel cleansed and somehow redeemed as I stumble up the trail to my car.

The Harvest

"It's a drearysome day," Uncle Earl said, hunching his jean jacket tighter around his shoulders," but maybe it'll clear up before three tomorrow."

I looked out the windshield and had a notion otherwise. Fog could linger in our valley for days. It was like the mountains around us poured the fog in and set a kettle lid on top. You'd feel the grayness not just outside but seeping through the walls and into the house. Bright things like a quilt or button jar lost their color and footsteps sounded cold and lonely.

The road curved and the Tilson farmhouse appeared on the right. Two cars were parked beside Mr. Tilson's blue pickup.

"That's Preacher Winn's car," Daddy said. "Probably best just to go on to the field."

Daddy eased the truck onto the opposite side of the road and we got out. I knew people were inside the house but no one came to a window or door to peer out from within it. Daddy and Uncle Earl took the butcher knives and sacks from the truck bed and we walked down a slope and through a harvested cornfield, damp stalks and shucks slippery under our feet. The cabbage patch was beside the creek. Two of the rows had been cut but four hadn't.

"We may have need of a couple more sacks than we brought," Uncle Earl said.

"Tim can fetch some from the shed if need be," Daddy said.

Uncle Earl nodded across the road. At first I thought to show me where the shed was but he was pointing out something to Daddy, not me. The fog was thicker here in the bottomland and it took me a few moments to see what I first figured a trough or hog pen was a tractor. It lay on its side, one big black wheel raised up, the harrow's tongs like long fingers.

"He shouldn't have been on a hill that steep," Uncle Earl said.

"No," Daddy said. "But there's many of us who got the chance to learn it."

Daddy and Uncle Earl set down the sacks and kneeled at the two closest row ends.

"Stay between us," Daddy said to me. "We'll cut and you sack them."

They began cutting, left hand on the cabbage head while the butcher knife whittled underneath.

"We'll be filthy as hogs by the time we finish," Uncle Earl said, brushing wet dirt off his knife hand.

"Stay clean as you can, son," Daddy said. "There's something else I got need for you to do when we finish."

I dragged the sack behind me up the row, feeling it stick harder to the ground each time I put another cabbage inside. Daddy and Uncle Earl stopped every few minutes to help catch me up. I followed Uncle Earl and Daddy as they carried six full sacks to the row ends.

"Let's ease up a minute," Daddy said.

"Fine by me," Uncle Earl said.

Daddy put his hands flat above his tailbone and leaned backwards. Uncle Earl sat down cross-legged and took out a pack of rolling papers and a tobacco tin from his bib pocket.

"A day like this you feel your aches more," Daddy said.

Uncle Earl nodded as he sifted tobacco onto the paper, twisted the ends and lit one end. A car engine came up at the farmhouse. In a few moments a car drove away, quickly invisible except for its yellow headlights.

"We best get back to it," Uncle Earl said, and picked up the last four sacks we had. "I can cut and smoke both."

"We'll need two more sacks, three to be safe," Daddy said to me. "You willing to go get a couple."

"I guess so," I said. "Should I ask first?"

"No," Daddy said. "There's no cause to do that. Just go to that shed by the barn. They'll be some in there."

"Three?"

"Yes," Daddy said. "Three's plenty."

I left them and made my way through the cornfield and up to the road. The fog thinned as the ground slanted upward. I fixed my eyes on the shed and kept them there so I wouldn't see the tractor. I had to use both hands to swing the shed door open, then wait for the dark to be less dark. In a back corner, burlap sacks hung above a mound of potatoes. I smelled them as I lifted the sacks off the nail. It was a dusty, moldy smell, but a green alive smell dabbed in it too. I stepped out and shouldered the door closed. Across the road, the bottomland had disappeared. It was like the fog had opened its mouth and swallowed the cabbage patch whole.

The sacks were in my right hand. I squeezed them tighter as I made my way across the road and through the cornfield. Soon after, Daddy and Uncle Earl came out solid from the gray. The last cabbage were cut and gathered and Daddy and Uncle Earl hefted a sack over each shoulder and walked to the truck. Three trips and it was done.

"Twelve full sacks," Uncle Earl said when he and Daddy had loaded the last one in the truck bed. "You still of a mind to take it to Lenior today?"

"Yes," Daddy said, "but I need to ask her if she wants some for canning."

"Then we better go see," Uncle Earl said. "The Preacher's gone so it's likely as good a time as there'll be."

We walked across the road and into the yard but Daddy and Uncle Earl stopped in the yard.

"Take your shoes and socks off, son," Daddy told me. "Then go up there and knock."

I did as he said, brushed off my feet as best I could and went up the steps and knocked. The woman who came to the door was a lot older than Mrs. Tilson.

"What is it," she asked.

"I need to speak to Faye a moment, ma'am."

"She's in a bad way right now," the woman said.

"Yes ma'am, I know," Daddy said. "The thing is, I come by yesterday and told her we'd get Alec's cabbage in. We'll take it down to Lenoir and sell it, but I wanted to see if she had need to save some for her canning."

The woman looked at us for a few moments. I didn't know to leave the porch or not but then footsteps came up the hall and Mrs. Tilson came and stood beside the older woman. She had on a black dress and I could tell she'd been crying a lot. She looked at me like she didn't know who I was, then fixed her eyes on Daddy and Uncle Earl, who stood in the yard with their hands in their overall pockets.

"We cut the rest of the cabbage, Faye" Daddy said. "It's in the truck yonder. We didn't know if you wanted to keep any for canning. If you do, we'll put it in the root cellar for you."

Mrs. Tilson put her hands over her eyes, held them there. Then, real slow, she let her fingers and hands rub hard against her skin, like she was pulling up a mask to see better.

"Sell it," she said when her eyes opened. "That's what Alec always does. Done."

"We'll do that then," Daddy said. "We'll see you at the funeral tomorrow but if there's anything you need done before that, let us know."

Mrs. Tilson didn't say anything or nod. She just stepped back inside and the older woman shut the door.

"You done good today," Daddy said to me when we got back in the truck. "Mrs. Tilson, she's grateful to you for helping out. She may never say that though. It's a hard time for her and she'll likely not want to ponder anything about these days."

"Anyway," Daddy said. "You done good."